Blood and Carnations

Blood and Carnations

Lily Izadi Monadjemi

ELDORADO

While this novel is a work of fiction
the backgrounds are authentic

First published in Australia in 1993 by Eldorado Publishing Pty Limited (ACN 059
757 587) 34 Burton Street Kirribilli NSW 2061, Australia.

National Library of Australia
Cataloguing-in-Publication data:
Monadjemi, Lily Izadi
    Blood and carnations
    Bibliography
    ISBN 1 86412 002 9
    I. Title.
A823.3

Typeset by Midland Typesetters Pty Ltd.
Printed in Australia by McPherson's Printing Group.

This book is for my beloved parents, Princess Monir Agdas and Hassan Izadi, both of whom died in foreign lands and who are each at rest in a different hemisphere – 'Victims of a Revolution'

Acknowledgements

This novel was begun as a result of several sessions with my psychiatrist, who suggested that a written recollection of the traumatic events in my life might help to cure my deep depression. Little did he know that the task would become an obsession - an obsession to become a voice.

I spent one year researching the historical events which influenced the lives of those who lived during the Pahlavi era.

First and foremost I would like to thank my friend and initial editor Dr Catherine Runcie, of Sydney University, who gave so much of her valuable time and advice at the first draft stage of the book, and my friend, colleague and final editor Anne Lawton for her helpful suggestions, patience and hard work. I would also like to express my gratitude to my friends and colleagues: Bernie McGeorge, Geoff Baggett, Jemil Melik and Catherine Raymonds who each, in their own way, contributed to the creation of this work.

Finally, I offer my everlasting devotion to my brother Mahmoud, my husband Mehdi and my two daughters Betsabeh and Parrisa, whose patience and encouragement have been the foundation stones of all my achievements in life.

Author's Note

I wrote *Blood and Carnations* in the spirit of reconciliation, to voice the echo of my heart and of those Iranians who feel as I do - yearning to have the freedom to visit Iran again, but fearing 'prohibition from leaving the country' until found innocent by whatever committee has a warrant for their arrest, for whatever crime that committee accuses them of.

I hope that someone in the government of the Islamic Republic of Iran will read my book, feel the agony and consider a national reconciliation.

Enshallah!

Nineteenth century satirical map depicting Russian imperialistic designs
on Persia

Part I

MY IRAN

We shall exult, if they who rule the land
Be men who hold its many blessings dear
Wise, upright, valiant; not a servile band
Who are to judge of danger which they fear
And honour which they do not understand.
Wordsworth

Chapter One

Sunday July 7th, 1946 was an exceptionally hot day. It took my poor sweating, screaming mother five hours to give my father absolute joy by giving birth to his long wished and prayed for baby daughter – me. He already had two sons – Amir, 12 and Ali, 10 – but he had desperately wanted a girl. Now, he was so overjoyed that he gave a gold Pahlavi coin to every visitor who came to see his beautiful Laila.

At the age of 42 my father, Assad Yazdi, was tall, slender, elegant and good-looking.His light complexion was typical of people from the Gilan region, a rice province in Northern Iran. His father was a prominent sugar merchant with offices both in nearby Rasht and in Baku in Russia but his family, compared to my mother's, were commoners.

Mother, a blue-blooded aristocrat, was the granddaughter of Nasser Al-Din Shah Gajar, Shah of Persia from 1848 to 1896 and daughter of Princess Khadijeh and Prince Ehtesham. The prince owned many forests and around a hundred villages in and around Rasht. Because of the estate's proximity to the Caspian sea, the cool climate of the region and the attraction of lion-hunting in the forests, the family took their summer holidays in Bousar, the seat of the estate.The grand house accommodated the family, the retainers and, to be precise, 35 servants, valets, nannies and cooks.

It had been during one of these vacations that Mother had met Father, a friend of her younger brother's. Theirs was love at first sight. For Assad this was, indeed, a great honour. Soon, as tradition demanded, his father contacted one of the family members to see if it was acceptable for a merchant to approach the prince for Khasegari*, matrimonial proposal. In due course, the message was conveyed to the prince. The idea in itself was appealing and practical. Prince Ehtesham needed someone he could trust to manage his affairs in Rasht – who better than a son-in-law? His Highness condescended to the proposal under the condition that the groom remain in the province and act as his representative.

Within a month the wedding arrangements were made, the trousseau prepared, jewellery chosen and Rasht was witnessing the most magnificent wedding festivities of the decade. Five hundred nobles from Rasht and the neighbouring towns were fed and entertained for seven days. Various groups of musicians, singers and magicians performed. It was a true Gajar extravaganza.

The Gajars, originally a Turkoman tribe, had first been seen in the Mughan steppe around 897 AD. During the course of history the Gajar Khans, or chiefs, became increasingly powerful until eventually, in 1796, Agha Mohammad Khan succeeded in uniting Persia sufficiently to found the Gajar dynasty. He then moved the capital from Shiraz to Teheran. A year later, this cruel Shah was assassinated by some of his servants and was succeeded by his nephew Fath Ali Khan, who went on to reign for 37 years. It was during this period that the gradual encroachment of British Imperialism and Russian expansionism began to cause problems for the Shah – and changes began to take place which were to reshape Persia's history.

Nasser Al-Din, the fourth Gajar Shah, ascended the throne in 1848 and my grandmother, the princess, was born two years before her father's assassination in 1896.

The next Shah was Grandma's brother, Mosaffer Ed-Din. It was in 1906 during his reign that Persia became a constitutional monarchy. The constitution established a parliament to rule with the king as figurehead. This bold national move so displeased the Russians and the British that

---

* This is where the groom's family meets with the family of the bride to ask permission for the marriage, and to settle the terms of the marriage contract, including a bride price

4

they signed a convention to formalise their division of Persia. Russia took the North, the centre became a neutral zone, and the South was given to the British. The last of the Gajars was Ahmad Shah who inherited the throne at the age of 12.

Meanwhile Persia, a feudal and religious society, was moving towards modernism and secularism. Oil had been discovered by Australian William Knox D'Arcy and, in 1909, the Anglo-Persian Oil Company was formed. The terms of the agreement granted D'Arcy the right to exploit natural gas, petroleum, asphalt and Ozokerite throughout the country, except in the Northern provinces which were the Russian zone of influence.

In the Persia of 1923, the concept of a honeymoon was non-existent so, after their lavish wedding festivities, my mother and father began their married life in a small, rented house in Rasht. This new, modest life was difficult for Mother. Her companions were a single maid, a young aunt and a mean mother-in-law. The aunt, Khaleh Joon*, was a beauty married to a beast of a man who was extremely wealthy. Their marriage had been arranged. After two years of struggling to adjust to life in the province, both ladies decided they had had enough of misery and boredom. They demanded of their respective husbands that they move to Teheran – or else. Needless to say, their wishes were granted and both families packed up and left for Teheran.

While Khaleh Joon's husband was so wealthy that he had never worked in his entire life Father, who was not rich at all, indulged in the modern venture of setting-up a printing business. However, in 1925, the political situation was again unstable; this time, the cunning political manoeuverings of a giant were shaking the foundations of the Gajar reign.

Reza Shah, founder of Pahlavi dynasty, had been born around 1878 somewhere in the mountains of Mazandaran, one of Iran's Northern provinces. His mother, recently widowed, had carried her baby on a mule over the mountainous paths to Teheran, where they settled down to live in abject poverty.

* Colloquial for 'dear'

A teenage Reza, in love with soldiering, enlisted in the Persian Cossak Brigade, a regiment introduced to Persia by the Russians to safeguard their own interests. At the age of 20 this ruthless Cossak, already a lieutenant, was given the title of Khan, a chief.

As he matured, Reza Khan began to realise that the foreigners were here to exploit Persian resources and that, while nothing was done to stop them, the lot of the Persians would get worse. Fired with the desire to stop this exploitation, but realising that he could not do so as an illiterate, he began to educate himself. In the process, he became increasingly aware of and influenced by foreign current events, in particular the Westernising reforms being attempted by the Young Turks, a political party led by Kemal Ataturk. Ataturk was later to prove a great inspiration to Reza Shah.

In 1914, World War 1 broke out and, within a short period, Persia was divided between the Russians, the British and the Turks. Eventually, two events occurred in Persia's favour. The plague took care of the Turkish army, and the October Revolution caused the disintegration of the Russian forces. The country was left to the British and, in August, 1919, an official accord deemed Persia a British Protectorate.

Five years of war had caused famine and misery in the country. As though this was not enough the Bolsheviks, in pursuit of the Russian army which had tried to seek refuge in Persia, landed in Enzeli on the Caspian Sea and formed an alliance with a local rebel named Kutchek Khan. Together, they created the Socialist republic of Gilan.

Meanwhile Colonel Reza Khan, never idle, had formed a close and opportune friendship with Sayyid Ziaeddin Tabatabai, a young, cultured journalist who was experienced in politics. Tabatabai, son of a mullah (priest), had easy entree into influential circles. In order to realise their political ambitions in a country divided between two occupying armies they had to make a choice. That choice was the British, who were particularly opposed to Ahmad Shah. In February 1921, as a result of a successful coup d'etat against the government,

Reza Khan was promoted to general and war minister and Tabatabai was made the new prime minister. Within a few days, the Russians signed a treaty with the new government renouncing all concessions and zones of influence and promising to respect the country's independence. Shortly afterwards, the republic of Gilan was liquidated and the British pulled back to the Persian Gulf where lay the country's rich oil fields.

At some stage after that, the alliance between the two men faced a conflict of interest and Tabatabai, found to be a British agent and fearful of the general's wrath, fled to Mesopotamia.

The 1919 Accord was repudiated by Ahmad Shah in 1919 and the British were forced to accept the Shah's decision. In the process of aggrandisement the all-powerful Reza Khan proclaimed himself the prime minister and, quite audaciously, suggested the young king take a trip to Europe. Ahmad Shah named his brother regent and left the country for France. He never saw Persia again.

Meanwhile, Reza Khan was planning to establish a republic and submitted his proposal to the parliament. He faced no objections there, but the top Shiite clergy fiercely opposed his project. The people wanted Ahmad Shah back but the young monarch, afraid of a civil war, did not return. Eventually, on October 29, the parliament deposed the Gajar dynasty and handed power to the regent Reza Khan. A few days later, the Gajar Shah's brother and the rest of the royal family (Ahmad Shah's immediate family) were shipped to exile in France. Ahmad Shah died in 1930, a heartbroken fallen monarch – a fate, so it seems, that neither of the Pahlavi Shahs were able to avoid, either.

After the departure of the Gajars, well-monitored elections were held to set up a new assembly and, on 21st December 1925, the members unanimously bestowed the Peacock Throne upon His Highness the regent, General Reza Khan. The infant who had been driven on the back of a donkey through the mountanous paths of Mazandaran had become the Shah of Shahs, empowered to shape the history of modern Iran.

The new Shah, inspired by Ataturk who had become President of Turkey, commenced the modernisation of his country. His first reform was to abolish native dress. His greatest opponents, the clergy, protested loudly but without success. To get rid of the chador, the Iranian Islamic cover for women, Reza Shah at an official inauguration presented his wife and daughters wearing Western clothes. He had them photographed and ordered all Iranian women to follow suit. The mullahs and the bazaaries, the traditional merchants whose offices are in the bazaar, the commercial section of the city, resisted and faced savage retribution. It is said that the police made the rebellious mullahs drink their own urine. In fact, the government did everything possible to denigrate and crush the influence and the power of the clergy. Soon the chador became an absurdity of the past. But the Pahlavis were later to pay dearly for their imprudence.

Meanwhile, Reza Shah also changed the name of the country from Persia to Iran, which means 'the land of the Arians'. Persia had been the name given to the plateau by the ancient Greeks and, later, by other Europeans.

World War 11 broke out in 1940 and Reza Shah, a pro-German, proclaimed Iran's neutrality. Germany's role in the country's foreign trade was massive and its influence on Iran's army crucial. Thousands of German engineers and technicians were working in Iran after helping to construct the trans-Iranian railroad from the Persian Gulf to the Caspian.

On June 22, 1941 Hitler invaded Russia and it became apparent that the Allies wanted to use the Trans-Iranian railroad to get supplies to the Russians. This meant another invasion of Iran. In late June, the British and Russian Ambassadors suggested that the Shah expel all German nationals and open the railroad to the Allies. The Shah refused to oblige. A month later, however, the government was forced to co-operate and, shortly afterwards, the Russians and the British again divided Iran into three zones: the North went to the Russians, the South to the British and the narrow band in the middle to the Shah. Forced by the Allies, Reza Shah abdicated on the

15th of September 1941 in favour of his son Mohammad Reza. The old Shah was exiled and, three years later, died in Johannesburg, another heartbroken, fallen king.

Iran became an occupied country and the Tripartite Treaty of 1942 was signed to clarify the Allies' position in the country during the war with Germany. The Treaty respected Iran's territorial integrity, sovereignty and political independence and guaranteed the evacuation of foreign forces from the country within six months of the end of the war. While in Iran, however, the British and the Russians did whatever they liked, from looting to rape. They even went so far as to replace unsympathetic elements in the government with their own partisans. In the North, the Russians replaced the Iranian governors with their own political commissars and, through communistic propaganda, were able to create the Tudeh, a party of the masses. In a matter of months, the entire Russian zone became a separate region making secession from Teheran inevitable. This was a real threat to national unity.

Mohammad Reza Shah's saviour was Franklin D. Roosevelt, another interested politician in the affairs of Iran. Roosevelt perceived the communist threat and realised the importance of saving Iran, the most strategic zone between Russia and the Persian Gulf. A special command was created and, during the course of 1942, thousands of Americans arrived in Iran. Now the country had three occupiers, each with its own particular interest and intelligence network.

In late 1944, the Tudeh triggered a general rebellion. Azerbaijan in the North fell. The Shah appealed to the British and the Americans, who had already honoured the Tripartite Treaty and evacuated their forces from Iran. The Russian forces left Iran only after US President Truman issued an ultimatum to Stalin and Iran's ambassador in Washington pleaded Iran's cause before the United Nations Security Council.

In December 1946, Azerbaijan was recaptured from the Tudehs. The cold war was on and Iran's importance for the West undeniable. So, Washington granted Iran a huge credit to help arm its troops.

Chapter Two

By the summer of 1947, Father's printing business had picked up and we had become the proud owners of a modest house in the prestigious Avenue Kakh. Although he was from a relatively humble background, Father's character was completely devoid of complexes and the airs and graces of his in-laws never seemed to bother him. He knew that they were jealous of his financial success. In fact, he had become their bank, from which they often borrowed money for their extravagant journeys to the gambling and spa centres of Europe. Very few of the Gajars ever worked. They usually lived off the income from their land, or pawned their valuables for ready cash. Those with the remotest claim to the throne had already either been exiled or killed, and the rest had to make do with what was left them by the now very rich Pahlavi Shah, who confiscated whatever caught his fancy.

Luckily, Grandpa's villages were not by the Caspian shore, the area most desired by Reza Shah, so his rice fields and tea plantations were safe. He was one of the few aristocrats who remained wealthy throughout his life.

After father left Rasht, Grandpa's affairs became mismanaged, making him short of cash. For major purchases he resorted to barter economy; for instance, in partnership with two friends he bought Darous, a village in the North of Teheran at the foothills of the majestic, snow-capped Albourz mountains. In exchange, he gave the vendor a village in Rasht. Grandpa's only source of cash was Father, who was always willing to lend him money as long as the interest rate was high enough! In those days, there were no banks to borrow from. The only people with cash ready to lend were the bazaaries, who did it discreetly, usury being forbidden in Islam.

Father was not an orthodox Muslim. He performed his daily prayers regularly, but he loved gambling, women and Arak too much to abstain from them. However, moderation was one of his virtues and was employed even in his indulgences. He was envied by his gambling partners for his discipline in controlling his impulses; the drinking of Arak was limited to two glasses per night; but only God and Mother knew about his women. Mother was very much in love with him and, throughout her life, bore the knowledge of his many infidelities with dignity and patience. Mother's beauty was gentle and appealing, and there were many men who desired her – but she never capitalised on her looks. She favoured subtle elegance, modesty and whatever pleased her husband. For her, there was only one man and that was her Assad.

Mother's daily routine revolved around her children and the social activities of her large, parental family, all of whom spent Thursday evenings and the whole of Friday (the Muslim weekend) at Grandpa's home. This usually included my four aunts and two uncles, some of whom lived at Grandpa's house. The evenings usually began with the older generation sitting together reminiscing about the good old days, talking politics and smoking hookah or opium. The younger ones would challenge one another in a game of Bakara, while listening to musicians playing romantic music and singers crooning sad songs. They drank Arak and often smoked opium. Uncle Homayon, the apple of Grandpa's eye, was both an addict and an alcoholic.

Father was aware of the environment to which his children, especially his two sons, were being exposed and made the wise decision to send the boys to boarding school in England. A relative living in London made the necessary arrangements for their enrolment at a private boarding school near Norwich in Norfolk. At the time, Amir was 13 and Ali, 11. Neither knew any English. The brave little boys were dressed in their best and sent to London, a city drastically hit by the war and still on food rations.

From then on, I was treated as the only child, except during the summer holidays when they returned to Teheran and became the centre of attention! I hated those long, hot summers when I was benignly neglected and the limelight was stolen by my athletic and handsome brothers. Fabulous parties were given. Vacations were taken in the grand hotel at Ramsar, a sophisticated seaside resort frequented by high society. Ramsar is extremely picturesque. The Elbourz range facing the Caspian is lusciously green and the hotel is situated on an elevated site among manicured gardens thick with citrus trees which slope down to the sandy shores. Avenues running into the beach are lined with tall palm trees, mimosa and rhododendrons. The sea, sometimes tempestuous, sometimes calm, is blue-green with white, fluffy waves washing the shores. The hotel is white, built in art deco style and on sunny days it shines like a large pearl surrounded by emeralds. Here, the peasants' mud huts with their shingle roofs are lost among the orange groves.

In those days, on the hotel's beach, floral umbrellas provided shade from the burning sun. Hurrying waiters served iced pomegranate and grape juice in tall glasses set on silver trays. Ladies in colourful bathing suits and straw hats sat together, gossiping or talking 'mine is better than yours', while the men eyed each other's wives or daughters.

Around noon, when the heat became unbearable, everyone retired to their rooms to take showers and prepare for lunch, a short siesta afterwards and, perhaps, a stroll in the garden. Dinner was formal. The women wore expensive haute couture outfits and the men appeared in smart suits, set to merrymake until dawn.

My brothers had the most wonderful times at Ramsar, but for me those summer days were lonely. Swimming and making sandcastles were my only consolations. I was a sad, desolate four-year-old, preoccupied with the question of why I had been so heartlessly abandoned. In retrospect I have to be fair.

Nobody had meant to hurt me. My parents were doing what any normal Iranian parents would do - seeing to it that their sons had a good time. However, children live in a world of fantasy and judge according to their sensitive perception of that world. When, suddenly, love and attention are withdrawn or diverted, their whole world crumbles into pieces. Fear replaces trust, anxiety wipes out self-confidence and the world becomes demonic.

Fortunately for me, as my brothers became used to their English way of life, made more friends at school and began to excel in sports, they began to take their vacations on the Continent. Father approved of their choice because, once again, Iran was going through a politically unsettled period.

The young Shah, who had married Fawzieh, the sister of King Farouk of Egypt, and had a daughter, Princess Shahnaz, was inexperienced and too frivolous to be effective. He was more preoccupied with his carnal affairs than the affairs of his state.The young playboy king was especially fond of tall, blonde Europeans who came to Teheran by the planeful. The time not spent with his women was spent horse-riding or flying. He was both a fearless pilot and a keen horseman. Not surprisingly, his marriage with Fawzieh ended in divorce.

In 1949, while attending an event at the University of Teheran, the Shah narrowly escaped an assassination attempt. The assailant, Fakhr Arai, a young member of the Tudeh party, was shot on sight taking with him to his grave the secret of the daring plot. Martial law was imposed. Most of the known agitators were rounded up and jailed.The communists went underground. And meanwhile, people poured into the mosques to thank Allah for their king's escape. The Shah took advantage of the emotions surrounding the event and made a series of political moves consolidating his power. These initiatives included passing a law limiting freedom of the press, curtailing the powers of parliament by making the senate, the parliament's inactive chamber, equal to the elected and active Majlis. Half of the senate would be appointed by the Shah, who would have the right to dissolve both houses singly or together by a farman, a simple decree. The curfew was lifted once order was restored.

The attempted assassination of 1949 changed the hitherto playboy into a monarch with ambitions to introduce revolutionary social and economic reforms. The Shah's new strength, and his success in crushing the Tudeh, impressed President Truman enough to persuade him to grant Iran a huge amount of financial aid. Elated by his new position of power, the Shah met and fell in love with Soraya Esfandiary, an 18-year-old beauty from the Bakhtiari tribe. They married on Monday February 12, 1951.

I still remember that cold, February day. Teheran was deep in snow and an excited crowd, of which mother and I were part, had lined up on both sides of Pahlavi Avenue to catch a glimpse of the new bride on her route to the Marble Palace, where the wedding ceremony was to take place. When the car conveying the bride approached us, the jubilant crowd began to clap and shout 'Zendeh bod Soraya! Zendeh bod Soraya!' (Long live Soraya!) Her car was moving very slowly and I managed to squeeze myself out to the front of the crowd and get a good look at the most beautiful green-eyed creature I had ever seen in my life. It was very sad that this queen was not able to give her king an heir. The marriage ended in 1958 and Soraya, given the title of Princess – and, apparently, a generous monthly allowance – left Iran for Europe.

1951 was an auspicious year both for the Shah and Iran. It was in this year that Mohamad Hedayat Mossadegh, a Gajar aristocrat born sometime around 1881, pushed through the nationalisation of Iranian oil. Mossadegh had entered politics early in life, dedicating his career to fighting against corruption. A devout nationalist, he had turned his attention to addressing the problem of the country's oil and stirring up violent attacks againt the British. In 1922, he became minister for finance.

During Reza Shah's reign, he was frequently jailed, the awful conditions of prison permanently impairing his health. After the war, he formed the National Front, a party with only nine deputies. In April 1951,when he became prime minister, this handful of men succeeded in imposing the law which nationalised Iranian oil. The nationalisation, naturally, infuriated the British, but in our house there was great jubilation. Everybody loved Mossadegh. Grandma was his great aunt and his mother was in constant communication with her.

I was Grandma's favourite grandchild and she took me everywhere with her, including to Mossadegh's residence. I spent every summer with her at the new palatial house which had been built at Darous. A well-kept lawn shaded with weeping willows surrounded the house and a bubbling spring ran into a blue-tiled pool whose fountains freshened the dry summer air. The garden was sheltered by ten hectares of fruit and nut trees. A true paradise for a lonely little girl. There were fifteen other children of around my age who belonged to the live-in servants, nannies, cooks and gardeners. I also had seven cousins, who often visited but never stayed the whole summer.

One June day, Grandma had the car summoned for us to go shopping at the bazaar. I was too young to understand what was happening, but I noticed people buying lots of dried provisions like rice, lentils, tea and cooking oil. The town had an air of excitement about it. Small groups of people were gathered, talking and arguing, at street corners, in shops and by electricity poles. The police seemed unusually vigilant. On the walls of every shop I noticed pictures of Mossadegh hung side by side with the Shah's. Grandma spent a long time shopping – so long that I got through three ice-creams purchased for me by the driver! It was dark when we arrived home to find my Aunt Firouzeh and her husband Uncle Hussain sitting with Grandpa, speculating on the latest political events. Gathering to discuss politics became a routine custom that summer.

As autumn approached, the air grew cool and the leaves on the trees began to change colour and fall. The family left Darous for their house in Kushk Avenue, while I went home to my parents. Father was happy to have me back and Mother, practical as ever, was preoccupied with filling our own basement with food. I loved the excitement, especially now that I could play my favourite game 'supermarket' with real food and not toys. I also began to develop the habit of inspecting mother's wardrobe, going through her bags and pretending they were mine. On one occasion I discovered something new, bright and shiny. A sack full of gold coins! I emptied the sack onto the floor, making pretty patterns with the coins on the carpet. Unexpectedly, Mother entered the room and, seeing the coins on the floor, her eyes widened and she screamed hysterically, 'What are you doing? Where did you find them?'

'In your wardrobe, behind your shoes, Maman.' Sensing retribution, I began to cry.

'Put them back in the sack at once, and don't tell anyone – not a single soul – about what you found!' she scolded.

Obediently, I picked up the coins and dropped them back in the sack, secretly enjoying the jingling sound of the precious metal mounting up in the container, and oblivious of the meaning of my mother's hysterical reaction. Those coins were father's security in case of trouble. Now, looking back, I admire his sense of foresight. Trouble came.The rial lost its value, gold went up and high inflation followed. When Mossadegh nationalised the oil, Britain sent paratroopers to Cyprus, gathered the troops she had based in Iraq on the Iranian border, and asked the International Court of Justice in the Hague to appoint an arbiter in the oil dispute and to impose an economic blockade on Iran. She also appealed to the United Nations and, on September 30, the Security Council voted to look into Britain's complaint against Iran.

During this critical period, the Shah was politically inactive and indecisive. However, Mossadegh wasn't. On the morning of October 7, the prime minister, thin and pale, and with his ever-running nose, left Mehrabad Airport for New York accompanied by his advisers and leaving behind a crowd of supporters chanting 'Allah Akbar' (God is great). Once in

New York, he was taken to New York Hospital where he feigned illness until the Security Council voted to postpone examination of Britain's request until the International Court came to a decision regarding the issue. A few days later, the fully-recovered Mossadegh met with President Truman in Washington and asked for financial aid. He received only a very small loan.

The economic situation in Iran was deteriorating rapidly and the country was on the verge of bankruptcy. Nevertheless,on his return to Teheran, Mossadegh was greeted with hysterical joy. For the first time in modern history a leader had given Iranians a sense of identity. Although in a miserable economic situation, Iran owned its own natural resources, its own wealth and had a prime minister who stood by the rights of his nation. Iran had found a defender in the person of Mohammed Hadayat Mossadegh.

To manage the money problem, he floated a loan of two billion rials and started printing money. Inflation followed, but the people supported and stood by him. Uncle Hussain was one of his most active followers and a member of the National Front. In an attempt to solve the country's political problems, the prime minister asked the newly re-elected Majlis for six months of absolute power. This request was granted. He also asked for the portfolio of war minister, but the Shah refused to oblige. Mossadegh resigned. Riots broke out. Four days later Ahmad Gavam, the Shah's newly-appointed prime minister resigned and the Majlis voted for Mossadegh's reinstatement. He became war minister, took over the crown's budget and exiled many of the Shah's friends and meddlesome family, including Princess Ashraf, the Shah's shrewd twin sister.

Tension was ruling the nation. The grown-ups were all concerned about the political situation. Many couldn't decide whether to be self-concerned or patriotic – whether to choose the Shah, whom the powers seemed to be backing, or Mossadegh the hero of the common man. Rumours began to circulate that Mossadegh was going to sell the country to the Russians. The Tudeh Party was beginning to resurface – and nothing scared the average Iranian more than the threat of communism, especially at times of economic crisis.

The youngsters were left to their own devices but were infected with the same mass hysteria: Shah or Mossadegh. Our games were all based on politics. We would form into two groups, those who were pro-Shah and those who were pro-Mossadegh. I always chose the Shah because of Soraya. We would each take the longest stick we could find in Grandma's garden and chase each other around pretending to fight for our hero. Usually a real fight would break out, someone would get hurt and, sulking or crying, he or she would run to the servants' quarters to be comforted.

Mossadegh's popularity began to decline and with it, Iran's chance of ever attaining democracy. When Churchill became prime minister of England and General Eisenhower was elected American president, the two men sided with each other to put pressure on Mossadegh and bring about the catastrophe which eventually followed.

By the summer of 1953, Teheran's population had proliferated and the town was beginning to sprawl towards the North, where the climate was cooler and the environment green and lush. Avenue Kushk had lost its prestige as a residential area and was becoming increasingly commercial. Foreigners were pouring into Teheran and there was only one luxury hotel to accommodate them: The Park. One of Grandma's nephews had just returned from Europe, full of fresh business ideas and keen to persuade Grandpa to turn the Kushk residence into a modern luxury hotel. Grandpa succumbed to the idea and, when summer came, the family vacated their house to take up permanent residence at Darous. I was ecstatic about this decision as it meant I could take my Norouz holidays there, too.

Norouz is the Iranian New Year, which begins on the first day of spring after the stroke of the equinox (March 20 or 21). The festivities continue for 13 days. Norouz is an ancient celebration of the rebirth of nature. The ceremonies represent the two ancient concepts of End and Rebirth, Good and Evil.

A few weeks before the New Year people thoroughly clean and decorate their homes, buy new clothes, bake pastries and germinate seeds as a sign of renewal. On the eve of the last Wednesday (Shab-e Chahar Shanbeh Soury, The Red Wednesday) bonfires are lit and people leap over the flames, believing the blaze will burn the bad luck, sickness and unhappiness of the year to come. A day before the actual turn of the year a special cover called a Sofreh is spread either on the floor or on a table and is decorated with goods representing the seven symbols of life, rebirth, health, happiness, prosperity, joy and beauty. These symbols, which begin with the letter 'S' are: Sabzeh (represented by sprouts), Sib (apples), Samanou (a wheat germ dish), Sonbol (hyacinths), Senjed (fruit of the Jujube), Seer (garlic), and Somagh (sumac). Also placed on the Sofreh are a copy of the Koran, some coins (usually gold), a bowl of water, painted eggs, a mirror, candles, plates full of pastries and pictures of the family members not present.

At the stroke of the equinox verses of the Koran are recited and the family, including the servants, gather by the Sofreh, hugging and kissing and exchanging greetings and, of course, presents. Families and friends visit each other in accordance with age and social standing. On the 13th day groups of loved ones picnic in the fields and by the riversides and throw away their sprouts, thus removing bad luck from the house where they were grown. Norouz was the best time of the year for us children. It meant gold coins from the grandparents, money from the rest of the family, new clothes and lots of delicious pastries.

The house in Darous was huge, a square building on three levels with 14 bedrooms, mirrored halls and marble bathrooms. A turquoise pond with a dancing fountain took prime position in the grand hall. During the day, sunbeams penetrated the hall through the French windows, creating colourful patterns on the marble floor. The rays were so bright that thousands of floating particles of dust could be seen suspended in them. A crystal chandelier lit the hall at night. Chaise longues were set on each side of the pond, perfect for reclining on and dozing off during the long, hot summer afternoons. A separate row of rooms lodged the servants and the retainers.

Uncle Hussain, much-respected by Grandpa for his French education, law degree and modern ideas, convinced his father-in-law to turn the village into a modern suburb by subdividing the land into residential acreages to be sold to trusted friends and relatives. Within a month the plan was approved by the municipality of Shemiran and the wheatfields had been turned into a well-planned suburb bearing Grandpa's name, Avenue Ehteshamieh. Each son received two hectares, each daughter one, and each grandchild half-a-hectare. At the age of seven I owned half-a-hectare of land! The avenue connecting the Assadi's land to Ehtashamieh was named after me, Avenue Laila.

But Grandpa's act of generosity had a string attached to it. All the adult recipients had to build on their land to help develop the new suburb. First to build was Uncle Hussain himself. His house was a simple, Swiss-style cottage with a large swimming pool in which he later taught every one of us to swim. Soon, the others followed suit, including Father. Though he had no intention of moving house as yet, he believed that once the political situation had stabilised, foreigners would flood the country and the cost of rented accommodation would rise. Father was always right. The problems did get ironed-out, foreigners did flood the country and rents rose sky-high.

On July 6th 1953 Kermit Roosevelt, son of Theodore Roosevelt, an agent of the Central Intelligence Agency, and a specialist in Middle East affairs entered Iran to tackle the Mossadegh menace. Only three people knew of the plot: the Shah, General Zahedi, a favourite of the Pahlavis, and his son Ardeshir. Zahedi was to act on behalf of the Shah from an underground position. The initial plan was for the Shah to initiate a decree to remove Mossadegh and replace him with Zahedi.

On August 10th the Shah decided to leave Teheran with Soraya for a short holiday at Kalardachte in the mountains.

Colonel Nematollah Nassiri, commander of the Imperial Guard, was elected to deliver the dismissal decree to Mossadegh. Through a leak, however, the prime minister became aware of the plot. Nassiri was arrested but Zahedi, warned in time, escaped. Early the next morning, Mossadegh went on radio and broadcast the news of the unsuccessful coup d'etat against his government. The entire press attacked the Shah, pronouncing him 'the foreign puppet'. At Kalardachte, the royal couple panicked and hurried to Ramsar where the king's aircraft was waiting for them. They fled to Baghdad, where they requested and were granted asylum. Iran, it seemed, wasn't worth fighting for.

On August 17th, 1953, the fall of the Shah of Iran made international headline news. The Iranian ambassador in Iraq demanded the Shah's extradition, but King Faizal refused and the couple left for Rome. Back in Teheran, the conspirators, who had been lying low, were regrouping, biding their time for the right moment to set their plot into motion. The following events all worked against Mossadegh. First, the Tudeh resurfaced singing communistic songs; then rumours began to spread that Mossadagh was selling the country to the Bolsheviks; and finally, Teymur Bakhtiar, the chief of the Kermanshah garrison, in support of the Shah allied himself with Zahedi.

In Darous, scared to death, everyone including the servants was sitting around their radios waiting for news. Conspiracy was in the air – though of course, at that time, no-one was aware of the C.I.A. plot which was only revealed decades later. Nevertheless, the atmosphere was electric with anticipated trouble. People loved Mossadegh, but feared the Tudeh. They also loved the Shah. For as long as they could remember they had had a king. It was part of their culture, part of their heritage. Now he had fled and left them fatherless. To hell with the foreigners: the British, the Russians and now the Americans! What did they care for the Iranian people? For the peasants who toiled the land, sleeping hungry at nights? For the bazaari whose credit was diminishing? And for the landowners, whose land was being confiscated? The foreigners did not want to help Iran.They wanted to exploit it. The Shah had already gone. Mossadegh, the old man, was he really planning to betray his country to the Russians? Those Godless Russians?

During those history-making August days everyone was restless, unhappy, anxious, indecisive and tired. No doubt it was this confused state of mind that induced the people to turn from Mossadegh to the Shah. On the 17th, a deal was struck between Roosevelt and a man nick-named 'Brainless' – an athlete and leader of a gang of louts from the south of Teheran. This group was to supply Zahedi with enough men and tanks to make another attempt at a coup on the 19th.

On the morning that the Americans were plotting to change Iran's destiny, Grandma and I were shopping in Avenue Islambul, the main shopping centre of Teheran. Small groups of men, shouting 'Long live the Shah!' were slipping ten rial notes bearing the Shah's portrait under the windshield wipers of cars as they passed by. People, cautiously at first, then boldly, began to cluster around them frantically stretching out their hands for a ten rial bill. This was creating a terrible traffic jam. Cars could not move. Our driver had gone white with fear and tears were running down Grandma's normally composed face.

I was petrified, even though I was unable to comprehend the gravity of the situation. The crowd was turning wild. Everybody was waving the notes around, shouting hysterically, 'Long live the Shah! Long live the Shah!'. Their hysteria was, no doubt, the manifestation of their pent-up frustrations. All the streets converging on Parliament Square, including the one we were in, now swarmed with masses of moving black heads and outstretched arms waving the notes like flags on a joyous occasion. Except that this occasion wasn't joyous at all. It was a time to be remembered with shame.

Mossadagh supporters were now mixing with the demonstrators and were snatching the notes and tearing them up. Fights broke out between the different factions.The situation deteriorated and I became so terrified that I buried my face in Grandma's lap and began to weep, silently, scared of attracting the attention of the crowd. After what seemed an eternity, our car escaped the jam and we headed speedily towards Shemiran.

At home that night we heard from one of the servants who had been caught up in the riot that, around noon, a gang of disguised roughnecks had crowded into Parliament Square. Suddenly, throwing off their disguises, they had taken out guns, revolvers and clubs, forced their way into the ministerial offices, beaten and thrown out the occupants and locked the doors. Soon afterwards a tank carrying Zahedi and his son appeared, dividing the crowd into two groups – on one side the Mossadegh people and on the other the C.I.A. As the tank approached, a collaborator shouted 'Long live Zahedi!' and 'God protect the Shah!' In Rome that same day the Shah was informed that his people wanted him back. The struggle for true democracy, the right of a nation to decide for herself, had been dashed by the mercenaries of the United States – the country which supposedly cherishes, above all, liberty and democracy.

The Shah returned, welcomed by the cheering, flag-waving crowds which had lined up along his route from the airport to his palace, lulled into believing that they genuinely wanted him back. A few days later Mossadegh, the man who had defeated the British in nationalising Iran's oil, the man whose aim had been to eradicate corruption and injustice and rule within a true constitutional monarchy, was arrested and placed in a cell with common thieves. His house was looted and ransacked.

Mossadegh's era ended swiftly. Yet the spirit of the old man has survived the demise of the Pahlavi dynasty and will be remembered with pride. The key players in the coup were handsomely rewarded by the Shah but, with the exception of Ardeshir, none of them escaped the curse of Mossadegh.

Chapter Three

It was a beautiful, sunny Friday in January. Snow had been falling for days and outside, in the bright sunlight, the glare was intense. To the North, only a couple of miles away, the foothills of the mountains were completely white. The Albourz range appeared so close and so high that they seemed about to crush the city. Mother and I were walking on Pahlavi avenue, taking our daily exercise. I didn't feel well. My bones were aching, my throat felt dry and I felt very cold. I began to shiver uncontrollably and asked Mother if we could return home. She took one look at my face and hailed a taxi.

Back home I went straight to bed and Mother called the family physician who arrived half-an-hour later carrying his big, black leather bag. After asking me some questions and giving me a thorough physical examination he turned and, whispering to my mother, led her out of the room. A little later she returned with tears in her eyes, her face drained of colour. She helped me out of the bed, took my nightdress off and dressed me in warm clothes. I felt weak and could hardly breathe or swallow. Mother lifted me up, pressing my tiny body to her chest as though trying to protect her little girl from the angel of death.

Out of the house, she walked very fast , splashing around in the melting, muddy snow. Fortunately the pharmacy at the corner of Kahk and Pahlavi Avenue was open. Mother asked for the chemist himself and, when he appeared from behind a partition, she handed him the doctor's prescription and told him I had diphtheria. The man led us into a tiny room behind the counter and helped me onto a clean bed. After a few minutes of fiddling with various little bottles he gave me two penicillin injections. The ampoules were to be repeated twice a day, so Mother made arrangements for him to visit our house and give me the injections at home.

It took six awful months to recover from the disease. Indeed, I was lucky to survive considering the rudimentary medication available at the time. I missed much of my schooling that year and really hated to fall behind, but with the help of a tutor I worked hard to catch up and finished the year with good grades. From then on, with the exception of my first few years in England, I passed all my examinations with honours.

Autumn in Teheran is a short, sad season with dusty winds, tempestuous storms, quick, heavy showers and long, curved rainbows.The trees lose their leaves, the swallows migrate to the South and the sparrows rummage in the gardens for food. There is a sense of melancholy in the air. It was on one such autumn afternoon that, returning from school hungry and looking forward to my snack, Nanny divulged some startling news. We were to move to Germany! I did not believe her and asked her where my mother was. She had gone to the bazaar to purchase the necessary luggage for the trip, I was told. I ate my snack and sat at my desk trying to study, but it was impossible to concentrate. Hours later, Mother arrived home in a van loaded with a variety of different-sized suitcases and hand luggage.

I was then told that Father had decided to set up an export business in Hamburg and that we were going to live there. As Germany was so close to England, my parents speculated, my brothers would be able to visit us frequently. In the meantime, we were going to sell our home and move to Darous to live with my grandparents. Although I was very excited, I had my doubts. None of us knew any German. How would I be able to study and make friends?

Within a short period of time the house of my childhood, with all its furniture and valuable, custom-woven carpets, was sold and we moved to Darous to wait for Father's business partner to set up office in Hamburg and find us proper accommodation. Darous again – and with no school!

26

What I can remember of that month revolves mainly around the fun I had with the servants - especially my Nanny, who was lodging in the servants' quarters. It was winter again and a very cold one. The main building was heated with oil heaters but the servants had to keep warm in the traditional way - under the Korsi, a low table covered with quilts and blankets under which a charcoal brazier slowly burned, its embers covered with a layer of ashes to ensure an even distribution of heat and prevent burning. They sat on mattresses round the Korsi, their feet under the covers, leaning against cushions. At night, they simply stretched out sideways and slept, warmed by the heat imprisoned under the quilt cover. At mealtimes the top, covered by a Sofreh, served as a table.

Every morning after breakfast Uncle Hussain, Grandpa's neighbour, gave father a lift to the city, leaving mother to attend to the household chores - which really meant ordering the servants around. I was left alone to do what I pleased. I passionately enjoyed historical novels and, when tired of reading, I hung around Nanny. She was devoutly religious and never tired of telling me stories about the Shiite Imams and their martyrdom, heaven and hell, Allah and Shaytan (Satan) and how the unbelievers would burn in seven hells. This pious woman taught me my daily prayers and made me perform them every afternoon and after dusk. I was allowed to miss the early morning ritual as, Nanny assured me, since I hadn't reached the age of nine (from which daily prayers become compulsory) God would forgive me for not rising before sunrise, the time of the morning prayer.

At noon, Nanny would spread a clean white cotton cloth over the Korsi and bring my tray of food, dished out by Grandma herself. The princess had a chair in the main kitchen on which she sat and supervised the dishing out of food for the many families living under her roof. She knew I liked taking lunch with the servants, so she made sure I didn't miss out on anything good. The servants' meals were not as lavish as ours.

Other maids joined us under the Korsi, happy to rest from

the morning's running around. Watching them eat gave me great pleasure. They seemed to have enormous appetites and thoroughly enjoyed their glasses of freshly-brewed tea. A boiling Samavar was a permanent feature in Nanny's room. Everyone, from the masters to the servants, took an afternoon nap. I used to lie under the Korsi, comfortably warm, and think about the new country in which we were going to live.

Eventually I would fall sleep, only to be woken by the clattering of the tea glasses on their saucers being passed around to freshen the sleepers and prepare them for submissive obedience to the orders of the mistress of the house. Clearly there was a class difference: the masters and the servants; the haves and the have-nots.

Afternoons would be passed taking walks down the Ehteshamieh. Grandpa loved to inspect the young plane and poplar trees which were planted on each side of the avenue. He used to walk ahead of everyone else, tall and erect, slender and elegant, moving with a certain grace unique to himself. Occasionally he would point with his gold-handled cane at a dying tree and reprimand the master gardener, who followed a step behind.

Grandpa was very goodlooking with refined, delicate features, a thin, well-groomed moustache and a scintillating smile. Unfortunately I was not one of his favourites. NeNe, Aunt Firouzeh's daughter and two years my junior, was. Grandpa loved displaying his preferences. One afternoon, cousins NeNe, Behrooz and myself were gathered in his large bedroom which was furnished with two single beds, one in each of two corners, a brocaded sofa facing the beds and an ivory-topped coffee table. As was his habit, Grandpa was sitting in his bed listening to our childish talk about the servants. He loved to listen to domestic gossip. Relaxed, he asked his valet who was standing by his bed to hand him the box of nougat from the table. Once in possession of the box, he took out a large piece and began eating it with relish. We sat watching him, our mouths watering in anticipation of receiving a piece of the delicious confectionery. He took his time, enjoying his sadistic act then, finished eating, he carefully took another piece and held it out to NeNe who jumped from her seat to fetch the treat, tripping on her long skirt as she went. After her, Behrooz received his share. When I thought my turn had come he looked at me with a malicious smile and said: 'Sorry Laila, there is only one piece left and that I shall eat after my dinner.'

I felt a dreadful pain in my heart and tears began rolling down my face. Feeling humiliated and hurt, unable to bear his cruel eyes still fixed on me and his obvious enjoyment of his inflicted pain, I dashed out of the room to seek sanctuary in the servants' quarters. The following morning Grandma, having been informed by Nanny about the previous night's mental torture, summoned me to her room and, to make up for her husband's mischief, gave me a box of Swiss chocolates – a rarity in those days. I loved her even more than before.

Grandma, short and plump with a bright smile and a pair of large, mesmerising Gajar eyes, was the epitome of kindness, dignity and generosity. An extremely wise and sensible lady, she knew how to manage people – especially her unfaithful and malicious husband. In those days, when men were permitted to have four wives, Grandpa remained monogamous. However, his extramarital activities were no secret. Indeed, he had been such a renowned playboy in his youth that, when his father went to Mosaffer Ed-Din Shah for the hand of his sister in marriage to his son, the Shah granted permission only on condition that the young prince prove his fertility by first taking a Sigah (concubine). In fact, His Majesty was not concerned with the possibility of infertility; rather, he was worried about the risk of venereal disease.

The Imperial request was obeyed, a concubine was taken and, soon afterwards, became pregnant. In due course, a healthy baby girl was born. Two options were presented to the concubine. She could either receive a hefty sum and leave, taking her child with her, or take the money and leave the child to be brought up in its father's household. The wise lady chose the second course.

A wet nurse was employed to look after baby Taji, who years later became my favourite aunt. Among the first women emancipists, her life was far more interesting and rewarding than her other sisters', with the exception of Aunt Firouzeh. She was tall, elegant and voluptuous. Men desired her, but I don't believe any of them had any luck in seducing her. She eventually married and mothered two children, a girl and a boy. Unfortunately, the passion of her life was gambling. As time passed and her political activities subsided, she gambled away first her husband's fortune, then her own immense inheritance from Grandpa. She was one of those individuals whose star never shone. Her husband became addicted to opium, her son to heroin. They took turns in frequenting clinics to rehabilitate themselves, only to return to the habit once released. One day in 1967, when she was crossing a busy road to visit her son in a clinic, a taxi hit her and she died instantly. I mourned her death for a long time. In my thoughts she lives, kind and gracious. Perhaps it was meant for her to find luck in death. She certainly didn't have much of it while living.

Does luck exist? Or are we responsible for the direction our destiny takes?

Chapter Four

In early March, the snow-covered Elborze announces the arrival of spring by revealing patches of green vegetation on its otherwise white foothills.The bare fruit trees prepare to dress in colour. Gradually, the muddy plains begin to dry out, becoming first green then patterned with purple bluebells, pink daisies and wild, deep blue violets.

In private gardens, roses bloom in the hedges, curl around the tree trunks and foam over the smaller plants in exuberant abundance. Violets and primroses fill the flowerbeds. The flowers and shortlived blossoms exude their exquisite scents, filling the air with intoxicating perfumes which attract myriads of bees, butterflies and singing birds.

It was on one such heavenly day that we left Iran. My parents and I rose early – so early that I could hear the Muez singing the Azan, calling the faithful to rise and salute Allah. Soon all the servants were up, keen to be of service and hoping to receive handsome gratuities for services rendered during our stay.

At around 9 am, a tearful Nanny dressed me in my travelling clothes and, with a hug, bade me goodbye predicting she would never see me again. How did she know that within six months jaundice would claim her and take her to heaven?

Just before our exodus we went to express our gratitude to Grandpa for his hospitality and generosity. The farewell was short, courteous and loveless.

Grandma and most of the family accompanied us to Mehrabad Airport where our emotions were expressed, tears shed and kisses exchanged. The plane took off at two in the afternoon, carrying us to an unknown future. Throughout the flight, Mother whispered verses from the Koran, blowing the prayers around to ensure a safe journey for us. Father, on the other hand, was enjoying himself eating, drinking and flirting with the blonde hostesses.

In Hamburg we were welcomed by Father's partner, a rather old and obese man named Mr Malek and his short, corpulent and domineering young wife. After we had collected our luggage, they drove us to our lodgings, a bedsitter in a boarding house which housed a common toilet and bathroom. Shock and disappointment flashed across my parents' faces, but they said nothing. Before she and her husband took their leave, Mrs Malek told Mother about a nearby corner shop for the purchase of immediate necessities.

Shortly after the couple had departed Mother, jetlagged and disillusioned, threw herself onto one of the three beds and began to cry. Father sat on a chair nearby, looking drawn and thoughtful as though, suddenly, he had realised the enormity of his mistake. The choice of lodging was demeaning and an indication of Father's position in the partnership.

I was so exhausted that nothing mattered except bed. The following morning I woke up feeling alert and fresh, determined to make the best of whatever was ahead of me. After a simple breakfast bought by Father from the corner store, I dressed myself, went out of the room and, with a timid smile, stood in the corridor ready to make friends.

The first person to enter the hall was a young woman wearing a clean apron and holding a bucket and a large broom. I presumed her to be the maid, come to clean the bedsitters on our floor. She had a bright, smiling face and I took an immediate liking to her. The feeling must have been mutual because when she noticed me she came close and, kneeling down to my level, lifted my tiny chin up and uttered something in German. I didn't understand what she said but guessed it to be a question about my identity. Pleased, I pointed to my chest saying, 'Laila'. She laughed, pointed to her own chest and responded, 'Helga'. Instantly a bond was formed and soon, with her help, I acquired enough rudimentary German to enable me to interpret for my parents.

Occasionally after finishing her work, Helga took me to a small park near the apartment. The playground there became my Darous and I made many friends ranging from children to old women. I desperately missed Grandma and Nanny. Mother kept herself busy housekeeping and Father tried to come to grips with the complexities of his new business venture. Neither of them was happy and the atmosphere at home was one of melancholy.

It did not take my parents long to realise that travelling from Britain to Germany, though the distance was not great, was not quite the same as travelling from Teheran to Ramsar. Travelling to and fro between the two countries needed visas and money. Amir's and Ali's single visit to Hamburg was a disaster. They slept in our room, taking the beds in which my mother and I normally slept, while we slept on the floor. In the absence of any income, Mother had become disturbingly frugal.

Our situation was totally different from that of Father's partner. Mr Malek knew German well; he owned a large house; his children went to school in Hamburg; and his wife enjoyed the companionship of her parents who lived in the same vicinity. We, on the other hand, were desperately lonely and unhappy and leading a life of unaccustomed poverty. Father, an observant man, soon realised that the company funds were being swindled, but because of his difficulties with the language he couldn't do much to ameliorate the situation. This sense of inadequency frustrated him and made him extremely moody. His frequent temper tantrums caused a great deal of tension in our small room and made Mother even more miserable. She had lost her appetite and developed a worrying pallor.

Naturally enough in these circumstances nobody was in any frame of mind to consider me, let alone think of enrolling me at a school. So I had to fend for myself. Eventually, Mother gathered enough courage to propose a return to Iran. Father jumped at the idea, as though he had been waiting for her to make the suggestion. Perhaps he was ashamed to suggest it himself, as though it would be an admission of failure. In any case, once the decision to return was made the air cleared. The city of Hamburg seemed suddenly beautiful. German food, especially the famous sausage, tasted good. Even our room looked bigger.

My parents sought advice from the Iranian Embassy as to how the partnership could be legally dissolved. The interpreter and lawyer recommended by the embassy were approached and once the affairs were sorted out amicably, we bade farewell to Helga, our sole friend, and left Germany.

The flight back to Teheran was comfortable and seemed short. I passed the time eating and daydreaming about Darous, where we were to stay until an appropriate house could be leased. Our villa in Avenue Ehteshamieh was to remain rented out and the income sent to my brothers.

At Mehrabad Airport we were met by Grandma – who was radiantly happy – and my aunts. Passing through the city on our way to Shemiran, we noticed how much the city had changed. Everything looked more alive. The shops were crowded with customers, and their windows were bursting with displays of imported goods. New buildings were being constructed everywhere we looked, but in particular on each side of the Avenue Ehteshamieh. These multistorey villas surrounded by high walls conveyed a new sense of affluence. Grandpa's trees had grown tall and the once barren fields had disappeared.

It was a real joy to be back among family and friends. To · my delight, within a week I was enrolled at the local school and life resumed its pleasant, secure course. I particularly enjoyed weekends, when all my cousins met in Grandma's garden to play. As long as we did not bring our mischief inside the house we were allowed to do whatever we wanted, with the exception of going near Grandpa's special pear trees. The fruit of these trees was reserved for His Highness, who loved to pick them with his own royal hands. These trees were our targets at night when the gardners were busy with their wives. During the day we either chased the hens to find eggs or ransacked the walnut trees. Our booty was sold to Grandma, our sole source of income.

My cousins were NeNe, Aunt Firouzeh's daughter, Behrooz and Mehram, Aunt Zinat's sons, Ahmad, Khaleh Joon's youngest son and Homa, Grandma's great granddaughter. (Grandma had married at the age of 11 and the marriage was consummated soon after her first mensturation – so her firstborn was only 14 years younger than her!) The rest of the cousins were much older than us.

We went through childhood together, playing, fighting, quarrelling, competing and compromising. There is much to be said for the extended family system. It nurtures compassion, loyalty, a sense of belonging and security. Children grow up within a society of loving and caring adults; adolescents go through the trying period of identification as part of an accepted peer group; adults tackle life secure in the protection of their clan and the aged pass their retirement days cared for and respected by their offspring. Usually, death is an end to a fulfilled life. Of course, all this is achieved by forfeiting independence.

Maturity brought about for us children a growing awareness of sexual differences. Usually, sexual knowledge was acquired discreetly and haphazardly, as sex was a forbidden subject .It was referred to as 'Kar Bad', which literally means 'the bad action'. We lived in a society with a double standard of morality. It was tacitly accepted that men participated in this 'bad action' but for women, outside of marriage, it meant dishonour or even stoning to death.

The initial source of my sex education was Sadat, Grandma's personal maid. She was an elderly woman with kind, tranquil eyes and shiny, silver hair covered by a long white scarf. She reminded me of Nanny. One day when I was skipping with a rope she came running out, beating at her head as though something dreadful had happened.

'Laila Khanum*, stop it at once!' she cried. 'You can lose your virginity by jumping!'

I was dumbfounded and truly frightened.

* lady

'Sadat, how can I lose my virtue by jumping?'

'Virginity is just a curtain of blood, ready to be dropped by any kind of penetration or jerky movement,' she replied, her voice filled with anxiety.

That was the end of any physical activity for me for a long time. The point was drilled so vehemently by Sadat and, subsequently, by my mother that the fear was absorbed strongly enough to make me a dreadful sportswoman for life.

We were growing fast. Our games were changing from the childish activities of climbing trees and roaming the garden to listening to music and playing married couples. Sex had become an important issue, to be sensed but not mentioned. We began to have crushes on one another, the neighbours and on the movie stars.

My suitor was Ahmad – tall, thin, good-looking and with a great sense of humour. He was thoroughly spoiled by his father and not in the least interested in intellectual pursuits. Ahmad wooed me with his stare and took advantage of every opportunity to touch me. His attention was flattering and I was fond of him.

Our elders were becoming conscious of our maturity and matchmaking was being contemplated. By 1956, I was tall,slender and looked much older than my age of 10. Although boys were beginning to notice me, however, my attention was solely focused on learning. I was at the top of my class and with each yearly report Father rewarded me with a generous present. I was already in possession of a jewelled Omega watch and a gold Parker pen.

The family was happy and I was happy. Uncle Hussain had just built a country house in Goldonak, his village in the foothills of the mountains about half-an-hour from Shemiran. The house was simple, comfortable and well-suited to the rustic environment of the village he had inherited from his brother. One Friday towards the end of the summer, he gave a housewarming party and invited the whole family. We were all excited and looked forward to the occasion for days.

At ten in the morning, four cars started out from Darous

for Goldonak. After a bumpy drive along dirt roads we arrived at the village. The house was set in the middle of a neatly-mown lawn, facing a bubbling spring which poured its icy water into a large, rectangular swimming pool. The clear water looked very inviting in the heat of the summer's day. A large tent spread its canvas to provide protection from the burning sun and a thick tribal kilim* decorated the area in the shade. Behind the tent a fertile apple orchard sloped down to a dry river bed.

The dirt drive connecting the main road to the house was bordered by hazelnut bushes heavy with ripe fruit, their green skins hidden among the wide, curly leaves. You had to look closely to discern the nuts from the leaves.

Aunt Firouzeh's Nanny had been assigned the responsiblity of disciplining the children and preventing them from disturbing the adults' card games. Accordingly, the tent was reserved for us and our lunch. Once the group had gathered in the tent, Mehram the oldest cousin, titled Khan, assumed leadership and suggested a search for hazelnuts. No-one dared to question his authority or oppose his suggestion. The attack was quite civilised. Once our pockets were filled and our hands could not hold any more we retired to the shade of a tree and began to skin the nuts, breaking the hard shells with a stone. Then, bored with the nuts, we turned our attention to the apple orchard. Mashallah, the master gardener, was nearby busy picking the fruit. Spotting us, he anticipated our intentions and put down his basket of fruit. Looking churlish and meaning business he approached and forbade us to pick the apples which had already been sold to a fruiterer. Obediently, with bent heads and chins drooping, we returned to the tent where a sumptuous meal was laid on a white Sofreh.

During lunch, Ahmad sat next to me, devouring me with his dark brown eyes and complementing me on my beauty. As usual his adulation was both embarrassing and pleasing. He was about to utter something else when Mehram Khan

* rug

37

suggested mountain-climbing. Everybody rose, and in groups of two or three headed towards the dry, slippery hills which led to the majestic mountains. Each of us found a sturdy stick to help with what we knew would be a slippery descent on the way back down. We decided to climb to a lone tree which was growing on top of the tallest hill. After an hour of exercise, panting and sweating, we reached the solitary plant, which turned out to have too few branches to provide any shade at all. Tired bodies collapsed on the stony ground. While resting, I enjoyed the dusty, hazy view of Teheran outstretched below like a cancerous cell with no shape or purpose. It was hot. An occasional sandy breeze brushed my burning cheeks. My dry mouth longed for a cool drink.

I was not yet fully rested when Mehram Khan got up and ordered us to descend. Like obedient soldiers we rose, ready to follow our general. Suddenly, Ahmad yelled: 'Let's see who can get down first!' and, leading the way, he began running down the steep, slippery slope. Suddenly, to our horror, we saw his body toppling down the hill, pulling with him a blanket of earth and stones.Then the tiny, whirling particles of dust which arose created a curtain of clouds and obscured the rolling figure from sight.

For what seemed like an eternity we stood there, devastated and paralysed with fear. Mehram was the first to run down towards Ahmad, whose body now rested on the edge of the dry river bed. From the distance, we saw him bend over, hesitate, then run towards the villa.

I began my descent with shaking legs, trembling with emotion, tripping over the stones and falling face down on the rough, thorny slopes. Hurt and bruised I reached the bleeding body. His face was colourless, his eyes closed. The expression on his lovely, kind face told of the pain he must have endured.

I knelt beside him and lovingly lifted his bloodstained head, gently placing it on my lap. I stroked his moist, sticky, curly hair, burying my face in it and feeling his blood on my skin. I hardly heard the sound of the approaching hurrying footsteps and the screams of Khaleh Joon. When the poor mother reached the lifeless body of her son she collapsed unconscious. Luckily, someone caught her, preventing a second tragedy. Ahmad's father stood some distance away covering his face with his hands, crying silently. As Uncle Hussain approached me I offered him the body. He knelt on the ground, holding the corpse and searching for a sign of life. Failing to find one, he nodded his head in regret.

The men gently carried the body to the tent, laid it down and covered it with the same white cloth on which lunch had been served. Those in control of their emotions began making the necessary arrangements. The village doctor, police and mullah were sent for. The women attended to the grief-stricken mother and the silent father. We, the cousins, sat in a corner crying, waiting for punishment. A disconcerted Mehram looked drained. Poor boy! To have to bear the burden of such guilt!

The servants were busy serving tea and Turkish coffee to the mourners. Father, realising the depth of our sorrow and guessing that we feared retribution, came over to us and sat down. Without looking at any of us he said: 'A senseless accident has brought tragedy to the family.' Then, looking straight at Mehram he continued: 'However, no single person is responsible for what has happened. We have to accept the will of God with grace and pray for our beloved's soul which is in heaven.' He paused, trying to control a sudden sob. 'Now you must get up, go and wash your faces and wait by the car for the prince's driver to take you to your homes. We will follow you shortly.' Having made this statement he rose and went to leave instructions with the chauffeur. We sighed with relief. But though Father's speech had erased our fear of punishment, nothing could lift the burden of guilt and sorrow we were going to feel for a long time.

I could not leave without saying a final goodbye to my beloved cousin and admirer. Slowly, I approached the tent. I waited until the people inside were absorbed in their tasks then, creeping close to the body with a pounding heart, tight throat and trembling hands I lifted the cover from Ahmad's face and looked at him for the last time. Quickly, I placed a kiss on his forehead then pulled the cover back over his face. I could not help wondering what he had been going to tell me when Mehram Khan had suggested the fatal climb.

Khaleh Joon never fully recovered from the loss of her favourite son. She developed diabetes and, unfortunately, a small scratch on her toe eventually led to gangrene and the amputation of her leg. She died a few years later. Her husband tried to commit suicide but was saved by the family physician. He survived the Revolution and lived till 1986 when he died of old age.

Chapter Five

General Teymour Bakhtiar was an attractive man in his late 30s. As the military governor of Teheran he was charged with the responsibility of tracking down Mossadegh's supporters. A man without pity, he was ardently opposed to Mossadegh and an impassioned anti-communist.

Bakhtiar wasted no time in filling the Ghasr prison with Mossadegh's former ministers, known supporters and Tudeh members. His prisoners were all interrogated and tortured. It was rumoured that thousands of officers were arrested. In Teheran alone, many caches of red propaganda, secret arsenals and crates of ammunition were found. This relentless pursuit of the communists led to the identification of most card-carrying Tudeh members and placed hundreds of them, including two of Father's cousins, in prison. Much later, many of these asked for pardon and were released to become high-ranking officials, particularly in Hoveyda's cabinet.

Bakhtiar imposed a curfew and harsh restrictions on consumer goods, resulting in public dependency on the black market. A period of repression followed and once again the country was on the verge of bankruptcy. This time, the Shah acted quickly and appealed to President Eisenhower for aid. He was granted millions of dollars. Diplomatic relations with Britain were re-established and after protracted negotiations an international consortium consisting of American, British, French and Dutch companies was created to replace the former Anglo-Iranian Oil Company. Slowly, money began to flow into the country. With the state of the economy improved, the Shah launched programs to upgrade agriculture, communications, industry and social services. The influx of American dollars produced a boom from which not everybody gained. While Teheran saw many changes, the desert and the villages remained almost untouched.

Corruption was rife. Under-the-counter deals, hush money and bribes became a fact of daily life. Merchants and businessmen made enormous profits. New movie palaces, department stores and commercial buildings mushroomed all over the city, whose population had grown to a massive one-and-a-quarter million. Yet the city had no sewage system, no proper hospitals and not enough schools.

Shemiran, with its sumptuous villas, nightclubs and restaurants became a millionaires' retreat and imported luxury cars became the new status symbols.

But in the lower city, where people lived under tin sheds with no sanitation and no electricity, poverty levels remained unchanged, as did the conditions of the workers and peasants. Workers earned an average of $8 a month while the cost of living crept up and the shortage of housing raised rents sky-high.

In the meantime, with the technical help of the Americans, Bakhtiar created a security organisation called SAVAK (Sazemane Atelaat va Amniate Kechvar – The Organisation for Information and Security of the Country.) Gradually and carefully, Bakhtiar had the agency penetrate every aspect of the public and private lives of the regime's opponents. He also connivingly accumulated files on everybody of the slightest importance. This formidable bank of information was to serve an important political purpose for Bakhtiar.

Over the years, SAVAK grew to become one of the largest secret services in the world. It was everywhere. Every high-ranking official was followed by a SAVAK shadow who monitored his every move. The same held true for all the country's large business enterprises, in particular the National Iranian Oil Company and the universities, where every dean was expected to cooperate with SAVAK. At people's houses, at dinners and receptions, one was never quite sure if those sitting on one's left or right were SAVAKI. No Iranian dared to express an opinion about this monstrosity.

SAVAK possessed the most sophisticated, cruel and inhumane instruments to dehumanise the opponents of the regime. In 1979, after the collapse of the monarchy, a television program presented a report on the organisation. Surviving victims were interviewed and told of the sadistic deeds which had been carried out by the SAVAKI – how these maniacs had even gone so far as to decapitate their fellow countrymen and women to keep the Pahlavis in power.

SAVAK also watched over all Iranians abroad, particularly students attending universities. The Shah, fully aware of this organisation's operational methods, had sanctioned its existence believing it to be indispensable to his own survival. How wrong he was!

The monarchy had been an inherent component of Iranian culture for as long as history remembered. Every Iranian, right up to the revolution, was brought up to respect the concept of 'Khoda, Shah, Mihan' (God, Shah and Country). The coup d'etat of 1953 was proof of America's acknowledgement of the popularity of the Shah, even against such a man as Mossadagh. Why then did the sovereign sanction the existence of such an organisation as SAVAK? Why did the Shah allow his relationship with his subjects to deteriorate to such a degree, and his regime to grow so corrupt that its very survival depended on the vigilance of SAVAK? Was it a weakness of character? Was it because he had grown up under the shadow of a domineering father? Or was it because of an immature ego which craved to be nurtured by the glorification of his sycophants who, for their own selfish purposes, let him live under an illusion?

Perhaps during the process of Westernising Iran the Shah had lost his Iranian identity and developed contempt for his own people. Or could it be that he imagined himself to be surrounded by traitors? Possibly, as up to the premiership of the late Hovayda, most of the men he trusted betrayed him! Even Premier Zahedi, an ambitious politican, was found to be harbouring dangerous intentions and was discreetly asked to resign. To keep face the general pleaded ill health and asked to be relieved of his duties. The request was granted and Zahedi left for Geneva to become the Iranian representative of the European section of the United Nations.

Grandma didn't like Zahedi because he had divorced one of her relatives to marry a younger, more beautiful woman. We all enjoyed gossiping and, recently, our favourite topics of conversation were the public dissatisfaction with the government's suffocating repression and Soraya's infertility. This latter problem was compounded by the accidental death of Prince Ali Reza, the Shah's brother and heir to the throne. People were worried about the future of the dynasty but no-one seemed to be concerned about Soraya herself. She had become a very unpopular queen and Grandma was of the opinion that she was more German than Iranian.

In spite of all the bad news Grandma and I were very happy. She had recently acquired a residential property in Avenue Saadi and was going to let us live in it rent-free until Father's financial situation improved. Luckily for me, Grandpa was spending most of his time in town planning the grand opening of his hotel. The construction had been completed a month earlier and the decorators were now busy furnishing it. Grandpa's new companion was his middle-aged nephew Prince Nasrollah, a chronic gambler who had wasted his vast fortune and, penniless, had sought refuge in the patronage of his generous uncle.

For some reason I disliked this intruder. There was something evil in his eyes, especially when he looked at me. On one occasion when the family was sitting on the floor by the Sofreh having lunch, he sat next to me crossing his legs as widely as possible so that his knee was touching mine. Automatically I moved sideways to make room for him but, shamelessly, he moved closer. The warmth of his bony knee disgusted me. I was squashed between him and Behrouz. When I couldn't bear the proximity of the two bodies any more I rose and ran to Sadat's room where she sat comfortably on the floor beside a large board cutting freshly-kneaded pasta into hair-thin strips for the evening meal. The wise woman detected my anxiety and asked if there was anything amiss. I did not know what to tell her and so I feigned a stomach ache and sat quietly by her side soaking up the comfort of her black-wrapped motherly presence. She attributed my pain to a probable overconsumption of unripe fruit then, with no response forthcoming from me, she began a religious lecture about MOHARAN, the month when Iranians commemorate the martyrs of Karbella, a town of pilgrimage for the Shiite Muslims in Iraq.

She began by saying, 'Many hundreds of years ago, on such a month, 40 brave men led by Emam Hussain, the third Emam, the son of Emam Ali, the Lion of Islam and the grandson of the prophet, went to war against the massive army of the ungodly Caliph Yazid, successor of the usurpers of Caliphat (rulership of the Muslim state) from the line of the prophet. Outnumbered, these men of God were slaughtered and beheaded by the army of Satan. The brave martyrs embraced death to save humanity from corruption on earth.' (The order of the succession to the Caliphat is one of the principles on which the Shiite dogma differs from that of the Sunni's. Shiites believe that before his death Mohammed named Ali as his successor. However ,after the prophet's death, Abubakr was elected as the Caliph of all Muslims. Eventually Ali was elected to become the fourth Caliph).

Exhausted, Sadat paused to take a deep breath and, with moistened eyes, promised to take me to the mosque that evening. This was the eve of Tasua, the night of the commemorated event for which she was dressed in black.

After dinner, covered in our chador, we headed for the mosque which had been sponsored by an endowment from Grandpa. At the entrance we took off our shoes and entered the threshold of the sacred house. The interior of the mosque was divided into two levels, the lower level accommodating the men and the upper level retained for the women. A white-bearded turbanned mullah seated on his elevated bench was recounting the story of the war. With sorrow in his tone and sadness on his countenance, he repeated each sentence at least twice in order to play on the emotions of the listeners. The story told, the mullah rose from his wooden bench and sat on the floor, giving the platform to a younger mn who had stepped forward calling for his slain Emam: 'Ya Hussain, Ya Hussain!' After a sudden commotion, all the men stood up and began beating on their chests to the rhythm of the chant. Gradually the chanting became more excited, provoking a frenzy of hysterical emotions in the Dasteh (the flagellating group).

Women watching the scene were equally aroused. They were crying and under their chador were gently beating on their chests to the same rhythm. Intermittently the flagellation stopped. The participants would sit on the floor, wipe the perspiration off their faces with black handkerchieves then take a cup of tea and a piece of date served by a donor. After a short recess, the mourning would resume. This continued until the time came for our congregation to leave for the mosque in the next suburb of Golhak.

Outside in the street, the Dasteh started off in an orderly procession. The men were chanting, beating on their chests and waving the green flags of Islam and banners proclaiming 'Ya Hussain, the slain of Karbella!' The women and children followed. On the road more people joined in the procession and the procedure repeated itself until, at midnight, the last designated mosque (usually the largest in the district) was reached. Then, well-satisfied with their performance of religious duty and assuming all sins to have been forgiven, the worshippers broke up to gather again the following morning, the sacred day of Ashura. On Ashura all activities in Shiite communities come to a complete standstill. It is a true day of commemoration, tears and prayer. Sadat and I had returned home after our Dasteh left for Golhak.

The activities of these two days may seem fanatical and uncivilised to a Western reader. But for the believer, it is a day of remembrance of great heroism, an adulation of the concept of justice for the principle of which, all those centuries ago, those 40 brave men of Karbella gave their lives. Perhaps it was because of the intense emotion the commemoration stirred up that the organisers of the procession which led to the Revolution of 1979 chose these two days for their most massive demonstrations against the Shah's regime?

My first religious education was rudimentary, obtained from the household staff – especially Sadat, whose exaggerated versions were modified by Mother's more rational explanations. The clergy were ordinary people with a blind faith, who believed what was handed down to them as absolute truth. The Koran was read in Arabic, with some verses being memorised to be whispered in times of trouble. The majority of people didn't even know the meaning of their daily prayers. As time passed, however, the people became more educated. The Koran was translated into Persian and the clergy had to attend Divinity College before they could preach. Very slowly, blind faith became a thing of the past.

For me, nothing has ever been easy. With only fragmented knowledge about Islam, at the age of 12 I was thrown into the world of Christianity to learn and comprehend the concept of the Trinity! It took me many years of living in doubt, searching for the truth, fearing the fire of hell and the acquisition of two university degrees before I felt able to choose my religion. I chose Islam because in its philosophy I found an appealing sense of equality, justice and, above all, simplicity in the relationship between man and his God.

Chapter Six

It was a hot summer afternoon. The burning sun blazed out of an azure sky, only an occasional breeze making the heat bearable. While the household was taking its siesta I sat waiting for Behrouz on the tiled edge of the swimming pool, cooling my sunburnt legs and thinking about Grandpa's illness which they said was angina. Earlier that morning, resting in bed with down pillows piled behind his head, he had looked pale and listless.

Except for NeNe, none of us was even allowed to pass near his bedroom without permission, though once or twice Grandma had asked me to come and massage her arthritic legs. At the end of each session she had sent me off with a ten rial note to buy myself an icecream. She loved having her legs massaged. Her usual masseuse was Sadat, who was never thanked and was lucky to get out of the room without being reprimanded for not performing with enough zeal. Traditionally servants were not treated as equals. However, my grandparents treated their staff better than most other aristocrats.

The custom of acquiring new help took place annually when the peasant elders came from Bousar to bring the landlord's share of the crops. They also brought their grievances about the season's poor harvest, their need for a small loan to see them through the coming winter and their inability to feed their family. Most of them wanted to know if His Highness could relieve them from the burden of feeding an extra mouth. At first their benefactor would express his displeasure at their lack of productivity, blaming it on their laziness. But eventually His Highness would show charity and grant them a small loan, as well as agreeing to allow the extra mouth which accompanied them to live under his roof. Elated and rich they would return to Bousar. The Gilaki dialect-speaking youngsters would then be placed in the charge of a senior servant until they learned proper Farsi and acquired some sort of skill in return for a small salary. The majority of them remained part of the household until their dying day.

It was not unusual for the servants to marry among themselves. In such cases the wedding was arranged and Grandma gave a small dowry to the bride and an adequate salary increase to the groom. In many ways their lot was much better than that of the young peasants who remained in the provinces.

The heat was becoming unbearable and Behrouz was late for our diving practice. I was becoming restless when I heard the sound of approaching footsteps. I turned towards the direction of the noise and, to my disappointment, saw Nasrollah approaching the pool. Grinning, he sat down next to me and let his hairy legs dangle in the water. Feeling awkward, I sat motionless. I knew instinctively that something dreadful was about to happen. With a malicious expression on his face, the prince asked after my health. Curtly, I replied that I was well. He inched closer and put his left arm around my shoulder, squeezing it to his sweating side. My heart missed a beat and I began to tremble with fear. There was no-one else around. Nasrollah nudged even closer and said: 'Little girl, why are you so frightened of me? Today I am going to play with you and you are going to like it very much. But you must keep it a secret – our secret.' Speech over, he put his other hand on my thigh and began stroking it gently; then, sliding his long, crooked fingers inside my swimsuit he began to play with my pubic hair and penetrate further down. I locked my thighs together to restrict the movement of his fingers. My chest was bursting with rage and apprehension and I could hardly breathe. His fingers were moving fast now and he was panting heavily. His hot breath was nauseating. I felt clammy and unclean. The only thing I could think of was my virginity and the fact that I was about to lose it. I had to save my honour!

The urge to escape impelled me to wriggle out of his grip and slide into the water, dragging him with me. Trying to break loose I began kicking the monstrous molester, but the determined bastard kept on clutching the fabric of my costume, pulling me to him. The straps were cutting into my skin. Dragged close, I summoned all my energy to my knees and pumped them into his testicles again and again. With an agonised shriek he let go. I pushed myself under the water and swam as fast as I could to the far corner of the pool. Reaching the edge, I pulled myself out and ran towards the building and my room, praying that I would not meet anyone on the way.

Luckily Mother was not in. Breathless, without bothering to dry myself, I dropped onto the bed and, burying my face in the pillow, began hysterically beating the mattress. What was I going to tell Mother? If I had lost my virginity would Father kill me, like Prince Zellian who had shot his dishonoured daughter? Would I have to run away to Shahre No (the red light district) to become a prostitute like all the other violated girls? How would my parents bear the humiliation of having a fallen daughter?

It was dark when I opened my eyes to see Mother's placid face smiling at me. She asked me why I had not dried myself after swimming and why I had been crying. I told her that I had been fighting with Behrouz and had been so upset I had forgotten to dry myself. Frowning she scolded, 'You will catch cold. And you are too old to get mixed up in fights!' After she had gone I rose reluctantly, straightened my bed and headed for the bathroom to try to wash off the touch of the evil man and, perhaps with it, my shame. The long, hot shower relaxed my shattered nerves.

I decided to try to find out whether or not I had lost the curtain of blood that protected my virginity. To do this I took Mother's magnifying glass from the vanity drawer and, squatting on the floor, placed the mirror in front of my vagina and began searching for any sign of change. No apparent difference. Where could the curtain of blood be? Or had I lost it? Not satisfied, I stood up, put the mirror back in its place and pulled my pants up. How could I discover what had happened to me? Perhaps Sadat could help.

When I entered the kitchen I found her preparing Grandpa's soup. She did not appear to be in a chatty mood and so, to help her, I offered to take the meal to the patient. She prepared the heavy silver tray and handed it to me, warning me to go slowly so as not to spill the contents. The bedroom was dimly lit by a single bedside lamp. Grandma was sitting on her bed whispering to Mother and Aunt Firouzeh, their elongated shadows on the wall creating a mysterious atmosphere in the stuffy room. Grandpa seemed to have dozed off. Grandma smiled at me and turned to her husband. 'Aga*, your dinner is here,' she said softly. There was no response.

Aunt Firouzeh rose from her chair and took the tray from my arms. She carried it to her father whispering: 'Aga Joon, your soup will get cold.' There was no movement. Carefully, she placed the tray on the ivory table and returned to the bed. She began to shake her father gently to wake him up. Grandpa did not stir. Worried now, she took his hand and searched for his pulse. Her wail broke the silence. She dropped to her knees and started to kiss the body. Grandma and Mother hurried to the bedside, beating their heads and tugging at their faces, crying 'Aga Joon, Aga Joon.' I stood there motionless, not daring to look at yet another lifeless face.

The loud and bitter lamentations brought in the servants. One of them had the sense to telephone the other members of the family who lived in their own apartments on the property. Soon Uncle Hussain arrived, accompanied by the family doctor and a mullah. The doctor diagnosed a heart attack as the cause of death.

In the adjoining room a mattress covered with a white sheet was placed on the floor facing Ghebleh (Mecca). Uncle Hussain and Father carried Grandpa out of the bedroom and placed him on the mattress, covering his body with another white

---

* sir; also a term of respect for the clergy

sheet. The mullah sat on the floor over the head of the corpse and began reciting verses from the Koran. The recitations continued until dawn when, in accordance with the wishes of the prince, his body was washed with water from the garden spring, splashed with rose water then shrouded in white fabric from Karbella which had been purified at the shrine of Emam Hussain.

Grandma's grief over the loss of her husband was profound. She had loved him dearly all her life and had carried the knowledge of his infidelities with patience and dignity. Not long before his death I had overheard the cook telling Sadat about His Highness' designs on the new teenage maid. If Sadat knew, then Grandma knew too. Sadat was her 'eyes and ears'.

The following morning everyone rose very early, as arrangements had to be made for the funeral and guests were expected. By nine o'clock the house was full of relatives and close friends attired in black who had come to pay their last respects. The washing ceremony had taken place after the morning prayers in a tent erected for this purpose near the spring. The body was now ready to be taken to the family mausoleum. At ten o'clock the sons lifted the shrouded body of the patriarch onto their shoulders and slowly carried it to the hearse. The entire party except for the children and the servants left for the mausoleum where, after the burial, lunch was to be served in the courtyard.

The mourning rites lasted for seven days culminating in the reading of the Will, a private affair with only the beneficiaries present. Grandma presided over the gathering, looked aged and pale in the black she would wear for one year. The duty of opening and reading the document was given to Uncle Hussain, Grandpa's favourite son-in-law. After the envelope had been opened and the contents revealed, no-one seemed satisfied except the two sons. They had inherited the bulk of Grandpa's inheritance, including Bousar and the grand residence. Only the remaining land in Darous and the new hotel were to be divided according to Islamic law: the male beneficiaries receiving twice the share of the females, with a special provision for Grandma to inherit the same as the daughters instead of the usual one-eighth. Even in death the old man had the last laugh.

I was sitting in a corner hating Grandpa when Nasrollah, my abuser, casually cornered me and threatened to break my little neck if I ever divulged to anyone anything about the pool incident. Impetuously I summoned all my courage and spat on his ugly, moustached face. Taken by surprise he took a handkerchief out of his trouser pocket and wiped his face. Then, with hatred in his voice he retorted, 'How dare you, you little brat.' Giving me another venomous look he turned his arrogant face and walked away. That was our last encounter. He left the family soon afterwards to live with his brother.

Chapter Seven

The pale autumn sun was just about to set making the horizon a yellowish red. A chilly wind was disturbing the dead leaves as they lay in their mounds on the ground. The swallows had already left for warmer climes. My parents and I were about to move to our own home in Avenue Saadi and I was standing on the veranda feeling depressed about having to leave Grandma. I was going to miss those afternoons when, together, we would drive to the bazaar at Tajrish, a neighbouring village at the foothills of the mountains, to shop.

Grandma was very generous to me and, occasionally when she inspected her treasure chest full of rare gems, she would give me a special gift. My most recent acquisition was a four carat emerald ring. Although we were very close, I never dared to tell her about the pool incident. Frightful nightmares and a deep sense of guilt were haunting me throughout the crucial period of my adolescence. I felt secure only in Grandma's presence, and now I had to leave her.

A summons from Father interrupted my thoughts. The time to depart had arrived. Inside, Grandma was standing by the door with Sadat, holding a volume of the Koran for us to kiss and pass under as we left. This ritual was observed to bring us safe conduct and good luck. Trying to hold back my tears I hugged and kissed her compassionate face and soft hands. Sombre but composed, she promised to have me stay with her every weekend and during the summer holidays. Thus consoled, I turned to Sadat, kissed her and gave her a quarter sovereign. She had always wished for a gold trinket. Now she could have the sovereign made into a ring or pendant. I wanted her to remember me forever, just as I would always keep her memory alive.

Our new house was modest with no architectural merit; a square block of land built on all four sides, rooms leading to rooms with roofed verandahs serving as corridors. The garden, tiled in terracotta, contained a large pond which was used as a small pool. In one corner sultana vines crept over an old trellis, their bird-bitten grapes hanging over a weed-ridden flower bed. A lonely persimmon tree graced the courtyard. Mohammed Ali, the cook, and his wife Zahra, the maid, were to help Mother in the house. The building, conveniently located directly in the centre of the city, was surrounded by shops and cinemas whose neon lights attracted large audiences to their dubbed Hollywood films.

My main sources of entertainment were watching an hour of television after my homework and an occasional visit to the movies. Being thrown back into the bosom of my family needed some readjustment on my part. Father was hardly ever at home. As manager of the family hotel, he spent most of his time working and in the evenings he went to his club. So it was just Mother and me. Most afternoons, hand in hand, we went shopping. She used to buy me freshly made piroshki, a Russian savoury, or Zaban, a kind of sweet puff pastry from the Armenian patisserie in front of our house. I loved these treats and I loved being with Mother again.

I often wondered why she never complained to Father of her loneliness. She looked after me with the utmost care and generosity, but somehow I could not communicate with her in the same way as I did with Grandma. The love of Mother's life, besides Father, was Amir. Even from as far away as England he dominated her thoughts.

As I grew older, I became more immersed in my studies. Father expected me to be the best and so I had become so, always top of my class and finishing each year with distinctions.

Weekends were a welcome relief. Every Thursday afternoon Grandma came to collect me from school. On Fridays, as usual, the family gathered in her house for lunch and a game of cards. The success of the family hotel was the main topic of conversation and a recent pastime was to spend the evenings lounging in its busy lobby. We usually sat in a prominent position, feeling important as the owners of such a grand establishment, expecting respect and demanding first-class service from the waiters who spoilt us with trays of caviar on toast and glasses of chilled Smirnoff vodka.

It was during one of these gatherings that I found myself being whispered about, but however hard I tried I could not hear what they were murmuring. On the way back to Shemiran, I asked Grandma why I had been the subject of discussion. At first she feigned ignorance, but eventually my persistent pleading and sulking persuaded her to divulge the news of the appearance of a Khasegar, a suitor wishing to take me as a wife.

The parents of a young man from a prominent family had telephoned Mother for an appointment. They had told her that they had been searching for a suitable wife for their eighteen-year-old son Mansour, and a mutual friend had suggested me as a perfect match. This friend, knowing which school I attended, had brought the young man in question there one afternoon as I was leaving and had pointed me out to him. After seeing me, and having then followed me to school repeatedly, Mansour had fallen in love with me and wanted to marry me and take me to America, where he intended to further his education. His parents were thrilled with his choice and wanted to see mine at the earliest opportunity.

I was flabbergasted. To marry at the age of twelve!

'Grandma, princess, surely Mother won't want me to get married now?'

'No,' she replied. 'I don't think so. I believe your parents are planning to send you to England to study.'

This was another shock.

'Why, Grandma?' I asked.

She answered in a matter-of-fact tone, 'Because they want to give you a good education. You are a very lucky girl to have such thoughtful parents. It is a great sacrifice to be separated from your children.'

That night I could not sleep. Another fear had been added

to my cornucopia of apprehensions: loneliness among strangers.

The following day, as soon as my parents arrived for lunch, I asked them about the Khasegar and England. Father looked at me with teasing eyes and said: 'Laila Joon, we are going to marry you off to a good-looking boy who is going to take you to America.' I shivered at the thought and began to cry. Mother came to my rescue and reprimanded him for teasing me. She explained that she had refused to grant an appointment to Mansour's parents and assured me that an arranged marriage was out of the question. However, they were planning to send me to England to a private boarding school. There, my brothers would supervise my affairs and look after me. Relieved that I was not to be forced into marriage, I went into the garden where my cousins were playing. They had already heard about my marriage proposal and, spotting me, they began to make joking remarks. I joined them in laughing at the idea.

The task of finding a suitable school in England had fallen on Amir's capable shoulders. He was a young man now and had finished his first year of studying medicine at the University of Durham. Amir was a hard-working student, a first-rate athlete and a responsible elder son. I had grown to love him dearly. During the summer holidays that my brothers had spent in Teheran he had shown me a lot of affection.

Soon we received news of a school in Cardiff, South Wales, which took foreign students and undertook to teach them English within one year. Arrangements were made for Mother and I to travel to London at the beginning of the summer. Lately, Mother's menstrual cycle had become abnormal and she wanted to have a check-up at Amir's hospital in Newcastle. Father was to join us later.

Chapter Eight

Teheran was in a state of jubilation. The recent royal wedding had caused much excitement and the populace was busy gossiping about the new young queen, Farah Diba. She was not particularly beautiful but was tall, striking and graceful. The Shah had met her in Paris while on a private visit in May 1958.

Farah came from a respectable family. Her father, Sohrab Diba, was a diplomat and Farah had been born in Rumania where he was posted. Sohrab died of tuberculosis in 1948 and in order to be able to support her only child Mrs Diba had taken up employment, something quite unusual and daring for a woman at that time.

Farah, a capable student, won a scholarship to study architecture in Paris. At a student gathering at the Iranian Embassy she met her future husband and impressed him with her bold criticisms of the way overseas student scholarships were handled. Subsequent private meetings were arranged by Ardeshir Zahedi, the Shah's son-in-law, and the couple married on December 21. The wedding photographs were splashed across the front pages of every newspaper and magazine in the country. The bride wore a magnificent Dior gown and a stunning diamond crown with matching earrings.

During the two decades she spent as Shahbano (Empress) of Iran the country benefited immensely from her conscientious fulfilment of royal duties. One of Farah's greatest qualities was her passion for everything Persian. Her tireless efforts initiated a revival in Persian culture and arts. Museums were enriched, historical monuments which had been left to ruin were restored, and artistic talents were sought and supported. However, as was the nature of the system, it did not take long for Farah's

59

family to ingratiate themselves with the royal couple, demanding respect and favours. The Diba clan, with the exception of Sagatdouleh Diba and one or two others, were unrenowned with little merit of their own except their royal connection. Her Majesty committed the unforgivable sin of allowing them to take full advantage of her name in making deals, winning contracts and generally competing with the Pahlavis in robbing the country.

Gradually, the excitement of the royal wedding died down and the real problems affecting Iran resurfaced. Prime Minister Eghbal's government was corrupt, the elections were phoney and the state treasury was empty again. Adding to the chaos were the vehement criticisms of Ali Amini, an old politician and leader of an opposition party called the Independents. In an attempt to rectify the situation the Shah promised that the twentieth Majlis would be freely elected. When the manipulated returns of the elections of the Majlis came in, Eghbal's party polled 75% of the votes – a real joke. The Shah asked for Eghbal's resignation, the parliament was dissolved and a new election brought Jafar Sharif Emami into power.

The situation became impossible. Strikes and demonstrations broke out in all the larger cities. Thousands of students demonstrated at Teheran University. There were riots between the students and the police with hundreds of the participants being injured. Meanwhile, Amini's regular press conferences focused on the need for thorough change. The boiling pot was near bursting. The Shah dissolved this parliament too and Amini, as the newly appointed prime minister, immediately announced on the radio that the treasury was empty and the nation's cooperation essential.

Political upheavals aside, unpleasant changes were also taking place in our small household. Mother's family, jealous of Father's success as manager of the hotel were making trouble for him, accusing him of dishonesty and mismanage-ment – neither of which was true. Father was the most honest man in the world. Always a wise man, in order to preserve his dignity, he resigned. What were we going to do now that

Father was out of a job, with two sons at university and me about to attend a private school?

Ali was at Trinity College in Cambridge studying petro-chemistry. We were proud of his achievement but it was costing Father a lot of money. Tuition aside, Ali was extravagant, particularly when thrown into the company of people far richer than himself. I felt very sorry for my father.

One evening, I overheard Mother weeping and asking him what was to become of us. She was particularly concerned about our education. She said, 'True, we have land. But we need cash to support the children overseas. Amini has brought us nothing but economic stagnation and we cannot even sell our land. How are we going to take care of the children?' I knew that Mother was not worried about herself. She could survive on bread and cheese if necessary; but she could not bear the thought of depriving her children of a good education. Patiently, Father listened to her worries and reassured her that he had enough savings to take care of everything.

My parents' financial problems and Mother's anxiety for the future took their toll on me. I began to have nightmares about becoming poor: another fear, another neurosis.

The day of our departure for London arrived. Once packed and ready, Mother and I bade farewell to the rest of the household. Grandma, sad but composed, accompanied us to the airport. As we kissed goodbye she told me that no-one would ever replace me in her heart. I hugged her close, praying to God that she would have a long life and that I would see her again.

At Heathrow Airport we were met by my excited brothers. After exchanging warm greetings we jammed ourselves into Amir's small Saab and headed for the Cumberland Hotel at Marble Arch. We stayed for two days in London – that grey, gloomy, majestic city with which I instantly fell in love. Cambridge, where Ali lived, was our next destination. The city, with its magnificent buildings, beautiful river and gowned students and professors, looked like something out of a history book. To our surprise, whereever we went people greeted Ali

61

with a smile and a reminder of his debt to them. Albeit reluctantly, Mother paid them all.

From Cambridge, we drove to Newcastle where Amir was studying medicine at the Royal Victoria Infirmary. Newcastle was the ugliest city I had ever seen – foggy, cold and provincial. There we met Pat, Amir's steady girlfriend. She was plain and humourless and none of us liked her. Doctors' appointments were made for Mother and medical examinations indicated the need for a hysterectomy. A date was set for after the trip we had planned to the Riviera.

My two brothers gave us a grand tour of Northumberland and the neighbouring counties. Our sightseeing took us to the beautiful Lake District where we had many enjoyable picnics by the sides of the smaller, less popular lakes. I particularly liked Ullswater in Glenridding, a lake surrounded by green hills dotted with fluffy sheep grazing on the long grass. The hills were often almost obscured by the mist rising from the lake. Plumes of smoke from the chimneys of nearby houses drifted upwards to become one with the clouds. Even though it was summer the weather was always cold. We stayed at the Ullswater Hotel which was built on the shore of the lake and Mother and I had our first taste of fish and chips at the local pub. No-one guessed my age.

None of us regretted leaving Newcastle. In Amir's Saab we set off for Dover to cross the English Channel by boat. The crossing was rough, as always, and most of the passengers were seasick. I felt giddy for three days afterwards. But even in this nauseated state I could not help feeling awe-struck at the beauty of Paris. Its magnificent architecture, majestic monuments, the wide streets with their elegant shops, and the smart, arrogant Parisian people made a great impression on me.

My uncle's residence in Neuilly, facing the Bois de Bolougne, was luxurious and well-suited to his high diplomatic rank. Aunt Azy was a lady of great taste and elegance and her hospitality helped make our short stay in Paris very enjoyable.

Our next destination was Geneva where we spent three

days with NeNe and Aunt Firouzeh who, after ten years of trying, had become pregnant again. NeNe was at boarding school and hating it. She hoped to return to Teheran at the end of the summer holidays. I envied her.

The drive to Cannes was pleasant. I loved the Mediterranean, which was so different from the Caspian. It was much calmer and bluer, so blue that from a distance the sea and the sky seemed to join and become one. Our rented villa overlooked the beach and a mooring site. It was also close to a produce market which boasted a great variety of delicious and interesting foods.

Every morning after shopping for our lunch at the market Mother and I walked to the Carlton Hotel's beach. It was more expensive than the other beaches, but also more exclusive. Mother's cousin and Father's friend, Amir Hushang, had a suite there. He was one of the Shah's closest friends and His Majesty had given him the international monopoly on the sale of Persian caviar. He was a hospitable man who enjoyed an occasional puff at the opium pipe and his suite was always open to his friends.

A few days after our arrival there, Father joined us in Cannes. He loved the beach, not because he was a keen swimmer (as a matter of fact he could not swim at all) but because he liked to lie on the sand watching the nude bodies of the sunbathing beauties. During the afternoons we lost him to Amir Hushang and his clique of friends.

Amir and Ali were busy with their many friends. Pat had been forgotten and Amir had become infatuated with one of our second cousins, the daughter of a stingy senator who did not mind enjoying our hospitality without ever reciprocating. The affair did not last long. Janet, Ali's English girlfriend had also joined us, consolidating what was to become Mother's permanent dislike of all English girls. The boys played tennis in the afternoons and I usually accompanied them to the club. Among the celebrities who frequented the centre was Prince Karim, the future Aga Khan. I developed a mad crush on him and could not wait for the afternoons when I could watch him play. He probably never noticed me.

We ate dinner either on the balcony of our small villa or at one of the small local restuarants. Invariably the focal point of the evening for the rest of the family was a session at the casino, but I was not allowed to join them. My place was at the casino's cafe, where I sat alone and ate as many icecreams as I could accommodate until the grown-ups returned either happy or disappointed. That summer, we travelled along the entire coast of the French Riviera. I was not looking forward to returning to England as it meant separation from my parents. They were to leave for Teheran a month after Mother's operation.

Happy times fly. Our wonderful holiday ended and, two days after our return to England, I was packed and ready for school. I spent my last night in bed with Mother. None of us slept. We wept all night – even Father. The next day, just before I climbed onto the train he held me tight and said, 'Laila Joon, remember this sacrifice is for your future. Life has many faces. One day our inheritance may not be enough to see you through life – but your education will.' How right he was!

Part II

GETTING OF WISDOM

It will have blood, they say; blood will have blood:
Stones have been known to move and trees to speak;
Augurs and understood relations have
By maggot-pies and choughs and rooks brought forth
The secret'st man of blood. What is the night?
                                    Shakespeare

Chapter Nine

St Peter's School in Cardiff, South Wales lodged one hundred students, many of whom were foreigners who had come to master the English language. The school's 18th century sandstone building was the property of a Welsh aristocrat. In the absence of any means of heating, the inside of the building was always cold, and at nights we were forced to rely on hot water bottles to keep us warm; unfortunately, however, the tap water was never quite hot enough and, since no-one was allowed into the kitchen to boil water, we shivered in bed as we tried to adapt to the Welsh lifestyle. I shared a dormitory with six other students, one of whom was an Iranian girl with a little knowledge of English. She had been assigned to help me settle in, but unfortunately we never became friends.

Not knowing the language of the people with whom one lives is terribly frustrating. In the early days I found life at my new school very difficult, but gradually my determination to learn got me through the initial barriers. With single words and broken sentences I managed to communicate with my peers. Fortunately, I never suffered from shyness, a trait which is an impediment to the acquisition of any new language. I tried to communicate with everyone and laughed along with those who teased my mistakes.

St Peter's was a Catholic school, with compulsory chapel attendance twice a day and one hour of church every Sunday. Goli, the Iranian girl, attended willingly, pretending to be a Christian. I didn't approve of her attitude towards her own religion. I felt she was a degrading example of a Muslim. How could she expect other people to respect her religion if she herself didn't? I reasoned that if I was to venerate Catholism and attend prayers the school should, in return, respect my faith and allow me time to practise it. To this end I made an appointment with the school's headmistress. With my rudimentary English I made her understand that I wished to perform my daily prayers and needed permission to enter my dormitory during the free period after lunch. (The students were not allowed to enter the dormitories during class hours.) I intended to perform my morning and noon prayers together. This way I would not disturb my roommates at dawn.

The headmistress gazed at me for a while then, with the shadow of a smile on her wrinkled face, nodded her permission. From the expression on her face and her friendly pat on my shoulder I knew that I had won her respect.

Goli hated me for this and accused me of being an old-fashioned Iranian. Annoyed and insulted, I asked her for an explanation. She believed most Iranians were religious fanatics and, thus, backward. She suggested that I take advantage of my situation, Westernise and forget about the archaic Islamic traditions. I disagreed with her and pointed out that one could adopt suitable Western traits without losing one's own identity. Eventually, our disagreement turned into animosity. At the time I was too young to realise that a good number of Iranians, especially the new rich, shared Goli's logic regarding native culture and Islamic traditions.

The only good memory I have of my one year stay at St Peter's is of our daily walks in the woods, particularly during spring when the woodland was a mass of beautiful daffodils and primroses. On sunny days, breathing the sweet fragrance of the flowers, enjoying the occasional glimpse of a small rabbit darting here and there, or a sharp-eyed squirrel in its tree, I felt as though I was treading some heavenly pathway.

Letters were my only means of communication with the outside world and, recently, they had been bearing good news. Father, in partnership with a friend, had leased a large, modern hotel in the heart of the commercial centre of Teheran. Together, they had renamed it The Mirabel. Mother had allowed him to mortgage everything she owned to raise the necessary funds for key money and furnishings – an act of great generosity on her behalf. Islam, contrary to common Western belief, not only allows women to own property, but also to retain it after marriage. She had undertaken a great risk, particularly during the austere Amini era.

Another important item of news which had been broadcast all over the world was that, on the morning of October 31st, 1960 Shahbano Farah had given birth to a long awaited heir to the Pahlavi throne. For one week the country had been in a state of jubilation.

Blessings come in threes. A letter arrived confirming my acceptance, depending on an interview, at Felixstowe College in Suffolk, one of the most highly acclaimed public schools in England. This meant I would be near Ali, who had finished university and was working in Felixstowe.

The term finished in due course and I rushed to Felixstowe for my interview. Miss Jones, the headmistress, was tall, intelligent and rather corpulent. Somehow, I must have impressed her with my ambition, aiming to take eight subjects for the Ordinary-level examinations with only one year of English behind me. I was accepted and enrolled to start the following autumn.

During the summer holidays I joined the Erna Law agency, an organisation which arranged Continental holidays for teenagers. Along with a dozen or so other teenagers, I spent a glorious two weeks mountain-climbing, staying in a picturesque village near Geneva. It was not until after the holidays that I found out that Father's financial affairs were in an appalling state. Amini, in his crusade to bring about the necessary economic and social reforms, had broken all contracts with foreign companies, declaring that Iran had no money to spend on its own development. This had drastically reduced the number of foreign visitors to the country and had badly hurt the hospitality industry. Mother had written to Amir requesting us to economise. I felt very guilty about my trip to Geneva and wondered why I had been allowed the luxury. Later on, I discovered that Father had forbidden

Amir to let me know about his financial troubles. He wanted me to enjoy life.

Another school year started. At Felixstowe College I was placed in Latimar House under the supervision of Miss Cowly, a spinster housemistress with a huge chip on her shoulder. She was a woman feared for her bad temper and severe punishments. Miss Cowly's main interests in life were her cat, which the captain of the house had the dubious honour of feeding, and chemistry, the subject which she taught. As bad luck would have it (and unaware of the consequences), I chose not to take her subject, bringing upon myself her rage and dislike.

The school complex was made up of five houses which accommodated the 300 students and the main school building. There were also ten tennis courts and two playing fields, one for hockey and the other for lacrosse. Unfortunately, during the four years I attended the college, I failed to acquire the necessary skills to perform well at either of these sports. I loved horse-riding, but this activity was forbidden to me; in Iran, it was believed that riding accidents were frequently responsible for the loss of virginity! The only other sport I enjoyed and could play moderately well was tennis.

Scholastically, I had begun a tough struggle. To study eight subjects with very little English was next to impossible so, after a few months, I decided to limit my load to five. I eventually passed all of chosen subjects, achieving the lowest grade of 45 per cent. Without really understanding what I had been reading, I had simply memorised the text books. It was ironic that I had chosen modern history as one of my subjects. Certainly my fascination with the history of the French and Russian revolutions, as well as my disgust for the abominations of Nazi Germany, greatly heightened my sensitivity to the events which later, in Iran, were to shatter our lives.

Biology – in particular anatomy – provided me with the knowledge that, thankfully, put an end to the burning doubts that had caused me so many sleepless nights. So after all, no harm had been done on that hot summer afternoon by

70

the pool! It was a wonderful relief to realise that no physical damage had occurred – but, sadly, the psychological trauma left a permanent scar.

In the summer of '61, I asked Father's permission to take my holidays in Teheran. He refused. The country, he said, was still going through troubled times. Bakhtiar had become increasingly powerful and it was believed that the Americans were backing him against the Shah. The head of SAVAK was openly promoting a military coup against Amini, whose reforms the Shah supported. Disturbed by this, the sovereign's agents began watching Bakhtiar's every move. Eventually, his threat became so serious that, to save his sovereignty, the Shah dismissed him. A purge of Bakhtiar followers ensued. The borders were sealed off; no travelling was allowed and no transfer of funds was permitted, except for students with appropriate visas. Fortunately my brothers and I held student visas, so we were able to continue to receive our monthly allowances.

Iran's financial problems were enormous, in particular the appalling imbalance in the country's foreign trade figures. Then, towards the end of 1961 the Bakhtiar menace reappeared. The Shah learned that Bakhtiar had visited President Kennedy whose administration, he knew, was unfriendly towards his regime. Apparently, the US government was now very concerned about the nation's growing discontent and instability. Enjoying the support of Washington, Bakhtiar began stirring things up again and new events took place at the University of Teheran which resulted in a call for Amini's dismissal. On January 26, 1962, the Shah summoned Bakhtiar to the palace and, this time, exiled him from the country.

Three months later, the royal couple visited the United States in search of financial aid. On his return, the Shah discovered that Amini had plans to curtail his power and, so, yet another prime minister was summoned to the palace and asked to resign. Assadollah Alam, one of the Shah's most faithful friends, was elected to replace Amini. Naturally, in such a climate, a trip to Teheran would have been neither safe nor pleasant.

Chapter Ten

At seventeen I looked older than my age and many of my brothers' friends had begun to make passes at me. Unfortunately for them, I was not particularly interested in the opposite sex.

Amir was my acting guardian and I spent some of my holidays with him in Newcastle. His affair with Pat had come to an end and he was now courting a nurse called Susan. This new girlfriend and I disliked each other intensely. She was jealous of the attention my brother paid me and, naturally enough, I disliked her for the same reason. It seemed to me that she had stolen my idol away from me and made him insensitive to my needs and demands. Gradually, the closeness which had existed between my older brother and myself evaporated.

As I grew apart from Amir, Ali began to take a more active interest in my welfare. He was living in London and was mixing with some very interesting and intellectually stimulating people, mostly Cambridge graduates. His love affair with Janet had come to a tragic end because of my parents' insistence that he marry an Iranian girl. Ali was leading a hectic social life in which I became involved whenever I visited him. Looking back, I realise that living with my older brothers and socialising with their friends deprived me of the company of people of my own age. I grew up too quickly and many of my English friends thought I was too mature and sophisticated for my age.

Summer was approaching and I was to go to Teheran in July. News from Teheran had been good and bad lately. With Amini out of the way, the Shah had committed himself to his 'White Revolution'. The country's doors were once again open to foreigners and The Mirabel was prospering. Father's financial affairs had picked up and there was no longer any reason to worry about expenses.

However, the political situation was once again volatile, this time stirred up by an Ayatollah named Khomeini, who was attempting to launch a religious coup. Khomeini had violently opposed the Shah's agrarian reforms and the emancipation of women. His vociferous sermons attacking the regime had agitated the faithful out of the mosques and into the streets where they shouted anti-Shah slogans. During the unrest in the holy city of Gom, Khomeini had been arrested and this news had led to further demonstrations, turning Teheran into a battleground. The army had intervened and the demonstrators, in their frustration, had set fire to the bazaar. Martial law had been proclaimed and the SAVAK had become busier than ever. The rumours pointed to a Bakhtiar involvement in the orchestration of the rebellion.

Mother's letters were full of grievances about the agrarian reforms, which had deprived her relatives of the income from their land. Another reason she gave for hating the reforms was that they had done nothing for the peasants, who were now without the protection of the landlords. The Shah had distributed among the peasants the 518 villages he had inherited from his greedy father, who had confiscated them from the people long ago, but Mother was not at all convinced that the Shah's motives were as altruistic as they seemed. He was only doing this to buy himself popularity, she wrote. I thought her remarks were silly. Surely it didn't matter what the Shah's real motives were. What mattered was that the reforms were good for the country. The feudal system was unjust and obsolete. I had witnessed the plight of the peasants who had come to Grandpa year after year trying to offload their children because they could not feed them. Grandpa had been a generous landlord, but there had been many who were rotten and downright cruel.

Much later, when I became more socially-conscious, I went through the twelve points of the 'White Revolution' outlined in Gerard de Villiers' The Imperial Shah (1976):

74

1. The abolition of tenant farming and the redistribution of uncultivated land among the peasants.
2. Nationalisation of all forests.
3. The selling of all government industrial enterprises to cooperatives and private people.
4. The sharing of profits from these enterprises between the employers and the employees.
5. A revision of the electoral law to provide for universal suffrage.
6. The creation of an Army of the Educated, for high school and university graduates who do their military service as teachers.
7. The creation of an Army of Health, made up of medical and dentistry graduates who practise their professions in the countryside free of charge.
8. The creation of an Army of Development to promote agriculture.
9. The establishment of Equity Tribunals in all the villages.
10. Nationalisation of all water resources.
11. A national plan for urban and rural reconstruction.
12. Reorganisation of all government units, administrative decentralisation and total recasting of national education.

In truth the above program, had it been exercised properly, would have rivaled that of any socialist party. But what was ever exercised properly in Iran, with all its corruption and nepotism? Nothing.

As an example, I escaped national service (the completion of which was required for employment at all government organisations) because Aunt Firouzeh, a courtier with a member-of-parliament husband, knew the head of the Education Corps for women. Everything depended on who you were, and who you knew. If you wanted to survive, or to accomplish anything, you had to become a sycophant dependent on a Pahlavi or a Pahlavi favourite. Healthy competition was non-existent. Talent, hard work, education and experience counted for little if you were competing against a favourite. This was very frustrating, particularly for the

75

country's young people whom the Shah's own reforms had educated, and who were now professionally qualified and ready to work for their country.

To give no mention to the positive aims of the reforms would be perhaps unfair to a king who had grand dreams for his country but who, unfortunately, had lost touch with his people – indeed had never tried to know or understand them. Sometimes I think he must have been ashamed of his people. Perhaps, like Goli, he thought them 'religious primitives'.

The reforms did lead to a great economic boom, especially in the petrochemical industries, with Khark Island becoming the world's largest petroleum port for the exportation of oil. Various natural resources were explored and mined. Iron and steel mills were built. The Aryamehr complex near Isfahan produced, besides gas, over a million tons of steel a year. There was great expansion in transportation and most of the country was covered by a new telephone network. Huge dams were built to irrigate vast areas of land, at the same time boosting the country's electricity supply. In 1974, with a production of six million barrels of oil a day, Iran became the world's fourth largest producer of oil.

But economic prosperity, modernisation, development and new-found wealth did little to erase the blatant discrepancies which existed between intent and result. The rich grew richer, the poor remained poor. Taking the country as a whole, more than half the population lived below subsistence level. The countryside changed little. There were no longer any peasants as such, but the farmers remained poor and diseased, with insufficient health care. The doctors in the Army of Health refused to leave the larger cities. As far as education was concerned, half of all Iranians were still illiterate. The majority of people were badly affected by inflation, and disappointed that their rising expectations of a better quality of life were not met. A brutally enforced repression alienated the educated younger generation, the intelligentsia and the mullahs, who were the traditional guardians of Iranian society and of the bazaar. It is heartbreaking to look back and see the tragic mistakes which were committed by this regime, which failed to motivate the nation to march towards the 'Great Civilisation'.

In the meantime, July came and I went to Teheran, to our own house in Darous. We now had two properties, one in Avenue Laila recently built and rented out, and the older house where my parents lived. This house was substantial, set in three acres of beautifully landscaped gardens dominated by a large swimming pool. A unique feature of the garden, placed next to a lovely weeping willow, was a huge, square timber bed with four ornamentally carved legs and a set of steps leading to its timber base. This unusual piece of carpentry had been Nasser Al-Din Shah's summer bed, roomy enough to accommodate His Majesty and at least four of his wives! It had been a present to Mother from Grandma.

That summer I spent many memorable moonlit nights on that bed, its wooden surface covered with a thick carpet and spread with comfortable cushions, sometimes alone, sometimes sitting with my family. We would drink vodka, eat yoghurt mixed with cucumber, listen to Persian music and simply enjoy the moonlight and the balmy air of those summer evenings.

Iranians love the moonlight, and the Teheran sky before the city became smogridden was truly beautiful; a clear, deep blue dotted with gently drifting milky clouds which passed over a galaxy of huge twinkling stars, and everything bathed in the golden light of a large moon. I often miss those nights sitting on that bed: alone, relaxed, without a care in the world, I savoured the cool evening breeze and gazed at the sky trying to find God to thank him for all his blessings. I never dreamed that, one day, I would lose it all.

The holidays passed quickly, with most of my time spent with my family. All of my cousins were visiting Teheran for the holidays. Mehram Khan was home from England and was planning to go to America to Utah State University; Behrouz was to join him there when he had finished high school. NeNe was back from Switzerland and was to go to London after the break, and Homa was home from France where she had been studying. Grandma was ageing, but her spirit was as strong as ever. Now we were next-door neighbours and I visited her every day. During this trip home she gave me a wonderful present – her father's horse cover, a real museum piece. Among the few family treasures still in my possession is this beautiful tapestry.

At home, Mother seemed very unhappy when, with all her financial worries over, she should have been content. One day, in as casual a way as I could muster, I asked her what was wrong. After a long pause she confided: 'I am worried about Assad. I think he has become an opium addict.'

I was horrified. 'An opium addict!' I exclaimed. 'How do you know, Mother?' Looking grim, she replied, 'He goes to Homayon's regularly before going to the club. My brother is always sitting by his brazier smoking the pipe. His house is a nest of corruption.'

I felt sick at the thought of my own father joining the parasites of our society. I urged Mother to make him seek professional help. She nodded her agreement and left the room.

In the afternoon, when Father came home, Mother asked him what his plans were for the evening. He replied that he was going to his club and that on the way he would drop in to 'say hello' to the princess and Homayon. Mother, rather unwisely, looked him straight in the eye and said accusingly: 'You are going there to smoke opium, aren't you?' Father became very angry and replied, 'I am not – but even if I was, it wouldn't be any of your business.' Mother was about to erupt again when I interrupted. 'Father,' I said gently, 'your health is our concern. You are the head of the family, the breadwinner. What would happen to us if you did become an addict?' He looked embarrassed and replied, 'I will prove it to you. I will not go to Homayon's for a week. Now, if I was an addict I wouldn't be able to go without a smoke for a week, would I?' Mother and I exchanged glances and agreed to the suggestion. But after he had left the house she said she did not believe him and was going to order the driver to report on his every move – from the time he left the house in the morning, to the time he returned home in the evening.

A week later, Mother was proved right. Father had not visited Homaydon's, but the driver reported that he was smoking in another addict's house. We decided to write to Amir, the oldest son and the doctor-to-be of the family, for help. As we had expected, a week or so later a very serious letter arrived addressed to Father, who then admitted to his addiction and booked in to rehabilitate himself at Mehre Hospital. Most people have no idea how hard it is for an addict to give up this deadly habit. Father almost died before he recovered.

While he was convalescing in the hospital, Mother was shattered by the news that Father had a second wife and a child! She was stunned. She had always known of his casual affairs – but a wife and a child were an entirely different matter. Poor woman; she had been her husband's rock, always generous, faithful, forgiving and, above all, patient. Surely she deserved better. I had to help her! To this end I organised a spy network of my own and, to my relief, found out that the story was a vicious lie fabricated by one of my aunts, who happened to have designs on Father herself. A carefully tailored report omitting the sister's role in the rumour was submitted to Mother who, enlightened, could have taken flight with joy. I also made sure Father realised what a lousy husband he had been. The result was a five carat diamond ring for Mother, and more nights spent at home. With Father back at work rid of the fatal habit, and Mother happily settled in the routine of married life, I returned to Felixstowe.

Chapter Eleven

The years between 1963 and 1965 passed without event. I took a couple of skiing holidays in Austria and France, both of which failed to make a good skier out of me. During the summer holidays, my parents came to England and we took vacations in Spain and the South of France.

In Teheran in January 1965, Prime Minister Ali Mansur was assassinated by Mohamed Bokharai, a student of theology. The subsequent interrogation of the assailant had revealed a right wing and also a Bakhtiar connection. After a short trial, Bokharai was executed. The new prime minister appointed by His Majesty was Amir Abbas Hoveyda, Mansur's finance minister, a cultivated, French-educated political scientist. Hoveyda proved himself to be totally devoted to his Shah, serving him faithfully for the next thirteen years.

Three months after Mansur's assassination there was an attempt on the Shah's own life at the Marble Palace. The assailant was killed on sight by the palace guards. The investigations which followed pointed to yet another Bakhtiar conspiracy. Most people's reactions to the attempted assassination were that of bewilderment at the extent of the infiltration of traitors into the impregnable palace security, and joy at the failure of the attempt.

I often wondered what would happen if someone did kill the Shah. The prospect was frightening. There would be a total vacuum in the absence of an adult heir to the throne or a strong decision-making body. The Shah was the centre of power, the sole decision-maker. All the elements of government – the Army, the Navy, the Airforce, the Police and SAVAK – worked independently of one another, each reporting only to the Shah. Obviously, such a system would not lend itself to coherence, so what would happen if this powerful figurehead was removed? Probably total chaos.

I left Felixstow at the end of the '65 school year and began a course at the St James' Secretarial College in London. Father had bought a lovely four-bedroomed freehold house in Fulham and my brothers and I were living there together. Amir was studying for his fellowship at the Royal College of Surgeons and Ali was working for a petrochemical company. I hated secretarial work. I had wanted to go to university but my parents had considered the idea ridiculous. The only ambition they had for me was that I should find myself a suitable husband. We had fought, I had lost – but not totally. They had agreed to let me take a modelling course in my free time, perhaps because they thought it would improve my prospects in the marriage market!

Living in London was exciting. I did not like the secretarial course very much, but I loved modelling. I was not tall enough for the cat-walk but my face was photogenic and I was in great demand for photographic work. My daily routine consisted of going to St James' in the morning then, at 5 pm, catching the train to Leicester Square to attend the modelling school, whose principal also acted as agent for the students. The class was held for two hours every evening, after which some of us went for a drink at the corner pub. Weather permitting, I usually walked home through St James' Park then Knightsbridge, stopping off at Harrods on Wednesday evenings for a little indulgence. By the time I got home I was ready for a snack supper, a hot bubble bath and the comfort of my bed.

Although my brothers and I lived under the same roof, for the main part we lived separate lives, only getting together at weekends. Amir was studying conscientiously, his girlfriend Susan visiting him every fortnight. On these occasions I made myself scarce. Ali, as usual, was out every night.

My brothers' friends had begun to treat me like a young lady, some even asking me for dates. I refused them all. My college friends did not understand why I was not interested in boys but, of course, they did not know about my first experience with the opposite sex and how revolting it had been for me.

One evening one of Ali's Cambridge friends, an English earl, asked me out for dinner. I accepted his invitation because he seemed to be a gentleman and, of course, his title impressed me. Punctually, he presented himself at the door with a beautiful bouquet of lily-of-the-valley. We had a wonderful dinner at Annabels, and after coffee he asked me whether I would like to dance or whether I would prefer to go upstairs to the casino. I chose to go upstairs because it seemed safer.

For the rest of the evening the poor chap stood watching me lose all my money until, both of us now in a thoroughly bad mood, we left for my house. At the door he bad me goodbye, kissed me on the cheek and left. I never saw him again.

Not long after that I met Count Antonio Speroni, a good-looking, charming Italian who was studying at Cambridge for his doctorate in economics. For Antonio it was love at first sight. As for me, he was the first man I really liked. He was in the habit of coming to London most weekends, where he would drive around in his grey Lancia sports car looking very chic. We met at a dinner party and after the meal he danced with me all night, never taking his eyes from my face. I liked his manners and his immaculate appearance, and we embarked on a platonic relationship. I do not know how, as a hot-blooded Italian, he tolerated such a chaste relationship, but from then on whenever we both were in England he would come to London on a Saturday night to take me out. At the end of the evening I always sent him off with a single goodnight kiss.

This comfortable relationship with Antonio was giving me self-confidence and I was beginning to lose my fear of men. My parents knew of our friendship and, because his background complemented mine and his intentions seemed honourable, they voiced no objections.

No man ever showed his love for me as much as Antonio did. I was the centre of his universe. He wanted to be with me all the time, which of course was not possible for a respectable Iranian girl. Sometimes I felt sorry for him; he loved me so much and I felt guilty for not being able to reciprocate his devotion. I loved being with him but I did not love him, and did not have the heart to tell him. Slowly, I began to distance myself from the relationship. After all, we could never have married, he being a staunch Catholic and I a faithful Muslim.

My secretarial course was due to finish in July. The modelling course had already finished and I was regularly employed for cinema and television commercials. I revelled in the limelight, but my parents did not approve and, to put an end to what they conceived to be an embarrassing situation, they decided I should return to Teheran immediately.

I wondered how I was going to tell Antonio. An emotional farewell would be too hard to bear. I decided that a letter would be the best solution so, while he was at Cambridge writing his thesis, I wrote to him informing him of my parents' decision. I gave him my address in Teheran, wished him luck in his studies and said that I hoped to see him sometime in the near future. Then, with a heavy heart, I left London, the city in which I had found peace of mind and contentment.

Teheran had changed considerably since my last visit. The city had grown in all directions. High-rise buildings were being constructed everywhere. The roads were jammed with cars, mostly owned by the blue-collar workers. The population explosion, the number of vehicles on the roads and the newly erected factories near Teheran were contributing to a serious air pollution problem in a city which was walled in by high mountains.

Both of my family's hotels were doing extremely well and Father was building three new houses, one for each of his children. There was no prospect of a career for me in Teheran. It would have been deemed below my dignity to become anyone's secretary and, of course, modelling was out of the question as it was not considered to be a respectable profession. So I was forced to become a lady of leisure, waiting for my

Prince Charming. With my hyperactive nature though, it did not take long for me to become bored and I began searching for something useful to do.

I started painting portraits and still lifes, as well as playing tennis, swimming, mountain-climbing and becoming involved in charity work. Aunt Firouzeh was my shining example of an achiever, interested in a variety of sports, politically active and heavily involved in charity work. I volunteered to help with her community work, and together we supervised the running of the Red Crescent Medical Clinic in Goldonak, and organised charity balls and many other fund-raising activities. Soon I became quite a socialite, invited out every night.

It was during a dinner dance at La Residence, the most fashionable restaurant in Teheran at the time, that my first 'Prince Charming' presented himself. The invitation was for eight-thirty and, as was usual in Teheran, most of the guests arrived late, intent on making a grand entrance. I arrived just before nine and told my driver to come for me at the curfew hour of midnight. As I entered the restaurant, I was greeted by the committee members who were standing at the door to welcome their guests.

The restaurant consisted of three large, adjoining rooms with an oblong table set in one corner for the buffet dinner. The rooms were packed with guests, the women elegantly dressed in the latest haute couture and the men in their black ties looking stiff and arrogant. The air was thick with smoke and the mingled smells of expensive perfumes. Waiters were circulating among the guests carrying trays loaded with drinks and caviar on toast. It was apparent that the guests were 'la crême de la crême' of society, with many government dignitaries present. There were also some rather odd-looking characters present, who did not seem to fit in. I guessed them to be either bodyguards or SAVAK agents.

I spotted an old friend standing in a corner and began to make my way over to her.

As I did so I could feel the approving glances of several men following me. I had not been talking to my friend for

85

very long when a rough-looking man approached us. He bowed politely and asked me what my name was. I introduced myself and was about to introduce my friend when he bowed again, turned on his heel and disappeared. My friend and I looked at each other in amazement at this unusual behaviour. A few minutes later Bahman, one of Ali's closest friends, made his way towards us accompanied by a middle-aged, immaculately dressed and handsome man. Smiling, Bahman kissed my cheek, shook hands with my friend then, turning politely to his companion, introduced the gentleman as His Excellency, Dr Kamran Nezami. The man bowed and kissed my hand, keeping his eyes on my face.

After exchanging some trivialities, Bahman took my friend's hand and pulled her towards the dance floor, leaving me alone with Dr Nezami who was still devouring me with his eyes. After a prolonged and uncomfortable silence he whispered, 'Miss Yazdi, may I call you Laila?' I smiled and replied, 'Of course.' He returned my smile and continued: 'You are the most beautiful woman I have ever seen in my life.' After a short pause, during which he seemed to be waiting for some kind of reaction from me, he went on, 'Michael Angelo himself could not have sculptured a more perfect profile.' By this time I could feel the blood rushing to my face. Trying to avoid his eyes, I thanked him for his compliments.

'Please, dance with me?' he begged. I was about to refuse when he grabbed my hand and gently pulled me towards the dance floor. The band was playing Frank Sinatra's Stranger in The Night. He pulled me close to him so that we were dancing cheek to cheek. I found this enforced intimacy distasteful and tried discreetly to pull slightly away from him, but without success. His heavy breathing and bulging organ pressing against me were making me feel nauseous.

The dancing continued for what seemed like an eternity. When I could not stand it any longer, I decided to forego politeness and asked him to stop. 'Only if you promise not to dance with anyone else tonight,' he replied. Hastily I agreed, and when he let me go I thanked him and almost ran towards the spot where I had left my bag. Picking it up, I rushed to the restroom where I was promptly sick. Bad memories were returning with a vengeance. It was only eleven- thirty, so I decided to remain in the restroom till midnight when my driver was to pick me up. The events of the evening seemed bizarre. First, the roughneck inquisitor, and then His Excellency, who happened to be a cabinet minister. Suddenly, everything made sense. The rough-looking man was a SAVAK agent assigned to the minister and he had been making sure of my identity before his charge made his move! This realisation made me feel even more sick and scared. At twelve sharp I headed for the exit where my punctual driver was waiting.

All the way home I could not stop thinking about the events of the evening. I wondered whether or not I should tell Mother what had happened. I decided to keep the incident to myself, at least for the time being. But next morning, while I was taking a shower, Mother came into the bathroom and told me that Bahman was on the telephone asking if I would have dinner with him the following Thursday evening. I asked her to accept on my behalf. When I had finished showering she returned to the bathroom, looked at me inquisitively and said, 'Since when do you keep secrets from me? Why didn't you tell me you met Kamran Nezami last night?'

'So what if I met Kamran Nezami?' I snapped back. 'I meet a lot of men when I go out. What's the significance of meeting this one?' Of course I was fully aware of the significance, but preferred to feign innocence.

'What's the significance of meeting a cabinet minister?' Mother echoed incredulously, then went on, 'Anyway, Bahman said the dinner is in Nezami's honour and he has asked him to invite you as a special favour to him.'

At once I regretted accepting the invitation. 'Mother, I've just remembered,' I exclaimed. 'I can't go to dinner on Thursday. I've promised to take Grandma to see a movie.' Sadly, this ploy did not work. Mother insisted that I keep my engagement and promised to take Grandma to the movies herself. I made a mental note to warn Grandma of the little white lie I had concocted to try to escape this unwelcome situation! As she left the room Mother commented that I was very lucky that such an important man was interested in courting me. 'Yes, Maman' I said meekly, but to myself I said angrily, 'Court me, my foot!'

Thursday evening came all too soon and I duly made my way to the Persian Room, Teheran's most expensive nightclub at the time. The head waiter showed me to a table at which were sitting a group of people. When Bahman saw me he rose, gave me the customary kiss on the cheek, then invited me to sit between Dr Samie, the minister for health, and another man whose identity I did not know. Kamran, as guest of honour, was seated at the head of the table. The band was playing Latin American music and the floor was packed with dancers moving to the rhythm of the cha-cha. Relieved not to be anywhere near the guest of honour I felt relaxed enough to make conversation with Dr Samie. Dinner was served, accompanied by the best of French wines.

When the band began playing soft music Kamran rose from his seat and came over to me. Tapping me on my shoulder he requested the pleasure of the next dance. I did not want to dance with him, but I could hardly refuse and we moved towards the floor. He held me tightly and began whispering amorous words in my ears. I was beginning to feel very uncomfortable, and when the band began playing The Twist I grabbed the opportunity to tell him I disliked this type of music and wished to sit down. He kissed my hand, then led me back to the table where he took the vacant chair next to mine, still holding my hand and occasionally squeezing it. I was enraged at the impertinence of the man but could not do much about it within the bounds of politeness.

Escape presented itself in the form of dessert, which the waiters were beginning to serve. Eating requires both hands! I have never eaten so quickly in my entire life. When I had finished my sweet I stood up, bade farewell to my neighbours, headed for the host to thank him for his hospitality and left the room. Kamran did not have time to react. This time I had asked my driver to remain in the parking lot.

At home, Mother was sitting up in bed waiting for me, full of questions about the evening and the minister. I told her everything, including my honest opinion about the man she hoped I would marry. 'Maman, he is twenty years older than me!' I said. 'And above all, I don't like him!' At this, Mother became angry and remarked cruelly, 'Perhaps you don't deserve him.' Deeply hurt I retorted, 'Maman, I deserve a better man than him!' And with a lump in my throat I ran to my room, banging the door behind me.

For the next four days all my telephone conversations were monitored. On the fourth day the call that Mother was waiting for arrived. Dr Nezami was on the telephone and wished to speak to me. I took the call with Mother listening in on the extension in her bedroom. It was a formal conversation, during which he invited me to attend a dinner party at his house the following Thursday evening. Knowing the consequences of a refusal I accepted, making Mother happy at least.

On the appointed evening, both for Mother's and vanity's sake, I took great care with my appearance and, appropriately dressed and made up, set off for the party. On the way I gave strict orders to the driver to not, under any condition, move from the front of Nezami's house.

When we arrived, the lack of parked cars surprised me. I wondered if perhaps I was too early, but a quick consultation of my diary proved me to be right on time. Suddenly, I felt frightened. I got out of the car and rang the bell; an elderly maid wrapped in a chador opened the door. I could not hear any party noise. I asked the maid if this was Dr Nezami's residence; she replied that it was and ushered me inside. As I entered, Nezami emerged from a nearby room, casually dressed in black trousers and a white shirt with several of its buttons undone, exposing a tanned chest covered with grey hair. In front of the maid he greeted me formally and led me into a dimly-lit room where soft, seductive music was playing.

We sat on the sofa and I asked him when the other guests were due to arrive. He gave me his usual romantic stare and whispered, 'There are no others. Tonight it is just you and me, darling.' I smiled at him, but under my breath I muttered, 'You bastard.' He asked me what I would like to drink. I felt like a scotch on the rocks but, instead, asked for some soda. He frowned, objecting to my choice: 'My darling, aren't you going to celebrate our first night with a glass of champagne?'

Impudently, I remarked, 'What do you mean, our first night? This is our third night.' His face lit up with anticipation and, putting his hand on my thigh he squeezing it lightly and whispered, 'I have been waiting for this moment since I set eyes on your beautiful face.' Suddenly, he remembered our drinks and went over to the bar to pour them. He handed me my glass of soda then sat down close to me. We drank more or less in silence, listening to the soft music. He played with my hair and, occasionally, kissed me lightly on the tip of my ear.

I hated myself for being there. Somehow, nothing this man did aroused any sexual desire in me. My body was rigid. After a while the maid entered, announcing that dinner was ready. In her presence he became formal again and withdrew his hand from my shoulder. We went into the dining room and ate our meal in virtual silence, then returned to the sitting room. Plans for a quick escape were racing through my mind.

We sat down on the sofa again and he put his arms around my waist and whispered, 'I want you, Laila.' As though I had not heard him I tilted my head back and asked him for a brandy. Irritated, he got up, went to the bar and poured two large brandies. He offered one to me and gently rubbed his own brandy glass to warm the contents. Then he sat down again and resumed his unsuccessful attempts at seduction. I was enjoying his frustration and wanted to prolong his agony. I gave him a long, sexy stare and began languidly moistening my lips. I moved towards him and, intentionally missing his opened mouth, began licking his cheek. When he was sure that he was about to have me, I suddenly rose from the sofa and smiled down at the astonished man. Picking up my handbag I said tenderly, 'Darling, I must go now. My curfew

90

is up and my mother will kill me if I am late.' Still in a state of shock, he got up and offered to give me a lift. I thanked him politely and told him this was not necessary as my driver was waiting at the door. I detected a flush of anger in his stubborn face as he showed me out.

On the way home I took a handkerchief out of my bag and carefully wiped the taste of his revolting perfume and sweat from my tongue, then leaned back, calm and satisfied. I could not wait to see the expression on Mother's face when she heard about the behaviour of her imagined Khasegar!

Chapter Twelve

I will never forget the expression of astonishment on Mother's face when I told her what Kamran had been planning for me. 'God forbid!' she exclaimed. Neither of us mentioned him again.

Winter was upon us and the skiing season had begun. Most of my friends were skiing at Dizin, the best resort – and with the longest slopes – in Iran. The slopes were only about an hour's drive from Teheran, so it was possible to ski every day if one was keen. I was not, but I did make the trip every Friday to be with my friends and, of course, to be seen.

Our group did everything together. We played sports, went to the movies and took turns in giving dinner parties. Two of the girls in the group were my special friends: Shirin, a Gajar and Pari, who was half-German. We were so close that we were nicknamed the 'three musketeers'. Pari, a pleasant-looking girl with lovely long, blonde hair was in love with Kami, a handsome young Harvard graduate who was, at present, working for his father. Shirin, exotic, refined and cultured, was not attached and I was planning to introduce her to Amir when he returned to settle in Iran.

Every Thursday evening a dinner party was held at one or another of our houses, and it was at Shirin's one evening that I met my first true love. The hostess had asked me to come early so that we could have our usual private chat before the other guests arrived. The night was still young when I reached her home. At the door I was greeted by the butler, who took my mink coat and ushered me into the sitting room where Shirin was standing next to a tall, slim, handsome man of around forty. As I approached her, I caught his glance and was at once mesmerised by his striking grey eyes. My heart began beating as it had never done before. Spellbound, I felt a rush of blood to my face. Shirin came to greet me with open arms then, taking my hand, she led me towards the handsome stranger, who she introduced as her Uncle Feraydon. With my free hand I shook his. His touch sent a peculiar sensation of shock down my spine. A kind of magnetic energy kept us together for the rest of the evening. This sort of experience was new to me – and it was wonderful. I did not even notice when the rest of the guests arrived or when they departed; only he mattered. We danced the night away wrapped in each other's arms, not talking much; somehow, words were not needed. At the end of the evening when it was time to leave, he asked if he could call me the following day. I squeezed his hand, winked my permission and left him. What a wonderful feeling it is to be in love!

The next day, and every day after that, he called. He became part of our group, participating in all our activities. I felt relaxed and happy in his presence. Sometimes, when we wanted to be alone, I visited his house for a cosy dinner by the fire. We would sit on the sofa for hours, talking, drinking wine, kissing and watching the amber flames until they died away. When I told Mother about the relationship she was delighted. After all, my suitor was a Gajar and extremely wealthy.

Feryadon had had a tragic first marriage. His wife had commited suicide and his brother-in-law, the prime minister at the time, had taken him to court accusing him of murder in order to get custody of his baby nephew. Feraydon was acquitted ad deemed fit to keep his son, but for a long time after the trial he had led the life of a recluse – until a few years ago, that is, when he had re-entered society to capture the hearts of its most beautiful socialites! These affairs, of which there had been many, had all ended when the lady in question had begun to show an interest in marriage. Now it was my turn. Modesty never having been one of my virtues I considered myself more beautiful than the others, as well as being his equal as far as our family backgrounds were concerned. I was not sure whether my age was an asset or a liability – but I was certain I would succeed where others had failed.

As time passed, more and more of our acquaintances and family friends became aware of our relationship. People who liked me invited us to social events together, while those who were jealous of me invited him alone and introduced him to other girls. My parents began to get worried about my reputation and doubt the honour of his intentions.

But we were in love, and to me nothing else mattered. I adored being with him, talking to him, walking with him and just gazing at him. Every day I waited by the telephone for his call; on the odd occasion that it did not come, I went crazy with worry.

Time passed and there was still no sign of a proposal. The pressure Mother was putting me under was not making life any easier. One evening, when we were dining with a group of friends at the Persian Room and all our dinner companions were dancing, a rather conniving idea hit me. I turned to him and said sadly, 'Feraydon, I am going back to London.' Surprised, he took my hand, kissed it and asked me why. I explained, 'People are talking about us. Our relationship cannot go on like this any longer – and I love you too much to be able to live in the same town without seeing you.' I stopped, to see the effect of my news. He thought for a moment and then said, more to himself than to me, 'I am planning to send my son to boarding school next year. Perhaps we can talk of marriage after he has gone?'

'Next year will be too late,' I replied sombrely. Just then, a couple of our friends returned to the table and we stopped talking about personal matters.

The next day I repeated our conversation to Mother. She was not impressed with my scheme and, after giving the subject some thought, she offered her own suggestion. Sadly, though, I did not have the opportunity of putting her plan into action; two days later, she asked me to go for a walk with her – an unusual request, and one that worried me. We waited until the afternoon siesta was over then set out towards the mountains. The weather was freezing and we had to walk quickly to keep warm. For a while we walked in silence and then she began, 'Laila Joon, what I am about to tell you is not pleasant. You must try to be sensible and look at it philosophically.' My heart began pounding.

'I had tea with Mehri, Feraydon's sister yesterday,' she went on, 'and we talked about her brother and you. Because she is my good friend, and because she likes you very much, she was honest with me. Feraydon has sigehed* his son's nanny so that she won't leave his household. Apparently the little boy loves her very much. She is like a mother to him. Feraydon will never marry anyone else – especially someone so much younger than himself.'

I was shocked to the core. 'Maman, please stop,' I cried. 'I don't want to hear any more.' Choking back a sob, I turned and ran back home, racing upstairs to my bedroom and locking the door behind me. I collapsed onto the bed, crying hysterically. A little while later, I heard Mother trying to open the door and asking to be allowed to come in. Stifling my sobs, I told her I wanted to be alone for a while. Sighing, she moved away from the bedroom door.

Alone in my room, I plunged into despair. My heart was aching; my body was trembling and the room was spinning round and round. My world had crumbled around me. The man I loved so dearly was a liar. He had betrayed me. He, too, had wanted to use me. Why, oh why? How was I going to live without him? How would I face tomorrow? I did not believe that I could. Suddenly, I remembered Amir once telling me that the best way to commit suicide was to take a handful of tranquillisers. It occurred to me that death would end my loneliness and all of my worries.

I rose from the bed and, very quietly, unlocked and opened the door and headed for the bathroom where the medicine cabinet was kept. Mother heard me and came in, her face

* Sigeh is the term for an Islamic 'temporary marriage', which can be prolonged for as long as the husband wishes.

kind and concerned. Putting her arms round me, she stroked my untidy hair and said gently, 'Men are not worth it.' I kissed her and began washing my face and, assuming that I was going to be alright, she went downstairs to the kitchen to organise the evening meal.

When she had gone, I dried my face, took out the bottle of Valium from the medicine chest and emptied it into the palm of my hand. I looked at the pills for a moment then crammed them into my mouth and tried to swallow them with a drink of water. It was harder than I had anticipated. As the tablets were going down they were making me choke. I drank some more water, then started coughing some of the tablets up. The coughing was getting worse and I was beginning to feel dizzy. I did not hear Father walk into the bathroom. 'Laila, are you alright?' he asked, concerned about my coughing. Trying to look normal I nodded, then went to him, put my arms around his neck and kissed his cheek, thinking as I did so that it was for the last time. I loved my parents very much, but I just could not face the world without Feraydon.

Father patted my shoulder and asked me why I had been crying. I did not have the courage to tell him about Feraydon and his Sigeh, and I began to cry again. He gently led me to my room, settled me on my bed and left the room. I knew he was heading for the kitchen to find out why I was so upset. I changed, got into bed and closed my eyes, hoping that I would never have to open them again.

The next day, sometime in the afternoon, I felt Mother's gentle touch as she tried to wake me up. I stirred and she said, 'Laila Joon, haven't you had enough sleep?' I opened my eyes blearily, feeling totally disoriented then, gradually, I recognised Mother's worried face. 'Maman Joon!' I whispered drowsily. Mother asked me if I had taken any sleeping tablets before going to bed. Suddenly, everything came back to me. Tears began running down my face. A dreadful fear welled up inside me and I could not speak.

Father entered the room. In my semi-conscious state I could hear him and Mother talking, but could not understand what they were saying. I must have gone back to sleep, or slipped into unconsciousness again, because the next thing I was conscious of was the family doctor leaning over me asking me questions. It took a lot of concentration to understand what he was asking, but at last my befuddled brain made sense of his words. He wanted to know what I had taken and how many. With difficulty I whispered, 'Valium. The whole bottle.'

'Young lady, you are very foolish and extremely lucky,' he said, his familiar voice sounding stern. I heard him telling Mother that the best thing for me to do was to sleep the tablets off. 'Ha! As though I wanted to get up!' I thought to myself as I drifted back to sleep.

It took me two months to recover from my failed suicide attempt and the subsequent depression which left me with chronic spastic colitis. During my convalescence Feraydon called many times, but Mother told him I had gone to Ramsar. As the days went by, I went over and over our relationship in my mind, trying to understand why Feraydon had not told me about his Sigeh. Gradually, out of love for him, and to excuse him, I began to rationalise his behaviour. After all, he was a dedicated father. His life revolved around his son, not his girlfriends. In his situation I would have done exactly the same, I told myself.

As stability returned, I asked my parents to allow me to go back to live in London, at least until summertime when Amir was planning to return home to settle. They saw the rationality in this request and agreed to let me go. In the meantime, Feraydon kept calling, demanding to know why I was ignoring him. Each time, I made up a suitable excuse then, finally, a few days before my departure, I agreed to have tea with him in the lobby of The Mirabel. The meeting was very sad. I still loved him, but I had been deeply hurt, and my self-confidence and self-esteem had been shattered.

As we said goodbye, he gave me a pocket Koran to guard over me, and a card on which he had written: 'Laila – I have never loved anyone as much as I have loved you, and if I have failed you it is because there is a reason. Darling, forgive me and remember me as what I wanted to be to you, not as what I had to be!'

In his own way, he had made a confession.

Chapter Thirteen

Back in London, away from the anxiety which had surrounded my last few months in Iran, life became more settled for me. I enrolled at St James' for a refresher course which was offered to 'Old Girls', and also joined a modelling agency hoping to pick up some casual work. I was lucky; there was a lot of photographic work available and, soon, modelling absorbed most of my time. It was good to be back in London, and good to be busy, but I still missed Feraydon dreadfully and neither work nor social life compensated for the loss of his companionship.

Antonio was in London. He had been calling Ali regularly enquiring about my whereabouts. The poor man had received only one letter from me in reply to the many he had sent me over the past few months. I was toying with the idea of calling him when I received a long letter from Shirin bearing tragic and incredible news. Feraydon was dead – killed by his own son. Apparently the boy's uncle had given him a hunting rifle for his birthday. The boy, unaware that it was loaded, had playfully directed the barrel of the gun at his father saying, 'Daddy, I am going to shoot you!' – and he had done just that. Feraydon had died instantly and the son had been sent to a psychiatric clinic in Switzerland.

So. The love of my life was gone. Shot dead by his own son. Numb with grief I sat for what must have been hours, wondering at the cruelty of life. When I could think no longer, I picked up the phone and called Antonio. I had to think about something and someone else, otherwise I would go mad. At that moment, I needed love. I needed someone to care for me, and I needed a positive element in my life.

Antonio was overjoyed to hear from me and instantly asked

me to have dinner with him. I accepted his invitation. Here was a man who loved me and me alone. Soon, we were seeing each other regularly again and the pain of my abortive relationship with Feraydon, and the subsequent tragedy of his death, began to fade from my mind and my heart.

After a few months, Antonio began talking about marriage and told me that he wished me to meet his parents. I tried to talk him out of the idea by reminding him of our religious differences. To counter my objections, he suggested a civil marriage ceremony. This was out of the question as far as I was concerned. According to Islamic faith a marriage ceremony such as this would constitute nothing better than living in sin and would bring upon myself and my children eternal damnation.

I wrote to my parents for advice.They, too, objected to a civil marriage and suggested, instead, two ceremonies – one Islamic and the other Catholic. This would keep both my and Antonio's consciences clear. The idea sounded reasonable but I was still reluctant. The trouble was that, emotionally, I was not ready for a serious commitment to Antonio.

Amir was now a Fellow of the Royal College of Surgeons in urology. To my delight, his affair with Susan had fizzled out and he was ready to go back home and marry a nice Iranian girl. Ali was also planning to return to Iran to work as the Iranian representative of the British company he was employed with. So our days in London were limited.

Iran, it seemed, was undergoing an economic boom. Factories, dams, roads and refineries were being constructed everywhere and there was a lot of money to be made by foreign investors. Because there had been a huge influx of foreign visitors and businessmen into the country, hotels were prospering and Father was doing even better than before.

In June my parents arrived in London. They were planning to lease out our London house now that we were all going to live in Teheran, and they also wanted to buy a Mercedes Benz in which we were going to drive back to Iran via France, Italy, Greece and Turkey.

When he heard about our proposed trip, Antonio invited me to break my journey and join him in Venice for a few days to meet his family. I spoke with my parents and, after agreeing to include Venice in our trip, I accepted his invitation. When everything had been organised we packed and freighted most of our luggage, including the silver and the antique paintings Mother had bought to include in my dowry. (Marriage for her children was Mother's predominant concern and she was constantly looking for suitable matches for us.) Then, according to plan, we set out for Dover and crossed the Channel, this time by hovercraft instead of the awful ferry.

We spent a few days in Paris sightseeing, shopping and eating the deliciously-rich French food. After that, we took a direct route to the South and spent a blissful month in a magnificent rented villa at the Cap d'Antibes. Most mornings found us at the beach, while we spent our evenings at the casino in Cannes or Monte Carlo. I looked older than my age and, since no-one at the entrance asked me to show any identification, I mingled with the crowd and lost most of my money.

Antonio telephoned me every day, impatient to have me in Venice. Eventually, my parents relented and agreed to allow me to fly there three days before we were due to set off for Italy. This meant I would have one week alone with him.

In the meantime, we were all enjoying our holiday. Amir had always been quick to charm the opposite sex, and a few days after our arrival at the Cap d'Antibes he picked up a married Canadian girl called Liza. From then on, she spent most of her time with us, leaving her two children in the care of their nanny.

At last, it was time for me to fly to Venice to join Antonio. To my surprise, after boarding the plane, I found that Liza was travelling on the same flight, alone. We sat together and she told me that she had sent her children back to Canada and was looking forward to continuing her holidays with Amir. I was shocked, and felt rather sorry for her husband.

At Venice Airport I was met by a tanned and handsome

Antonio. I introduced him to Liza, and when we discovered that she was going to be staying at the same hotel, Antonio offered to give her a lift. Together, we drove to a parking lot where we left the car and took a boat to the Lido and the Excelsior. Venice – that gorgeous, ornamental city with its magnificent architecture, its rocking gondolas and romantic canals – is a paradise for lovers. Antonio was so happy to have me there that the warmth of his passion nurtured my own worn, confused and hurt heart and I found myself rejoicing in his company. It was good to feel wanted.

After we had settled into our separate rooms at the hotel, Antonio told me that, unfortunately, his parents had had to cancel their visit to Venice as his father had to attend an urgent business meeting in New York. Fate was at work again. Antonio may have been disappointed that his parents were not coming, but for me, the news was welcome!

The days passed quickly, as all good times do. We visited the surrounding islands, ate the best Italian cuisine at the most renowned restaurants, and drank delicious wine. The annual film festival was on and we saw many of the movies and met most of the participating stars. It was late summer, so the evenings were pleasantly cool and lit by a romantic moon. I was very happy.

My family arrived on schedule and booked into the same hotel. Liza's presence was a pleasant surprise for Amir, but left Ali feeling rather lonely. Antonio sensed his frustration and arranged a date with an attractive young woman for him. The pair hit it off and saw each other several times during our stay. We all had an unforgettable time in Venice. Father was his usual generous self and provided us with the best of everything.

On our last night we had dinner at a particularly fine restaurant. Ali was totally enraptured with his new companion, and midway through dinner he informed us in Persian that she had invited him to her home for a nightcap. The next day, he revealed that while he had been enjoying his drink, her father had arrived home unexpectedly. Poor Ali, yearning and unfulfilled, had been shoved out of the kitchen window into the street below, just missing the canal!

On the day my family and I were due to leave, Antonio and I sat by a window in the lobby of the hotel holding hands and finalising our plans for the future. He wanted us to be married as soon as possible and adhered to my mother's suggestion that, to satisfy both parents, we would have two religious weddings, one Islamic, the other Catholic. I agreed, but refused to set a date. I told him I would let him know once I was back in Iran. I needed more time to think. I had to be sure that I was making the right decision.

Our farewell was sad. Somehow, I sensed that the final chapter of a very special relationship was about to end. It had been my misfortune to have fallen for Feraydon instead of Antonio. Liza left for Canada on the same day and I could not help envying her lack of scruples and her capacity to enjoy life.

Our next destination was the ancient city of Rome, where we spent two nights at the Excelsior. We strolled along the Via Veneto, visited the famous historical monuments and threw coins into the Fountain of Tivoli, wishing for happiness. From Rome, we drove to Naples and then, again by hovercraft, ventured to Capri, a large green island set like a jewel among the blue waters of the Mediterranean. One of the nearby attractions was the Blue Grotto, an underwater cave to which tourists traditionally made a pilgrimage either by dinghy or the local bus. We made the mistake of taking the dinghy and the motion of the boat made me feel very seasick. Unfortunately, the giddiness associated with the nausea lingered for days and ruined the rest of my stay on the island.

From Capri, we went to the port of Brindizzi and, from there, cruised to the island of Corfu - a disappointment compared to Capri. We cut short our stay and sailed to the mainland of Greece, where we headed for Athens. Unimpressed, we did not stay there long and set off on the drive South to Turkey. Amir was not interested in historical monuments and refused to stop at most of the magnificent sights we passed on the way. But even he could not fail to be impressed with the city of Istanbul. It was an experience not to be missed and I loved it even more than I had loved Rome. The Byzantine architecture, the Topkappi and the Aya Sophie mosque were fantastic and, to me, brilliantly conveyed man's desire to show his love for his god through his art. There is a great contrast, though, between the European and the Asian sides of this city. When the Strait is crossed and the traveller leaves behind the continent of Europe and enters Asia, everything changes. Turkish poverty and the appalling lack of hygiene become a striking part of the landscape.

In Ankara, a crowded, unattractive metropolis, we decided to be on the safe side and buy some provisions for the journey to Mount Ararat. The scenery by the Black Sea and on the mountainous roads was breath-taking, but the route was dangerous. The roads were in poor condition; at one stage an earthquake had destroyed part of the road and, if we had not been travelling in such a solid car, we would not have been able to continue. We were also warned not to drive after dark because of bandits. In the motels where we stayed on route, we ate our purchased food and slept in our clothes because the bedding was filthy and infested with lice.

At Arzerom, on the border of Turkey and Iran, the Turkish customs officer made us unpack everything we had and searched the car as though we were smugglers. Once safely on the Iranian side, the Iranian customs officer did the same thing, though in a friendlier fashion. While we were waiting, the appetising smell of kebab filled the air, wafting from a nearby restaurant on the Iranian side. We had not had a decent hot meal for three days and our mouths were beginning to water. I was even hungrier than the others, because I had not eaten anything substantial since we had left Istanbul. When I felt I could not wait any longer, I approached the detaining officer and begged him to speed up the formalities. He smiled, nodded his head and, his suspicion aroused, promptly increased the meticulousness of his search for possible smuggled goods. After another hour, when the intoxicating smell of the kebab had faded, along with my diminishing hope for a good meal, he stamped our passports and permitted us to officially enter our own country. Relieved, we wasted no time in driving to the restaurant for the most delicious meal of our lives. We spent the night at a hotel in Tabriz and, the following day, headed for Teheran and home, driving on the Shah's new highway linking Arzerom and Teheran.

Chapter Fourteen

Darous was more welcoming than ever. Perhaps it was I who had changed. Antonio's love had given me back my confidence and self-respect. I began painting again and started looking for a job. Within a week or two, I had found a position with the School of Social Welfare, acting as a bilingual interpreter for Iranian students and their American lecturers. The school had been founded by Satareh Farmanfarmian, a distant relative and a friend who had been the first educated social worker in Iran. Satareh had been instrumental in the establishment of several female adult education centres located in various slum areas of Teheran. The most successful of such centres was Javadieh in the South of the city, where the poor lived in appalling conditions without water, sewage or any other means of sanitation.

During my free time, I continued helping Aunt Firouzeh in her extensive charity work. Realising how the 'have-nots' lived had made me more socially conscious. The gap between the living standards of the rich and those of the poor was enormous. Surely a regime which sustained such social injustice could not survive? Then again, I thought, how could it fail while protected by America?

One day, while Father was giving me a lift to the school on his way to the hotel, I asked him if he ever did anything to help the poor. He told me that every year he bought the jail sentences of ten prisoners who had been gaoled for bad debts. I had not been aware that such a practice was possible. I increased my charity fundraising by constantly appealing to the benevolence of my own family members. Mother and Grandma were my most generous donors.

Grandma had become almost bedridden, but her spirit was

as strong as ever. Every afternoon, her bedroom became a gathering place for the family to drink tea and chat. From the flock of household staff who had served her over the years, only ten remained. The others had left and been absorbed by the expanding workforce; most had remained loyal enough, however, to visit every No Rooz, to kiss their Lady's hand and receive their Aidy (present).

My two uncles had sold Grandpa's house. Uncle Homayon had lost the bulk of his enormous inheritance at the gambling houses of Europe and had been left with one house which he rented out. He was now living in a self-contained apartment built for him in a corner of Grandma's garden. She was supporting not only him, but also his two children from his third wife, from whom he had recently been divorced. To his dying day in Paris in 1988, Uncle Homayon never earned a living.

Uncle Hussain was now an elected senator, vociferous in his criticism of the corruption of the regime. His attitude had so displeased His Imperial Majesty that he was banned from court.

NeNe was back at home, studying for a degree in French at the University of Teheran. Mehram Khan had married and was working for the Ministry of Electricity, later to be renamed the Ministry of Energy. Behrouz had received his bachelor degree in statistics and was returning home in the summer. Homa, meanwhile, had married a French aristocrat and was jetsetting between the capitals of Europe.

My brother Ali was courting Suzie Hashemi, daughter of one of the most influential men at the National Iranian Oil Company (NIOC). Dr Hashemi was a millionaire who did not believe in investing in Iran. The family lived in a huge rented villa two streets away from us. Suzie was two years my senior, already divorced from an English husband. She was extremely intelligent, well-read, gregarious and striking. Her father was a pleasant, rather regal, highly-educated and extremely clever man. He had been among the first group of distinguished students sent by Reza Shah to Europe for

110

tertiary education. Dr Hashemi had gone to England and studied engineering. He had started at the bottom of the ladder in Abadan during British supremacy, persevered through the process of nationalisation and, through sheer hard work and foresight, had worked his way up to gain one of the most important positions at the NIOC.

Mrs Hashemi was something of an enigma. She was petite, attractive, always-bejewelled – a highly-intelligent and conniving lady who was better informed than any SAVAK agent. To her friends she was hospitable and generous; to her enemies she was lethal.

In no time at all, the courting couple were talking about marriage. Party after party was thrown by the Hashemis and their friends, to give the couple the opportunity to get to know each other better. They seemed very much in love. Mrs Hashemi was already introducing Ali to her friends as her future son-in-law, and Dr Hashemi was full of promises of oil contracts which would come Ali's way. Mother was on the top of the world. Father was cautious. Amir was hesitant and I was simply enjoying the parties.

Antonio was inundating me with amorous letters. He was missing me and could not wait for the day when I would return to Italy to become his wife. In all honesty, I told myself, he had a lot to offer me and perhaps, with time, I would grow to love him. Feraydon was dead and my heart had bled enough. It was time to start living again and Antonio was a good choice.

Soon, Ali informed my parents that he and Suzie had decided to get married. Mother was delighted but Father, on hearing the news, called a family conference. He thought that their decision was hasty and that they should give themselves more time to get to know each other. But Ali believed he knew all he had to know and he was very sure of his choice. Finally, after all aspects of the union were explored, the decision was made to go ahead with Khasegari.

On the appointed date our whole family, dressed in our best, arrived at the Hashemis' house. We were shown into the main salon, where three musicians played softly and the Hashemi family were gathered to greet us. The family's solicitor was also present, which seemed odd. After the two families had exchanged formalities and taken tea, the musicians were sent to another room.

As was expected by tradition, Father began praising Ali's qualities, his income and his dedication to Suzie. Then he asked what conditions were set for the bride. Mrs Hashemi requested a bride price of ten million rials because, she said, Prince Mahmoud Reza, the Shah's brother, had set the same amount for Dr Egbal's daughter when he married her – as well as presenting her with a beautiful, flawless five carat diamond wedding ring (Dr Egbal was managing director of the NIOC).

My parents were silent, but I detected a malicious flicker in Father's eyes. After a few moments, he cleared his throat and said: 'Madam, with all due respect, I am not Reza Shah and my son is not Prince Mahmoud Reza. Would you please set a more reasonable price?'

Mrs Hashemi's chin dropped and she exchanged hesitant glances with her husband and the solicitor, who immediately intervened and said, 'Madam, please permit your humble servant to express his humble opinion.' Not waiting for permission he continued, 'These two distinguished young people are in love, and Ali Joon is a refined young man from an excellent family – and about to make his fortune under the guidance of His Excellency, Dr Hashemi. It would displease God to let money interfere with the happiness of these two young people. Please Madam, be gracious enough to agree to the sum of five million rials.'

Now it was my parents' turn to exchange questioning glances. This time Mother, who was not going to let anything endanger this grand alliance (which had already become the subject of much envy among family and friends) nodded her head in agreement and added, 'Marriage is sacred and a joyous event. Talk presupposing unhappiness will bring bad luck.' Having said her piece she rose, went over to Suzie and kissed her. Congratulations were in order. The waiters, as though they had been standing behind the closed door eavesdropping, appeared immediately with bottles of chilled Dom Perignon and bowls of caviar set on ice. The musicians were called back and began playing the wedding song 'Yar Mobarak Bad'.

The only person who did not seem happy was Ali. The wedding date was set for November 11th. From now until then, life would become one big party.

Chapter Fifteen

Mother was busy buying jewellery for the bride and ordering the customary sweets and cakes for Sofreh Agd*. To bring good luck, happiness and fertility to the bridal couple the Sofreh is adorned with a pair of candelabra, a mirror, some seeds and a volume of the Koran. These items are presented to the bride by the groom before the day of the wedding ceremony. Great care must be taken in the decoration of the Sofreh.

Avenue Manuchehri is the area of Teheran most popular for antiques and it was here that Mother was searching, from shop to shop, for the best she could find for her first daughter-in-law. For the Sofreh, she was going to lend her own large Soozani+ which had been given to her by Grandma on her wedding day.

In the meantime, Father had leased and furnished a surgery for Amir. Amir was not, in fact, supposed to practice medicine until he had completed his two-year compulsory medical service for the Army of Health. This required that he use his expertise in a village in rural Iran for two years, and attend concomitant army camps in the summer. By using our connections and by bribing the right people, we had been able to have him exempted from village service, but camp attendance had proved to be inescapable so he had dutifully enrolled. The first camp requirement had been for him to shave his head. The removal of his beautiful black hair and

---

* Agd is the actual wedding ceremony and registration. The couple sit on small stools in front of the Sofreh facing Mecca, while the mullah reads the Koranic verses which bind them in matrimony.

+ Embroidered mat

the resultant white skull had not enhanced Amir's looks, but now the hair was beginning to grow back and he was not looking too bad.

The night before the wedding, we all went to the Key Club, the newest nightclub in town. On the way home, after dropping Suzie off at her home, Ali took out a cigarette and lit it. He smoked only when he was upset. I asked him what was the matter. Hesitantly, he began to express his doubts about his decision to marry Suzie, and said that he now wished he had abided by Father's request to postpone the wedding till they could get to know each other better.

In an attempt to cheer him up Amir said flippantly, 'It's too late to get out of it now, brother – but don't worry, if it doesn't work out you can always divorce her.' This suggestion infuriated me. 'How can he divorce her with a five million rial bride price?' I objected. An aggravated Amir snapped back: 'No-one asked for your opinion. So shut up.' Hurt and surprised, I decided this was no time for an argument and kept quiet. But I was worried. I loved Ali very much. He was kind and gentle and people took advantage of him too often. Perhaps his sixth sense was warning him of problems to come? The next morning, Mother and I went to the hairdresser early. The ceremony was to begin at five in the afternoon and there was much to be done before then. At three o'clock the handsome groom, dressed in a smart suit and having kissed the Koran to bring him luck and protect him from evil, left for the Hashemi residence. The rest of us were to follow half-an-hour later.

When we arrived at the house we were greeted by the bride's father, who was standing near the entrance. Inside, an assortment of roughnecks reminiscent of those who had been present at La Residence were mingling with the elegant guests – a sure sign that many government officials were to attend.

The house was overflowing with enormous baskets of rare flowers, exquisitely arranged. In the main salon, the same musicians who had entertained us at the Khasegari were

116

playing happy songs, and the waiters were circulating carrying trays of drinks, caviar and other cocktail savouries. Mrs Hashemi was expensively attired in a diamanté Dior outfit. A pair of dangling emerald earrings complemented her olive skin. The bride, standing by the groom, looked exotic. Ali was all smiles; apparently the jubilation of the day had washed away the doubts of the previous night.

A little while after our arrival, Prime Minister Hoveyda and three ex-prime ministers honoured the couple by agreeing to act as witnesses for the Agd. (Islamic law requires only two witnesses but Mrs Hashemi insisted that if only two of Their Excellencies had been asked, the other two would have been offended.) The religious verses were to be recited by the Emam Jumeh, who had performed the wedding rites for the Shah.

Sharp at five the bride and the groom were seated on two cushioned stools covered with silk lace and placed in front of the Sofreh Agd. A brocaded lace veil covered the bride's face. Three ladies, known to have happy marriages, were rubbing two pieces of sugar cane together, the dust dropping onto a white cloth which was held over the bride's head. This tradition is believed to bring sweetness to married life.

The Emam read the selected Koranic verses and then asked the bride if she would take Ali Yazdi as her wedded husband. After the question had been repeated the customary three times, she whispered 'yes'. A joyous murmur filled the room. The rings were exchanged and the groom lifted the lace from his bride's face and kissed her. Then the guests, in accordance with their closeness to the family and their social standing, kissed the bride and groom and gave them gifts. Mother, on behalf of our family, gave her a set of diamond jewellery. Considering the number of important people present, the bride must have collected a small fortune in jewellery. The party went on till the early hours of the morning, then the couple were driven to a suite reserved for them at the Royal Hilton Hotel.

The honeymoon was to be spent in Abadan, the site of

Iran's biggest oil refinery in the province of Khosestan, and the honeymoon party was to stay at the residence of a top-ranking NIOC official. Two of Suzie's best friends, myself and a journalist were to accompany the couple. The following day after lunch, we boarded a private airplane and headed for Iran's black gold centre. At Abadan airport we were welcomed by our host and hostess, along with a number of company officials whose sole interest in coming was to be mentioned to Dr Hashemi. The journalist who accompanied us was to report the events of the trip in his social column in the Keyhan International, Teheran's English evening paper.

We were driven to a large villa on the estuary of the Karoon River, which flows into the Persian Gulf. From the villa the view of the river, graced by lines of palm trees, was truly poetic. All the company's VIP employees' residences were located in this once British zone, which was completely segregated from the actual town. The people of Khosestan are mostly of Arabic origin, with very dark complexions, and the staff at the villa brought to mind the romantic tales of *One Thousand and One Nights*.

Close association with Suzie was uncomfortable for me. In her company I was on the receiving end of very negative vibrations. Somehow, there was an insincerity in her attitude and an insinuation that my brother was lucky to have become Dr Hashemi's son-in-law. To me, this was an insult. Well, I have never taken insults lightly, so I began a Yazdi promotion focusing on my family's background and education. It was on this campaign that I struck a dangerous chord.

It happened one afternoon when we were sitting in the lounge having tea. An enormous framed picture of the Shah, standing on a globe with a broad American smile and an outstretched arm as though he owned the world, dominated the entire wall. I had just about had enough of the gathered parasites' praises of Hashemi greatness achieved under the shadow of his Imperial Majesty. The last stroke had been a criticism of Ahmad Shah, the king who had stood against the British until they had persuaded Reza Khan to agree to their oil terms in exchange for the prize of the Gajar throne. A flash of memory had brought to mind an old photo of Ahmad Shah standing beside Reza Khan, who was holding the rein of the monarch's horse. Grandma had had the picture framed and given it a prominent place on the mantlepiece in her bedroom.

Family loyalty and frustration with what was going on induced me to look at Mohamad Reza Shah's picture and comment: 'How regal of a man whose father used to hold Ahmad Shah's horse reins.' As soon as the remark was out I realised the enormity of my folly. There was a long silence. The journalist rose and left the room. The hostess saved the hour by suggesting a walk along the river.

Three hours later I received a telephone call from my hysterical mother, who shouted, 'What have you said, you fool?' Astounded, I asked what she meant. In a sort of coded language she made me understand that she had received an anonymous telephone call warning me to be careful of what I said in future, or I would face severe punishment. Shocked, I almost dropped the receiver. So SAVAK was among us; only a handful of people had been present when I had made that remark.

The rest of the stay became a frightful nightmare. Who was the spy? Many subsequent events made me suspect the journalist. Having toured the famous Abadan refinery – one of the largest in the world – sailed on the Gulf and partied every lunch and dinnertime, we caught the same plane back home.

Ali was temporarily residing at his in-laws until the house father was building for him and Suzie was ready. Now people were inviting us for Pagosha (parties given by close friends and relatives in honour of the newlyweds). The last Pagosha dinner was at our home, in spite of the fact that the groom had gone to Canada on business.

After dinner had been served the older folk left and my father retired to bed. I was supervising the Mirabel waiter who had been helping for the night when the maid entered to inform me that there was a call for Miss Hashemi. I corrected her: 'You mean Mrs Yazdi.' She protested that she had not made a mistake and that the man on the telephone had asked for Miss Hashemi. I said nothing more and informed Suzie that there was a call for her, and the maid showed her to the study where there was a telephone extension. A few minutes later the maid reappeared, this time approaching Amir. She whispered something to him and, together, they left the room. Suzie returned and told us she had to leave.The rest of the guests departed soon after her and I went to bid them goodbye.

Returning to the salon I noticed Mother and Amir whispering together, both with concerned expressions on their faces. I asked them what was wrong. Amir, in his usual annoying fashion, evaded my question – he liked to exclude me from becoming involved in family affairs – but mother ignored him and told me that when the telephone had rung, Father and the maid had simultaneously picked up the receiver. When he had heard a man asking for Suzie at that hour of the evening, Father had become suspicious, so he had hung on to the receiver to find out who the caller was. The man, whoever he was, was waiting for Suzie at the Key Club.

'Miss Hashemi' now made sense.

Amir proposed that he call our cousin Mehram, who had been at the party and had just left, and ask him to go to the club and find out the identity of the 'boyfriend'. Mehram agreed and the four of us sat in my parents' bedroom waiting for him to call us back. Time ticked by. No-one talked. The tension was at a breaking point when the call came. Suzie had been dancing in the arms of a young man named Bahram Bazari.

Amir's immediate comment was: 'The bitch isn't even discreet!'

A bewildered silence filled the dimly-lit room. Our hearts were bleeding and our pride was hurt. Mother began to cry.

I was astonished. Why in the name of heaven did this intelligent, already once-divorced woman marry Ali when she was in love with someone else? Questions raced through my mind to which I had no sensible answers. We were too emotionally distraught to reach a rational solution that night – if one could be found. The shock was too great and the wound too deep.

Chapter Sixteen

This family crisis had upset everybody deeply. We discussed the situation for many days before deciding to keep the discovery of Suzie's paramour a secret from Ali. We would wait to see how the marital relationship developed.

With the excitement of the wedding behind me, I settled back into my own routine with my friends. Shirin was desperately looking for a beau. I had tried to match-make her with Amir, but my brother had become attracted to another friend of mine, a rather quaint but charming lady called Haleh. Haleh was 20, tall and blonde, with rosy cheeks and a creamy complexion which she had inherited from her Hungarian mother. She was the only daughter of a respectable physician and her father was extremely possessive of her and jealous of any male who showed the slightest interest in her. For some reason, though, he had had no objections to Amir. According to Haleh, this was because Amir was a medical man like himself.

One evening while a group of us were dining at the Darband Hotel's Terrace Nightclub, Amir proposed to her and she accepted. Mother was told the next day and an appointment with Dr Honari, Haleh's father, was arranged for the following Monday for Khasegari. I was pleased with Amir's choice and happy at the prospect of having Haleh as a sister-in-law.

When Monday came, we all set out for the Honari residence. Their house was a grand old building surrounded by ten acres of manicured gardens, the interior enriched with precious Gajar antiques. Dr Honari was an extremely good-looking man, immaculately dressed and expensively cologned, but his wife was a plump, good-natured Hungarian with, in my opinion, no class at all.

Very formally, we were received in the salon which, to merit the occasion, had been decorated with vases full of flowers. A male servant served tea and the patriarchs of both families began to discuss the marriage contract. Dr Honari indicated that no bride price was necessary and Father, impressed by this noble gesture, offered to give the couple the new house he was building in Avenue Laila. Dr Honari showed his pleasure at this generous gift by offering to furnish the house. Haleh said that she would like to take a trip to Munich where the family had a residence, to shop for her trousseau. Her father thought this was an excellent idea and added enthusiastically that he would accompany his daughter.

The date for the wedding was to be settled after Amir had completed his national service, and the Nomzadi (engagement party) was to take place the following Wednesday with only family members and a few close friends present.

Now mother's only worry was me – still single and with no Iranian prospect around. Mother coud not tolerate this situation for long. Consequently, the number of dinner parties given at our house increased dramatically, and there was always a different young man for me to meet. I hated the boring parties and wondered why my mother was so keen to get rid of me.

Life is full of surprises. It was at a dinner dance given by my cousin Mitra that I met a real prince charming – an unattached Pahlavi prince. He was tall and handsome with large, dark eyes which radiated an irresistible hypnotic glow. Mitra, an alert hostess and a matchmaker by nature, must have noticed the prince's attentive glances, because she made her way over to me and said teasingly, 'Laila, you look terrific. No wonder the Vala Hazrat (His Royal Highness) can't take his eyes off you.'

Embarrassed I objected, 'Don't be silly Mitra, he's probably looking at someone else.'

'No, he's not,' she replied, then left me for a little while to reappear hanging onto the arm of the same journalist who had been with the honeymoon party in Abadan. We greeted each other and began to make small talk. Mitra's comments had made me very conscious of the prince and I was aware that he was trying to make his way towards me. Soon, he was standing next to us. The journalist bowed and Mitra asked His Royal Highness' permission to introduce me to him. A smiling prince stretched out his hand. I took it and curtsied. He was gracious, serious and, very formally, asked me to dance with him. I felt like Cinderella. His hold was gentle, he smelled delicious and I felt as if I was sailing in Paradise. It was terribly flattering to have been chosen by Vala Hazrat. I did not want the dance to end.

Dinner was a buffet affair. We served ourselves then went to sit in a secluded corner where we made light, pleasant conversation. The rest of the guests had noticed me with the prince and had begun to whisper among themselves.

The evening came to an end all too soon. The prince offered to give me a lift home but, though I would dearly have loved to accept, I had to decline his offer. My parents did not permit me to accept lifts from other people (not even from royalty!); I had to travel to and from parties in our own car.

That night, sleep was impossible. Beautiful thoughts carried me through till dawn, when I rose and went up onto the roof terrace to watch the sunrise – something I often did when I was happy. The sun, with its golden rays spreading over the horizon, reminded me of the glory of God. Every morning at dawn the Muezzin* standing on the minaret of the mosque facing Mecca calls the faithful to prayer. His voice that morning was music to my ears. While listening to the call I prayed and made a single request: 'Please God, don't let me get hurt again.'

I knew that this time I was playing with fire and that if I was not careful I could ruin my reputation forever. I also knew that by mid-morning people would be gossiping about me and Vala Hazrat. I was right. That day, and for the few

* The man elected by the mosque to sing the Koranic verses at the times of the daily prayers: before sunrise, at dawn and at noon.

days following, the telephone never stopped ringing. Acquaintances and people who hardly knew me called to invite me to their parties, to which I guessed the prince was also invited. Almost every night for one month I saw him. His behaviour was always the same, formal but totally attentive. We talked and danced, but we hardly ever laughed.

My parents were in the dark; I had been afraid to tell Mother about this latest turn of events. However, one evening Aunt Firouzeh called, inviting me on behalf of Princess Ashraf's lady-in-waiting to a dinner in honour of the princess. I was hesitant in accepting the invitation until Aunt Firouzeh told me that my presence had been requested by Vala Hazrat himself. In that case, I could not refuse. Mother, who was in the room at the time, became suspicious and wanted to know why I had been invited to this party and not her and Father – who were, after all, friends of the hostess. I told her the truth, thinking she would welcome the news but, surprisingly, prudence took precedence over pride and she said warningly, 'Laila, this affair is dangerous.' Taken aback by her comment I told her not to worry, and to trust me, and she said no more about it.

We had arranged that I should accompany Aunt Firouzeh to the party. I was very excited, because to meet Princess Ashraf was a great honour. She was beautiful, intelligent, clever, notorious – and, reputedly, the most powerful woman in Iran. Her friends were blessed and her enemies doomed. For the occasion I dressed tastefully. Aunt Firouzeh collected me in good time and, once we were seated in the car, inundated me with all sorts of questions regarding my relationship with the prince. From her tone, I detected a slight hint of jealousy.

At the party we were greeted by the host and the hostess. The prince had already arrived and, very tactfully, the hostess guided me towards him. I curtsied and stood by him making the usual, rather boring conversation. I liked the prince, but I suspect that I liked him for what he was, rather than for who he was. I was beginning to find his constant formality irritating. I was an extrovert who loved to communicate with

126

people, tease them and make them laugh. This royal rigidity was beginning to play on my nerves. I thrived on warmth and affection, but the prince was as cold as ice. He was not a talkative person, which made communication even more difficult. In my naivety I could not decide whether it was simply in his nature to be cool, or whether he was hiding behind the demands of protocol. I decided that all I could do was be myself – natural and straightforward.

This was the first time in the prince's company that I was not really enjoying myself. There was a lot of noise and I could smell opium, which meant that there was a room allocated to the use of drugs. I hated drugs. Rumour had it that opium and heroin were used by some of the royal entourage. Another rumour being circulated was that the prince owned a poppy farm. Considering that the punishment for opium smuggling was hanging, this was a rumour which I preferrred not to believe.

We were sitting in a secluded corner when the sound of a bell created a sudden commotion. Everybody rose except the prince. I did not know what the bell was for and so, since the prince remained seated I did, too. Soon a short, plump man entered the room announcing the arrival of Vala Hazrat Ashraf. The sweet smell of Diorissimo filled the room, preceding the entrance of the princess and her courtiers. She was petite and strikingly beautiful, with eyes which were even larger and darker than her brother's. People who knew her said that she was the only Pahlavi who had inherited Reza Shah's strength of character. Indeed, the princess' very presence commanded respect and obedience and her quick, sharp glance in my direction indicated her displeasure at my misdemeanour. I could feel the heat of my blood rushing to my face. The prince must have noticed the change in my colour, because he took my hand for the first time that evening and squeezed it as though to reassure me.

The entertainment for the evening was Persian-style, which meant that the guests sat on cushions spread on the floor. White sofrehs were spread on the carpets and a single, short table set in front of the princess. Plates full of different foods were laid on the sofrehs and, at intervals, the waiters brought round trays laden with steaming kebabs.

After dinner, some of the guests left the room and soon the sweet smell of opium intensified. The musicians resumed playing and the prince and I remained sitting together in our corner talking of trivial things. The princess left at 2 am, accompanied by her most recent favourite who had just been made a deputy minister. Shortly afterwards, the prince followed suit and the guests were free to leave. On the way home, Aunt Firouzeh was non-communicative and Uncle Hussain was in a thoroughly bad mood. He disliked parties at which drugs were used, but because he was a politician and involved with the court again, he sometimes had to swallow this distaste.

For a while the invitations stopped, and I was just beginning to wonder what had gone wrong when a call came from the journalist inviting me, on behalf of the prince, to dinner. This was the first time His Royal Higness had invited me to have dinner with him and I was thrilled. To accept, however, I had to have my parents' permission. I knew they would not allow me to go alone and told the journalist this, so he suggested bringing Amir along. As Amir was not yet home, I asked the journalist to call me back in the evening.

When my brother had returned from work, had his bath and was sitting, relaxed, in front of the television with my parents, I told him of the prince's invitation and asked him if he would accompany me to the dinner. To my surprise, he erupted, 'You fool! Do you expect me to act as a pimp for my own sister? What do you think people will say when they see the three of us alone, huh? Do you think he wants to marry you? Have you forgotten the stories about all those innocent girls who have been taken advantage of by the Pahlavi princes and left to become whores? Don't you know that the man who invited you on his behalf is his pimp? Dear sister, if you think he wants to marry you, you are wrong. He just wants to screw you!'

For the first time in my life, I hated my brother. Why did

128

he have to take so much pleasure in degrading me? Surely he could have discussed the situation with dignity and respect. Mother broke the silence and, as usual, stood by her eldest son. It seemed to me that no matter how hard I tried to please Mother she could find no room for me in her heart. At that moment, I hated them both.

When 'the pimp' called, I asked him to express my apologies to the prince and tell him that, due to family circumstances, I would not be able to accept his invitation. I only saw Vala Hazrat twice after that, and on both occasions he completely ignored me. Perhaps my honourable brother had been right?

So, it seemed that the prayer that I had uttered on the terrace had been heard. The termination of the relationship had not been traumatic. I was disappointed, of course, but I was able to take it philosophically. And in the meantime, life went on.

130

Chapter Seventeen

Amir's engagement was a small, private and rather rushed affair. Dr Honary was suffering from a serious eye problem which needed surgery, and he wanted to have the operation performed by his German eye surgeon in Munich. So, after a small party to celebrate the happy occasion the family left immediately for Germany.

My life was becoming rather boring once more. My work at the school had become monotonous and I needed a change of environment. Perhaps an Italian wedding would create some excitement? Antonio's letters were full of plans and promises and I was more or less ready for him.

With my parents' permission I made the necessary arrangements to travel to Italy in July. Father was keen for me to make the trip because several recent political events in Iran had again given cause for worry. In spite of a period of economic prosperity and political calm, there had been two more attempts on the Shah's life, both pointing to involvement by Bakhtiar who was now living in Europe. The man had simply become too dangerous and everyone wondered why SAVAK could not take care of him.

Many years later when the regime had changed, I met one of the men who did eventually shoot him. The assailant was from the Bakhtiari tribe and the story he revealed was rather interesting. In 1968, SAVAK became sure of Bakhtiar's anti-Shah activities in Lebanon and on the Iran-Iraq border. Consequently, Beirut was flooded with SAVAK agents employed to observe Bakhtiar's movements and wait for an opportune time to either eliminate or expose him. When the right occasion presented itself they tipped off the Lebanese police, who arrested Bakhtiar on charges of trafficking in arms. He was sentenced to three month's imprisonment. The Shah demanded his extradition but Charles Helou, president of Lebanon, responded by extending the sentence, thus avoiding the Shah's request.

In Teheran meanwhile, a military tribunal tried the former general for treason and passed a death penalty. The Shah renewed his demand for extradition but his request was ignored by Helou, who permitted General Bakhtiar to leave for the country of his choice. Under escort, the released prisoner left Lebanon for Rome and, eventually, Iraq. Iran broke diplomatic relations with Lebanon and recalled its ambassador from Beirut.

Bakhtiar was not to live for long, however. In August 1970, an Iran Air plane flying over the Iraqi-Iranian border was high-jacked by two passengers claiming to be Bakhtiar supporters. They ordered the pilot to land in Baghdad where, on landing, they demanded to be driven to their hero's house where they were received with open arms by the general himself. A few days later a hunting party was arranged near the Iran border, during which one of the 'friends' shot Bakhtiar in the back. The two SAVAK agents, having at last rid the Shah of his dangerous enemy, then returned safely to Iran.

By 1967, Teheran was growing fast. It had become a paradise for foreign businessmen and tourists. Sidewalk cafes flourished along both sides of the tree- lined Pahlavi Avenue, which joined the prosperous North to the poverty-stricken South. Elegant nightclubs in Shemiran entertained the Westernised Teheranis and downtown cabarets featuring Iranian singers and belly dancers attracted the louts, as well as the new, middleclass businessmen with cash bulging out of their pockets. But the trendiest entertainment centre in Teheran was the Bowling Club, a grand set-up with twenty bowling alleys, a brasserie and a movie house showing films in English. Pari, Shirin and myself were in the habit of going there every Sunday night to have dinner and see a movie.

One evening, just as we were leaving the restaurant, I noticed my cousin Behrouz sitting at a table with a handful of his friends and went over to say hello. Seated next to him was an extremely good-looking man with a bright, attractive smile. He flashed a quick glance in my direction then dropped his head and began fiddling with his fork. The rest of the boys were undressing me with their eyes. I lingered a little longer than necessary, to see if the attractive young man would pay me any more attention. He did not, and feeling crestfallen and slightly ashamed I left for the movie house.

The next day, just as I arrived home from work, Behrouz called to see if I would like to go to his house for a game of pasour, an Iranian card game. Homa and a friend were already there, he said, and they needed a fourth player. I told him I would join them after I had changed into more comfortable clothes.

I took a shower and, feeling refreshed, I decided to walk to Behrouz' house which was about ten minutes from ours at the top end of Ehteshamieh. Near the front entrance of the house stood an old blue Comet, which looked as though it had been driven by many bad drivers, so many dents did it have on its side panels. Suddenly, a sixth sense warned me that my fate was somehow connected to this old dented car. Was it possible that it belonged to the good-looking man I had met at the Bowling Club?

Feeling excited, and at the same time a little nervous, I rang the doorbell. Behrouz' nanny opened the door and showed me to the family room where my relatives and – yes – the man from the Bowling Club were sitting comfortably chatting. As I entered he rose and was introduced to me as Iskandar Mahdavi. We shook hands. His were very soft, and his bright smile was so enchanting that I fell in love with it.

The group had been waiting for me to arrive to start the game, so without more ado we sat down at the card table and drew cards for partners. The cards decided that Iskandar and I would play against Behrouz and Homa. We chose to play for dinner at the Kolbeh, a restaurant and nightclub in the mountains on the outskirts of the city. As we played, I was conscious of Iskandar's surreptitious glances in my direction, quickly followed with a lowering of his head as he pretended not to be interested. I was enjoying the situation. In the meantime, Homa was trying to attract his attention. She had divorced her French husband and was not bound by social expectations of virtuousness. Her attempts at flirtation did not bother me.

Iskandar and I won the round and I left to go home and change into something more formal for dinner. Homa was Behrouz' next door neighbour and Iskandar lived in Karadj, where his father was a professor of physics lecturing at Karadj University. He had come prepared to spend the night at Behrouz'.

At home, I groomed myself carefully and put on a provocative gown. I was going to indulge in a little competition with my cousin. At eight-thirty the door bell rang and I went outside to join the others. Since I was going out with family members, the usual rule did not apply and I did not have to be chauffeured in our own car. True to my premonition, the blue Comet did belong to Iskandar and my feeling of excitement grew as I climbed in.

As we chatted on the way to the restaurant, I discovered that he was, in fact, a distant relative. I also discovered that he had just graduated from Utah State University in the field of economics and was holidaying in Iran while trying to decide whether to return to America for post-graduate studies or find a job in Teheran. He, like everybody else, had to enrol for compulsory national service and this he wished, by hook or by crook, to avoid.

Kolbeh is situated half-way up a hill just before the ascent becomes too sharp for cars to go any further. It is a picturesque venue. Waterfalls gently spray the surrounding rocky escarpments before merging with the river and rushing downhill towards the South, and the mingled sounds are like music to the ears. The evening air is always cool and pleasant in Darband and, on that particular night, it was chilly. I was shivering and Iskandar gallantly took off his jacket and draped it around my shoulders. However, during dinner he amused himself with my flirtatious cousin, completely ignoring me. She was sitting beside Iskandar, while I was seated across from him. Well, I mused, she wasn't a virgin any more - so why not? He was, after all, very charming. Resigned, I amused myself with Behrouz, listening to his plans for a trip to Paris where he could be with his beloved girlfriend Sharzad. Feeling a little jealous, I could not help wishing that I, too, was loved as wholeheartedly.

After dinner, annoyed and bored, I suggested leaving for home; at this, Iskandar interrupted his flirtation and suggested that we go to a party at his aunt's house. He had been invited and had promised to call in after dinner. Both Homa and Behrouz agreed and, since it would have been very rude and unsociable of me to refuse, we left the restaurant and headed for the party.

On the way, I discovered a little more about Iskandar's background. It seemed that his mother was my mother's third removed cousin on Grandpa's side. So we shared the same great grandfather! His grandfather had been a prominent lawyer who had owned a lot of land; he had divided this between his children - hence his family, like mine, all lived in one vicinity.

Iskandar's aunt's house was full of people when we arrived, mostly the 'nouveau riche'. The host and hostess already knew Behrouz and, when Homa and I were introduced to them, they welcomed us with affection. I was introduced to Iskandar's cousin, who was Behrouz' friend and also a graduate from the Utah State University. The majority of the guests were much older than us and within a short while all the younger people present gathered round us, no doubt bored with the company of the older folk. They, typical of the new rich, all seemed to be trying to impress and outdo each other with grandiose talk about their residences, their cars, their children's schools, their jewels, the number of servants they had, their trips to Europe and, a more recent trend, their beach houses by the Caspian sea. Flaunting riches was becoming a way of life.

We were listening to the boys' conversation about their lives in the United States when Iskandar, who had disappeared, returned accompanied by a plump and pompous woman who he introduced as his mother. A tall, silver-haired, pleasant-looking gentleman followed. He was Dr Mahdavi, Iskandar's father, and I took an immediate liking to him.

It was getting late and I was worried that Mother would be waiting up for me so I insisted that, this time, I must go home. In the car, I found out that Iskandar liked playing tennis as much as I did. I found it rather strange that he seemed to be preoccupied with Homa while remaining fully aware of me; but, I told myself, it did not really matter. I was going to marry Antonio and Iskandar was simply a charming man playing a little game. Why not play along? I realised I was enjoying a sense of adventure.

I felt strangely elated that night and somehow knew that the next day would have a surprise in store for me. I was right. Iskandar called, inviting me to play tennis. I accepted and told him I would book a court at Veisies, a nearby club. He suggested that I make a permanent booking for every afternoon. Every afternoon? He must be really interested! But what about Homa? Had he simply been trying to make me jealous?

Iskandar and I played tennis every afternoon for one month. Every time he came from Karadj his car was full of artichokes which had been grown at the Karadj agricultural centre. He knew I loved them and his gesture displayed a thoughtfulness and simplicity I was unaccustomed to.

Time was passing too quickly. The date of my planned departure to Italy had already expired and the trip had been postponed until September. Poor Antonio was upset, but there was nothing he could do about it. The thought of an Italian wedding was receding in my mind. I was having fun with Iskandar and there was definitely a physical attraction between us. For the first time, I really enjoyed being with a man without feeling nervous or worried. His tranquil nature had a calming effect on me. There was a quality of pure kindness and a

136

gentility about him that instilled a sense of trust, respect and peace in me. At nights I went to bed without a care, knowing that I would be woken by his soft voice on the telephone wishing me 'good morning' and wanting to know my plans for the day.

Mother liked him very much. Father, however, was concerned about his financial situation. He had no work, his father was a university professor with only a small income and, by our standards, they were not at all affluent.

After two months of going out together, still in the company of my cousins, Iskandar asked me to go to America with him. His request struck me as being silly and I told him so. What was I going to do with him in America? Did he merely wish to sleep with me, but lacked the courage to seduce me in Teheran? I was offended and told him so. I also told him that I was going to Milan in September to marry Antonio. He already knew about my commitment to the Italian count and, as I pretended to become more serious about my trip to Italy he, in turn, became more serious about his relationship with me. His youngest aunt's husband was my mother's cousin and a good friend of my father's and this gentleman took it upon himself to play matchmaker. One day, Father called from The Mirabel to inform Mother that Dr Moshiri, Iskandar's uncle, had called and wanted to make an appointment for Iskandar's grandparents, parents and the aunts and the uncles to come to our home for Khasegari. This must have been the best news that Mother had heard since Father's proposal to her!

It was the tradition of the older families for the whole clan led by the patriarch or the matriach – whichever was still alive – to go for Khasegari. I had guessed this was coming, as Iskandar had mentioned to me that his grandmother wanted to visit my mother – though he had omitted to mention anything about Khasegari! I had got to know my man a little better. He was modest, honest and obstinate, an introvert with a very composed temperament. Always immaculately dressed, he had a cultivated taste in almost everything. It was most unfortunate that he had no money! On the other hand, money had never really been an issue in my life. Father had always made sure that I had everything I wished for and he would continue to do so whether I was married or not. So why worry?

I was sitting outside having tea when an exultant Iskandar arrived. He greeted Mother, who kissed him with delight. He asked if his uncle had called. I told him that he had and asked him whether or not he lived in the twentieth century. The question surprised him then, as understanding dawned, he looked at me with his bright, teasing eyes and said, 'Well, you wanted to know what you would be doing if you came to America with me. Now you know.'

'What if I don't want to come to America with you?' I asked, 'Then we stay here and I will find a job after my national service.'

'Who is going to pay for our living expenses in the United States?' I asked. He thought for a while and then said, 'I will find work, and my father will support me.' I laughed, but I felt suddenly uneasy. I realised I would have to start penny-pinching and I hated the idea. A pleasant game had suddenly become serious. It seemed strange that this was what fate had in store for me. I had experienced romance with a government minister, two princes and a count; now it seemed that it was my destiny to marry a penniless graduate with an uncertain future – who also happened to be a charming, patient, intelligent and lovable man.

I was not yet in love with Iskandar, but I was certainly attracted to him more than I was to Antonio. I reasoned that if marriage is a contract based on trust between two committed individuals, and if each honours their responsibilities and does well by the other, then the relationship will be sealed with a bond of love. I saw no reason why Iskandar and I could not aim towards building such a bond. So, against all odds, I decided to marry him.

Chapter Eighteen

One week after Khasegari, Father gave a lavish engagement party in the roof-garden restaurant of The Mirabel. Mahasti, a famous Iranian singer, entertained the hundred and forty family members and close friends who had been invited to celebrate the happy occasion. The venue was simply decorated with white flowers in their pots dug into the flowerbeds of the otherwise Japanese-style garden. An artificial waterfall splashed into a small, rocky pool, the surface of which was strewn with white rose petals. Baskets of flowers were scattered here and there and the sweet scent of tulip roses permeated the air.

According to many of the guests Iskandar, in his smart navy-blue suit, and I in a short, straight, white lace shift made a handsome couple. The hairdresser had pulled my hair back and up, arranging it in a tight bun fixed high on my head with a large taffeta bow, a style which gave me a few more inches in height.

Just before dinner, Dr Mahdavi took the platform and, after announcing the engagement, summoned us to exchange rings. It was a happy moment. The band played Yar Mobarakbad and the guests cheered, kissed and congratulated us. The capacious dinner table was laden with a variety of steaming, exotic dishes which exuded a delicious blend of mouth-watering aromas. A giant multi-layered cake adorned a small table near the waterfall. After dinner, Iskandar and I cut the cake with a pastry knife and made a wish for happiness.

Our wedding was to take place on September 14th and I suddenly realised that I had not yet written to Antonio. Quite simply, I did not know how to break the news to him. I did not have the courage to tell him of my infidelity. Selfishly, and feeling ashamed, I decided not to write at all.

Our celebration was not the only one in town. The Shah's coronation was set for October 28. The Iranian constitution lacked provision for a regent in the absence of an adult heir so, during the Shah's absences, provisional power was vested in a commission. Considering all the attempts on his life, the Shah needed to appoint a trusted regent till his son came of age. Accordingly, he had certain points of the constitution modified so that only he could designate the regent. The right choice was Farah, but first she had to be crowned.

Teheran was in a jubilant mood, and so were we in Avenue Ehteshamieh. Mother was busy preparing my trousseau, and Father was planning a source of income for me. Iskandar's mother, an excellent cook, was baking the traditional pastries for the Sofreh Agd and his father was bargain hunting for the diamond wedding ring. Iskandar's father and I had grown quite close. He was a charming man, frugal and a master bargainer. He would bargain so persistently that the vendor would lose patience and let him have the merchandise for whatever he was prepared to pay. Iskandar and I went out shopping regularly with him, but as soon as he was ready to bargain we would hide ourselves from the vendor's sight.

Iskandar also had a brother, Parviz, but the two were totally different. Parviz was a passionate revolutionary, totally against the monarchy and anyone with any money. Naturally, he hated my very existence. I represented the aristocracy and wealth, both of which were repugnant concepts to a dedicated Tudehi. Mariam Khanum, my future mother-in-law, bore an extraordinary love for Parviz so it was quite natural for her to dislike me, too. I did not care, as long as she did not interfere in my life. Unfortunately, she did – right from the start. Poor Iskandar was to be torn between the two of us for a long time.

From the 10th to the 14th of September our house was carefully prepared for the afternoon Agd ceremony, to which the elders of both families were invited. The wedding party was to be held on the evening of the same day, again at The Mirabel's roof-garden.

Unfortunately, Ali and Suzie would not be able to attend as they were now living in London. A malicious so-called friend had informed Ali of the rumours surrounding his wife. Shocked, he had consulted our parents and, after much deliberation, had decided to bury the knowledge. He had also realised, however, that it would be wise to separate his wife from the source of his misery and so he had requested a transfer back to England. His request had been granted and, surprisingly, Suzie had made no objections to the move. Father and Dr Hashemi had each given the couple a residential property in London and they had chosen to live in Suzie's rather grander house and sell Ali's, spending the proceeds on furnishings. So far, the marriage seemed to be working well.

Amir was still completing his national service and attended his successful surgery only during the afternoons. Haleh, Amir's fiancee, was still in Germany waiting for her father to recover from his eye operation and would be away for another two or three months.

September 14th was the day that Mother had been waiting for most of her life. The servants set to work at the crack of dawn. The furniture in the family room was removed to allow space for the large Sofreh Agd. Iskandar had sent me a huge 18th century gilded mirror, a pair of Gajar glass candelabras and a volume of the Koran to safeguard our union. The room was filled with white flowers and numerous dishes of pastries draped with jasmine were spread out on the Sofreh. Two small, lace-covered stalls were prepared for the bride and the groom. The salon and the garden were organised to accommodate the guests, with three of The Mirabel's waiters serving.

After lunch my hairdresser and the make-up artist began to transform my rather naive appearance into something more sophisticated. By four o'clock I was a beautiful bride dressed in a long, white silk taffeta gown, my face hidden behind a pleated white lace veil which was attached to a bun on the back of my head. The guests began to arrive for the five o'clock Agd.

141

Tradition holds that the actual vows should be taken before sunset, otherwise the marriage will be doomed. To my dismay, by five o'clock there was no sign of the groom or his family. I was going out of my mind, confined to my bedroom and not allowed to leave the room before the arrival of the groom. My parents were insulted. Time was passing and sunset was approaching.

At last, at around five-thirty, an apologetic clan arrived and Iskandar came up to my room to claim his bride. I was exasperated, but decided that the occasion did not merit a scene, so with a smile I took his arm and entered the hall. The musicians began playing the Yar Mobarakbad as we walked slowly in and took our seats in front of the Sofreh. Aunt Azi and Mrs Moshiri, Iskandar's aunt, began rubbing the cane sugar, the dust falling into a cloth held over our heads, and while the mullah was performing the marriage ceremony Mother threw handfuls of gold coins and sugar candy over my head. The guests rushed to pick up the coins from the floor. Iskandar and I exchanged rings and my new husband lifted the lace veil and kissed me. Mother gave me her magnificent emerald necklace and matching bracelet – a gift to her from my father on her own Agd. All eyes were on my neck and wrist. The rest of the presents were nothing in comparison. I realised how deeply happy my mother was.

The guests left at seven and we had one hour to rest before setting off for The Mirabel. Three hundred guests feasted and danced at our wedding party. I loved the festivities, but at the same time I could not help thinking that the whole extravaganza was ridiculous and that, as a young couple starting out, we could have put all that money to a much better use.

By the time the guests left , Iskandar and I were exhausted. We spent our first night together at The Mirabel and we were both so tired that we went to sleep in one another's arms. In a way, I was glad. The tension and repulsion that I had experienced from my brushes with sex in childhood had led to a sort of apprehension on my part of the nuptial night. Fortunately, later, my husband proved to be a sensitive and considerate lover, which helped me overcome my fears. Trust and kindness engender love.

We took our honeymoon in Isfehan, staying at the magnificient Shah Abas hotel. We spent the days sightseeing, taking in the majestic, historical sights of this beautiful city. At nights we had fun – laughing together and simply enjoying our youth and our growing closeness.

After our honeymoon we settled into Dr Mahdavi's house to wait to hear whether or not the university Iskandar had applied to had accepted him for a postgraduate degree.

In the meantime, Teheran had been inundated with excited crowds from all over the country, come to witness the coronation. What seemed like millions of flags emblazoned with the Imperial Lion rampant hung from every public building. The houses along the path of the procession were being refurbished and huge triumphal arches graced every intersection. Rumour had it that the SAVAK was taking stringent security precautions by locking up the 'undesirables'.

On the morning of the 28th, Mother, Iskandar and I watched the historical event take place on the television in Grandma's bedroom – my small, private world looking on at history being made. We did not know then that history was to touch this little world of ours with devastating effect.

In the great Hall of Mirrors at the Golestan Palace the Shah sat on the Peacock Throne. Seated one on each side of him were Farah in a Dior white satin dress and the young prince in his uniform. Suddenly, the trumpets blared and the Imperial flag was hoisted above the throne. The Imam Jumeh, chanting Koranic verses, stepped forward and handed the Koran to the monarch to kiss. Then the Shah put on his belt, slung Reza Shah's sword into it and placed his father's jewelled mantle around his shoulders. A group of dignitaries then marched forward and offered the crown to the Shah, who took it and crowned himself.

The attendants who were carrying Farah's crown and green-bejewelled mantle then approached the throne. The queen knelt before her husband and the attendants draped the mantle over her shoulders. The sovereign crowned his wife then, turning to his son and pointing to the assembly, he pronounced young Prince Reza as his heir. At that moment I found myself hoping that the crown would bring him more luck than it had his father.

Chapter Nineteen

Iskandar and I began our married life living with his parents in their house at Karadj, about half-an-hour's drive from Teheran. My new husband was kind and considerate, but he was also vulnerable and jealous. One evening when we went out to dine at the Chemineh, Teheran's newest nightspot, I bumped into an old friend who had just returned from England. I was truly happy to see him. He had looked after me as affectionately as a brother would have done while I had been studying in London. We embraced and I duly introduced him to Iskandar. My husband gave him a cold nod, then rudely propelled me away from him and over to our table. His behaviour embarrassed and angered me. I did not retaliate straight away, but for the duration of the meal we did not exchange a single word.

In the car on the way home I gave vent to my anger. I reminded him that I had spent most of my adolescence in the company of two much older brothers, whose friends had been in and out of our house all the time. I had even stayed with these young men on occasion during the school holidays, I explained. He must understand this, and accept these people as my good friends – not my ex-lovers. There was nothing wrong with my having male friends, I maintained vehemently. Iskandar listened in silence. In fact, it took him many years to learn to modify his attitude and accept my gregariousness.

Meanwhile, my mother-in-law's busy tongue was making life unbearable for me in the small town of Karadj – and, in any case, my new home was much too far from Ehteshamia for my liking. I was dreadfully unhappy and, one day, when I had had enough of my mother-in-law, I packed my suitcase and asked Iskandar to take me home and live with me there.

He was angry and insulted, but I told him that I could not take another dose of his mother's animosity, nor could I bear the boredom of being confined to a small town. As was his habit, he lapsed into a long, thoughtful silence then agreed to my request. I was very relieved to be able to spend the remainder of our time in Iran at my parents' house.

Away from my mother-in-law's domain and free from her interfering influence, my relationship with Iskandar deepened and strengthened. There was so much that was good in him: his honesty, gentleness and generosity. Gradually, I won his trust and, being the more ambitious of the two, began to take charge of our lives. In a way, our characters complemented each other: he, the conservative advisor with a commercial sense and me, the risk-taker. We began planning our future and thinking of worthwhile investments.

The city was growing towards the North, and in the flourishing economy the price of land was rising. At the same time, the growing flood of foreigners into the country was causing a hike in the rental market. One had to have foresight, and land seemed to be the best and the most secure investment. With the money Father had given me I was limited to buying in areas like Goldonak on the periphery of Shemiran so I asked Uncle Hussain, whose family owned the village, if he knew of anybody who wanted to sell. Within a couple of weeks I became the proud new owner of a large plot of land situated by a river which flowed down from the mountain and rushed to fill the new Lattun dam under construction. The adjacent lot belonged to Uncle Hussain's gardener, Mashalah, who promised to cultivate and look after my land while I was in America.

Fortunately, it did not take long for Iskandar to receive an acceptance from the University of Southern Illinois in Carbondale, where he planned to take a doctorate degree in economics. He would then be able to lecture on our return to Iran at the newly inaugurated National University, which was built on the hills of Evin looking down on the ugly, sprawling metropolis that Teheran had become. Uncle Hussain was a member of this university's board of trustees.

146

We were to leave for the United States on February 20th. We planned to stop en route in London to see Ali and Suzie, before flying to New York where we would buy a car and drive to Illinois. Our last few weeks in Iran passed very quickly. We spent our last evening at the Persian Room where Amir threw a goodbye party for us. The guests were all close friends with the exception of a petite, elegant and very beautiful young woman who had arrived with one of Amir's friends. All evening she kept darting alluring glances at her host. Iskandar noticed this, too, because he remarked: 'Haleh should come back soon, otherwise she might find herself without a fiance!' I agreed.

A friend of mine who was sitting beside me was able to shed some light on the identity of the beautiful stranger. He told me that her name was Kobra and that she was the daughter of a retired merchant involved with SAVAK. She had, it seemed, been married twice before, to two of the most eligible catches in Teheran. She had sued her first husband for impotence after one year of marriage; scared of the SAVAK connection, he had divorced her, granting her a huge bride price. This man had remarried and sired a son by his second wife – so much for his impotence. Kobra had not been so fortunate with her second husband, a prominent Christian who had married her without his father's consent. The father had threatened to disinherit his son and the immensity of the fortune which he stood to lose had overshadowed the son's love for Kobra and brought about her second divorce.

There was a certain sensuality about Kobra that attracted all of the men at our table – including my husband. Feeling a little jealous, perhaps, I was secretly laughing at her credentials: 'Daughter of a SAVAKI; already twice divorced – who would want to marry her?' I was in for a great surprise.

The next day, blessed by all our family and close friends, Iskandar and I left Iran to begin a new life. At Heathrow Airport, Iskandar met his second brother-in-law for the first time and the two men instantly took to each other. In the car on the way to his home, Ali told us that Suzie had gone to Paris to study French. From his tone, it was obvious that things

147

were not right between the two of them, but he seemed reluctant to expand on the subject. Ali and Suzie's house was truly magnificent, six storeys high and served by an elevator. The interior was tastefully decorated with antique furniture and fine Persian carpets. One could feel the meticulous touch of the interior decorator.

This was Iskandar's first visit to London and I was determined to make him love the city as much as I did. On our first day I took him on a grand tour of the city, and in the evening my brother took us to the Clairmont for dinner and gambling. The following day, a sunny Sunday, Ali invited us and a golf partner to the R.A.C. club in Epsom to play golf and have lunch. The clubhouse is an old, graceful building perched high on a lovely green hill surrounded by the beautiful golf course which stretches undulatingly away as far as the eye can see. I have always loved the English countryside and I think from that day on Iskandar began to share my sentiment. While Ali was golfing, we took a long walk and explored the area. The air was icy, but we were well wrapped up and were soon warmed from the exertion of the exercise. When the golfers returned we had a drink at the bar then entered the elegant dining room to enjoy an excellent roast beef and Yorkshire pudding lunch. The next two days were spent in much the same way, enjoying a happy and carefree time.

New York was a totally different experience. It was too modern, too crowded, too busy and too dangerous, and I had not yet developed a taste for American culture. We stayed there only one day, and as soon as we had bought our car, a navy-blue Mustang convertible, we set off on the long drive to Illinois. Carbondale was a typical college town which boasted nothing out of the ordinary except its beautiful campus. We stayed at the Holiday Inn until we found a one-bedroom furnished apartment close to the campus.

Winter in Illinois is freezing, but I did not mind this. I liked the snow and the crisp, cold days on which, after my daily house chores, I would go for long walks. To my disappointment, I was a dreadful cook. Poor Iskandar was forced to consume many uncooked rice dishes in those early days and, gallantly, never criticised my cooking. As time went by, however, I became quite a crafty cook and a master at utilising short cuts.

Every morning, Iskandar went to the university and I was left alone to do the housework – which amounted to virtually nothing. I loved my small, humble abode and strove to make it a haven for both of us. To my surprise, I discovered that I had green fingers, and in no time the apartment was full of healthy, flowering plants. Soon I made friends with the neighbours and a few other Iranians who were studying at the university. At the end of the first term, my husband achieved high enough marks to qualify for an asistantship, which added a bonus to our monthly allowance and provided for a comfortable lifestyle.

Iskandar spent most of his time at home studying, while I read or watched television. After a while, the monotony of this lifestyle led to frequent irritability on my part and Iskandar proposed that I, too, enrol at university. This seemed like a sensible suggestion and I wrote to my parents to see if they would pay for my tuition. They welcomed the idea. I applied and was accepted to take a degree in social welfare – a cause that had been dear to my heart through all the years of parties, feasting and carefree talk in which I had indulged, and which had been reinforced by the charity work I had done. I knew what poverty was, and I wanted to do something about it. True to form, I acted on my decision immediately and wholeheartedly and the pursuit of knowledge in my chosen subject, once a hobby, now became a goal. Life became more pleasant as we each sat on our favourite chair and studied in the evenings. Our conversations became more academic and we competed for excellence in our fields. For a while, life was pretty much perfect. Then I became pregnant.

What was I going to do with a baby and studies? I was too sick to think. Iskandar was thrilled at the prospect of fatherhood and began looking after me with great care and dedication. After several consultations with my parents I decided that the best thing to do was to return to Iran for my confinement. In the meantime, however, I had to continue my studies until the end of term so that I could gain the credits which were due to me. Iskandar had decided to transfer from a doctoral degree to a masters, which would be finished by the time the baby was due. On the way back to Teheran I planned to stop over in London to break the long flight. Suzie was back in England and it seemed that things were a little better between her and Ali.

Iskandar and I spent our last day together in Chicago where I was to catch my plane to Heathrow. We were very much in love and hated to separate, so our farewell was very emotional. During the miserable flight to London, I experienced some bleeding and several sudden, painful abdominal spasms. The combination of pain and the fear of losing my baby were intolerable and I was so scared and anxious that the stewardess gave me a tranquilliser.

At Heathrow Airport, I could not find Ali so I caught a cab to their house. Suzie welcomed me with open arms and, concerned about my condition, immediately called in an obstetrician. His examination revealed that further flight might be dangerous so, after several telephone conversations with my husband and my mother, I decided to take a long rest in London and then return to America. This change of plan was a welcome relief for both Iskandar and me; we were miserable apart. Mother agreed to come to Carbondale for the delivery and to stay and help until I fully regained my strength.

Suzie was extremely hospitable and caring towards me for the duration of my stay in London. Coincidentally, her family were staying at the Carlton Towers and, once I had recovered, we went out together almost every night. I began to get to know Mrs Hashemi better. A very shrewd lady, she also had a great sense of humour and, for an Iranian of her age, was extremely cultured and intelligent. On my last Saturday evening, just as we were about to leave the apartment to have dinner at the Carlton Towers Rib Room, the telephone rang. Ali picked up the receiver. It was Amir. The ensuing conversation was one-sided. with Ali on the receiving end.

Silence reigned in the room until at last he put the receiver down and exclaimed: 'My God!' Suzie and I, almost at the same time, asked him what was wrong. He did not answer straight away, but dropped into a chair, holding his head between his hands and repeating over and over, 'My God.' After a few moments, he composed himself and, looking a little dazed, glanced up at our anxious faces and told us the shocking news. Amir had eloped with Kobra and our parents had disowned him. He had called to ask Ali to telephone Haleh and give her the news.

We were astounded. How could he do such a thing? Did he have no principles? How could he marry that woman? I kept on thinking of Kobra's large, black determined eyes and Haleh's innocent face.

Part III

Not in Utopia - subterranean fields,
Or some secreted island, Heaven knows where!
But in the very world, which is the world
Of all of us - the place where, in the end
We find our happiness, or not at all!
Wordsworth

Chapter Twenty

As she had promised, Mother arrived in Carbondale shortly before the baby was due. It was wonderful to see her after two long years. Once she had recovered from her jetlag, she zealously took charge and ordered me to rest. Her presence, her help and support, were like a precious gift to me. She was the very essence of motherhood – loving, generous and selfless.

My first contractions occurred on a freezing evening when I had just returned from a short walk. As the frequency of the spasms increased, Mother recognised the signs and, together with Iskandar, she took me to the hospital. My daughter, a healthy baby with rosy cheeks and a head covered with black hair, was born at 1 am on the 18th February, 1969. For a newborn baby, her features were very well-defined, promising great beauty. Iskandar was disappointed at first. He had been hoping for a son to perpetuate the family line. But Betsy was so sweet, so gorgeous, that nobody could help but adore her, not least her disappointed father.

A few days after being released from the hospital my stitches became infected and I was placed on a course of strong antibiotics. Tirelessly, and without complaint, Mother took care of me and Betsy who was a hyperactive baby with no love for rest. This meant, of course, that Mother did not get much sleep and she began to lose weight. Her state of health worried me, but I was so sick myself I could not do very much to lessen her burden. I do not know what I would have done without her.

Meanwhile, back in Teheran, Amir had sought Grandma's assistance to act as mediator to mend the rift between him and my parents. Through her, he asked my parents to forgive him and to accept Kobra as his wife. My parents had been waiting for such an appeal; they loved Amir deeply and, in spite of the fact that he had insulted, hurt and failed them, they were ready to embrace him again. They had decided to give him the key to the house they had built for him, and Mother was going to present her own diamond wedding ring to the six-months-pregnant Kobra who, it seemed, had turned out to be a good wife. The reunion had been arranged to coincide with Mother's return to Teheran so, when I had fully recovered and Mother was sure that I could manage by myself, she left for Iran very excited at the prospect of seeing Amir again.

With Mother gone, it seemed to me at first that I would never manage. Taking care of a difficult baby, along with domestic chores and a full load of credits per term seemed impossible, but with meticulous planning and lots of hard work, I managed to establish a manageable routine. Unfortunately, Iskandar was useless around the house and, at times, seemed hurtfully inconsiderate. His selfishness threw us into a trying period in our marriage and, as a solution, I suggested marriage counselling. The counselling did not last long; after a few sessions he abandoned it, vigorously announcing his disbelief in the curative power of psychoanalysis. However, we both wanted the marriage to work, so to that end we began to try to modify our behaviour and our unrealistic expectations of each other. Sometimes we succeeded; sometimes we failed. Nevertheless, we went on trying. Our only objective was to finish our studies as quickly as possible and return to Iran.

The media was full of news about the Shah and his super-extravagant celebration of the twenty-five-hundredth anniversary of the Persian Empire at Persepolis. Needless to say, the millions of dollars spent on this extravangaza had brought a multitude of criticisms from people all over the world, especially those who were aware of the extent to which poverty still existed in Iran.

The anti-Shah student body in the United States had become

vehement in its verbal attacks on the regime and their members were present in all universities, including ours. By chance, I met one of these students at a meeting and we became involved in a political dialogue. It did not take long for me to realise that there was no way I could win in my arguments in favour of the regime because he was so much better informed about the system than I was. His judgements were based on his experiences of living with the masses; mine were based on living with the upper classes. We came from a different world and saw what was happening in Iran from a different perspective. Even though we agreed on nothing, I was very impressed by his political knowledge, which was supported by facts, and concerned at the extent of his hatred for those involved with the regime. We did not part as enemies, but before he left the meeting he turned to me and said: 'Laila, we have a list of who we are going to execute when we overthrow the blood-sucking Shah – and your Uncle Hussain is on that list.'

I laughed at him rather hysterically. Who could overthrow the Shah while the administration in Washington backed him so firmly? People were saying that just recently, during a trip to Teheran, President Nixon had given him carte blanche to purchase any American military equipment he wanted, short of nuclear weapons. It was speculated that Iran would constitute the main force for stability in the Persian Gulf zone, making the Shah indispensable to the West. No, my dear fellow; no-one will be able to topple the Shah – and no-one will execute my uncle.

Sometimes happy sometimes wretched, overworked but successful, we studied and saved money. We toured the length of the United States by car, brunched at Nickelson's Farms, gambled at Las Vegas, lunched at Fisherman's Wharf in San Francisco, dined at the Russian Tearoom in New York, stayed at the Hilton on the Michigan Boulevard in Chicago and, finally, in late 1972, completed our courses with honours and returned to Iran.

We spent our first few months in Teheran at my parents'

house, waiting for my tenants' lease to expire so they would vacate the property which had been given to me as my dowry. Father kept his promise and had an interior decorator furnish the house to my taste. Iskandar, with his doctorate in economics, applied for a lecturing position at the National University of Iran, but not until we pulled Aunt Firouzeh's connection with the president of the university was his application considered and approved. The pay was low, but I assumed that this was just the beginning of what would become a lucrative career.

Through Amir's influence with the Minister of Health and Welfare I became the principal social worker at the Reza Pahlavi Hospital in Shemiran. It was there that I witnessed first-hand the farce of the regime's propaganda which bragged about the benefits bestowed upon the nation by the Pahlavi regime. Reza Pahlavi Hospital was a government institution with a social work ward, the function of which was to provide home care for children from poor families. On my first day at work I presented myself to the assistant of the president of the hospital who was to introduce me to the social work team. After offering me a cup of tea, which I refused, she got up and led me into a long corridor at the end of which was the social services office. In this room sat a young girl who immediately rose from behind her metal desk to greet me. The assistant introduced her as Miss Shirazi, the principal social worker.

Assuming that she was leaving her job and that I was replacing her, I asked her the reason for her departure. Cautiously, she hinted that I was replacing her not because she was leaving, but because of my U.S. degree, and that she would be working under my direction. Her words and her subservient attitude embarrassed me. Trying to be as natural as possible, I assured her that we would work as a team. I told her that I would appreciate her support, welcome her suggestions and needed to draw on her experience. This approach seemed to break the ice a little, because she became less tense and more friendly as she briefed me on the duties and functions of the office. As she explained how the system worked, she stressed that most of the patients' needs were financial. She pointed out that some people abandoned their sick children to the care of the hospital, while others were so poor that they could not take care of or feed their children in convalescence. In the former cases, the social worker had to find the parents and persuade them to collect their children, and in the latter she had to determine which patients qualified for a token of the dried provisions available for the purpose. I was horrified at the thought of mothers abandoning their beloved children because they could not afford to look after them.

Miss Shirazi took me to the ward where the bulk of our patients lay. The large room was packed with children of all ages, some suffering from malnutrition, some from burns and many from infections caused by lack of hygiene. She told me that when there were no available beds, the gardeners often found breathing bundles which had been left inside the hospital grounds. My introduction to the job ended. At home that afternoon, I took the longest shower of my life, scrubbing myself as though to wash away the social guilt I felt for being affluent. I could not touch food that night as I thought of those poor children lying in their beds waiting for parents who might never return.

The next day I was to look after my first case. The patient was ten years old, semi-recovered from typhoid fever, and her mother had disappeared after learning of her coming release. My task was to locate the mother at an address given as: Near the silo in Javadieh. Javadieh was the concentrated slum area in the South of the city, a vicinity where there were many silos. How was I to find this woman?

I was told that I could use the hospital van, but a telephone call proved the driver to be on an errand for at least another hour. While I was waiting for him to return, sheer luck brought the mother into my office. She was a thin, haggard woman dressed in rags. Her face, though not old, was heavily wrinkled and her blistered hands told of much hardship. I greeted her warmly and asked the janitor whose responsiblity it was to serve tea to look after my visitor. At the sight of food, she brightened up and I let her enjoy her treat. After she had eaten she sat looking at me meekly, as though waiting for a reproach. I returned her gaze until she became uncomfortable enough to begin talking.

Sixteen years ago, she told me, she had married a peasant and given him three daughters. Two years ago the family, like so many others, had left their village and come to the city in search of a better life. After one year of trying without success to find permanent work, her husband had left their room one morning and never returned. It did not take too long for the unpaid landlady to learn of the flight of the breadwinner and throw the family out into the streets. Not knowing what to do, the young mother had taken her children to the nearby silo site in search of work. The foreman there had taken pity on her and offered her employment. Her wage was dependent on the number of bricks she collected – ten rials (about seven US cents) per hundred bricks – and as an incentive to start work immediately he had allowed her to collect enough bricks to build a shelter for herself and her children. With the help of her oldest daughter, she had erected four walls and roofed it with a sheet of tin given to them by the foreman. Their dwelling, which she referred to as a tin hut, was without any means of sanitation or water. Their drinking water was either joob water (water from the gutter) or was drawn from the nearby well. Their toilet was a hole in the ground which she had dug outside the hut. When finances permitted, she took the children to the neighbouring public baths.

Her oldest daughter, aged fifteen, was also working at the silo. Her second daughter, fourteen, had been sold for five thousand rials to a pimp from Shahreno (the red light district). He had promised her the girl would live well and wear good clothes. Now she did not know what to do with the third one, who was in hospital.

The story was heart-rending. What could I offer this woman?

160

What would truly benefit her – Freudian counselling, or a couple of kilos of lentils? How many hundreds – indeed, thousands – of such desperate souls existed in our society?

Suddenly, my thoughts were interrupted by the woman, who was asking me what I could do for her. I apologised and told her I must see her room before I could make any decisions. I had to make sure she was telling the truth. I called the driver again. He was in; I led the woman to the parking lot, where we got into the van and headed for what can only be described as the shameful underworld of the Pahlavi paradise. After one-and-half hours of driving in the horrific Southern Teheran traffic, we reached the site. It was a huge shambles of a place which most human beings could not conceivably imagine to exist in a modern capital city. Scattered rows of tin huts provided shelter for the people who scraped a pathetic living from the silo. The stink of human waste permeated the air, and swarms of flies were feasting on dung everywhere. A few diseased dogs, thinner than the people they were watching over, were scavenging around on the barren land. A handful of children were playing next to one of the huts and a couple of babies were crawling with bruised knees on the muddy, contaminated ground. A little baby girl was sitting in a corner trying to suck at a broken brick.

The woman guided me to her so-called home. The floorspace was just large enough to accommodate four bodies stretched side by side. The inside was immaculately clean. The ground was covered with an old, faded, many times mended kilim. A thin mattress lay folded up in a corner. The only cooking apparatus was a gas burner, next to which some tin and plastic bowls and plates were neatly stacked. Some tin cutlery and a wooden spoon filled an old shoe box. This was her share of the Pahlavi paradise.

I could not control my tears. The woman looked at me as if I was mad and asked me why I was crying. I stared back at her, not knowing what to say. Then it dawned on me that this individual had accepted her fate and was trying to make the most of it. Such was the lot of those who were not caught up in the whirlwind of the march towards the Great Civilisation. On the way back to the hospital, I told her I would make arrangements for her to receive five thousand rials in cash per month, plus ten kilos of rice and lentils, if she took her daughter with her when we returned to the hospital and rented a decent room. The look in her eyes was worth a million rials. For the dried provisions, she was to go to the hospital each month; for the money she was to go to the reception of the Mirabel Hotel.

The next day I resigned. The social problems in Iran did not need social workers with U.S. degrees. They needed a system which aimed at eradicating the problems from their roots up. They needed a revolution. The woman remained on my payroll until she found herself a bricklayer husband who could take care of her and her children. Meanwhile, the oil money was pouring in and construction was booming.

Chapter Twenty-One

It is every young couple's dream to move into their own home, and Iskandar and I were no exception. With much excitement, and brimming with hope and happiness, we settled into our beautiful house which had been lovingly decorated with our precious Gadjar antiques and tapestries.

Our first major problem was to find a trustworthy servant. It was becoming increasingly difficult to find good domestic help. Nobody wanted to slave in the house anymore; the factories were employing people by the hundreds, offering good salaries and all sorts of benefits. Industry was expanding and business was booming at an undreamed of pace. At the same time, prices were soaring and wage-earners were finding it difficult to cope with rising inflation.

Iskandar's salary was not adequate for our means, and even though Father was giving me a generous monthly allowance, I realised that if we were to maintain the standard of living that was enjoyed by our peers absorbed in the private sector, I would have to find work. I no longer wished to pursue a career in social welfare; instead, I wanted to teach. Iskandar's cousin, head of the department of psychology at the National University of Iran, liked me and when I told him of my desire to lecture at the university he invited me to join his department.

I could not teach psychology with only a master's degree; however, I was qualified to lecture in the compulsory English courses which were run to enable students to follow English texts sufficiently well to either enrol in post-graduate programs, or further their studies in English-speaking countries. As people were becoming more affluent, and the Western-educated graduates were capturing the job market, most young people aspired to study abroad and, hence, needed to know English.

I was assigned to three courses: preliminary, child and abnormal psychology to years one, two and three respectively. I cherished my position and wholehearted devoted my time and energy to my job, part of which was to summarise the English texts of the translated versions taught in the classrooms, so that those students already familiar with the theories could learn the concepts in English. In reality, I was teaching both the language and the field of psychology.

Initially, those students registered at the university had been from the higher income groups who were able to pay the annual fees. As time passed, however, and more money came into the country, the government took the positive step of abolishing this fee. Naturally, the socio-economic backgrounds of the students changed as the original students went abroad and vacated their places to applicants from the lower income groups. As time went by, I also noticed an increase in the number of female students who wore the traditional chador. I thought nothing of this trend. As a matter of fact, I welcomed it as a sign of increased literacy and general prosperity among the lower classes.

Each college had a dean who was responsible for the welfare of his students and who was also, because of the close contact he had with them, expected to cooperate with SAVAK when required. Most, though not all, obliged and SAVAK vans were a permanent feature in the campus parking lots. From whispered rumours, I gathered that any dissent among the students was severely and savagely punished. In retaliation, the students would look for the slightest excuse to start a riot, and often took their anger and frustration out on the university windows. It was not unusual for us to go through an entire winter with a piece of cardboard covering our class window as a substitute for the broken glass. I was not politically minded, and it did not really matter to me what the students did to the windows. My life was comfortable and I enjoyed my job. Iskandar, like most of the other lecturers, was supplementing his income with extra lecturing in a number of other institutions. It seemed as though everybody was making money.

Amir had settled into his grand house next door to us. It was pleasant being neighbours. His naughty little son Dara was Betsy's playmate and Kobra, a lady of leisure, was actively managing their extensive social life. Her successful husband had recently been appointed president of a major public hospital. Every Friday, we gathered at my parents' home for lunch and lazily gambled the afternoon away. The cunning Kobra, now well-accepted by the family, considered herself to be the Queen of Ehteshamieh. A narcissist with no scruples, she always got what she wanted, no matter what the cost. She mixed with the obnoxious new rich, mostly contractors and middle men. Among them, morality was blase, indulgence synonymous with being modern, and the taking of hashish and marijuana the norm. Amir hated her lifestyle but he loved her too much to stop her from indulging herself. Meanwhile Ali, who was living between Teheran and London, was still unhappy. His marriage, although blessed with a daughter, was on the rocks again. In my opinion the conquest of his Suzie's heart had become a blinding obsession with him.

In Teheran, life was prosperous. The Mirabel was always full and Father had bought a beautiful waterfront property on the shores of the Caspian Sea in his children's names. For some reason, Kobra felt a special sense of ownership towards this property and regularly spent long weekends there. She was pregnant again and Amir was very attentive towards her. Their social circle included cabinet ministers, high-ranking government officials and one very good-looking aristocratic admiral who was particularly fond of Kobra and a regular guest at the house by the Caspian. His undaunted attentions to her had become the talk of the town, making Amir extremely uncomfortable – but, as usual, she did what she wanted and got away with it. We were, thankfully, seldom included in her high-society circle.

My cousins, who I saw frequently, were all doing well. Behrouz, now married to his beloved Shahrzad, was a board member of a bank; Mehran, a high-ranking engineer, was employed at the ministry of electricity; and Ne Ne had married into a family with court connections. Her husband, Tari, was a highly educated, ambitious and successful civil engineer. Unlike many favourites of the court, he was extremely competent and hardworking. Uncle Hussain, senator by royal appointment, was busy turning one of his villages near Goldonak into a modern residential suburb.

On the whole, the family could not have been better off. My only source of unhappiness was my housekeeper's lack of competence to manage the house, but this problem was duly solved when the flow of foreign skilled and domestic help into the country enabled me to hire two hardworking Philippino servants.

Meanwhile, our megalomaniac monarch was exultant at his success in masterminding the oil price rise of 1973. Massive capital was being injected into the economy. The rich were becoming richer – but the poor saw no change. Teheran, already overcrowded with cars and people, was buried under a thick cloud of pollution. The city was pulsating with activities of all kinds: construction, commerce, festivals and conferences. It had become a city of neurotics searching for wealth and success. The relaxed traditional customs and courtesies were being wiped out by the onrush of civilisation – that is, the Shah's idea of civilisation. Yet, contrary to expectation, people did not seem to be happy; nor were they enthusiastic about the transformation of their society, or the fact that Iran had become more than just a spot on the world map.

The international press was full of praise for the Shah. Foreigners were greatly impressed by his total dedication to turning Iran into a Western industrial state. But to his detriment, as he became more prominent on the international scene, he also became more isolated from his people. The strict demands of protocol, together with the tremendous security measures which surrounded him, shielded the monarch from direct contact with his subjects. His SAVAK had become ubiquitous and repression of the people had intensified. We only ever heard the Shah's helicopter fly over our heads. The Shah's 'people revolution' was a myth. There was the

Shah - and there was the people. But never the two together.

I was of a generation and a class which had benefited from Pahlavi Iran. I had been brought up with the notion of loving the Shah and, indeed, I had loved him once. But there was something about the Pahlavis which was repugnant. The airs and the graces, the pompous poses in their photographs, their arrogance, all gave the impression of ownership rather than comradeship or benevolence. The 'father of the people' image - which to some extent had existed during the early part of Mohamed Reza Shah's reign - had evaporated as he became more dictatorial. The Pahlavis did not rule Iran; they owned it.

Among the populace, the privileged, the pampered, and the arrogant armed forces - the base of his power - were loyal. The rich entrepreneurs, the up-and-coming middle class, the high-ranking technocrats and the middle men whose numbers were increasing, acquiesced. The clergy, the intellectuals, the students and the bazaaris were covertly critical and hostile, and the sullen, silent passive majority tried to make the best of their poverty and anxiety stricken lives. It seemed to me that what was lacking was trust. How could the nation trust this regime and its government, when rumours pointed to millions of dollars paid as commission into Swiss bank accounts owned by the royals and their government officials? The extravagant lifestyles of the recipients proved the validity of the rumours.

Such was life in Iran. Even we, a class which lived in perfect affluence, felt the wrongness of it. Yet whether we liked it or not, we were living in a land of bewildering contrasts, going through a process of dynamic economic, social and cultural change which influenced every aspect of our lives. We were part of a gigantic wave sweeping across the country, crushing all obstacles in its quest to become part of an ocean of prosperity. Now we even had a minister for women's affairs. Divorce laws were being changed, their Koranic origins being discarded to give more rights to women. No longer could men divorce their wives simply by saying 'I divorce thee' three

167

times. There were family courts to protect the female's rights and women were becoming a huge and remarkably efficient force in the labour market.

Almost everybody I knew was employed, with two or three different jobs. Iskandar had become an executive board director of a government bank with a good salary and a chauffeur-driven car. I was ecstatic about his new position; I saw it as a stepping stone towards a much higher rank. The way we were working, and with the people we knew, there was no reason why I might not become the wife of the minister for higher education, or the chancellor of a university. In the Shah's Iran, the sky was the limit. Iskandar was such a brilliant lecturer that the university had agreed to keep him on full-time, in spite of his position with the bank. He now conducted his lectures during the evenings which meant that we never saw him before nine o'clock at night. This did not matter. 'Workomania' and progress were the moods of the time.

I was teaching extra hours myself. The two Phillipinos I had employed in place of the Turkish housekeeper were managing the house very efficiently and looking after little Betsy. My daughter, now aged five, was growing tall, slender and beautiful. Both she and Dara, who now had a baby brother, were attending an international kindergarten where they were learning English and Farsi. It was a great advantage for the children to be neighbours.

Amir's wife, meanwhile, was becoming involved in some rather suspect business deals. Cashing in on connections was bringing her in big money. Her tiny figure was always wrapped in chinchilla and her fingers adorned with precious stones. Rumour had it that she was involved with the officials in charge of the purchase of naval armaments, in particular the good-looking admiral who was at the centre of it all. People were talking about the affair and Kobra had become a source of embarrassment to the family. We could do nothing but wait for Amir to realise his folly. Fortunately, the wait was not long.

One Thursday afternoon, after taking my usual walk to visit Grandma, I stopped at Mother's house. As I entered the sitting room a ghostlike Mother was hanging up the telephone receiver. I asked her what was wrong. She whispered: 'It was a police officer looking for Amir. I gave him all the contact numbers I had. What do you think the police want with him?' Trying to hide my own alarm, I replied, 'I don't know, Maman. We are all clean, none of us have any dossiers with SAVAK. Perhaps they want to ask him questions about one of his patients.'

I sat down beside Mother and took her cold hand. On reflection, I wondered if perhaps something had happened to Amir's children. I called his house, but the nanny assured me that they were playing in the garden. Relieved, I asked her to tell my brother to call us as soon as he arrived home. In the meantime, I had to calm Mother down; she was becoming hysterical. I called home and left instructions with Fe, Betsy's nanny, to let my husband know where I was and to tell him to join me as soon as he returned home.

Father arrived at about five thirty and when he heard the news he immediately called his nephew, a colonel in the army, to see if he could help us. Unfortunately, he was not at home and we could do nothing but wait. The minutes crawled by. The only sound which occasionally broke the silence was Father's whisper of 'Allah Akbar' – God is great. Then, just before eight in the evening the intercom buzzed. It was Iskandar. He urged me to hurry down to the car as something dreadful had happened. I hung up the receiver, waited for a second to compose myself, then told Mother that Iskandar was at the door and wanted me to go home as he was very tired. Mother was too agitated to care.

At the gate, Iskandar disclosed that Kobra had been murdered. The police had found her naked body lying side by side with the admiral's; they had both been shot dead. Horrified, I asked how they had known who she was. Apparently, he continued, an anonymous caller had tipped off the police, who had immediately gone to the apartment and found the bodies. They had then tried to contact Amir and, when they could not find him, had called Mother. My shattered brother was at our house, Iskandar went on. He did not feel able to go home and face his children in the state he was in.

In the car we were silent . Suddenly an attack of nausea made me throw up. There were no tears; the trauma was too terrible for tears. The whole story seemed like a scenario out of a movie. It could not possibly be true – and happening to real, beloved people.

God does give us courage in times of trouble. The children were told their mother had died in a car crash. Luckily, they were too young to ask questions. We moved them into my house while the police investigations continued. Mother had a nervous breakdown and had to spend some time in hospital; Father appeared to be philosophic about the event, but I know that he took to opium again for a while. Amir, after that first horrific night when he drank himself into oblivion, took charge of his shattered life with courage, dignity and an admirable self-discipline and came out of the affair with his family honour and integrity intact.

The murder still remains a mystery. All we could discover at the time was that the admiral had had a male servant who had disappeared after the murder, and that the shots had been fired from close range. The press only told of the murder of a navy admiral in bed with a socialite. No names were mentioned. The whole affair was very professionally hushed up by SAVAK and the police. We were powerless and, in a way, reluctant to pursue the matter. What was the point in digging for dirt? However, the mother of the dead admiral did not give up so easily and luck was on her side. Some time later, when the Shah commenced his anti-corruption campaign to please President Jimmy Carter, many high-ranking officials were rounded up and jailed. Well-connected herself, she found out that one of those who had been jailed was responsible for the murder of her son. This man had been involved in a multi-billion dollar project relating to the purchase of some highly sophisticated equipment for the navy, and this project had needed the admiral's approval. Millions of dollars in commission had been involved. The man had become aware of the admiral's love for Kobra and had befriended her, offering her an astronomical bribe to persuade her lover to sign the deal. The servant had been his watchdog. The admiral was an honest man and, when Kobra failed in her mission, she in effect signed their death warrants. So tightly woven was the web of corruption that the admiral's mother did not dare to pursue the matter any further.

Amir, disgusted with the system, sold his house and took his children and their nanny to live in London. A year later he married a decent woman.

Chapter Twenty-Two

Once a week we were expected to have lunch at my in-laws' place. They had moved back to their house in Teheran and Dr Mahdavi was commuting to work in Karadj. Parviz, who lived with his parents, had married an Austrian girl and was working for the government. He was a hot-headed communist who believed all capitalists should be rounded up at Shahyad Square and shot. Our meetings often ended in an angry dispute between him and myself, which spoiled the day for all of us. I hardly ever enjoyed these visits; they were a sacrifice to please my husband and often, hurt and angry, I would take out my fury on Iskandar as we drove home.

At times I felt really unhappy with my choice of marriage. But my problems were nothing compared to what Ali was going through. He and his wife had finally divorced and he was trying hard to adjust to life without Suzie and his lovely daughter Yasmin. My heart bled for him because I knew how much he loved them both. The news of the divorce affected my parents badly and they became very depressed. I thought a change of environment might do them good, so I encouraged them to take a trip to London to enjoy the house they had recently bought at Rutland Gate. The idea appealed and they invited me and Betsy to accompany them. I declined the invitation as I was pregnant again and could not face the six-hour flight.

In any case, life in Teheran was at its best. We had made a new friend who was a cousin of the queen's and, through him, we had been introduced to Madame Diba. He often invited us to functions at which she was the guest of honour. We were moving in the 'right' circles and meeting the 'right' people. Iskandar was popular among professionals and I was certain that he would soon move into a more prominent position.

The Shah was at the pinnacle of his power. Recently, in his arrogance and dislike for Arab influence and its spiritual concomitant Islam, he had changed the calendar from its Islamic origin of Hejrat, the Prophet's emigration from Mecca to Medina, to the twenty-fifth century of the Persian Empire. This whim was intended to stress the Aryan identity of the Iranians and meant that all legal documents beginning with one's birth certificate had to be changed. The decree was a bureaucratic blunder and a direct affront to Islam which, quite rightly, infuriated the clergy. However, people were enjoying the boom of '74 and it was to their advantage to keep quiet. There was so much money, so much activity and so many grand plans in the air that no-one thought of complaining about anything except the Teheran traffic.

The empress, as active as ever on the cultural scene, was patronising the controversial annual International Cultural Festival at Shiraz, where talent from all over the world entertained royalty and those who could afford the tickets. The festival was popular among the jetsetters and the very rich. I was not inclined towards avant-garde art and so, to my friends' astonishment, I never attended this famous event. The festival encouraged tourism and did help the city of Shiraz in a commercial sense, but it also offended the traditional section of the city's society.

What I admired most about Farah was her love for everything Iranian. She did much to preserve the best of Iranian heritage, especially where architecture was concerned. Under her direction, old houses in the provinces were bought, restored and opened to the public. Beyond doubt, she was the most respected member of the Pahlavi family. Although I saw her on many formal occasions, I was never introduced to her.

One of the events at which I sat in viewing distance of the Imperial couple was the opening ceremony of the 1974 Asian Games in the colossal Aryamehr Stadium. Around 100,000 people saluted the Shah with well-drilled enthusiasm. To an outsider, the greetings may have appeared genuine,

174

but we all knew how the crowds were gathered. Usually, when spectators were needed at an event, invitations were sent to public servants and official dignitaries whose attendance was then meticulously monitored by SAVAK. A missed occasion was noted and the official reprimanded and, sometimes, dismissed. These so-called invitations became more frequent when, in March 1975, the Shah arbitrarily decided to abolish the multi-party system and create Raztakhiz, a single party of national resurgence to which all Iranians had to belong.

I never wanted to understand the purpose behind Rastakhiz and, like millions of others, accepted it as another political gimmick.

Once or twice a year I received an invitation to attend the meetings. My summons always landed into the wastepaper basket under my desk in my office. Fortunately, for some reason, SAVAK always overlooked my absences. Some of my more important colleagues, however, could not escape the boring gatherings during which speakers shouted their phoney appraisals of the Shah-People Revolution while the audience yawned or snored, clapping puppet-like when they heard the Shah's name mentioned. Poor Iskandar could not evade the meetings as easily as I did but, because all his classes were in the evening, he often had a legitimate excuse not to attend. His work at the bank was progressing well and he was being kept very busy.

The Shah, meanwhile, had introduced another ploy in the guise of an industrial reform. A decree had been passed which compelled all industrialists who owned plants over a certain size to sell forty-nine per cent of their ownership to their workers within a certain time limit, with a greater share to be sold to the workers in nationalised industries. This sudden reform led to panic and uncertainty among the entrepreneurs, who became reluctant to invest any more capital in Iran. They began to send their money out of the country and, by 1977, billions of dollars had left Iran. The workers, lacking faith in the authorities, did not welcome the reform; nor did they take advantage of the generous offers of share acquisition in place of cash wages. Through lack of trust this reform, too, failed to have the desired effect.

Father, like most people, was getting worried about all these unpredictable changes. Cautiously he, too, began to send money out – for a rainy day, as he put it. I decided to sell my land at Goldonak, but when I went to the municipality to get the necessary legal forms, I found out that a city plan had been established for Goldonak, and that my land had become part of a park zone. Accordingly, it had to be sold to the municipality for a very small sum. Only already cultivated land was exempt from this law and could be sold privately. I was mortified and immediately sought advice from Uncle Hussain. He told me that only an order from the governor of the province could provide me with an exemption. Luckily, the governor was a relative of Iskandar's, so I made an appointment and went to see him with my request. He informed me that such an order was impossible, but suggested that if I was somehow able to fence the land and plant some trees on it during the night, I would have myself a garden and it would be very difficult for the municipality inspectors to prove that the land had once been barren. What a brilliant idea! I thanked him a thousand times and left.

That same day I drove to Goldonak in search of Mashalah, the gardener who had worked for my family for twenty years. I was certain I could trust him. I found him in my uncle's garden and asked him if he could execute such a plan, and how much it would cost. He quoted what I considered to be a totally unrealistic price, but I had no choice but to agree. First the trees were purchased then, when the angel of darkness had spread her wings over Goldonak, Mashalah and his five sons set to work to create my fenced garden. The work was so professionally done that I forgot all about my intention to sell the land. I mused that in due time, when Ehteshamieh became too crowded, I would build a villa on it, with a swimming pool and a tennis court. The perfect residence!

Not for a moment did it occur to me that anything might happen to the Shah. America was behind him all the way and he was inundating the country with social reforms. Of course, at the time I was not aware that the reforms were not working!

I loved Iran and I wanted to bring up my children in my own country. My second baby was expected shortly and, unwilling to take the risk of my waters breaking in the middle of the classroom, I had decided to have an induced labour. Dr Sabeti, my obstetrician, had made the suggestion when I had revealed my fears to him. Iskandar did not like the idea, but my persistent pleas had persuaded him to succumb. The date reserved for my labour was 14th May.

On the due day Mamad Aga, our faithful driver, drove me to the hospital. The poor man was bewildered at the idea of taking his mistress to the hospital before the pains had come. I did not think it wise to tell him what was really going on. If he had known that I was interfering with God's work, he would have condemned me as 'ungodly'. This would have been a gross mistake at a time when an unusual religious fervour was spreading across the country.

At the hospital, I was checked into a room and told to change into a hospital gown. Anxiety suddenly gripped me and for the first time I questioned the wisdom of my decision. What if something went wrong? What if something happened to the baby? I would never forgive myself. While I was anxiously searching my conscience, the door opened and Iskandar and the doctor entered. Doctor Sabeti was the best obstetrician in Iran – Swiss-educated, dashingly handsome and, not least, a Gadjar aristocrat. I could trust his judgement. Smiling, he asked if I was ready. I looked at him and suddenly burst into tears. Iskandar sat beside me on the bed and put his arm around my shoulders. Trembling violently I snuggled against him and let his warmth and kindness comfort me.

'Don't tell me you're chickening out?' the doctor teased. I shrugged. Iskandar continued, unsuccessfully, to try to console me. Suddenly a tall, bossy nurse waltzed in, smiled at the doctor, nodded at Iskandar and, without a hint of compassion, ordered me to follow her. Meekly, I obeyed.

I was taken to a small room in the middle of which was a single bed. Following the nurse's instructions, I lay down, trying to stifle my worries about what she was going to do to me. After fiddling around with various instruments, she connected me to an intravenous drip and told me to lie still until the pains arrived. I lay there for an hour – but the only pain I felt was in my heart. Suddenly, the door opened and the doctor came in. He looked at me with his teasing eyes and said it looked as if the baby might not be ready to be born after all. If the pains did not come within another hour, he went on, I would be sent home.

Most certainly that could not happen. Under no circumstances was I going to return home without a baby! I believe I willed that labour on myself. Just before the hour was up the pains began, and at one o'clock in the afternoon I gave birth to Parissima, a tiny, jaundiced infant weighing less than a kilogram. She was immediately placed in an incubator. All my joy evaporated and was replaced with a horrendous feeling of guilt. Had God indeed punished me for interfering with his work?

Chapter Twenty-Three

Parissima had to remain in the incubator for ten days; I was grateful that my doctor allowed me to stay in the hospital with her. My health was not robust at the best of times and after the birth I found that the slightest exertion made me extremely tired. One night when I woke up to go to the toilet, I noticed that my body felt unusually heavy. I dragged myself out of bed and was walking slowly towards the bathroom when, suddenly, I collided with the wall in front of me and fell to the floor. For a while I sat on the cold tiles as though glued to them, then, summoning all my strength, I pulled myself up and got myself to the bathroom. In the morning I told the matron about my fall. She assumed that it had simply been caused by physical weakness and assured me that all would be well in due time.

Two days later Parissima and I left the hospital and went home. It was clear that Betsy had missed me very much – and equally apparent that she did not take kindly to having an intruder in the house! I begged Iskandar to be especially attentive towards her so that she would not feel emotionally threatened by the new baby. I had been subjected to parental discrimination and I knew how much it hurt. No child of mine was going to be exposed to the same traumatic experience!

It was good to be home, but I was finding it difficult to regain my health; I felt very tired and not at all well. My maternity leave expired all too soon, forcing me to return to work before I felt ready. On my first day back at the university I experienced another fall, which was later followed by two others at home. Something serious must be wrong with me! I called Dr Sabeti who arranged for me to be admitted to Pars Hospital. There

I was told that I had an inner ear infection which was affecting my balance. It could either get better or it could get worse; whichever way it went, nothing could be done about it. I had to go to bed, to rest and to preclude the risk of more falls.

Iskandar talked to his cousin who, to my relief, agreed to arrange for a substitute lecturer to fill in for me until I recovered. Meanwhile, my condition was rapidly deteriorating until I experienced total loss of balance, forcing me to become completely dependent on the family and household staff for the most basic of functions. Everybody was very concerned about me, particularly as we did not know how long the malaise would last. Mother came to sit with me during the day, Father came after work and various cousins visited at different hours. It took me eight weeks to recover and I was to find out later that my balance was permanently impaired.

Father suggested that Iskandar and I take a trip to London to recuperate. I did not need much persuading and we took the children and Fe with us. In England, both of my brothers were content with their lives and we were all very happy to see each other. The holiday helped me to regain my spirit as well as my health.

Once I had fully recovered, we returned to Teheran and I recommenced lecturing. But the classroom environment had changed; the normally polite students had become impertinent. The cafeteria in which I sometimes lunched seemed fuller, noisier, the tables occupied by lively groups of students involved in heated discussions – which always changed to small talk when anyone in authority appeared on the scene. The almost threatening expressions on their faces made me uncomfortable. There was hate in their eyes. I stopped going there altogether.

Iskandar, a popular lecturer, had been appointed dean of the students. One evening, over dinner, we began to talk about the changed atmosphere of the campus. He divulged that SAVAK had intensified its vigilance, and that their representative had contacted him to ask for his co-operation in identifying dissident students. I was horrified and asked him whether he was going to resign or co-operate. He replied that he was going to do neither; instead, he would try to protect the students who were being picked up daily and sent to SAVAK headquarters. Some returned, others disappeared for ever. Many of those taken to headquarters could be helped, Iskandar said. By using his influence he could act as intermediary and try to secure their release. The suspicious looks, the anger and the hatred now made sense.

Naively, I had been wondering why the students were so against the regime, which seemed to offer them so much more than before. All the reforms targeted at the rich were to make the poor people's lot better. Wealth would trickle down, wouldn't it? Education was expanding, entering the remotest areas. University fees were being abolished and many of the students received grants. There was so much work that skilled labour was being imported from overseas. Relative freedom of speech was tolerated. People could travel freely. Iranians did not need visas for most countries. There was no exchange control; many people had apartments and houses all over the world, and for those who did not wish to shop abroad most consumer goods could be purchased in Iran. Why, then, were these young people – who owed their education to the Shah – so against him?

Iskandar had a completely different view of the situation. He did not believe that the majority of people were content. He believed that the oil money was the worst calamity that had ever hit Iran and that it would have serious repercussions for the regime. The result of the boom was an annual inflation rate of around twenty per cent. The Shah's dreams were unrealistic and most of his projects too grand to realise. Many companies, and the government, too, had indulged in excessive imports of all sorts of goods, whose transfer from port to city was impossible because of inadequate roads, fragmented rail links and limited means of transport. The infrastructure simply was not ready to absorb the pressures of an overheated economy.

The boom had also created a wide gap between rural and urban incomes, a situation which had persuaded many farmers to sell their land and drift to the already overpopulated cities, like Teheran, which could not accommodate them. This state of affairs not only damaged agriculture, but also worsened the spread of the city slums. To make matters worse, villages on the outskirts of the capital were being bulldozed to make room for modern towns, leaving the inhabitants homeless. The majority of them had no choice but to seek refuge in the poverty-stricken areas like Javadieh.

High wages and rising expectations tended to make the urban working classes, particularly industrial and construction workers, volatile in their political and social attitudes. Their lot had definitely improved. Now they were eating take-away pizzas and drinking Budweisers for lunch, instead of their usual bread, goat cheese and Coca Cola. The influence of American culture, once detested, was now embodied in the hamburger shops and pizza parlours which mushroomed on every corner. A chain of Kentucky Fried Chicken restaurants was installed, though without a legitimate franchise. The colonel definitely looked like an Iranian.

A kind of social vacuum was engulfing the populace, especially in the larger cities, threatening to endanger the existing social order. Everything was changing, but in the absence of logical goals, rational planning and trained human resources only God could predict the results.

Iskandar forecast a gloomy future. I knew he was right, but I did not want to admit it. What concerned me most at that particular time was the shortage of onions. The greengrocers were complaining that all the onions were rotting at Khoramshahr (the major Iranian port) because there were not enough trucks to carry the goods to the cities, and to aggravate the situation the government was trying to enforce an impossible price control in order to curb the embarrassing inflation. Needless to say, this situation had created a black market.

I did not let the lack of onions, an essential ingredient in Iranian cooking, bother me for long. Instead, I hunted the supermarkets for dried onion flakes and bought the entire stock of the local supermarket. I felt relieved about the eradication of this minor problem. The average Iranian did not even know such a thing as dried onion flakes existed. To be on the safe side, I began storing imperishable goods like rice, cooking oil, canned and bottled essentials. Both freezers in my kitchen were filled with meat and frozen vegetables. I was only half-conscious that I was preparing my household for trouble.

Norooz, the New Year, was approaching and my parents decided to take their vacation in the villa by the Caspian. I loved going to Father's villa. There I could swim and sunbathe all day, and gamble away the evenings at the casino in the Hyatt Hotel. This hotel had been built by the Pahlavi foundation, which had been created by the Shah in 1958 and which boasted its own bank, the Omran, to utilise the revenue obtained from the sales of crown land. The foundation invested in all areas, from industry, to hotels, to offshore investments. Initially, its profits were to be used for social services, but in truth the foundation acted independently of the central government. Its managing director, a Dr Rumm, had been chosen by the Shah himself from among his most trusted servants and appointed by a royal decree, putting him in charge of investing the Pahlavi wealth in the most lucrative businesses in Iran and abroad – especially in the United States.

The Omran Bank, the channel through which these financial transactions were made, was expanding under the management of Dr Rumm and had become the fourth largest commercial bank in Iran. One of the aims of its managing director was to stack the board with new, Western-educated professionals. A hunt was initiated and one of the preyed-upon was my husband. Iskandar was invited to meet Dr Rumm and, after the interview, a generous package including a brand new, chauffeur-driven Mercedes Benz was offered and accepted. Iskandar's new position made him an executive director of the bank at the age of thirty-two.

The bank's most recent investment was the creation of the

ultra-modern Shahrak Garb, a new suburb on the outskirts of the Evin Hills, spreading out from the West wing of the city. Naturally, the land belonged to the foundation and different international developers were contracted to construct residential complexes on the site. The apartments were advertised to be sold off the plan. It seemed like a good investment and we decided to buy two apartments, one for each child, from the Omran Techlar Complex which was being constructed by a Greek company.

1976 was probably the happiest and most secure year of my life. I had everything I had ever wanted and was living in the most exciting country in the world. Iran was preparing to celebrate fifty years of Pahlavi rule and, through the university, we were invited to attend the main ceremony at Reza Shah's mausoleum in the holy city of Ray, near the shrine of Emam Abdol Azim. This is a cold, isolated yet magnificent place situated on an arid desert plain. From the main road, one sees only a long, wide avenue leading to the main building, which is surrounded by nothing but dry, stony earth.

On the day of the celebration we got up very early. Women were to dress in long, formal gowns and the men were to wear black ties or uniform. Iskandar had to wear his black university gown. By nine-thirty in the morning we were both elegantly dressed and ready to leave for the hall at Teheran University, where we would be picked up by special security buses and driven to the site. Bayat, our new driver, arrived right on time to drive us to the university. I felt pleased with myself: riding in my new chauffeur-driven car, all dressed for a royal occasion.

The hall was full of excited academic dignitaries robed in their black gowns, which billowed around them when they moved; their wives wore long, chic, custom-made dresses and stood by their husbands feeling important, making intellectual jokes, trying to corner those who were more important than themselves and avoid those of lower rank. At ten-thirty it was announced that it was time to set off on the hour-long drive to the mausoleum.

When we reached our destination I was stunned. The dry desert had been transformed into a garden filled with flowers. Stands were erected on each side of the avenue leading to the steps of the building. Pot plants were dug into the ground to create a make-believe green border, and carpet runners smoothed the path for their majesties. Many important people from the upper echelons had been invited to celebrate the occasion: cabinet ministers, generals of the armed forces and diplomats shone in their uniforms, which were ostentatiously decorated with stars, medals and ribbons. The crowd made a magnificent sight. Here, rivalry, snobbery and sycophancy went beyond the imagination.

When all the buses had arrived and the numbers had been matched to the SAVAK's list, the guests were asked to take their places at the designated stands. Placement was in accordance with rank; the most important officials and diplomats were seated near the building and the lesser souls were allocated stands in accordance with their ranks. Our position, to my surprise, was not very far from the mausoleum.

The sound of helicopters announced the arrival of their majesties. I could not see their aircraft from where we were sitting, but a few minutes later a burst of applause and the movement of people rising told of their approach. The Shah, very erect, looked immaculately elegant, but the empress appeared sullen. I was so excited, and clapping so hard, that I could not feel the cold which a few minutes ago had been making my bones ache.

The Imperial couple, followed by their entourage, were nearing our stand and the crowd's excitement was rising. As they passed us, I caught the sovereign's hypnotic glance for a split-second and was mesmerised by its magnetic force. During that euphoric moment a surge of pride touched my heart. With smiles and waves of the hand they acknowledged the spectators' salutations as they walked the length of the path to mount the steps and enter the mausoleum. After a short while, they returned to their helicopter and flew back to their palace. This was to be the last grand Imperial event to take place in Iran.

That night, we watched the ceremony on television. I was astonished to see the Shah and the empress driving in an open, horse-drawn carriage for what seemed like many kilometres, waving to what seemed like thousands of cheering people. When had they driven in the carriage? Where had been the crowds of such apparent magnitude?

I concluded that the mass media and the propaganda machine had been at work again. An electronic montage had been cleverly created to give the impression of a popularity which simply did not exist. Such a gross lie felt eerie and I regretted my jubilation of only hours ago. I felt manipulated and naive. What deception!

Chapter Twenty-Four

The election of President Carter in November 1976 was a bad omen for the Shah. Democrat presidents had not favoured him in the past, as their foreign policies had frowned on corruption. President Carter's public devotion to the cause of human rights in the Third World countries, and his emphasis on the need to reduce the volume of sales of military equipment to them, gave the Shah ample cause to worry and led to a period of uncertainty in Irano-American relations.

The Shah, being a shrewd statesman, in order to endear himself to the new president – or perhaps for personal reasons known only to himself – initiated a considerable liberalisation of his regime. This breeze of greater political freedom was refreshing at the university campus. I remember conducting a lecture on the concept of 'freedom', purposely diverging from psychology and penetrating into the sensitive field of politics without being reprimanded by the head of the department for my endeavour.

Newspapers were becoming more readable and openly signed letters from respectable citizens such as lawyers, academics and members of the old National Front Party began to circulate. These letters were critical of the policies and performances of the regime but, surprisingly, no arrests were made. Friday mosques became crowded, the clergy using the occasions to show their hostility towards the Shah's modernising moves.

One Friday, we heard that a prominent Ayatollah was to speak at Gobad, a well-known mosque not far from us, so we decided to attend. After dinner we walked to the mosque. Cars were parked for kilometres on either side of the road leading to the house of worship and a huge crowd had gathered outside to listen to the sermon which echoed from the loudspeaker. Wrapped in my chador, I held tight to Iskandar's hand. Near the entrance, an elderly man turned to me and said: 'Sister, women are sitting inside.' I asked him what time he thought the preaching would finish. He replied: 'At ten.' I looked at Iskandar, who politely thanked the old man and told me to go inside and meet him by the entrance after the sermon.

Inside, the mosque was crowded with women chadored in black, sitting cross-legged on the carpeted floor listening intently to the speaker. The faces of the listeners were glowing with excited anger – not like the congregation at Ashora, when the women beat their chests hysterically to the 'Ya Hussain' of the chanter – but like angry tigresses ready to tear apart the body of the usurper Pahlavi.

The well-informed Ayatollah was professionally stirring up the audience by criticising the regime's anti-corruption policies – the way in which honourable merchants and poor street vendors were being rounded up and jailed for selling overpriced merchandise, while the government was powerless to stop the Pahlavis and their favourites from ransacking the country. He stressed the futility of removing Hoveyda from premiership, only to reappoint him as the court minister. If Hoveyda was corrupt, why maintain him? Was not this campaign yet another ploy used by the Shah to deceive the people? I agreed with him. I disliked what the Shah had done to Hoveyda, the man who had served him sincerely for thirteen years. Why humiliate a faithful servant? Or was the king trying to purify himself from the sins of his past by sacrificing loyal subjects?

Nobody seemed to like Dr Jamshyd Amouzegar, the new prime minister. He was supposedly brilliant, clever and able – but he was a cold and arrogant bureaucrat. Rumour had it that in order to save the government money, he had cut off the large subsidy which Hoveyda had used to pay the mullahs to keep them quiet. If this was true, it was a gross mistake. No-one had more power over the minds of the populace than the mullahs, and no tanks would be able to control a fanatically-aroused mob. Politically used, Islam, with its powerfully appealing notions of equality, liberty and fraternity, could become a lethal weapon at the hands of the increasingly estranged Shiite clergy, especially during this time of social and economic malcontent.

The Ayatollah, having exhausted the malaises of political policies, arrived at the shameless absurdities of the annual Shiraz International Cultural Festival. Apparently, the vulgarity of the artistic events of 1977 festival had been an affront to all Islamic values. An actual rape scene had been enacted on a pavement in a shopping centre. Even I felt ashamed. How could the Shahbano of a Muslim country allow such disgraceful events to take place in the name of art? If this was their Imperial Majesties' idea of modernism we did not want it. Why were they going against the grain of their society? Why such hatred for everything Islamic?

The crowd in the mosque was now highly aroused, and looked as if they were ready for a bloody battle.

The sermon went on until ten when the Ayatollah's 'Allah Akbar!', in unison with that of the congregation, shook heaven and earth with its power. The preacher then descended the steps of the Manbar (pulpit) and the excited crowd rose and began to swarm towards the sole exit. The passageway immediately became jammed and people began to struggle to get out. Chadors were slipping off coiffeured heads, clearly indicating that a large number of these women were unaccustomed to wearing the cover.

It was a frightful experience. As I tried to push my way through the crowd, images of the past flashed through my mind – of roughnecks angrily waving their clubs in the air, shouting 'Death to Mossadegh!' Cold sweat began to saturate my cotton shirt. The constant movement from all directions was making me dizzy and nauseated. A sudden shove from behind threw me outside into the street where bodies, cars, motor cycles and bicycles mingled together trying without much success to move. Iskandar was nowhere in sight.

As the road was one-way, the general push of the crowd was towards the North, in the direction of Avenue Ehteshamieh. Suddenly, I caught sight of my husband trying to locate me among the wave of women spilling forth from the mosque. I was just lifting my hand from under my chador to signal my whereabouts, when someone stepped on the fabric from behind, pulling it off my shoulders and onto the ground. I bent to pick it up and, suddenly, felt a heavy weight crushing me. Before I knew what had happened I was lying on the ground on my right side with the paralysing weight of a motorbike resting on my left leg, its cold metal handlebars jamming into my chest. For a moment I was stunned, then I felt an excruciating pain in my leg. Many heads were bent towards me, and hands stretched to lift the bike off my body. After what seemed an eternity, the weight was lifted and a kindly hand grasped mine and helped me to get up. At the same time, someone grabbed my shoulders from behind, intensifying my pain. In a state of shock I tried savagely to free myself, then I heard a gentle voice asking me if I was alright and realised it was Iskandar.

Surprisingly, in spite of the dreadful pain in my leg, I was able to walk. Iskandar acted as my support and, very slowly, we headed for home. Safely there, Fe helped me into a hot bath where I had time to reflect on the events of the evening. Gobad Mosque was in Shemiran, an area which housed the most affluent sections of society. Why had it been so crowded? Clearly, the people I had seen were not the discontented poor. What reason did they have to support dissent? Were we perhaps in the throes of a revolution?

All of what had been said at the mosque made sense. Was this sudden liberation movement by the regime logical, or was the Shah playing with fire? Why had SAVAK stood by and allowed the Ayatollah to say what he wanted? Was he perhaps going to 'disappear' in the night? Could it really be that the Shah, after so many years of autocracy, was going to let the people voice their grievances? Was he going to acquire a listening ear, even though he was not prepared to relinquish any power? After all, people just wanted to have a say in the issues which concerned their lives; nobody wanted drastic change or a revolution which involved bloodshed. Perhaps now the Shah will listen to the message of his people, I told myself, and before getting out of the bath I begged God to help Iran. But neither God nor the monarch listened to the voice of the Iranian people. Sooner than was expected, SAVAK's physical attacks on the moderate elements drove them underground.

A new development which people like me found it hard to understand, and which we could not stop, was the resurgence of religious traditionalism. Recently, there had been several disturbances at Teheran University, with threats being made against the female students for their choice of provocative Western dress. There had also been a strike against mixed cafeterias for the students. I had not visited ours lately, so I was not sure what was happening there.

In our circle, life was normal. My friends and I still had our regular buffet lunches on Thursdays at the fashionable Imperial Club, a sports complex used mostly by the upper classes and by high-ranking military officers, who impressed their importance upon observers by arriving in their helicopters to play tennis, golf or ride horses. The restaurant was excellent and the club's cinema showed foreign films in their original language. If anybody wanted to see or to be seen, the Imperial Club was the place to go.

After these lunches, we took turns to entertain the group with tea and a game of cards in our houses, a social arrangement called Doreh. One Thursday evening in the summer of 1977, when Doreh was being held at my house, the electricity suddenly went off while we were in the middle of a game of cards. Fe immediately went into the kitchen, lit the gas light (found in all Iranian houses at the time) and brought it back to the table. I told her to call the house of my cousin Mehram who worked at the ministry of electricity, to find out what the reason for the blackout was, and how long it would last. After a few minutes she returned and reported that he had not come home yet, but had advised his wife that Teheran would be without electricity all night. This news caused us some concern and we decided to stop the game. Later that evening, we found out that the national electricity grid had given way under the weight of expanded industrial and domestic demand.

This acute shortage of electric power in the towns and cities was to become a fact of life in the next few months, leading to drastic industrial damage and domestic distress. Of course, the Northern parts of Tehran, in particular Avenue Ehtesh-amieh, suffered least (Mehram had given our area priority to receive power), but many Southern suburbs went without light for days at a time. Soon, gas lights and candles became scarce and we all began to worry about winter and heating.

The cold season lashed at us with unprecedented severity. Yet people seemed to be coping with the power failures and all the other small difficulties which presented themselves daily. We went prepared to our Dorehs, sometimes sitting at the table dressed in our minks and with hot water bottles warming our laps. Ludicrous? Ominous? Or both, perhaps.

The latest gossip was that a son of Ayatollah Khomeini, who was still in exile in Najaf, a city in Southern Iraq, had been murdered by SAVAK. I had forgotten all about Ayatollah Khomeini. Apparently, certain cassettes were being distributed in the bazaar; rumour had it that he hated the Pahlavis so much that in his seminars he called them 'Reza Khan' and 'the son of Reza Khan'. I thought a man who dared to deny the legitimacy of Pahlavi rule must have exceptional guts.

In November of 1977, the Shah paid a state visit to Washington. People thought that the two statesmen would patch up things and that life would soon be back to normal. The ceremony at Washington was televised and we all sat down to watch it. What we saw was horrifying. There were violent clashes between the dissidents, the pro-Shah groups and the police, who were using tear gas. The Shah and Farah, together with President Carter and his wife, stood stiffly to attention for the playing of the national anthems, handkerchieves held to their eyes and tears running down their faces. What humilation. How could the CIA allow this?

Gradually, the atmosphere in Teheran changed to that of unrelieved sombreness and many people began to liquidate their assets, with the intention of leaving the country. Most of my friends were going to take long vacations overseas. Fortunately, my relatives stayed in Iran and Grandma's house remained a centre for the latest gossip. Uncle Hussain had not been reappointed senator; like many other long-serving servants he had been banished from favour. Luckily, because of his unblemished reputation, they could not accuse him of corruption so he had not yet been jailed. Now he spent most of his time in Goldonak, writing his memoirs. Land in Goldonak had appreciated in value quite considerably, and I decided to arrange for an architect to draw up a plan for a magnificent house. The trees on my lot had grown tall and the landscaped garden needed a house to complement its beauty. However, with the situtation being what it was, the construction of the house was postponed until after Christmas. Although Iran is a Muslim country, the Christian New Year is an occasion which is celebrated by many at hotels and resturants and most of the households in the North of Teheran, including ours, decorated a tree for the sake of their Philippino servants.

On New Year's Eve, I had Anniana cook whatever was customary in the Philippines and the servants joined us in the formal dining room to eat. After dinner I released them from their duties so that they could spend the evening with their friends. The children went to bed and we sat in the television room waiting for the news. President Carter and his wife were in Teheran celebrating the occasion royally at the Niavaran Palace. Nothing was broadcast that evening, but the next day the newspapers gave extensive coverage to President Carter's after-dinner speech. The Democrat president had called the Shah's Iran 'an oasis of peace and stability in a troubled region' and had confidently stressed the popularity of the Shah among his subjects.

This was indeed auspicious news.

Chapter Twenty-Five

We had just returned from a day's skiing at Dizin, and were sitting in the television room waiting for the news, when Iskandar threw his newspaper on the floor and exclaimed furiously: 'What infamy!' Taken by surprise, I asked him what it was that was infamous enough to provoke such fury? Grudgingly, he picked up the paper and handed it to me to read. On the front page was a long article by Daryoush Homayoun, the minister for information, detailing Ayatollah Khomeini's personal background, private morals and religious credentials and boldly discrediting the old man. I was devastated by the abusive tone of the article and frightened of the consequences of such an attack on an idolised figure. I wondered whether or not I should send Betsy to her school, which was located next to Niavaran Palace. What if there was a march towards that area or, worse, an attack on the palace itself? In desperation I turned to Iskandar for advice; he assured me that security in that vicinity was tight and that we should not panic.

The following day nothing untoward happened, except that tension mounted in the campus. Most classes were half-empty and those who were present were inattentive. Small groups of students whispered among themselves as they hurried from one building to another, their coat collars turned up, and knitted scarves protecting their faces from the lashing wind which whipped through the snowcovered hills. There was a feeling of foreboding in the air.

When my lectures were finished, I set off for home without returning to my office. I spent a few hours with the children, then took a brisk walk to Uncle Hussain's house. Inside, his male servant greeted me and ushered me into the formal sitting room. My uncle, looking haggard, but as elegant as ever, was sitting on a comfortable chair next to the fireplace where a limp flame burned dejectedly. I kissed him, then sat down on the other armchair. Our conversation almost immediately turned to politics. I wanted to know what he thought of the present crisis and what he thought the future held. I knew that he hated the Shah, and I also knew that he was not religious. Some years ago, he had been a member of the National Front Party, but after the coup against Mossadegh he had been reconciled with the Shah's regime and had managed to climb high in his political career. I asked him what he considered to be the best solution to the present problems. Without hesitation, he replied that the Shah must go.

'Go where, Uncle Hussain? If he goes, we will have anarchy.'

'What do you think we have now?' he asked sarcastically.

'I don't know. But why doesn't he act like a sovereign?'

He retorted with bitterness: 'He is waiting for his master's orders.'

'The Americans or the British?' I asked.

He rose, took a piece of wood from the antique brass tray and placed it on top of the last burning log. Then, with a poker, he played with the smoking ashes until the fire began to flicker. Satisfied, he rested the poker against its stand and returned to his seat.

Impatient with his silence I continued, 'I don't think the British are for him. The BBC (Persian language service broadcasts) is supporting Khomeini. Everybody in the country is listening to the channel's nightly broadcasts, which are definitely biased against the regime. Radios with FM receivers have become as rare as fresh meat.' (Fresh meat had become a scarce commodity. Apparently, a ship full of live stock from Australia had been thrown into the Persian Gulf because it had been impossible to unload it.) 'The British are very clever. They know the Iranian mentality and they know who to back.'

As though I had been talking to the wall Uncle Hussain cut in, 'An alternative for the Shah is to choose a prime minister from among the National Front Party.'

'Uncle, do you know of such a person? Someone who is willing to forgive and forget the past and help him?'

'Yes Laila, there are still people who prefer the constitution of 1906 to the Black Rule*. But they are not willing to co-operate with the Shah while he is still in the country because they believe his Imperial Majesty will never give up his autocracy.' I realised that my uncle definitely knew something. I heard someone enter the room and turned to see my aunt approaching, followed by the servant with a tea tray. He placed this on the table next to her chair. My aunt enquired about Iskandar and the children and, once satisfied that they were well, she handed us our steaming cups of tea and joined in the conversation. She was in total agreement with her husband, holding the view that the 'old vulture', the Shah, must hand over the executive power to a democratically elected prime minister and leave the country for good.

What she said made sense, but seemed unrealistic. Once the Shah had gone, he could never come back, and without him there would be no cohesion within the government. For the past thirty-seven years he had been the sole decision-maker; in his absence, surely, all would fall apart. I was surprised at the extent of her antagonism towards the monarch. Why the sudden change of camp? I did not agree with my aunt and uncle, but neither was I going to argue with them.

During the course of our conversation I discovered that NeNe and her two sons were going to go to London to live until the troubles were over. I mused that it was unwise of her to leave such a handsome husband behind. Suddenly, I realised that it was already dark and I had to walk home. Aunt Firouzeh offered to drive me, but I refused. The streets were still safe and I enjoyed walking. I bade my aunt and uncle goodbye and set off, a little disturbed by our conversation.

On January 9, in retaliation to the infamous newspaper article insulting Khomeini, serious rioting broke out in the holy city

* Black Rule was a phrase coined by the Shah himself to describe the rule of the clergy.

of Qom. Troops were called in and a bloody confrontation led to the loss of hundreds of lives. This incident shocked the entire country, leading to irreconcilable hostility between the religious leadership and the government. The religious leaders proclaimed the observance of the customary forty-day mourning period for the martyrs of Qom and their followers immediately expressed their sympathy and respect for the dead – and for their leaders – by covering themselves in shrouds and demonstrating in the streets. The purpose of the exercise was to show that dissent welcomed martyrdom, though I did not understand this at the time.

A deceptive lull followed, during which life resumed its normal course, until exactly forty days later when riots broke out in Tabriz, the capital of Azerbaijan and the home base of Ayatollah Kazem Shariat-Madari, the most respected clergyman in Iran. Groups of rioters stormed out of the mosques, burning and destroying anything and everything that was symbolic of Pahlavi modernism – banks, cinemas and liquor stores. The town's garrison was called in and the many killings at the hands of the army led to another forty-day mourning period. More martyrs. Soon, bloody riots in all the major cities became an acknowledged part of life.

One day, when Father had had enough of the tension and mounting problems, he decided we should all take a break in London. Obediently, we packed and the whole family, including Fe, flew to London. Under the circumstances, and after what seemed like a century, this family reunion was a tremendous morale booster, especially for the children, who loved being together again. Father was enjoying himself more than anyone else – living in London, the city he loved, and bestowing generosity upon his offspring, especially his favourite, the effervescent Parissima.

First thing every morning he and Parissima, hand in hand, headed for the local corner store to purchase doughnuts and newspapers, both Iranian and English. At home, the papers were scrutinised for news of developments in Iran. The Shah, it appeared, was diligently pursuing his anti-corruption campaign, and a new order had prohibited all bank directors from leaving the country without a pass from the Clearance Committee of the institution for which they worked. This decree applied to Iskandar and meant that when we returned to Teheran he would not be able to leave the country again unless cleared by the bank's committee. This put his freedom in jeopardy. We both became nervous and began to reconsider our standing in view of this order. Wealthwise, the only property Iskandar owned was the Omran Techlar apartment. He had never signed any incriminating documents, nor had he ever abused his privileges. In fact, during his entire banking career he had done nothing but help people. His enemies were few and his friends many. There was no crime of which he could be accused.

The most devastating news was that the Cinema Rex in Abadan had been set on fire, incinerating 400 people. The regime blamed the incident on the terrorists, while the opposition accused the government. This news shocked us deeply and Iskandar decided to return to Teheran immediately. I wanted to stay until the university re-opened in October so he, accompanied by Fe and Parissima, left two weeks before the rest of us.

My brothers were worried about our going back, but we simply had to return to our own country. I loved Iran and I did not want to live anywhere else. Besides, I truly believed that the Americans would never let the situation get out of hand. For the past thirty-seven years the Shah had served their interests in the area; surely the U.S. government was morally obliged to protect him? If they let him down, the rest of their puppets around the world would lose faith in them. In any case, it did not serve any of the powers to have a destabilised Iran in the strategically crucial zone of the Persian Gulf.

A realistic person, however, could see that the root of the crisis lay within the structure of Iranian society itself. The problem was that people like us never dreamt that the grass roots would be able to carry out a genuine revolution by themselves. We were like aliens living in sanctuaries, secluded by high walls and social class distinctions, deluded by comfort and a luxurious lifestyle, and totally insensitive to the traditions, values and hardship of the rest of society. We called the common people 'Bazaaris' and 'Dahaties' (which literally means 'coming from the villages', though the correct implication of the word is 'outdated') and they had tagged us the 'Taghoties' – the corrupted ones.

Yes, we were to be blamed as much as the king we worshipped, whose foot we kissed and to whose tune we danced while the going was good – and who we now called our fallen idol . . . the old vulture . . . the blood-sucker . . . as he gaolled our peers.

Life in Iran was changing, fast. Amouzegar, hated by the mullahs, resigned on August 27 and was replaced by Senator Jafaar Sharif-Emami, the president of the senate. Rumour had it that he had been chosen because he could count a couple of mullahs in his ancestry. This was another mistake. People had not forgotten that he had also been head of the controversial Pahlavi Foundation. From the start, it became apparent that his policies were going to be conciliatory towards the religious opposition. One of his first actions was to revert to the original Islamic calendar, cancelling the Shah's cherished Pahlavi version. Then all casinos, which he himself as head of the foundation had only recently opened, were closed. But none of these moves was powerful enough to check the rising tide of discontent. The more the government gave in, the less effective its manoeuvres became.

One afternoon, we were gathered at Mother's house for tea and a game of cards when Taghi, the cook, entered the room, obviously excited and bursting with some kind of news. Mother asked him where he had been all day.

He replied, 'Khanum, to obey your orders I rode to town this morning to do your grocery shopping. On the way back, when I was crossing Avenue Shah Reza, I was held up by a huge demonstration. When I discovered that the march was organised by the clergy, and that it was for Islam, I got off my motorcycle and joined in. From the man walking next to me, I found out that the demonstration had started off from the Shahyad Square and was heading South.'

He stopped to catch his breath, then continued: 'Khanum Joon, I must admit they were very daring with their anti-Shah slogans. But what was so wonderful was that they were so friendly towards the soldiers who were standing by their tanks watching us. Many people were holding carnations and on various occasions, with my own eyes, I saw them place their flowers in the barrels of the soldiers' rifles and call them "brothers". Khanum, I swear by Emam Ali that I have never been so proud in my life as I am now. With Islam in power, all will be well again.' The emotionally aroused servant stopped to wipe away his tears.

What a clever ploy, I thought, as I realised the meaning of the events he described.

'Taghi, why are you crying?' I asked.

He stared at me wide-eyed, as though questioning my sanity for asking such a ridiculous question and then, without uttering another word, he turned and left the room – something he would never have done before all these upheavals started.

Mother remarked that he and his wife were very religious and pro-Khomeini, and that we should be careful of what we said in their presence. Frustrated and frightened, I turned to her and remarked, 'The day I have to be careful in front of the servants will be the day I commit suicide.' Mother, in her considerate way, turned to Iskandar and said, 'You should make your wife listen to logic.' Iskandar smiled and replied: 'Mrs Yazdi, if you cannot put some sense into your daughter's head, what makes you think I can? You know how she is, stubborn as a mule and always does what she wants. I don't think she has ever listened to anyone in her life.'

Furiously, I retorted , 'I will only listen to reason and none of you, so far, has said one word which makes any sense at all.'

Father intervened and remarked sarcastically, 'Miss Know-It-All is talking now.'

Hurt and bitter, I snapped back. 'Yes, I am Miss Know-It-All. I am a damned sight more intelligent and have more guts than both your sons put together. It is so hard for you to acknowledge this, isn't it?'

Mother intervened sharply: 'Be quiet and leave your brothers out of this.'

I could not take any more. The tension, uncertainty and fear which surrounded us had made us all irritable. I realised that for the first time in my life I had raised my voice to my father – and for no good reason. Why had I brought my brothers into the argument? Freud would have said it was a slip of the tongue – but Laila would have it as shattered nerves. Ashamed of myself I rose, apologised to my parents and kissed them goodbye. Then, trying to hold back my tears, I left with Iskandar, only to have another hysterical outburst in the car. Iskandar, patient and loving as ever, eventually managed to calm me down.

The next day an edict was issued banning further assemblies without prior authorisation. Two days later, on September 8, I was woken up at about 5 am by a voice announcing something on a loudspeaker. Anticipating trouble, I listened hard, but could not quite make out what was being said. Hurriedly, I woke Iskandar and asked him to listen, too. Frightened, he jumped out of bed and opened the window. The voice was proclaiming martial law.

'Why martial law?' I asked. 'What could have happened last night, Iskandar?'

'I don't know. But something must have.'

We both became quite agitated and realised that the situation must be really serious for the government to take such drastic action. We sat in bed, drowned in thought, waiting for the next radio news at 7 a.m. Right on time I turned the wireless on. The newsreader announced that during the night, in defiance of the government's edict, another demonstration had taken place without permission. Therefore, to bring law and order to the city, martial law was proclaimed for Teheran under General Ovissie's capable auspices. Well, at last the government was showing a sign of strength. Martial law had been declared to stop these weird processions. I was confused, but relieved.

That day, a Friday, we decided that instead of going to my parents' house we would take the children for lunch at the Imperial Club. We had not finished eating when a friend entered the restaurant and came over to our table to say hello. After the usual exchange of pleasantries, he began to smile broadly as though he had conquered the world. Iskandar asked him what was making him so happy during these troubled times. He seemed surprised at our ignorance and, with a big, sinister grin lighting his ugly face, asked, 'Don't you know what is happening at Jaleh Square at this very moment?'

'No, we don't,' replied Iskandar.

'Well, you'll be happy to hear that at last his Imperial Majesty has decided to have the army burn the roots of those lice-infested mullahs and their followers. The troops are killing them like ants at the square because they defied martial law and gathered for another demonstration.' He stopped talking, but retained his grin in expectation of an approving response from us. To his disappointment, he did not receive it.

Civil war had started. Iranians killing Iranians. For what? I felt sick.

Unable to control my disgust at what the man had described, I glared at him with eyes full of hatred and said, 'Slaughtering unarmed citizens is not a matter for rejoicing. What if a brother or sister of yours was present at the square? Would you be laughing still?'

He was insulted by my question and shouted, loud enough for all to hear, 'My kin wouldn't be seen dead with those dirty black devils.' Chin up, he shot a contemptuous glance at me and, without saying goodbye to either of us, he turned and left. We did not stay for tea and, after taking care of the bill we drove to Mother's, hoping Taghi would be there and would know what had really happened.

Arriving at the house, I found my parents resting in bed watching television. I told them the story and asked where Taghi was. Apparently, he had gone out that morning and had not yet returned. Iskandar sat on a chair and I took my shoes off and climbed onto Mother's bed, cuddling up against her. We waited patiently for our informer to show up.

At around five in the afternoon he arrived. The man looked like a resurrected corpse in his bloodstained clothes. Iskandar asked if he had come from Jaleh Square. The trembling man began to sob. 'Yes Aga, I am coming from hell itself.'

'Taghi, why did you go to Jaleh Square when you knew that there was a martial law prohibiting assemblies?' I asked, terrified of what I might hear.

'Last night after the evening prayer, Aga (the mullah) informed the congregation that there would be a demonstration at Jaleh Square (South East of Teheran) and that it was the duty of all good Muslims to participate.'

He stopped to clear his throat, then continued, 'I try to be a good Muslim, so after my breakfast, even though I had heard the news about the martial law, I rode to the square. After parking my motorcycle at a secluded corner, I saw the troops standing around. I didn't take much notice of them because, like everyone else, I assumed that this march would be peaceful like the previous ones and that, as usual, the soldiers would stand aside watching us. None of us thought the soldiers would shoot at us. When the square became crowded, the sound of helicopters began shaking heaven and earth. At first, we thought the Shah was coming to watch us from his flying machine, but then we realised that the helicopters belonged to the airforce.

'As the choppers were circling the sky, loudspeakers began ordering the demonstrators to disperse. No-one paid any attention, because no-one believed that the soldiers would shoot at unarmed people. Suddenly, all hell broke loose. The troops on the ground, and those from above, began firing into the crowd. Bodies fell like autumn leaves savaged by a sudden storm. The blood of the martyrs running on the asphalt sanctified the square.' Taghi was moved to eloquence.

'The sound of machine guns, the wail of those going to heaven and the chant of "Death to the Shah, Khomeini is our leader" thundered through the air. Those still alive, never having been faced with such ferocious retaliation, desperately tried to disperse, but the soldiers wouldn't stop. They kept on firing and firing and firing.'

Taghi stopped again, the lump in his throat preventing him from continuing. The man was shaking. I got off the bed, took Father's glass and poured some water from the water jar which he kept on his bedside table. I gave it to Taghi and asked him to sit down on the floor. He took the glass, drank the water, thanked me and sat down, crossing his legs.

Taghi had survived because when he had heard the sound of the first shots, his legs had given in and he had fallen into a nearby gutter. When the noise had subsided, he had tried to move, only to find that he had been buried under a corpse. Horror had made him collapse again, but eventually he had managed to gather enough courage to push the body away and pull himself up. Then, oblivious to his surroundings, he had run as fast as he could to where he had parked his motorcycle. Luckily it was still there.

We were devastated by his tale. He must have detected our fear because he turned to Mother and said, 'Khanum, you and Master should go to England. This country won't be safe for you any more.'

Mother immediately replied: 'Taghi, we are Iranians like you. This is our country, too – and besides, we have never done anything which should make us afraid. Why should we leave?' Taghi shrugged his shoulders, rose from the floor and, again without permission, left the room. Islamic brotherhood was catching up fast.

After a short period of silence, Father shook his head and said, 'He is right. We should go to London.'

Mother asked: 'And live on what?'

'We could sell this house, and my apartment building which will be finished soon,' replied Father. He was building a block of twelve apartments in one of the best residential areas of the city.

I disagreed. 'Why should we sell two prime properties because people are daring to stand up against corruption?

If any changes take place, there is no reason to believe that they will be for the worse. The dissidents are not communists; they are ordinary people fighting for their rights. I am surprised that the soldiers did fire into the crowd. They are of the same rank and file as the dissidents and I cannot believe that they are going to fight their brothers for long. Then, with no army, there won't be any bloodshed. Some sort of civil solution will save the country, if not the Shah.'

I was still blind to what really was happening. The tide of the revolution had not reached Avenue Ehteshamieh. My territory had not yet been threatened.

My mother was wiser than me. Within a couple of months she sold the house and came to live with us until, at the end of her tenant's lease, she could take over her rented property in Avenue Laila. I did not have any cash savings, and I had to think about liquidating some of my assets. I suggested to Iskandar that we should try to get our money back from our two apartments at Omran Techlar, but he immediately rejected the idea, declaring that he would never do anything illegal. I pleaded with him, but to no avail. Nobody was in a buying mood, so there was no chance of selling any of my blocks of land. The only alternative was to sell my carpets. I had never sold anything in my life before, so I consulted Father, who was still in touch with the carpet dealer he had dealt with for many years. When he heard my request to be put in touch with the dealer he became very angry. To him, selling part of my dowry was demeaning. He forbade me to talk about it and offered to help us should we ever be in need. My husband and I were grateful for the gesture, though neither of us ever intended to take him up on it.

The only alternative to selling the carpets was to take some of them to London and leave them with Ali. I shared this thought with Iskandar who approved of the idea, and a trip was planned for the coming university holidays.

Meanwhile, even nature seemed to be against the regime. In mid-September, a tragic earthquake at Tabas, near Mashad in the Eastern desert, almost erased the town from the map killing close to 20,000 people. The army was put in charge of the relief operations but the mullahs, the theological students, and the students from the University of Mashad rushed into the devastated area and began working non-stop to supply food and shelter for the survivors. A belated visit by the Shah to the area was televised. In his bemedalled uniform it seemed to me as if he had gone to witness a military manoeuvre, rather than to share the sorrows and sufferings of his people, whose mud houses – their share of the Great Civilisation, the Pahlavi Paradise – had collapsed on their heads with the first tremors.

The film clip was disheartening and very revealing of the nature of the crisis. On one side stood the Shah among his soldiers, obviously uncomfortable at being so close to his people, and on the other, the clergy and the students, doing everything possible to help. Why did he not go into the afflicted area and show his sympathy for the suffering of his subjects? Why had God so hardened the monarch's heart towards his own people?

Allah had really cursed the plateau. With the speed of lightning, violent demonstrations spread throughout the country and strikes crippled both the private and public sectors. The worst strike was that of the workers and technicians in the National Iranian Oil Company. It meant there would be no petrol and, for those who used oil heaters, no fuel for the coming winter. Long lines began to form at all the petrol stations as people sought to fill their car tanks and stock up on bottles of petrol. The queues at the bus stops became longer and longer, and walking became the surest means of transport.

Gas for cooking purposes had to be purchased in containers and since the gas company had stopped delivering these, they had to be collected from their outlets. In desperation one day, I asked Bayat how many we could carry in the car. He told me four. We immediately set out for town and, after procuring the four containers and putting two in the trunk and two on the back seat, I asked him to drive me to the fruit market at Behjat Abad. We also had to collect Father from The Mirabel later on.

At the intersection of Avenues Ferdowsi and Zahedi, we came across a small, excited crowd sticking Khomeini's pictures onto the windows of cars which were waiting at the traffic lights. I was terrified. With four containers of gas in the car, what would happen if they decided to get violent? We could not turn back, so had to continue in the same direction. As our car stopped at the lights, two teenagers jumped onto the bonnet, while a third stuck his head through the open window and ordered us to say 'Death to the Shah'. We had no choice but to comply. Then he stuck a black and white printed picture of the Emam on the windscreen. When eventually the light turned green, the two teenagers sitting on the bonnet jumped down and I heard Bayat sigh with relief. We collected Father, forgot about grocery shopping and headed for home.

On the way to Shemiran I was thinking how good it was to have my parents living with us, even if it was only for a short time. Their plans had changed. They had decided to go and live in London until the troubles were over. I thought it was a wise choice for two older people, especially considering that Father had not been feeling well lately.

On October 7, the BBC announced that Khomeini had flown to Paris, where he had been joined by Abol Hassan Bani Sadr, Sadegh Ghotbzadeh and Ibrahim Yazdi, three of his most devoted followers. I had never heard of any of them. I wondered why he had chosen France. Perhaps the French and the British had decided he would be better off under their noses. Paris, the centre of liberalism to the world, would provide him with an excellent public platform from which to continue his campaign against the Shah. In Europe he would also have access to all the resources of modern communication. How very clever.

At the university the autumn term had started, but hardly anyone attended classes. Joined by high school children, teachers and some professors, the students were too busy demonstrating in the streets. Within the government, the prime minister was attempting to dramatise the anti-corruption drive by putting Hoveyda's ministers in jail. Some of them were our good friends. Even General Nassiri, the former head of SAVAK and presently the Iranian ambassador to Pakistan, was called in to face a military tribunal. Liberalising policies were being passed daily but, unfortunately, nothing seemed to work. Khomeini, from his platform in Paris, was stealing the show with his simple message: 'Mahmad Reza must go'.

The most recent rumour was that the military had become irritated by the guaranteed freedom for the press and was planning to take severe action against the revolutionaries. It seemed that the government had become a divided body. For the first time since the torrent of revolution had begun sweeping the country, the Shah appeared on the television talking about liberalisation and, in a way, apologising for the past mistakes. He seemed aged and dispirited. His confidence and arrogance had evaporated. The speech was so low-key that the appearance did not generate any confidence in him, or in what he was trying to do. In the past, he had never even tried to create trust in his subjects. What made him think that his promises were now going to be believed and trusted? I felt very sorry for him. His dreams for Iran had been too grand and too unrealistic.

My parents' last dinner in Teheran was eaten at The Mirabel's restaurant. We had a good meal and passed the time speculating as to what might happen next. Iskandar was of the opinion that the Shah would choose a prime minister from the old National Front Party – someone with a blameless reputation. The problem with this idea was that the choice was limited to a few very old men, none of whom were likely to accept the offer. Father disagreed with Iskandar and thought that Khomeini would win and topple the Pahlavis. Mother had no opinion at all, while I was simply afraid of communism.

At night I began having nightmares. My dreams were morbid and terrifying. Day and night I was preoccupied with the fear of having to flee the country without money. I felt desperate. I had to find a way of liquidating some of my assets and sending the money out of the country. Early the next morning, I drove my parents to the airport and stood on the balcony of the departure building watching the jet fly them to safety.

Chapter Twenty-Six

November saw the peaceful demonstrations throughout the country turn violent. Some people believed this was because Zbigniew Brzezinski had contacted the Shah to assure him of the United States' support for his regime. Apparently, this reassurance had encouraged the army's generals to push for a military coup. Many people supported the notion of a military takeover and thought of it as the only effective means of dealing with the uprisings, but I strongly objected to the idea and was frightened to even think of it. Nothing could sanction brothers killing brothers, and that would be what happened if power was given to the military.

Every morning we woke up expecting disaster. I was anxious about the safety of Iskandar and the children. Leaving the house was not safe anymore. Although Bayat, who was in charge of the children's transport, was very protective, the dangerous location of the school worried me. The vicinity of Niavaran Palace was not an enviable location anymore. The Omran Bank was also dangerously situated in the middle of the city, where demonstrations frequently gathered momentum. This bank, which belonged to the Pahlavi Foundation, was the perfect target for a frenzied mob with a penchant for arson. Fortunately I was safe, because the students had taken their angry outbursts to the streets and, for the moment, the campus was empty.

I was glad about this. Going to work had become nerve-wracking, and witnessing the change in my colleagues abhorrent. Most of the lecturers were now trying to link themselves with the dissent. As a kind of tokenism, the men had put aside their neck-ties and grown beards, while some of my sophisticated female colleagues had taken to covering their hair with scarves from Dior or YSL. Once, I asked one of them: Why the change? The reply was that the chador was to support the anti-regime movement, and that it would be worn until the country was rid of the 'old vulture'. My guess was that she counted on the fundmentalists winning and wanted to keep her job once they took over. I do not think many of the women who supported the revolution believed that they would be required to adhere to Islamic dress after the victory. A good number were educated, westernised women who were fighting against injustice under the unifying banner of Emam Khomeini; their cover was worn simply to signify their support for change.

On the other hand, others tried to look Islamic purely out of pragmatism. I could not be that pragmatic. It was tempting, but I could not go against my principles and pretend to be what I really was not. I was a Muslim by choice, but the Islam I had chosen did not put me in bondage. Yes, it required me to be modest – but modesty is a quality of character and does not need external cover. I liked to think of myself as a human being rather than a sex symbol. And after all, most whores living in the red light district of Teheran went about their business covered in the chador.

My Islam also taught me love and forgiveness. The Koran advises us to leave punishment to God because forgiveness is better than vengeance. Unfortunately, very early in the life of the revolution I learned that, on occasions, the Koranic verses were only selectively remembered and practised by those in power.

In spite of my apoliticalism, I knew why there was a revolution. But I could not be part of it until I understood what the revolutionaries stood for. There were so many factions united under the Khomeini banner that it was impossible to discern a cohesive set of goals or directions to which one could adhere. Apart from the Tudeh party, there were the Mujahidin-e-Khalg (the People's Fighters), an extremist militant group who had been engaged in guerrilla warfare against the regime for years, the communist Fedayin-e-Islam (Those Who Sacrifice Themselves for Islam) and of course, last but not least, the clergy.

I hated the Tudehs and did not know much about the other two. If, one day, I had to take sides, I would affiliate with the mullahs, simply because they stood for Islam - the Islam that respects the ownership of private property. At least I could count on the fact that they would not confiscate what we owned, I told myself. Little did I realise how totally ignorant and ignobly selfish I was being!

As the days passed, living became merely existing, and my time was spent either at work or hunting for food. Many people - especially the minority groups - were preparing to leave the country and were selling their homes and furniture. The bargain hunters were buying with alacrity. I was tempted, but somehow I associated the acquisition of material possessions with happiness, and this was not a happy time. Only the necessities were purchased. My freezer had enough meat and vegetables to feed an army, sacks of rice were piled up right to the ceiling of the cellar, and tins of cooking oil, kerosine, gas and petrol were stashed in safe places. The medicine cabinets were also amply stocked.

Our evenings were spent at home, or with those of our relatives who were still in Iran. Grandma's residence was our favourite meeting place and we visited her every afternoon. Aunt Zinat was looking after the hotel at Avenue Koshk and The Mirabel had a new manager.

I had given up going to the city after that horrific day when we were caught in the demonstration with the gas containers in the car, but one day a friend of mine persuaded me to join her in a shopping spree at Avenue Manuchehri, where the antique shops were bursting with rareties. We planned to make a day of it by first having lunch at The Mirabel and then walking the short distance to the shops. The date was set for November 5. I also made an appointment with my hairdresser for the same day, to save petrol and another trip to town.

On the morning of our date, I arrived at my hairdresser's salon, which was situated in the Avenue Takhte Jamshid near the American Embassy, gave my shopping list to Bayat and

213

instructed him to shop for me and to then go to The Mirabel for lunch. I told him I would walk the few blocks down to the hotel and meet him there.

My hair was finished by 12.30 and, after taking care of the bill, I descended the flight of stairs and opened the door to leave. To my amazement, I was confronted with an ocean of people – men, chadored women and children making their way along the street side by side in an ordered procession. I hesitated for a moment, trying to decide whether to leave now or wait for the marchers to pass. I estimated that with the number of people involved it would take hours before the last of them passed me. The crowd was very dense, but fortunately it was moving in the right direction for me, so I joined in.

With my make-up and coiffeured hair I looked odd and conspicuous in the midst of the chadored crowd, so to avoid trouble I surreptitiously pulled a tissue from my bag and rubbed it over my lips to remove the signs of sin. I did not have to worry about my eyes as they were covered by my large, tinted spectacles.

Gradually, after my initial fear wore off, the mob identity took over and I became part of the tidal wave pushing ahead. This feeling of unity lasted until I became conscious of the glance of the man walking next to me. I read hate in his face and intent in his expression. When my eyes met his, he thrust his head close to my face and whispered: 'You whore.'

God forbid. My legs began to shake like jelly. Frightened, I kept quiet and pretended not to have heard him. I doggedly fixed my gaze on the throng ahead. Ignoring my silence he said again, 'You whore.'

I began moving faster in a bid to lose the dreadful man. Suddenly, I realised I was passing the intersection of Takhte Jamshid and Avenue Zahedi, where I had to turn left. Hastily, I made the turn, stealing a quick look to see if the aggressor was following me. Thank God, he was not. Avenue Zahedi was just as crowded, and this time I had to move against the flow, which was very difficult. Eventually, after half-an-hour of pushing and squeezing, I reached the entrance to the hotel where Bayat, looking worried, was waiting for me.

Inside, I made my way to the lobby and collapsed into a chair. When the receptionist saw me, he left his desk and came over to give me the message that my friend had cancelled our lunch appointment. I was relieved because I was in no mood for socialising after my ordeal. I decided to have lunch by myself in Father's empty office, hoping that the streets would be cleared by the time I had finished eating. A flash of memory brought Father's kind face to my mind and tears to my eyes. He had always loved it when I had lunch with him here. Now he was gone, and I was lonely. So lonely.

I was still eating at around 2 pm when, suddenly, the building began to shake and the sound of several explosions shattered my peace. It sounded as though a bomb had gone off. I jumped from my seat and ran towards the broken window. The street was empty of demonstrators, but small groups of young men were feeding a large fire in which two cars were burning. Some other men seemed to be leaving the hotel, pushing armchairs out into the street.

Where was Bayat? Where had he parked the car?

Was it my car they were burning? I looked hard. No, it was not.

Why were the demonstrators in the hotel? I opened the window and fragments of glass crashed to the floor, the sharp edge of one shard cutting into my skin. I did not feel the pain.

I rushed downstairs to the lobby, where angry men were dragging whatever they could find outside and throwing it onto the ferocious fire. The hotel employees were just standing aside letting the vandals do whatever they pleased. Petrified, I joined the observers and watched. To my surprise, none of the violators was interested in the cash register. These were no thieves, and they knew exactly what they were doing.

From behind, Bayat's familiar voice whispered: 'Khanum, don't worry – the car is safe.'

Happy to hear him I murmured, 'Thank God for that.'

Gradually, the rioters' fever subsided and they left the hotel. The spectators gathered in groups to discuss the event and I ran to the telephone to find out whether or not my husband was safe. He was. I then called the school to see if there had been any disturbances in that area. There had not, but we only had twenty minutes to get to Niavaran and pick the children up.

Half-running and half-walking, Bayat led me to the car, which he had parked in a narrow lane a couple of blocks up the street. Safely in the car, we set off for the school. As we turned into Avenue Takhte Jamshid, I realised where the sound of the explosions had come from. Columns of smoke were rising from carefully selected buildings to the North of the American Embassy. As we drew nearer I saw that two banks, a cinema, a couple of office high-rises which belonged to prominent businessmen, and a supermarket had been turned into fiery rubble. Fires were still blazing everywhere. A large pile of paper money, probably salvaged from the burning bank, was fast becoming a mound of ash. The flames were burning the symbols of the Pahlavi regime.

Who was responsible for this atrocity? Who in the name of heaven was responsible? Further up the street, frenzied men were plastering the crawling cars with stickers which read 'Death to the Shah. Our leader is Khomeini.'

Very slowly, we left the crowd behind and entered the Old Shemiran Road. Free of the congestion, Bayat sped towards Niavaran where, half-an-hour late, we reached the school. My beloveds, looking anxious, were waiting at the gate holding hands. As the children glimpsed the car, they made a move towards the road, but were pulled back by the school janitor. I got out of the car, ran towards my darlings and with one arm around each, pressed them to my heart and began kissing them as though they had been lost and I had found them again. On the way home, travelling down Niavaran Road, I saw the black smoke rising to join the smog that hid the long-forgotten blue sky. The city was still burning.

At home, I took a shower and went into my bedroom, spread

my prayer mat on the floor, put on my chador and prayed. I prostrated myself on the floor, pleading with God to save my family and my country from disaster.

The next day, General Azhari was appointed the new military prime minister. The appointment gave rise to the suspicion that the city had been set on fire by the armed forces to justify a military government. Why else had the soldiers stood aside and merely watched? Nobody knew what to believe any more.There had been no loss of lives and no looting – only arson.

On the afternoon of the 6th I decided to walk to Uncle Hussain's house again. I felt more secure with a military government in charge. Faced with the army, the strikers might return to work, and some sort of political compromise might bring about national reconciliation.

At the house I was received cordially by my aunt and uncle. Tari was also present, and the three were discussing the Shah's latest televised speech during which he had told the nation that he had heard their message and had appealed for calm. He assured us that the days of corruption and tyranny were past; that in the future everything would be done according to the constitution of 1906; and that free elections were to be held in the immediate future. Tari was very excited about the speech and believed it was about time the Shah showed some sign of sovereignty and took charge of his country again.

I agreed with him, but his father-in-law did not. The old politician was as gloomy as ever and looked sick. Apparently his stomach was troubling him. Uncle Hussain believed that the military government was no solution at all, and that Azhari was a poor choice of leader. He argued that a military government was a thorn in the eyes of the people. It would simply incense them further and lead to more uprisings.

I had come hoping to hear good news and was disappointed. It seemed that nothing would satisfy my uncle except the Shah's departure from Iran. I did not hold to this view. Without the Shah there would be no army, and without the fear of the army there would be anarchy.

I was too agitated to stay long, and when Tari rose to leave I asked him for a lift. In the car I enquired after NeNe and the children. He told me that they had rented a small flat in Knightsbridge near the children's school, and were waiting for him to join them. He, however, did not want to leave Iran because of his vast financial involvements with the government. Besides, like me, he believed that the Americans would save the Shah. He dropped me off at home and went on to my cousin Shahri's house for a drink .

Uncle Hussain was right. The new government proved as powerless as its predecessors. Turbulence and strikes proliferated, especially in the provinces. The Central Bank became paralysed and people were queueing to take their money out of all the banks. What small savings we had were at home, wrapped in a nylon bag inside a large metal box which had been placed in a bucket and lowered into the well. My jewellery was also at home. It simply was not wise to keep anything in a bank safe anymore, so I had brought it home and found a second metal box in which to put it, along with the leather bag containing my gold coin collection. One Friday afternoon, when all the staff had their day off, Iskandar dug a large hole in a forsaken spot in the garden and buried it.

As the military government's ineffectiveness became more apparent, the Shah's obsession with persecution of his officials intensified. General Nassiri, the man who had helped him to power during the 1953 coup, and who had subsequently headed SAVAK, was arrested together with General Khademi, the head of Iran Air. The latter was said to have committed suicide in dubious circumstances, but rumour had it that he was, in fact, murdered by his captors because he was a Bahai. Bahaism, initially persecuted in Iran, had been accepted by the Pahlavi regime but was now being frowned upon.

There was also talk that Hoveyda was about to be jailed. He was living up the road from us at his old mother's house. For thirteen years, Hoveyda had served the Shah with devotion and loyalty. How could the monarch put him in jail? This act would condemn thirteen years of his own regime. The next day Hoveyda was arrested. When, a few months later, the Shah departed from his country he took his dogs with him, but left his loyal prime minister behind bars in Evin Jail. Hoveyda was executed shortly after the victory of the revolution.

The situation was deteriorating by the hour and I was becoming increasingly worried about the future, so I decided to take a week off and go to London, taking with me a couple of carpets and my jewellery. Iran Air flights were all booked out and I had to wait for ten days before I could get a seat. Two of my most valuable carpets were chosen and packed into two different suitcases. The metal box was dug out of the ground and the jewels removed. The box went back into the hole, now containing only the gold collection, our sole liquid asset in Iran.

On the day of my departure, just to be on the safe side, I sewed the jewels into the lining of my mink coat. Luckily, the custom officers were so busy that no-one bothered to check anything or anyone very thoroughly. The trip was short and pleasant. Father had aged, but Mother looked much the same. For the duration of my stay, Father thoroughly spoilt me and Mother gave me a long list of chores to do for her in Iran. She was as prudent as ever. A safe in the bank was rented and my jewels tucked away. I also left my mink coat and jacket in London.

Now I had something for our 'rainy day'.

Back in Teheran, I noticed that the city had changed, even in the short time that I had been away. Walls were defaced with slogans like: 'Yankee go home', 'Death to the Shah', and many obscenities addressed to the Shah and Farah. Avenue Ehteshamieh was deserted. Most of the residents had left the country, leaving their houses in the care of their servants. The only people I saw in our vicinity were some construction workers excavating the pavements for gas pipelines. To my surprise, I discovered that these workers were Kurds.

It was encouraging to see something constructive going on,

especially during this time of unending destruction and misery. Selective power cuts plunged Teheran into darkness daily. Pressure was building up against foreigners – particularly Americans – and there had been some killings in the provinces. The economy was in ruins and the foreigners whose technical expertise was essential to the running of Iran's various industries were starting to leave the country. Parliamentary sessions were being televised and the prime minister was submitting all government measures to parliamentary debate. Members of parliament seemed to have found their long-lost tongues and were expressing radical opinions.

Unfortunately, the Shah's liberalisation movements, his anti-corruption campaign and all the other concessionary activities seemed to be taking place in a vacuum. Khomeini's charisma had captured the heart of the nation and his simple slogan, 'Pahlavi must go', had become as revered as a verse from the Koran.

During one of my frequent homages to my avuncular political mentor I heard the first good news in months. Uncle Hussain had been asked by the Shah to contact his old friend Dr Shapour Bakhtiar, a respected member of the National Front, to see if he would form a government. Serious negotiations were underway, but one of Dr Bakhtiar's conditions for accepting the appointment was that the Shah must leave Iran indefinitely. I liked Dr Bakhtiar. He was a highly-educated nationalist with an impeccable reputation, whose aim was to reconcile the nation under true democracy.

After enlightening me about Dr Bakhtiar, my uncle asked if we would help him by inviting pro-constitution lecturers from the university to our house, where he would talk to them about the man who was to save the country. Bakhtiar needed all the support he could get. I agreed. To fulfil my uncle's request, we chose two dozen of our trusted colleagues and invited them for afternoon tea. The gathering was informal, friendly and took the shape of a political workshop. Constructive opinions were expressed, solutions were sought and the conclusion was that we should strive towards a trusted civilian government which enjoyed the loyalty of the armed forces. Only thus could a national reconciliation be brought about without further bloodshed. All the intellectuals present subscribed to the idea that the Shah should leave the country until everything was under control, and then return as a true constitutional monarch. None of them believed that the Shah could remain in Iran and not interfere with the government's decision-making.

When the last of the guests left, I hugged Iskandar like a little child and exclaimed: 'Iskandar Joon, it seems our country might be saved after all.'

Iskandar gently stroked my hair, gave me a quick kiss and said, 'Don't get too excited. Wait until Moharram is over.'

He was right. We had to wait for Moharram, the holy month, which would start on December 21. The days of Ta'sua and Ashura would create the greatest challenge to the authorities. Given the history of these two holy days, the emotional background would provide the most opportune time for a powerful religious drive to initiate the decisive push against the shaky structure of the Pahlavi regime.

There were omens, all pointing to a forthcoming challenge.

Some time in late November, fully aware of the martial law, Khomeini issued instructions to the people to hold the ceremonies and defy authority of any kind, indicating that Moharram was a month of blood and vengeance. In retaliation, the government banned public processions and instructed that religious ceremonies would have to be confined to the mosques and that a curfew would start at 9 pm every evening.

On the eve of the first of Moharram, we went for a short walk in the direction of Ghobad Mosque. The house of worship was full, and even though it was cold and wet, people were standing outside listening to the sermon. The sky was thick with black clouds and the atmosphere seemed ominous. To avoid the possibility of another entanglement, we immediatly turned back towards home. Shortly after we entered the house, the electricty went off. Inside, it was cold and quiet. To keep warm, Fe and Anniana slept in the same bed. Betsy and

Parissima slept together on the floor of our bedroom, warmed by an electrical heater – that is, when there was electricity. Fortunately, I had lots of blankets, otherwise we would surely have frozen that bitter winter. The children were already asleep, and with no electricity, there was nothing else to do but go to bed.

In the middle of the night I was woken by the sound of chanting in the distance. I concentrated hard in order to hear better and after a time I made out the words 'Allah Akbar', continuously repeated. The chanting seemed to be becoming louder by the minute. Hastily, I woke Iskandar and told him to listen. Trying not to disturb the children, we got out of bed quietly, put on our dressing gowns and slippers and went outside into the garden. It was very cold. I shivered. The black clouds had cleared, but the sky was lacklustre and there were no stars.

The chanting was getting louder and louder. Iskandar said that he would go up to the roof to see what was happening. I followed him. Apart from the twinkling lights of the city, nothing could be seen. But in the distance, we heard the sharp report of machine-gun fire. We stood there in silence, the wind biting our faces. I no longer felt the cold; fear had numbed my senses. We stayed motionless until the chanting and the sound of the machine-guns had died down.

The next day, the radio announced that in a clash between the authorities and the defying demonstrators, some people had been killed, many more injured and hundreds arrested. However, Taghi was of the opinion that the government was lying and that the incident had resulted in more than 1,000 casualties. No-one could pinpoint where the chants that had been simultaneously heard throughout the city had come from, but the general belief was that, at a designated time, the revolutionaries had gone onto their roofs and cried: 'Allah Akbar'. A one-day general strike followed and the schools were closed until after Ashura. Night after night the same scenario repeated itself. The cry of 'Allah Akbar', mixed with the sound of firing machine-guns, became our bedtime lullaby.

On December 2, in a communique issued from Paris, Khomeini called on all soldiers to leave their barracks and join the people. He expressed his gratitude for the general strike and ordered the strikes to continue until the government was paralysed. He also called any politician who planned to form a government under the oppressor Shah 'an opponent of Islam'.

The latest rumour was that it had not been real people who had been shouting 'Allah Akbar' from their roofs; the nightly chants had come from amplified tape recordings played through the loudspeakers of the mosques. Maryam Khanum and my brother-in-law laughed at the insinuations, because every night both of them were going onto their roof to sing, 'God is Great'.

The nation was anxiously waiting to see what would happen during the two holy days. To everyone's relief the authorities lifted the ban on processions in order to allow the Ta'sua and Ashura marches to take place. On these two occasions the troops were to be withdrawn from the streets.

On the day of Ta'sua, I asked Iskandar to accompany me to Avenue Pahlavi to watch the procession, which was to make its way towards Shahyad Square, a modern monstrosity which had been built near the airport. He would not hear of it so I resigned myself to watching the event on television. From what was televised, it seemed as though the whole city was on its feet. From early morning, crowds had set off from their various starting points and begun heading towards the Square. All streets feeding to the main route of the procession were overwhelmed with disciplined marchers carrying banners with different slogans: 'Death to the butcher Shah', 'Khomeini is our leader' and 'Islamic Republic'. The sheer number of the demonstrators was awesome, and they seemed to be brilliantly organised. Men and women carrying babies, or holding the hands of their children, walked side by side in orderly fashion.

The turmoil had changed to a tide, pushing the nation into an unbelievable unity between the forces of the extreme right and the extreme left and, in between, swallowing the moderates.

223

Even I, sitting in the safety of my home watching what was going on outside through the lens of the cameraman, felt proud of my brave countrymen. They certainly had more courage than we did, standing as they were against what they believed to be evil with nothing but a simple cry of 'Allah Akbar'. I felt ashamed that I did not have the guts even to observe the march from a street corner.

I wondered where the supporters of the Shah were. Those millions who had attended the stadiums on his birthdays, who had shouted 'Long live the Shah' in Rastakhiz gatherings, and whose bows had touched the ground. Probably most of them were marching up and down the Champs Elysees.

Contrary to the authorities' expectations nothing went wrong on that day.

On the following day of Ashura, when the procession reached Shahyad Square, a mullah climbed up the steps of the monument and read out a seventeen-point declaration on behalf of all opposition groups and parties, each of which was mentioned by name. The most important points stressed were that Khomeini was the leader, the Shah must be overthrown, strikes must be supported and the army must unite with the people. Ashura also passed in peace. However, the next day we heard that there had been a shoot-out at the headquarters of the Imperial Iranian Ground Forces. Some soldiers had shot at the guards. This was a very serious situation; it meant that the armed forces were divided among themselves.

Uncertainty continued.

Our only hope was Bakhtiar, who had by now become the black sheep of the National Front. The constitutionalists were waiting for him to be appointed the new civilian prime minister. Rumour had it that the Shah had agreed to appoint a Regency Council and leave the country. The crucial question was whether or not the army would back Bakhtiar in such situation. We also heard that Ardeshir Zahedi was back from Washington, where he acted as His Majesty's Ambassador, as the emissary of Brezezinski. His mission was to try to dissuade the Shah from leaving the country and to encourage him to take severe military action against the revolutionaries.

On December 31 it was officially announced that Bakhtiar would form a government and that the Shah would go overseas for rest and medical attention.

At last, what I had been waiting and praying for had happened. With Bakhtiar in power, the nation would reconcile and all would be well again.

How wrong I was.

Chapter Twenty-Seven

Shortly after his appointment, Bakhtiar announced his intention of having his government confirmed by both houses of parliament. Only a legitimate government, he said, could bring about the peace and order which the country was crying out for.

Secure in the thought that rosy days were ahead of us, Iskandar and I decided to take the children to London for a short holiday. The sleepless nights, constant anxiety and pressures of daily life had affected both of us. I was experiencing bad headaches and he was suffering from insomnia. Before leaving, I decided to throw a party to cheer us all up. Tari, Shahri (Aunt Azi's daughter) and her husband were the only cousins I had left in Iran so, naturally, I included them on my guest list.

A few days before the event, Shahri called and asked if she could bring her girlfriend, whose husband was overseas. Reluctantly I agreed; one had to be mindful of every mouth to be fed.

Iskandar and I were so looking forward to the party that we were ready many hours before the first of the guests arrived. I was very happy to see all my friends again; for at least a couple of hours we could pretend that nothing had changed. The last people to arrive were Shahri, her husband, Tari and Shahri's girlfriend. The woman looked cheap, with bleached blonde hair and false eyelashes, and from the way she behaved I guessed that she was more of a friend to Tari than to Shahri. To my disgust, after dinner, she started smoking grass, passing the joint to Tari after she had taken her share. I considered their behaviour to be disgraceful and could not bear to watch them. I was furious with Tari. How dare he insult me so thoughtlessly and spoil my evening? After all, his wife was my cousin. I was so angry that I left the guests for Iskandar to entertain and retired to my bedroom. All the joy had gone out of the evening.

The following day, Bakhtiar's appointment was rejected by the National Front Party leaders and the strikes intensified. The queues for petrol and kerosene grew longer. Often it took a whole day of waiting in the queue before anything could be procured. Bayat was responsible for the purchase of petrol for both of our cars. He would drive the Mercedes to the petrol station at 6 am and return, if he was lucky, at 4 pm with a full tank and several large bottles which he had filled for the Fiat.

Iskandar was very unhappy at the bank and was toying with the idea of resigning. I was against the idea. If he resigned, we would lose Bayat, the Mercedes and a good income. With Father gone and the hotel making virtually nothing, who would support us? My husband hated what was happening at the Foundation. The people in charge were trying to liquidate what they could of the Pahlavi assets by forcing some of the government institutions, like the National Iranian Oil Company, to purchase them at astronomical prices. The bank was then sending the money out of the country.

On the afternoon of January 3, Iskandar had just arrived home from his office when he received a telephone call from a well-wisher, informing him that he would soon receive a message asking him to return to the bank to co-sign a cheque for release to General Oveissi. The sum involved was one million dollars. The money belonged to the people, said the informer, and if Iskandar valued his life he would not answer the call.

Horrified, we decided to do as the man advised.

Ten minutes later the call came. I picked up the receiver. The voice on the other end of the line advised me that it was the secretary of the bank's managing director, wishing to speak with Dr Mahdavi. I informed her that my husband had not yet arrived home. She told me that his presence was required at the bank urgently and I assured her that as soon as he arrived I would convey this message to him. Iskandar did not return to the bank that evening and General Oveissi left Iran the next day.

On the same day, I received a call from Uncle Hussain, wanting to know if we would mediate with one of our well-known university friends to accept a ministerial position in Bakhtiar's Cabinet. Iskandar refused. I asked him why. He replied that he had chosen to remain apolitical. He believed that what was going on in the streets of Teheran was determining the future of the country. The parliament had become obsolete, the Constitution of 1906 was dead. People did not want democracy. They wanted another idol to worship and the cry was for Khomeini.

I agreed with my husband, especially in view of the conference which was taking place on the Caribbean island of Guadeloupe at which, it was believed, the leaders of the United States of America, Britain, France and Germany were deciding the political fate of Iran. The future of Iran depended on their decision, not on anything Bakhtiar did. In fact, the signs indicated that their support was for the Emam. The presence of General Huyser, the American Deputy Commander of the NATO Forces in Iran also pointed to the fact that the Americans were very much involved in what was going on. It was believed that his mission was to ensure that the decision of those present at Guadeloupe would be carried out.

On January 6, Bakhtiar presented his cabinet to the Shah and, soon after, the media news confirmed the Shah's intention of departing from Iran. Now all we could do was to wait for the 16th, to see if the free parliament would confirm the new government.

In the meantime, the food shortage had become acute. One day, quite by chance, I came across a smuggler who sold me three kilos of Beluga Caviar. Sturgeon fishing and the distribution of caviar was the monopoly of Shillat, the government fishing organisation which was managed by the Davalo family. It was against the law for ordinary fishermen to fish for sturgeon; however, some did and sold the caviar on the black market. Ludicrously, for two weeks we had caviar on toast for dinner. I often thought of the poor who could not afford the black market prices and who did not have freezers in which to store their food. From what Taghi told me, I gathered that the young people and the mullahs were taking care of feeding the needy. The food was distributed in the mosques, subsidised by money from the bazaar. Street activities indicated that the people themselves were in charge. Few police were seen and all one saw of the army were soldiers sitting on their tanks, smiling and waving at passers-by.

On the morning of January 16, 1979, Bakhtiar's cabinet and program were approved by both houses of parliament. That same day, at around 10.30 am, I heard the familiar sound of helicopters flying over our roof. This time, however, there were many, not the usual two or three. I ran to the roof just in time to witness a tragic historical moment. The Shah – the King of Kings, the Shadow of God on Earth – was leaving his land to become a wanderer. I kept my blurred gaze on the helicopters until they became mere black knots on the horizon. The king was running away again. But what about all the faithful servants he had left behind in his jails? What would become of them?

Very slowly, I descended the steps to the patio, went to my bedroom, put on my cloak and walked to Grandma's house. The sorrow I felt was too intense to bear alone. The street was even more deserted than usual. Suddenly, a colossal black cloud which had been following the helicopters burst into a downpour, and a savage wind whipped through the leafless branches of the gnarled trees. It was as though nature, too, was weeping for the fallen monarch – or perhaps for us, a class which was about to become extinct.

When I entered Grandma's bedroom, she was sitting in her bed with her lunch tray on her knees, totally ignorant of what had happened. Her dear, beautiful face brightened when she saw me. I bowed, kissed her hand and then her face, and told her that the Shah was leaving the country. She shrugged her bent shoulders and retorted that the Pahlavis had got what they deserved. Her maid brought tea and, at my request, turned on the radio. The 2 o'clock news announced the Shah's dramatic departure from Iran.

Within a few minutes of the announcement, the sound of honking car horns drove us out to the gate. The street, which had been deserted only a short while ago, was filled with cars, flashing their headlights, their drivers shouting, 'The Shah has gone!' I could not share in the jubilation and went back inside where I stayed with Grandma for another hour before walking back home.

That day was the end of an era for us – a good era.

The days that followed saw nothing but a deterioration of the situation. Statues of the two Pahlavi Shahs which had adorned most city squares were pulled down, smashed and urinated on. Strikes were rife, most of the shops were shuttered and closed and there were demonstrations everywhere. The whole country was rebelling. SAVAK nests were being discovered, ravaged and burnt and the soldiers had begun to fraternise with the revolutionaries. A couple of cabinet ministers had already resigned.

On January 19 the Arbain March, another sacred religious day, took place in Teheran. Millions of people participated in disciplined orderliness on the walk to Shahyad Square, the platform for the revolution. The soldiers simply looked on. At the square the opposition leaders, among whom was the revered, many-times-jailed Ayatollah Taleghani, read a ten-point declaration which stated that the illegitimate Pahlavi regime had been overthrown, and that in its place the Islamic Republic must be established under the leadership of Emam Khomeini, who was invited to introduce an Islamic Revolutionary Council and a provisional government; that Bakhtiar's government should not be recognised as it was illegal; that the army must join the nation; and that strikes and demonstrations must continue until total victory was attained.

Gradually, Iskandar and I began to realise that people wanted Khomeini and only Khomeini. From what we read in the newspapers, it seemed that the opposition's provisional government was made up of reasonable men – men like seventy-five-year-old Mehdi Bazargan, a European-educated secular leader who had been a faithful adherent of Mossadegh, and who had been imprisoned on many occasions by the Shah for his leadership of the old National Front Party. Bazargan was a good Muslim and, hence, highly respected by Khomeini and the bazaar. With people like him governing the country and with Khomeini, a man of God, acting as the spiritual leader of the nation, the Iranian revolution would surely be remembered as the most peaceful, disciplined, orderly movement of its kind in the history of the human race.

A democratic secular government working within an Islamic framework, we told ourselves, would bring about the desired social justice, equal opportunity and general prosperity for which so much blood had been shed. We had nothing to fear from the future. There would be no more killings – especially now that the Shah and his family were safe in Egypt.

This is what we told ourselves and each other. In times of extraordinary crisis, the human mind becomes cunning. It desires to create positive visions which are crucial to its survival. Under such dismal circumstances one cannot live without hope – however remote, however unrealistic. So, we hoped.

Every morning, we woke up to a new rumour. One day it was a military coup, the next, Bakhtiar was flying to France to meet with Khomeini – and so on, and so on. On January 29 at a press conference, Bakhtiar announced that the airports, which had been closed, would be reopened to permit Khomeini to return to Iran. I immediately called my travel agent and booked three tickets on British Airways for London departing on February 3, and one on the 11th for Iskandar, who could not leave the bank before then.

Passports had to be submitted to the office of the SAVAK prime minister three days prior to departure for a security check. To save time and travelling, I took Iskandar's as well, and handed the four passports to the travel agent who was responsible for the submission. On the date of travel, the documents would be returned to us at a special section of the customs area, after our tickets and luggage had been checked in.

The next two days were spent in speculation as to what might happen to the Emam Khomeini's plane. Some said that it would be diverted to the remote island of Qish in the Persian Gulf. Others believed that the generals were going to shoot the plane down, thus eliminating tens of thousands of his supporters in a single, massive attack. But the majority believed that the Emam would arrive safe and sound.

From the evening of January 31, crowds began to gather on what would be the route of the Emam's procession to Behesht Zahra, renamed the Martyrs' Cemetery. They were prepared to sleep on the pavements in order to secure a good position from which to see their leader.

On February 1 we stayed at home, sitting by the television, ready to witness yet another historic event – the return of the architect of the Iranian revolution. The Ayatollah, his advisors and many journalists arrived aboard a chartered Air France 747. In the airplane, he was interviewed by one of the reporters and asked the question: 'What do you feel about returning to Iran in triumph?'. The Emam did not even look at the reporter. With an expressionless face and a gesture devoid of any emotion he replied, 'Nothing.'

If the leader felt nothing, the crowds certainly felt something. Khomeini was greeted by jubilant mobs in their millions. Teheran was afoot again. All the streets leading to the route were full of people dancing with joy. The procession moved very slowly, the soldiers standing back and allowing the security to be handled by the revolutionary forces. Somewhere along the way, Emam got out of the car and climbed into a helicopter which took him to Beheshte Zahra. The cemetery, too, was a sea of living souls who had gathered to welcome their hero, the Idol Smasher, Bot Shekan.

The Emam took up residence in a small, inconspicuous school building in the South of the city. Ayatollah Khomeini

233

was to prove to be everything that the Shah was not – humble, true to his word and devoid of wordly interests. He was to give Iran a new identity – whether it was good or bad, only time would tell.

Relieved that the Emam was safely tucked away, I began packing again for our 'rainy day'. I fitted a small carpet and the Nasser Al Din Shah's horse-cover into one of my suitcases. With the new, tougher custom regulations, each traveller was allowed to take only one carpet out of the country.

On February 3, I went to visit Grandma to bid her a quick farewell. She cried, and forecast that she would never see me again. I promised her that this was going to be a short trip and that I would be back in no time at all. We left the house for the airport, Iskandar driving. We drove through the empty, littered streets which had witnessed so much in such a short time, past walls scarred with posters and slogans, past The Mirabel with its shattered windows, and the squares with their broken or headless statues, and we passed the Shahyad Monument, the rostrum of the revolution.

The airport was packed with excited, unruly people, each carrying more than the allowed weight. No revolutionary spirit was to be found here. Just the anxiety, impatience and fear of people on the run. At the counter where we were to collect our passports, two elderly men in front of me were denied theirs. They had become prisoners in their own country. I dared not think of their fate.

The flight was on time both at take-off and on arrival and at Heathrow Airport we were welcomed by my brothers and my parents. It was an unforgettable moment of delight. For one week we had a happy, even carefree, time. Then all hell broke loose. On the evening of February 9 in Iran the Homafars, the Western-educated airforce technicians (non-commissioned officers), who were in charge of the maintenance of the most sophisticated weapons systems at Doshan Tappeh Air Base on the Eastern outskirts of Teheran, demonstrated for Khomeini. Fighting broke out with the troops of the Imperial Guard and additional troops were brought in, escalating the fighting. Some time before morning, the Homafars broke into the base armoury and seized thousands of rifles, most of which they tossed over the fence to the revolutionaries outside. A curfew was imposed and ignored. Bloody demonstrations spread throughout the country.

Communication with Iran broke down. I had no news of Iskandar. For four days I sat by the telephone trying to dial home, and when I became exhausted, one of my brothers or the children took over. Desperate fear for Iskandar kept me numb, but focussed. The televised news was horrific. Fighting between the revolutionaries and the army was bloody, and there was no information about the whereabouts of Prime Minister Bakhtiar. For two days the shooting and killing continued, until the military withdrew to its barracks proclaiming its 'neutrality' in the political conflict.

At 3 am on February 15, after ten hours of dialing our number, I got through. Iskandar's gentle voice answered. I kept crying: 'Are you really alive, my darling? Are you alive?' For a few minutes, we both wept with relief, then we calmed down and began to talk sensibly. As we were exchanging news, I could hear the sound of shooting in the background and asked him where the noise was coming from. He told me that the revolutionaries from the Ehteshamieh Committee were shooting at suspects or into the air. I asked him what a 'committee' was. He chose not to answer and began telling me how he and his father had narrowly escaped death a few days beforehand.

On February 10, guessing that the airport might close again, he had decided to go there to collect his passport. He had picked up his father from his house, and they had driven to Mehrabad together. At the entrance, they had seen a large sign which read: 'The airways are closed to the thieves who want to run away.' Empty-handed, they had set off for home and, on the way, had been caught in a shoot-out. Luckily they had not been hurt, but back at the house the trauma had taken its toll. Iskandar's father had suffered a heart attack and had been hospitalised.

After thanking God that he was still alive, I asked my husband what he wanted us to do. He replied that we should stay in London until it was safe for us to return to Iran; otherwise, he would find a way to join us. We said goodbye and I promised to telephone him every day.

Over the next few days, the regime of Emam Khomeini was recognised by all heads of state and the Iranian revolution hailed. I was stunned. How had an inchoate reform movement turned into a full scale revolution in a country like Iran? A country with a sovereign like the Shah, protected as he was by such a formidable security organisation as SAVAK?

I suspect that the necessity for change in the Iranian body politic was a result of deep social, economic and historical forces that will take history a long time to understand. However, what has to be acknowledged is that Khomeini's skilful manipulation united these forces, and his charisma endowed them with a focus and purpose. He turned an ideologically divided reform movement with limited objectives into a genuine revolution with its own unique Islamic ideology. Whether or not this Islamic content was acceptable to the modern mind, and whether or not it was understood by the general populace, is beside the point. The fact remains that it appealed to the masses and the intelligentsia, as demonstrated by their presence in the streets and their willingness and readiness to die for the cause.

How the Shah must have envied the devotion his people were now showing his dire enemy. What a pity that while he had the opportunity he failed to mobilise such a loyalty towards his own White Revolution. Perhaps if he had become more involved with the real needs of his people – not merely effecting rapid economic development; perhaps if he had become more sensitive to their traditional values, more respectful of their religion and less concerned with his own glory and military might; if he had allowed political freedom instead of blocking all kinds of political dissent – even constructive criticism; if he had valued his intellectuals as much as he had valued his generals, he would still be sitting

236

on his throne and Khomeini might have remained an unknown recluse.

Well, now the events had taken their course and there was nothing for me to do but hope that this man of God would declare a general amnesty and bring about the paradise the Iranians had fought for. Two weeks later Mehrabad Airport re-opened and we were on the first flight home to Teheran.

Chapter Twenty-Eight

There were only a few passengers on our plane, so disembarkation was quick. At the bottom of the aircraft's mobile steps, we were met by a row of soldiers with machine guns who were patrolling the route to the airport building. Inside, bearded, tieless revolutionaries were in charge.

We met Iskandar in the visitors' lounge and, together again, headed for our car. Feeling rejuvenated, I asked Iskandar why he had not brought Bayat to help him with the luggage. He fell silent for a while then, looking guilty, admitted that he had resigned from the bank. This news was traumatic for me. It would mean many adjustments to our lifestyle. However, I did not know how to react without hurting my husband, so I did not dwell on the subject.

At home, our servants received us with affection. Anniana served a delicious Philippino dish and Iskandar opened a bottle of wine. In pouring the drink, however, his usual generosity was not apparent. He told me that there was a ban on alcoholic beverages and the Passdaran Enghelab, the revolutionary guards, were attacking the liquor stores and breaking the contents. We only had a few bottles left in the house and these were to be kept for special occasions, like tonight.

I asked Iskandar who the revolutionary guards were. He explained that komitehs, or local revolutionary committees, had blossomed throughout the country on the morning after the revolution. Many of them, it seemed, were extensions of the neighbourhood committees which had been formed around the mosques in 1978 to organise strikes and demonstrations, and to distribute food and kerosene to the needy. After the final fall of the regime, any sense of discipline had vanished.

The young people who made up the majority of the komiteh members became fully armed, taking their weapons from the thousands of rifles and submachine guns which had been seized from military arsenals on February 10 and 11. These committees were serving both as local security forces and as agents of the revolutionary authorities against the members of the old regime. In short, they had become a power unto themselves.

I asked if we had a komiteh in our neighbourhood. It seemed that we did. The guards, in fact, had already been to the house to check if the owners were in Iran, and demanding to see the deed to the house. Iskandar had told them that the house belonged to his wife, who was overseas and would be returning soon. They had given him a month to present both the deed and his wife to the komiteh, otherwise they would confiscate the property.

After dinner, when the children had gone to bed, Iskandar talked about the executions of the army generals and Nasiri, whose half-dead body had been roped to a car then dragged through the streets of Teheran so that the people could enjoy the punishment of the principal butcher of SAVAK. I did not like what I was hearing. I was too tired and disappointed to listen to any more morbid news, so I retired to bed.

The next morning I called Grandma, who sounded well and was impatient to see me. I promised to visit her in the afternoon, then tried Uncle Hussain's house with no success. It was a fine day. Spring was just around the corner and my weeping willow was beginning to turn green. The climbing roses were blooming and the violets in their different shades of purple covered the borders around the pool. The sparrows had returned from their winter holidays and were chirping cheerfully. I suddenly felt very happy and decided to walk to Uncle Hussain's house and surprise him.

Avenue Ehteshamieh was as soulless as before and the abandoned villas looked forlorn without their inhabitants. Most of the shops appeared to be empty and some were still closed. The streets were devoid of traffic and the occasional passers-by looked glum. There were very few women around and, of those, most were in chador. Only one or two were bare-headed like me. There was a peculiar sadness in the air. Clearly, the revolutionary euphoria had vanished.

I walked briskly across Saltanatabad Road and entered the Golestan 10th, at the end of which was my uncle's house. Even from this distance I could see that the gate was closed and I took this to be a security measure. As I drew closer, however, I saw that there was a board attached to the gate. This was unusual. I quickened my pace. The gate was padlocked and the wooden placard informed me that the house belonged to the Foundation of the Disinherited*. A solitary revolutionary guard holding a submachine gun was standing at the corner, picking his nose and watching me. I continued to walk, passing the house without looking at it and, when I arrived at the first crossroad, I turned right. My mind was a muddled blank. I could not think clearly.

Still in shock, I continued walking for some time, then decided to change direction and return to the house. When I reached the crossroad I saw that the guard was still standing on the corner. I was certain all of a sudden that he was watching the house. I approached him and asked: 'Brother, what is the meaning of this sign?'

Without looking at me he replied, 'This house belonged to an undeserving Corruptor of Earth. It has been confiscated for the Foundation of the Disinherited and soon it will be put to good use.'

'Yes, I am sure you are right. Justice must be done. God be with you, brother.'

'God be with you, sister,' he replied, still looking down at the ground.

I almost ran home. I called Iskandar at the university and demanded an explanation. He informed me in carefully worded sentences that on the night before my arrival from London Uncle Hussain, who had just had a stomach operation, had

* Disinherited was the new terminology for the poor.

been seized from the hospital and taken to Evin Prison. The house had immediately been confiscated. Aunt Firouzeh had been allowed to pack her necessities into one suitcase and had then been forced to leave. She had been staying with Tari ever since. Grandma did not know of the arrest, Iskandar stressed, and was not to be told.

Devastated, I replaced the receiver then, without a second thought, I ran out of the house and walked as fast as I could to Tari's house. My aunt was there. She looked aged, spiritless and very thin. Her aristocratic nose looked longer and her domineering eyes had lost their lustre. It seemed that she had no energy for talking. I went to her, gave her a hug, and we both began to cry silently. Prudence had not deserted her, however. She whispered in my ear that I should not ask any questions, nor mention any names. Obediently, I moved away from her and sat on a chair nearby. We began to talk, touching only on trivialities. On the opposite wall I noticed a large picture of the Emam. His penetrating eyes seemed to stare right through me.

I had not actually understood the necessity for precaution until I heard Tari's boisterous voice in conversation with someone else. The two men entered the room and Tari introduced the stranger as Ali Aga, a guard from the Darous Komiteh who was in charge of their safety. I greeted the young man and froze in my seat. So, they were under house arrest. Mamad, the cook, brought a tray of tea and, in silence, we occupied ourselves with sipping the hot drink. I was impatient to find out what had happened, but obviously this was impossible in the circumstances, so I invited my aunt and Tari to have dinner with me and politely extended the invitation to Ali Aga. He, fortunately, thanked me but refused.

Around 7.30 pm my guests arrived. My aunt looked more at ease, less nervous and willing to talk. She told me that, one afternoon, a group of guards bearing a command from the revolutionary tribunal had entered Uncle Hussain's hospital room and taken the patient to Evin Prison. No reason been given, no crime mentioned. One of the group had accompanied her to her home where she had packed her suitcase and left, leaving all her possessions behind her. The next day, their bank accounts had been seized and all their properties, including Goldonak, confiscated. She had been told to appeal to the office of the prosecutor-general (Dadsetan-e Kol),and the Foundation of the Disinherited to establish what property and possessions belonged to her and what was her husband's. Anything she had inherited from her father would be returned to her.

She and her son-in-law had already contacted some of their old friends from the Mossadegh era for help, and Tari was optimistic that he would find a way to secure Uncle Hussain's freedom. Their positivism lifted my spirits and we began planning how we could expedite matters. Before taking their leave, Aunt Firouzeh asked if she would be able to stay with us if need be. I welcomed the idea.

The new university term started, but for the first few days I found my classes without students. The head of our department had left Iran and a small committee of students had undertaken to do the planning for the faculty. The janitors had become the link between the student committee and those lecturers like myself who had not gone into Islamic cover or had not yet given up wearing neck-ties.

One day, feeling particularly frustrated, I asked Abas Aga, my favourite janitor, why the students were not attending my classes. He told me that they were boycotting them. I asked why. He gave me a friendly shrug and suggested I ask Dr Ahmadi, the new head of our department. Worried, I went to Dr Ahmadi's office and knocked on the open door. The bearded revolutionary rose from his chair and politely pointed to a seat. Without beating about the bush, I told him the reason for the visit and asked him if I was being 'purified'. He assured me that this was not the case. My dossier had been studied thoroughly and it was clean. However, the students had accused me of being a 'dictator' and 'in the habit of dressing inappropriately'. Neither of these was a crime for 'purification'. The problem was simply that the students of the School of Humanities had decided not to attend my classes, he went on. I had either to present myself and debate the issue, or find another college within the university where I could lecture. I accepted the challenge of a debate first, and told him that if the result was negative I would apply to another college. He acklowledged my decision as sound and saw me to the door.

Through Abas Aga, I made an appointment with the student body to defend myself.

The situation was humiliating and nerve-racking, but under the circumstances pride had to be swallowed and nerves soothed by tranquillisers. For the five years that I had been involved with the university I had done nothing but my best for the students. My lectures, I believed, were interesting, well-prepared and targeted to the cognitive level of my students, the majority of whom had entered American universities without any difficulties. True, I had failed without remorse those who had not studied enough, and those I had caught hiding text books under their chadors during examinations. It was, of course, to these students that I had been a 'dictator'.

The worst aspect of the situation, though, was Iskandar's repeated 'I told you so.' In his own way he was condemning me, too. He seemed to be enjoying my predicament; it was almost as if the students were punishing me for a crime for which he himself wished to accuse me. I had always been aware that he resented my forcefulness, but I had not realised he disliked it so much. I was a stubborn fighter, and a stickler for principles. Both qualities, if not properly understood, might be mistaken for a domineering trait . With a clear conscience I had nothing to fear from the student committee and, if necessary, I was prepared to fight them.

On the day of my so called 'trial', dressed in my usual choice of clothing, I entered the room, sat at the lecturer's pulpit, gazed at my judges and, defying their authority, smiled at them. I asked them to, one by one, give me their reasons for refusing to attend my classes. There was no mention of 'dictatorial behaviour', or 'provocative dressing.' They must have realised that they could not discredit me with accusations which they could not substantiate.

The sum total of their objections was that I had no qualifications to teach at the university and that my position had been acquired through favouritism. Thrilled that I could prove them wrong, I asked one of the students to be kind enough to go to the personnel officer at the employment bureau and ask him for my file. A chorus of muttered objections hummed through the cold room but, eventually, one of the students rose and left for the bureau. After half-an-hour of uncomfortable silence, the door opened and he entered with a thick green manila folder tucked under his arm. He handed the file to the student who had been acting as their leader, who proceeded to extract my degrees from among the other papers. He read each out loud then, satisfied, nodded his head, apologised for the group's mistake and rose, indicating that the session was terminated. I rose too. Looking directly at him I said, 'I hope I will see you tomorrow for the nine o'clock lecture.'

I received no response from the students. The silence was agonising. Eventually, the leader found his tongue and replied maliciously, 'Dr Ahmadi will inform you of the outcome of this meeting. Until then there will be no classes.'

With my chin up, and forcing a quivering smile, I left the room, beads of cold perspiration running down my back. For the first time I realised that logic counted for nothing with these young revolutionaries. It was, after all, a time for pure and utter vengeance.

Without wasting another minute, I headed for the office of the Head of the School of Economics. Having been ushered inside, I told the head of the department my story and asked him if he could find me a position. I was counting on Iskandar's popularity with the faculty and the students to persuade him to help me, and I was right. Fortunately, they did need an English lecturer. He asked me if I had enough knowledge of economics to be able to prepare and deliver the lectures. I replied that learning had never been a problem for me and that, after all, their best professor was my husband. We both laughed and this broke the ice. He assured me that as far as he was concerned the position was mine – but, he warned me, he had to discuss the issue further with the student body. He said that he would let Iskandar know of their decision.

Light-heartedly, I left his office and began to descend the three flight of stairs which I had climbed so anxiously only an hour ago. For the first time, I noticed the pictures of the different communist leaders, from Marx to Mao, which hung on the walls of the college. Small wooden tables stood next to the portraits, with stacks of books written by those leaders for sale. A couple of students stood by each desk ready to propagate or defend their ideologies.

Whoever would have dreamed that such freedom could exist in Iran?

At home, I told my husband of what I had done. He admired my audacity and made no objection to my working at his college.

The next day, Iskandar was informed that I could start my classes from the following Saturday (the first working day in Muslim countries). I had one week to prepare my economic lectures in English. Iskandar gave me the appropriate text books and I was well-prepared and fully organised for my first class. The students, unlike many of their peers, who generally started fidgeting fifteen minutes or so before the class was finished, stayed until after the bell rang then gathered around my chair, inundating me with questions. Soon, I had earned for myself a reputation equal to that of Iskandar's and the students became my friends.

Young people are very observant. It did not take them long to realise that I was not a Hezbollahi, a fundamentalist. The leftists, identifying themselves with modernism, thought of me as a sympathiser – yet I was far from being a communist. Nevertheless, I found talking with the leftists easier, and their arguments more rational than those of their religious counterparts. That was probably why they liked me.

Gradually, I began to favour the Kurds in my class. They

were a courageous tribe for whom I had always had the greatest respect and sympathy. Their lot was worse than all the other minorities, as they were a group which inhabited four different countries – none of which really wanted them. Now, agitated by the revolutionary leftist elements, they had initiated a movement for autonomy in Kurdestan. To crush their uprising, the central government was fighting them fiercely and with a cruelty which was unbecoming to a regime which called itself Islamic. The Kurds were also very poor. I still disliked the Tudeh, and never associated with my brother-in-law.

Iskandar's office was the meeting place of all the factions. The students loved and respected him. They had not forgotten how he had helped them in their dealings with SAVAK. He was the only lecturer with a known affiliation to the Pahlavi Foundation who had not been 'purified'.

The process of 'purification' was becoming very common these days. Every institution had a committee which was 'clearing' the organisation of the criminals of the old regime. Within a short period, hundreds of educated technocrats, engineers, doctors, professors, and, in particular, military officers lost their jobs, some for real but most for fabricated reasons. Personal grudges were being used to damage neighbours, business partners, employers, superiors, friends and family members. Revenge was devouring many innocent lives and causing many properties and businesses – the results of long, hard work – to be confiscated. Even the prime minister had confessed to a state of social disorder. He had called Teheran 'a city with a hundred sheriffs'. There were parallel governments of the revolutionary committees, courts, guards and the government of Bazargan all trying to rule according to their own perception of what was right and what was wrong – or rather, what should be right and what should be wrong. Security had collapsed. Society was on the verge of polarisation and we all had to fend for ourselves.

It is amazing how human beings learn to adjust to change. In the absence of Bayat, I had to collect the children from school and do the shopping myself. Food was scarce, but if you had enough money it could be found. I established good relations with the owners of the various shops in my vicinity, and occasional tips saw to it that I obtained the best available goods. Walking to the shops replaced walking as a form of exercise, and I enjoyed my afternoon strolls to Grandma's and then to the bakery to purchase freshly-baked Sangak bread for dinner. Foresight was paying off. I was well-stocked with frozen meat and out-of-season vegetables and was proud that, in my household, no-one felt the hardship that had been imposed on others. Imported goods were almost non-existent. The price of electrical appliances had increased tenfold and everybody was seeking freezers and refrigerators. Music tapes and videos could be purchased only from the black market. Female singers and actresses were either in hiding or had already left the country. Mrs Parssa, the first woman cabinet minister, was executed and the talk was that, soon, everybody would have to go into chador. All my sleeveless garments had been abandoned. Luckily, the weather was still cool.

One afternoon, when I returned from collecting the children from school, Fe handed me a letter which had been delivered to the house by a member of the local Komiteh. It requested donations for the families of the martyrs of the revolution. I gave the letter to Iskandar and we decided to make a monthly contribution. This meant that we had to go to the Komiteh ourselves, which presented a good opportunity to take the deed of the house to establish my ownership, and to let them know that I had returned from overseas and was residing in my own house.

For this occasion I had to look Islamic, but I was determined that I was not going to wear the chador. The next best attire was my blue cloak, with a white woollen hat which covered all my hair. Long boots and thick stockings would take care of my legs.

We walked to the Komiteh headquarters, where two armed youths in khaki parkas stood guard at the entrance. As was the traditional custom, Iskandar entered first, while I followed, pretending to be a meek obedient wife – which I certainly was not. I was laughing secretly at the whole charade. Inside, we were asked the purpose of our visit. I began to answer, but the man ignored me and looked at my husband. I had to learn to control myself. The new order was totally male-dominated and women were expected to accept their second class citizenship. This was something I would never learn to do!

We were ushered to the main room, in which wooden chairs were set out for visitors, and a distinguished-looking old man with white hair and a white beard was sitting on an aluminium chair behind a large aluminium table littered with papers, manila folders and an ashtray full of cigarette butts. Four unshaven, untidy-looking roughnecks were standing near him, carefully examining a pile of coloured photographs and making derogatory comments.

Iskandar and I took the two chairs closest to the table and sat waiting to be attended to. I was curious to catch a glimpse of the pictures which were attracting so much attention. Unobtrusively, I tried to steal a glance at the photographs which the man standing nearest to me was holding. Coincidence had him throw them on the table, well within my view, which unfortunately was a little hazy without my glasses. When I could not control my curiosity any longer, I leaned towards the table and took a good look at the photograph on the top of the pile. It was a picture of the empress and ten other women standing in a row dressed in bathing-suits, the tallest at one end and the shortest at the other. I guessed that it had been taken at the Noshahr royal residence by the Caspian. Excited, I addressed the old man humbly and asked if I, too, could look at the pictures. He picked up the pile from the table and handed them to me.

I knew most of the women in the photographs. One of them was my second cousin from Mother's side. She and her husband were successful architects, and her father had been the first radiologist in Iran and a president at Teheran

249

University. The family was well- respected. While looking, I was also listening. The guards, in their door-to-door inspection of the district's houses, had come across my cousin's residence which, in their absence, was being looked after by an old caretaker. To save his own skin, he had let them in and the inspectors had ransacked the house. The pictures were from her album and proved her connection with the court.

Now the men were debating whether or not the photographs were evidence enough to warrant the seizure of the property. After a long discussion, the resolution was that the husband and wife were guilty and that the house should be taken for the Foundation of the Disinherited. Suddenly, I became very frightened.

After the roughnecks had left, the old man introduced himself as Haj Sabaghi. I realised he was the father of one of Bazargan's cabinet ministers. Very politely, Iskandar introduced himself and me to the man and handed him the deed to the house, along with my birth certificate which we had brought in case they questioned my identity. The old man took the documents, examined them carefully and, satisfied, handed them back. He asked Iskandar what his occupation was and when he learned that he was a lecturer, the old man's tone became more friendly.

Encouraged, Iskandar began expressing sympathy for the families of the martyrs of the revolution and offered a monthly contribution of 5,000 rials. He laid the envelope he had been holding on the table. The old man opened it, took the cheque out, looked at the sum and then praised Iskandar's generosity. He asked us if we wished to have tea. We declined and politely took our leave.

Outside, a thin, pale moon hung in the sky. Young men, mostly in their teens and clutching machine guns, were being despatched to their posts at the crossroads. Their mission was to stop and search every car that passed, looking for anti-revolutionaries, drugs – especially opium – and breath-testing for alcohol.

These youths were responsible for the shootings we heard

nightly, the shots sometimes aimed at people, and sometimes no doubt simply a means of entertainment for the bored Passdaran, the guards.

At home, we both knew what to do first. We took our photograph albums out of the library and searched through them thoroughly. Any possibly incriminating photographs were taken out and, one by one, torn into tiny pieces. Then the remains of our cherished memories were flushed down the toilet. Not even the garbage bin was safe enough.

At dinner, I found Betsy very excited and asked her what was the reason for her happiness. She told me that her new teacher, an American married to an Iranian, was from Jackson County in Illinois. This made her and Betsy fellow countrywomen. Betsy was her favourite and she had been given a packet of American bubble-gum.

Suddenly, I remembered that I had to renew Betsy's American passport. After dinner, I took the document out of the safe and saw that it had already expired, so the following day I went to the U.S. Consulate to have it renewed. There was a long queue at the entrance and I cursed myself for having neglected this task. I had no choice but to wait five hours to be attended to.

Tired and hungry, I arrived home to discover that Anniana wanted to hand in her notice. She had decided to go and live in Paris. I could not blame her, but I was upset by this additional source of frustration. One by one, the agents of comfort were deserting us. The trimmings which had made our life luxurious were disappearing. The good times were dying and, with them, a part of us. I was amazed at my own calm. A short while ago, I would have considered Anniana's resignation a major disaster. Now, it was simply a nuisance to be shrugged off.

The next bad news was that seven families of the Disinherited had taken occupancy of Father's unfinished apartment building in the city. I could do nothing about this as I had no power of attorney from my father. I called London to give him the news. He replied that he and Mother would return home at once to claim the property, but I advised against their return. Comfort and safety were more important for an elderly couple than possessions. Father listened to me carefully, then told me that he had done nothing in his life which warranted hiding. I explained that no-one knew anymore what was right or wrong; the new values had not yet been established, and a society undergoing such dramatic changes was not safe for an elderly couple to live in. He should wait until the fervour for vengeance had subsided before he returned. Finally, he agreed to heed my advice.

Two days later, Ali called from London informing me that a man named Kaman had contacted him at his office and had offered to get his money out of Iran for a thirty per cent commission on the total value. This was a good rate in view of the government's strict exchange control. Ali asked me to contact the man's representative, stressing the need for utmost secrecy. Smuggling money out of the country was a criminal offence which incurred the death penalty.

I refused. He became angry. I grew angry in return then, eventually, gave in. Ali gave me the name, address and telephone number of the man in question and instructed me to call his representative Javad Aga immediately for an appointment. Both on the telephone and at the meeting I had to repeat a coded message for identification. When Iskandar came home, I told him of the telephone conversation. At first he was upset, then he was cautious and, finally, he agreed to accompany me to meet the man.

The next day I called Javad, introduced myself and repeated the coded message. An appointment was made for the following day at 11 a.m. At around 10 o'clock we set out for the meeting, which was to take place in the heart of the city. We both felt more than a little apprehensive about the whole affair. Ali was putting us in a dangerous situation. A pang of resentment passed through my heart. They, living in London, were safe and secure. They had no right to jeopardise the safety of our lives for their money. Now it is Ali's money, next it will be Father's, I told myself.

252

I regretted agreeing to see this agent. How did we know whether or not we could trust him? Would he remain discreet if his operation was discovered, or would he divulge our names to the authorities?

Somewhere between Shemiran and the city I suggested we return home. Iskandar was also in two minds about the situation but, somehow, the blood bond overcame our fear. We parked the car a block away from our appointed meeting place and walked the rest of the way to the office, which was located on the fifth floor of an unobtrusive building. The lift was out of order and we had to use the stairs. The door was open and we entered the empty room. An unshaven man in a khaki parka came to see who had ventured into the premises. He looked like a Pasdar. I felt cold. This must be a trap.

After a few moments, Iskandar gathered the courage to ask for Javad Aga. The man told us to wait. He disappeared into another room and, after ten minutes, a giant of a man, also unshaven and dressed in a khaki parka, presented himself and asked us to follow him into a small conference room. He closed the door, giving the impression that he did not feel safe in his own premises. Iskandar introduced us and repeated the coded message. The man smiled and asked: 'What can I do for you, Aga?'

In a semi-whisper, Iskandar informed him of the purpose of our visit. The man listened, watching us carefully as though trying to assess our worth, then declared that he would have to get in touch with Mr Kaman before any arrangements could be made. Iskandar asked him how they were able to get the money out in spite of the exchange control.

He replied, 'It is very simple, Aga. Mr Kaman is a businessman and has secured a foreign exchange line of credit with the central bank. Every time he wants to transfer funds, he presents the necessary commercial documents to the bank to secure foreign exchange for the purchase of imported goods. Once the fund is released to him he can do whatever he wants with it.'

'Doesn't the government hold him responsible for the goods

which are not imported into the country?' asked a surprised Iskandar.

'Aga, don't worry,' the man replied. 'Mr Kaman has a good many of the customs officials in his pocket.'

The procedure recommended itself to an economist.

I asked the representative how he would require the money and what security we would have that the money would be transferred. He replied that he would need the money in cash and that our security was our trust in Mr Kaman.

As we walked back to the car, Iskandar and I discussed whether or not we felt it was safe to go ahead with the deal, and also whether we should sell something of our own and send that money out, too. After examining the pros and cons of the matter, we decided to wait and see how this deal went. If all went well, we would sell the rest of our carpets and send that money out.

Three days later, Javad called and asked us how much money we intended to transfer. I told him the amount and he instructed me to put the money into a suitcase. He would pick it up from my house at an agreed time when no-one except myself or my husband were at home.

A day before the appointed date, Iskandar and I, carrying four large shopping bags, entered the branch of the Bank Meli where Ali's money was deposited, and cashed the cheque which he had given to a trusted traveller to deliver to us. Bundles of 10,000 rial notes were put into the paper bags. The cashier was looking at us suspiciously, probably guessing that the money was about to leave the country.

Trying to look like ordinary shoppers, bent under the weight of the shopping bags, we walked to the parked car on the other side of the street, keeping as close to each other as possible. We placed the bags on the back seat and drove straight home.

At the gate, Iskandar honked and Fe appeared, opening the garage door. Iskandar drove the car inside and we both got out. Assuming the bags contained groceries, Fe began opening the car door to remove them. Hastily, I stopped her, telling her that they were to be delivered to Grandma's house. She closed the door and went inside the house. I whispered to Iskandar that I would go in and ask her to come down to the basement with me to get some meat from the freezer. While we were down there, he should take the bags up to my bedroom and hide them in the closet.

The next day, an hour before Javad Aga was due to arrive, I sent Fe and the children to see Grandma. Ten minutes before his arrival, I stood gazing out of the kitchen window, which overlooked the street and, in the distance, the Albourz mountains. The snow had melted; only a white cap remained. How I loved those mountains.

Right on time, a blue Volvo drew up in front of the house and Javad Aga got out. He looked round carefully, then rang the bell. I ran downstairs to open the garage door and he climbed back into his car and drove inside. I ushered him into the house. He stood completely still as though awestruck. I asked him what had caught his attention. He replied: 'This must be the most beautiful house I have ever seen in my life. You are a lady of great taste, Laila Khanum.' I thanked him, shrugged my shoulders and remarked: 'Yes, the house is beautiful, but I have become its prisoner.'

He asked me what I meant. I told him that I could not leave the country because I had no money outside of Iran. I could not even take a holiday because, if I left the house, the komiteh would assume that I had run away and would confiscate it. So, I was its prisoner. He said nothing.

We entered the sitting room. He sat down on the light green armchair next to the marble fireplace, refusing my offer of a cup of tea. His eyes were darting here and there around the room, admiring the antique paintings on the walls and the Gadjar ornaments on the tables. I left him to appreciate my treasures and went to the bedroom to get the red suitcase containing the money. I brought the heavy case in, placed it on the carpet and opened it. I told him what sum it contained, assuming that he would trust me. I was wrong. He sat down on the carpet with his legs crossed, licked his finger, and began taking the bundles out and counting every note, one by one.

God Almighty, I thought to myself. He is going to be here for hours. Jokingly, I remarked: 'Don't you trust us?' Without lifting his head he replied, 'Mrs Mahdavi, I am only an agent.'

Fair enough. I sat next to him and began counting, too.

Two hours later, he left the house with the suitcase in the boot of his car. The money was to be in Ali's bank account within seven working days. Nine days later, a call from London confirmed the completion of the transaction.

Chapter Twenty-Nine

The referundum to decide the post-Pahlavi political system took place on March 30 and 31. We were sure that no matter what went into the ballot boxes, the Islamic Republic would win with a 99 per cent majority; therefore, on the afternoon of the 31st, we walked to our district polling centre, voted for the Islamic Republic, then went to visit Aunt Firouzeh.

By the time we arrived at Tari's house, it was late afternoon. I rang the doorbell and immediately, as though a guest had been expected, Mamad opened the door. He looked pale. I asked him what was wrong and the old servant replied: 'This morning at 11 o'clock they took Tari Khan to the Komiteh for questioning and he has not yet returned.'

We rushed upstairs and found Aunt Firouzeh in the sitting room. The poor lady looked like a breathing corpse. Her long, thin fingers were trembling and her eyes were moist with tears. We kissed her and sat down, waiting for her to tell us what had happened. After a minute or two, she whispered, 'They must have taken Tari to Evin.'

Iskandar, in an attempt to console her, said, 'Firouzeh Khanum, he might still come back.'

I asked, 'Auntie, do you know which Komiteh the guards have taken him to?'

'No, I don't know. I only know that the summons was from the prosecutor general,' she replied tearfully.

'Auntie, perhaps Ali Aga, the man who was posted to guard you, might know.'

'Oh, yes. I had forgotten about him. But he hasn't been here for the past two days.'

I suggested that she contact him for assistance.

The shaken woman rose, went into her bedroom and

returned with a small piece of paper. She sat down, took the telephone from the side table, placed it on her lap and began dialling.

Ali Aga himself answered the phone. She told him what had happened to her son-in-law and asked him for help. From the change in her colour I guessed what Ali Aga was telling her. Tari was indeed in Evin Jail.

We invited Aunt Firouzeh to come and stay with us for a while and the distraught woman accepted the offer gratefully. That night I told her about Kaman Aga, anticipating that one day she might wish to employ his services herself.

That night, too, I asked myself: Why all this hatred towards the members of a dead society? Was it a crime to live and work in your own country? It was not our fault, I told myself, that we had been born under the Pahlavi regime. Surely being born into affluence was determined by destiny, not choice. Islam does not frown on wealth, as long as it is earned with honesty and as long as one's religious dues are paid. So why were we being ostracised and persecuted like common criminals? Then I remembered that the revolutionaries were not all Hezbollahis; they were also from the Mojahedin, the Fadayan, and the Tudehs – all leftists who would love to gather us together in Shahyad Square and shoot us.

It was two months before Tari was released. His cunning nature had found an ally in one of the revolutionary guards who, for the love of money, had helped to facilitate his freedom. Two days after his release, Tari called my house and asked me for more information about Kaman Aga. I gave him all the relevant details then asked him if he had seen my uncle when he had been in jail. It seemed that he had, but it was apparent that he did not want to expand on the subject.

The reign of terror which had begun only months before was becoming more evident by the day, and it was obvious that the revolution was not leading us towards the promised paradise. Two of the most respected, democratically inclined Ayatollahs were already in their graves. Talegani had been found dead in his bed in suspicious circumstances and

Motahari, a distinguished professor of Islamic philosophy at Teheran University's Faculty of Theology, had received as his gift from the revolution an assassin's bullet.

While the revolution was devouring its most distinguished children, Ayatollah Khalkhali was taking great pleasure in the group executions of hundreds of men, women and children. Rumour had it that he had once been an inmate at the Chehrazi Mental Institution because of his bizarre hobby of hanging kittens. Now he was hanging the Kurds and opium smugglers by the dozen. Ironically, in some shops, his portrait hung side by side with that of the Emam.

The unity that had spanned twenty-five centuries of monarchy was disintegrating. Factions were killing and discrediting each other and even in the classrooms tension and rivalry were rife. I was beginning to fear for our safety.

The Mirabel had been confiscated and the house by the Caspian was under investigation. I had already presented myself twice to the town's Komiteh with the deeds of the property, and had informed them that my parents were in England for medical reasons. They had given Father six months to present himself or, they said, they would confiscate this property, too.

Construction on the Omran Techlar apartments had been stopped because the Greek contractors had disappeared; so, too, had their bank guarantees which had been placed as security for their performance. There was a rumour circulating that the Omran Bank director in charge of the affair had stolen the bank guarantees and given them to the Greeks in exchange for a handsome sum of money which was to be deposited in his American bank account. He, too, was missing.

I felt sorry for Iskandar. This apartment was the only possession he owned in the world. There again, I told myself, he only had himself to blame for its loss. I had asked him on numerous occasions to pull some strings to release the large deposits we had paid for the flats, before it was too late. But each time, he had rejected the idea. He was too honest for his own good. If we had been able to retrieve the deposits, we would have been able to send the money out of the country along with Ali's. Well, it was too late now and it was no use dwelling on the past. Fortunately, I still had a couple of carpets which I could sell.

Luxury had not only become taboo; it had also become a burden. In all likelihood I would soon have to take down the portraits of my ancestors and hide them in the basement with the suitcase Aunt Firouzeh had left with me when she had returned to Tari's.

My aunt had always been very secretive, but since her husband's imprisonment she had become very close to me, and one night she divulged that his trial was coming up shortly and that, for the first time in the history of the prosecutions, he and two other prisoners were going to face a public trial.

This news was a relief. It seemed to be a move in the right direction and we believed that there would now be a good chance that they would be pardoned. At 63, Uncle Hussain was the youngest of the three senators, the others being 72 and 80 years old. The trial was to take place in three weeks time.

In the meantime, Aunt Firouzeh had been allowed to visit her husband once a month at the jail. I loved my uncle and I asked if I could accompany her on her next visit. She agreed, and at half-past twelve on the set afternoon I collected her from Tari's house.

Evin Prison is situated on the outskirts of the Evin Hills on the upper-west side of the city. From outside the prison, only a large iron gate and high walls are visible. That afternoon, the vicinity was packed with parked cars and visitors of all ages who had formed a long line which stretched down the hill. Only immediate family members were allowed to see the prisoners and I was to pass as my uncle's sister. After an hour-and-half of waiting, we arrived at the identification kiosk where I was required to show my birth certificate to prove my identity. My shattered nerves made it easy for me to produce calculated tears. Pleadingly, I addressed the guard: 'Brother, misfortune has brought me absentmindedness. I forgot to bring the document with me. Please, for the love of your own sister if you have one, be gracious enough this once to allow me to see my brother. I have not seen him for the past two years as I have just returned to Iran from India.'

He looked at me for a while and then, without uttering a word, quickly stamped two passes and handed one to each of us. I thanked him profusely. At the gate, Aunt Firouzeh handed the parcel she had brought for her husband to the jailor to be inspected and delivered. Then we submitted our passes to a guard, who ushered us into the corridor of a single-storey building containing several small rooms, glass-partitioned in the middle and with telephones set on each side of these. The prisoners talked with their visitors through these bugged telephones.

We entered a cell and I saw my beloved uncle standing behind the glass partition waiting for his wife. He was dressed in a white shirt and brown trousers and it seemed as though he had aged a hundred years. His beautiful grey hair had turned white and his thin, lined face, though still handsome, looked little more than a skull.

Man and wife exchanged simple endearments.

My heart was bleeding. I was having difficulty controlling myself but, somehow, I managed. I did not have the heart to deprive my aunt of so much as a second of her brief communication with her husband; consequently, I did not utter a single word to the man I respected so much. I just stood there looking at him, crying inside. After a short time, a bell indicated that our time was up. My uncle looked at me, his kindly eyes communicating his appreciation that I had come. I blew him a kiss, then the old couple said goodbye and we departed.

For several days, the front page of every newspaper was covered with pictures of the three senators on trial. No lawyers were to attend, and the accused had to defend themselves. The proceedings were taking place behind closed doors and only the press were permitted inside.

We read the printed reports and listened to the news. Aunt

Firouzeh was optimistic and Grandma had bought a lamb to be sacrificed, the meat to be given to the poor in gratitude for the freedom of her son-in-law. Apparently, Tari had paid off the right people.

On the night before the end of the trial I had a peculiar dream. I dreamt of Grandpa, who seemed very happy. I asked him what was the cause of his happiness and he laughed and said: 'Child, don't you know that my dearest son is free? As free as a bird, and about to come to me. I am waiting for him.'

Elated, I woke up with heart palpitations. The dream had not seemed like a dream. It had seemed very real. I began to shake Iskandar to wake him up. He groaned. I shook him again. 'Iskandar! Tomorrow Uncle Hussain will be set free!' I told him excitedly. He groaned again and told me to go back to sleep, but I kept on shaking him until he listened to me. 'I dreamt of Grandpa,' I went on, 'and he told me my uncle will be freed tomorrow. When I was a child, Sadat told me that if you dream of dead people and ask them questions they will reveal the truth. It is true. My uncle will be free. You will see.'

By now, Iskandar was fully awake and replied, 'Laila, I hope by God your dream will come true.'

Confident that the next day would be a happy one I went back to sleep. The next morning, I dressed quickly and drove to the university. In my euphoria, I forgot to switch on the radio for the news. As I entered the staff room, I noticed that two of my colleagues started whispering and thought that perhaps the students had been creating more trouble for me. In the corridor on the way to my classroom I saw Dr Ahmadi, who was exceptionally gentle and friendly. But I was in such a hurry to get through the day that I did not pay much attention to what was being whispered around me.

I finished my lectures and, at around four, I left the university for home, hoping to catch a newspaper vendor somewhere on the way. At a crossroad, a young boy carrying a stack of Keyhans under his arm approached the car. I took out the ten rial coin which I had ready in my coat pocket and gave it to him. He handed me the paper. The traffic light was still red. I put the paper face up on the front seat and saw the large black heading: 'The execution of the three Corruptors on Earth, and the Enemies of God, took place at 3 a.m.' The pictures of the executed senators were printed in a row under the headline.

I screamed in disbelief and began beating my head against the steering wheel. No . . . No . . . No, I repeated over and over to myself. It cannot be true. It can't be! Where was justice? What, after all, was the difference between this regime and the previous one? Which holy religion sanctifies the execution of three old men? The Koran says it is better to leave vengeance to God. So why did this new Islamic order take so much pleasure in bloodshed – killing, and killing, and killing?

The honking of cars behind me made me realise that I had caused a traffic jam. With trembling hands, I changed gears and drove off like a maniac. Suddenly, memories of my dream of the night before came back to me. Free! Free! Grandpa had been right. His favourite son was free. Free from this cruel world which was devoid of humanity.

Somehow, I found myself at Tari's house. At the door, a sorrow-stricken Mamad informed me that everyone was at Aunt Azi's. I drove there. The number of cars parked outside the gate indicated that there were many mourners present. They must all have heard of the execution on the morning news, which I had missed.

The gate to the garden was open and I walked up the driveway to the house. Inside, the house was full of relatives both close and distant, all attired in black. Aunt Firouzeh, red-eyed but composed, was sitting on a sofa next to Grandma. As she saw me, she stretched out her thin, quivering arms. I ran to them and we both began crying. Grandma's soft hands stroked my back gently. She was crying, too. Aunt Azi came and helped me up and led me to another room. My teeth were chattering and my body was shaking uncontrollably. The servant brought me a cup of sweetened camomile tea and

I sat drinking the herbal concoction until the shaking subsided. Then I left to go home to change into black. At the gate, I met Iskandar who was just leaving the house. The sight of him released the pent-up anger I was feeling towards the world and I began shouting and screaming at him, scolding him for not informing me of the news in the morning. He stood there patiently until I had calmed down, then hugged and kissed me in an effort to comfort me. He waited until I had changed then, together, we drove back to my aunt's.

At least one hundred visitors paid their respects that afternoon and evening. Many stayed for dinner, which had been prepared by a catering service and paid for by Grandma. Aunt Firouzeh had joined the ranks of the disinherited.

After dinner, when the distant relatives had left and a semblance of life had returned to Aunt Firouzeh, I dared to ask how she had been informed of the news. Apparently, at 1 a.m., a telephone call from a guard had ordered her to present herself at the fortress immediately. At first she had thought the call was a bad joke. To make sure, she had rung the prison to check the validity of the order and was told that if she wished to see her husband for the last time she had better hurry to the prison. Tari had driven her to Evin, where a guard at the gate had taken her to her calm and resigned husband. Uncle Hussain had begged her to have courage. He had given her his watch but had not parted with his wedding ring. They had said goodbye, then one guard had taken him to the firing squad while another had accompanied her to her car. She had heard the shots being fired.

For a few awful days, we became lifeless souls. Our brains functioned and our hearts pumped the blood round our bodies, but it was as if we were only half-alive. We also had a major problem which required immediate attention; this was to secure Uncle's body and give it a proper burial. The corpses of the 'Corruptors of the Earth' had been deposited in the morgue, ready to be dumped into a mass grave. Some families of the executed had even been billed for the bullets.

We unanimously decided that we had to find a way to give our dead relative an Islamic burial. A few years back, when the Behesht Zahra cemetery had been built, a number of rooms had been sold to various families, to be utilised as eternal resting places for family members. Father had bought one of these halls for us and I now offered to give my grave to my uncle.

Aga Reza, a trusted employee, was present at this family meeting. He told us that he knew the morgue's doctor and offered to find out what this good man could do to help. The suggestion was welcomed by all and the loyal man left immediately.

I decided to spend the night at Aunt Azi's, where the mourning widow was staying. At around midnight, Aga Reza returned and brought the good news that the doctor would co-operate and let us have the body. We had to go to the morgue next day at 12 noon, which was when the guards usually left to attend their prayers at the nearby mosque. The plan was that Aga Reza and Tari would go inside, find the body among the hundreds of corpses which had been thrown together, then carry it out to an ambulance which would be waiting for them outside. Of course, the ambulance driver would have to be handsomely paid.

Early the next morning I went home, collected the deed and the key to the burial hall and returned to my aunt's. The house was again full of visitors. Just before noon, Aunt Firouzeh excused herself from the gathering, pretending to be suffering from a migraine headache. Then one by one, but at intervals, Tari, Iskandar, my oldest aunt, Zinat, and myself left the house and headed out into the street. Tari joined Aga Reza in his jeep while the rest of us climbed into our car.

When we arrived at our destination, Iskandar parked some distance from the entrance. Tari and Aga Reza parked near the building and walked inside. An hour later, an ambulance passed us and honked its horn and Iskandar, alert for this signal, started the car and followed. It was a forty-five minute drive to the cemetery but, luckily, the traffic was not heavy and we were able to move quickly. We passed the slums of Javadieh and the silos. Nothing had changed. The tin houses were still there, but there were no women gathering bricks. The factories had closed.

We entered the cemetery and the ambulance stopped at the mortuary. Tari got out and ordered us to remain in the car until he returned. The two men opened the back doors of the ambulance and gently pulled my uncle's body out. He had gone to his death in his white shirt and brown trousers. There were many bullet holes in his chest. His handsome face was white and his eyes were closed.

My aunt could not control herself any longer. She jumped out of the car and rushed towards the body, which was now inside the small building. I sat, transfixed, trying to imagine what the poor, innocent man must have gone through while waiting to hear the judgement of the jurists (not the jury).

How did he feel when he heard his sentence? Did he at once regret his connection with the Court? Or had he been executed because of his relationship with Bakhtiar? Why had he not left Iran when Dr Bakhtiar disappeared? What a silly question, I chided myself. My dear hero was a true nationalist. He had loved Iran and he had died for Iran.

Tari's voice interrupted my thoughts, telling me that we could go in and pray for our dead. In the room the body, cleansed of the stamp of human savagery, wrapped in a white shroud and sprayed with rosewater, had been laid on the carpet facing Mecca. My aunt, seated by his head, was crying soundlessly.

I sat at his feet, stroking his stiff, bony legs and began to pray for his soul. Then the mullah stood facing Mecca and commenced the death prayer. Our men stood by him and the women behind. I mused that the mullah was truly a good man. He had engaged in the prohibited task of washing and blessing the corpse of an 'Enemy of God' – something for which he would be punished if discovered. After the ceremony, he advised us against burying Uncle Hussain in the cemetery. He told us that the guards frequently checked new graves, and that if they suspected one to hold an executed body, they desecrated it, removed the corpse and burned it. It seemed that there were spies everywhere.

Aunt Zinat was in charge of the upkeep of Grandpa's mausoleum and she suggested a visit to the caretaker. We drove back to Shemiran through heavy traffic and reached the site just before dusk. Aunt Zinat and Tari got out of the vehicles and entered the mausoleum. After a long half-hour they returned. The caretaker had agreed to co-operate with us but had demanded two hundred thousand rials for his services. In the circumstances we had little choice but to agree to his demand.

While we waited in the mausoleum, the man went home to fetch the equipment necessary to remove the single, marble stone on which Grandpa's figure was sculptured, and to open the grave. At last, he returned with a large spade, a drill and some other tools. Our three men took off their jackets, rolled up their sleeves and began their laborious task. After three hours of non-stop labour our beloved Uncle Hussain was safely buried in the family mausoleum.

Happy, Grandpa? His favourite son was indeed free – and they were together now forever.

Chapter Thirty

The husband having been killed, the wife now became the prey. The hunt began precisely forty days after the execution of Uncle Hussain. Fortunately, the messengers of death knocked at her door when she was out of the house and a Godloving neighbour, who happened to be outside at the time, heard their conversation with Mamad and called Tari. The family and a few trusted friends hid Aunt Firouzeh while she prepared to flee.

I was feeling deeply angry with the recent course of events and the non-stop killings. I wanted to strike back, but I did not know how or at whom.

It appeared that the only construction going on in the whole of the country was the digging of our street for the gas pipeline. The workers were Kurds and, just to do something unrevolutionary, I began to lavish hot food and clothes on them. My sudden generosity bewildered the men, but created a rapport between us. One day, when I arrived home from the university, one of the men stopped work, climbed out of the ditch and asked to speak with me. I stopped by the gate, waiting to see what he wanted.

'Khanum, you and Aga are very generous. I thought perhaps you could help our people in the mountains. In Kurdistan, our brothers are being massacred both from the sky and on the land by Mostafa Chamran, the minister for defence. We need money and warm clothes urgently. Any help counts.'

The smile froze on my face. Suddenly, I was in a position where I had to make a politically dangerous decision - one for which I was not prepared.

I promised to see what I could do to help him and then went inside. Aunt Firouzeh was spending the night with us;

she could not stay in one place more than one night in case her persecutors discovered her whereabouts. After dinner, when the children had gone to bed, I told her and Iskandar about the Kurd's request and asked them for their opinions. We agreed that we should help by donating money and warm clothes and my aunt offered to give me all Uncle Hussain's clothing which was stored in our basement. That night, between us, we collected a trunk full of clothes and blankets and a gift of ten thousand rials. Iskandar cautioned me not to give the Kurd anything in our own vicinity.

The next morning, when I was leaving for the university, I took the roadworker aside and told him that I had what he wanted. He suggested I meet him at 5 p.m. in front of the hamburger shop in Avenue Ehteshamieh. He would wait for me there in a car, he said, and I should then follow him to a safe place where I could hand him the goods. I agreed to this plan.

Just before five I drove by the shop. The Kurd was there, sitting waiting in a Paykan, and when he saw me he started the car. I drove round the circuit of Marvdasht Square and began to follow him. He travelled up Rostamabad and made a left turn into Niavaran Avenue, heading for Tajrish. He passed the bazaar, entered Pahlavi Avenue and took the turning which led to Evin and the prison. Suddenly, it crossed my mind that I might be helping the wrong person. What if he was a spy, sent to discover anti-regime elements? What if he was taking me straight to the prison with the condemning evidence in my car?

I began honking at him hysterically and indicated that I was going to stop the car. The Kurd slowed down and parked some distance ahead. He got out of the car and walked back in my direction. I felt cold and frightened. When he reached me he asked what was the problem. I replied that we had driven far enough, and asked if he would now remove the trunk from my boot. He glanced around quickly to make sure no-one had followed us, then swiftly opened the boot, grabbed hold of the trunk and pulled it out. He began to walk away.

I ran after him and said, 'There is ten thousand rials in an envelope inside. Please send a prayer for my uncle when you use the money.'

He looked at me with his kind but tired eyes and said: 'Khanum, God bless you and yours.' I stood there, speechless, watching him as he hurried to his car, placed the trunk in the boot and drove away.

Gradually, I began to calm down and set off for home. Living had become dangerous and frightening, and I realised that the animal instinct in me had momentarily got the better of my civilised nature and that I had reacted accordingly. In a jungle where wild, wounded scavengers reigned the primary maxim was to survive, and that was what I was trying to do.

On November 4, I was preparing to go to my class when Ahmad Aga, the janitor, came to my office. He told me that there would be no classes that day as the students were celebrating the occupation of the American Embassy – that 'Nest of Espionage' – by the 'students following the Emam's line'.

I could not believe my ears. Anti-American sentiment was high, but I had never dreamed that anyone would ever attempt to occupy the embassy. This was tantamount to declaring war on America. Bazargan was a practical politician, and right from the beginning he had tried to maintain some sort of amicable relationship with the United States. The rumour was that only recently he had met with Zbigniew Brzezinski in Algiers. Who, then, was responsible for this daringly dangerous act? Was it perhaps a reaction to Washington permitting the ailing Shah, now dying of cancer, to enter the United States for medical treatment? What will happen now, I asked myself. How is Great Satan, America, going to retaliate to this insult? And what is peanut-grower Carter going to do?

In a way, I was glad. I hated Carter and his divided administration. I believed that they were responsible for everything that had gone wrong in Iran. How could they let down the man who had served their interests in the region for more than thirty years? Who would ever trust them again?

I called Iskandar's office to see if he was free to take me home. I did not dare to talk about the situation at the embassy on the phone. Unfortunately, however, he had a staff meeting to attend so I left for home alone. When I arrived at my house, I honked my car horn to ask Fe to open the garage door. Within seconds, the door was opened, but one look at her colourless face told me that something was very wrong. I drove the car in, parked it, then asked her what was the matter. She began to stutter then eventually, pointing to the basement, managed to tell me that there were armed men down there. I ran inside and quickly made my way down the stairs. Betsy and Parissima were sitting on the bottom step, hugging their knees and shaking pathetically. When they saw me they jumped up and, their arms clinging round my legs, began to cry hysterically. I held my babies tight and kissed their little heads, trying to calm them: 'Don't worry, my darlings. Everything will be all right. Mummy is here now.'

Two mean-looking, unshaven young guards in Khaki parkas, each holding a machine gun emerged, ghostlike, from the room in which Uncle Hussain's suitcase was. One of them came close and said: 'Salam, Sister. We have come from the office of the Prosecutor General to collect what your aunt has been hiding here. Could you tell us which suitcases are hers?'

Without a word I went straight to the empty one and kicked it: 'This is what my aunt has in this house.'

The older of the two bent over and opened it.

'It is empty.'

I gave him a sharp look and replied: 'Of course it's empty! What did you expect to find in it? Your men supervised what my aunt took out of her house. This suitcase contained the clothes she brought with her in the hope that, one day, her husband might need them again. I am sure you are aware of the fact that he is dead and so, not having any further use for them, she has given them to the needy.'

Suddenly, I remembered that I had not checked their letter of authorisation. I asked the man I was talking to if he could show me the document and he immediately took a folded piece of paper out of his pocket and handed it to me. It was genuine and bore the proper stamp, authorising him to search my basement for the executed man's possessions.

God almighty! I had a spy in my household! How else could they have known about the suitcase in the basement? I felt as though my heart was about to stop beating. I was having difficulty breathing and could not prevent my legs from shaking. Summoning all my self-control I handed the letter back to the man and waited to see what he and his companion would do next.

If they decided to search the rooms upstairs, they would find the antiques and the Gajar paintings on the walls, all my parents' carpets, my silver and all my other treasures which were so carefully and beautifully exhibited. Even here in the basement, if they looked into the other room they would find the wine. Oh God, help me, please. If they find the wine I'll die under their lashes.

Unexpectedly, little Parissima began to cry again. I lifted her up and pressed her tiny head to my shoulder, kissing her long, brown curls.

The two men began whispering to each other.

Parissima's sobs had now grown louder and Betsy was still clutching onto my skirt, fear written across her face. Perhaps the sight of the children's fright brought compassion to the men's hearts, for the one who had been doing the talking suddenly turned to me and said: 'Sister, there must have been some mistake. We were told you were hiding your aunt's valuables here. The informer must be your enemy. He will be punished.'

Relieved, and surprised that they had not demanded to search the rest of the house, I replied: 'Thank you, brothers. No need for apologies, you are only fulfilling your duties.'

I turned towards the stairs, deliberately guiding them to the side door, and they left the house disappointed and empty-handed.

Betsy and Fe followed me to my bedroom. I laid Parrisima on the bed and asked Fe how long the men had been in

273

the house before my arrival. She replied that they had been there for ten minutes. I asked her if they had entered from the main entrance or the side door; luckily, she had had enough sense to bring them in from the side door. The decor of the main entrance was very impressive and, these days, dangerously condemning.

Contrary to the dictates of logic, at that moment I decided to let the house remain as it was. Nothing really belongs to us, I mused. We are only the keepers, though some people are luckier than others and live and die with what they have. We come to this world with nothing and leave it wrapped only in a white shroud. Everything belongs to God. He gives and takes for reasons unknown to the human mind. It is wise to become detached from the material world, I told myself. It hurts less when they take it away from you. I sighed. No more can I believe that man makes his own destiny. After all, how am I responsible for what has happened to me, and to my family and my country? A force beyond my control is shaping the future. Suddenly, I remembered our Behesht Zahra's private resting hall and began to laugh. What a joke.

I was certain that the men who had been here already knew about my antique collection. Even if I took everything down and hid it, they would know where to find it. Who was the spy? It could not be Fe – she was not a man. And Bayat had not been in the house since long before the suitcase had been brought in. It must be Nematallah, the gardener, I reasoned. But he had loved the Shah! On the afternoon of the day that the King had left the country, I had found him crying in despair. I had asked him what was bothering him and, still sobbing, he had replied: 'My Shah has gone. I love my Shahan Shah.'

I had cried with him.

How could he have changed so quickly? I made it my business to find out about his political inclinations next time he came to do some gardening.

Meanwhile, the presidential election was ahead and everybody was talking about the two most prominent candidates. Admiral Ahmad Madani, governor-general of Khuzestan province, was the favourite of the upper-middle classes and Abol-Hassan Bani-Sadr was backed by the masses. It would be interesting to discover who Nematallah's favourite was. A week later, I found him busy shovelling the snow from the garden path. As usual, I discussed the garden with him and talked about the annuals I wished him to plant for the following spring. Then, gradually and meticulously, I steered the conversation to Bazargan's resignation on November 6 and the coming election. Nematallah had definitely become a Hezbollahi, and a staunch follower of Ayatollah Beheshti. He was proud of the occupation of the 'Nest of Espionage', as though he himself had participated in the event, and was very happy about Bazargan's resignation.

In the heat of the conversation, the gardener also informed me that his wife was pregnant again. I was surprised. He already had seven children. I asked him why the eighth. His answer was that he wished to offer Islam one more Martyr. My God. How had they managed to brainwash this Shah-lover so thoroughly? No, I realised after a moment's thought. He had not been brainwashed. It was simply expedient for him to belong to the system. His class had put him in the heart of it, and it had lavished on him provision coupons and all sorts of other advantages. Perhaps a large house had even been confiscated from the Enemies of God. I had to be careful. Very careful. Later, I told Iskandar about my discovery but his trusting nature made him doubt my assumption. I became furious at his naivety and decided not to involve him with domestic matters anymore.

The first presidential election took place in January 1980 and, as was expected, Bani-Sadr became the first president of the Islamic Republic. I had voted for Madani. I did not know much about Bani-Sadr and made a point of finding out about him from my colleagues, and those students who were familiar with his background.

The first Iranian president was born in 1933 to a moderately prosperous land-owning clerical family from Hamadan. He attended Teheran University, studying at both the faculty of theology and the faculty of law. In the early 1960s, difficulty with the authorities over his political activities forced him to leave Iran for Paris, where he furthered his education. It did not take him long to become a prodigious writer, concentrating on Shi'a Islam as a force against dictatorship. Throughout his exile, he remained a staunch critic of the Shah, an ardent nationalist and a self-proclaimed revolutionary with the conviction that the solution to Iran's political and economic problems lay in a return to some form of Islamic ideology.

He was initially drawn to Khomeini in 1962-63 when the Emam launched his campaign against the Shah's policies. He then met him in 1972 in Iraq and became Khomeini's devoted follower.

Before his presidency, I met him at a seminar, during which someone asked him what he thought his chances were of winning the election. He answered: 'If what goes in comes out, I will be elected.' At the time, we all laughed. But the statement, coming from a man who had been a revolutionary all his life and was now a presidential candidate himself, was horrifying. It meant that he did not trust the system. What had changed, then? So many dead, the economy in ruins, law and order vanished – for what?

A couple of months later, it became obvious that there was a serious struggle for power between the president and Ayatollah Beheshti, the strongman of the Hezbollahis. Now there was unrest everywhere. Hezbollahi club-wielders were breaking up Mojahedin meetings, and the Fedayan and the Tudehs were being called traitors and the 'Enemies of Islam'. My communist sympathiser brother-in-law was arrested and sent to Evin Prison, where he would remain for many years. The political situation was deteriorating fast.

Most of our friends and all my cousins had left. Shahri's husband had been 'purified' from the diplomatic corps and had gone to Geneva where he had landed himself a good job at the United Nations, but Shahri and her son were still in Teheran. Aunt Firouzeh had, thank God, managed to escape in style, though no- one knew how Tari had been able to send her out in an airplane. Most wanted people fleeing to Europe were taking the dangerous Mount Ararat route to Turkey either on foot or on horseback. The news of Tari's serious affair with the blonde girl had unfortunately reached NeNe and she and the children were returning home.

The television programs now being broadcast were all Islamic. Night clubs and all the good restaurants had been closed and there was a ban on music and video tapes. In the absence of alcohol, housewives were distilling Arak (a home-made substitute for vodka) from dates, rice and raisins. Apparently, Arak made with raisins was dangerous and had been known to cause blindness and even death. Not being a very good housewife I had, perhaps fortuitously, never mastered the art and we generally bought ours from an Armenian painter I knew.

Marijuana was being grown in most gardens. Adultery, in cases where one marriage partner was absent, had become common and almost accepted. Parties were given very privately, as there was no guarantee that the guards would not get wind of what was going on and come to raid the house, rounding up the sinners and bestowing upon them the appropriate penalties. One hundered lashes was a mild punishment for the smell of alcohol on one's breath and hanging was the due for smoking or smuggling opium.

One evening, I discovered that Shahri was having a dinner party. Fe, my most efficient neighbourhood spy, reported that Tari and his mistress were among the guests. This explained why we had not been invited. The guests were still there when I turned our lights off.

We were fast sleep when the shrill ring of the telephone woke us. I jumped out of bed, wondering what drama had occurred at this hour of the night. It was Shahri. Whispering, she asked me to go downstairs and unlock the gate and the entrance door. Someone's life was in danger, she said, and we had to help. The guards had been to her house. They had taken all her male guests to the Komiteh except one. Then the telephone went dead.

I relayed this strange request to Iskandar, who looked at me with bewildered eyes. He told me to stay in my room and ran downstairs to let the escapee in, but I could not possibly stay up there without knowing who was coming to hide in my house. I put on my dressing gown and went downstairs to welcome the guest.

I could not believe my eyes when I saw the trembling, breathless nephew of the Shah's closest friend enter our hall. What on earth was he doing in Iran ?

God, Shahri was a silly woman. Why had she put us all in such danger? If the authorities ever discovered that we had given shelter to this man, we would be rounded up, taken to Evin and executed there and then.

But somehow, the hostess in me took over. I greeted the shaken man warmly, welcomed him in and asked him what time in the morning he wished his breakfast? The question was also so I could find out how long he planned to hide with us. He told me that he would leave the house before sunrise, and said that if I would be kind enough to provide him with a flask of hot coffee and some bread and cheese he would be most grateful.

Perhaps the provisions were to see him through the mountains?

I went upstairs to the kitchen, made him a flask of very strong coffee and, in a plastic container, packed a loaf of bread, a large piece of goat's cheese and some dates. I put the flask and the container in a small carrier bag and took it to his room. He thanked me warmly. I smiled at him, silently speculating that he had missed the firing squad by the skin of his teeth, and left the room.

When I woke up the next morning he had already gone. Fe informed me that, at dawn, a man in a Range Rover had come for him. Shahri must have arranged the pick-up. Much later, I found out that he escaped safely from Iran.

During those crucial months, only hope for a better future

kept me from going insane. I sincerely believed that the people had revolted for a good cause under the leadership of a man of God. I believed that Ayatollah Khomeini would see to it that Islamic justice would be restored to our society and that, under his auspicious guidance, the nation would begin a period of reconstruction. My beloved Iran would, after all, become the paradise for which so much blood had been shed. I had not yet realised that, like all other abstractions, the concept of paradise was subject to interpretation.

To add to life's difficulties, Fe was demanding her salary in American dollars, which I had to procure from the black market at three times the official value. This meant that all my salary from the university went to her. Also, the government had made it difficult for Philipinnos to stay in Iran by reducing the usual one year work permit to three months. Now, every three months, I had to go to the Ministry of Labour to bribe the man in charge so that he would not create uncessary difficulties when renewing her permit. Fe was turning out to be a tyrant. After five years of kindness and generosity from our family she, too, was letting me down. But no matter what, I had to retain her. No-one else in the house could be trusted.

I was feeling lonelier and more scared than ever, and very depressed. Somewhere between trying to face reality and block out the glorious past I had lost the ability to enjoy life itself.

Chapter Thirty-One

The vigorous rivalries between the hardliners and President Bani-Sadr moved the American hostage crisis to the centre stage of domestic politics. Not only were Iran's demands for the Shah's extradition, the return of his wealth, and the admission by the United States to 'crimes' committed against the Iranian people not met by Washington but, in addition, the billions of dollars in Iranian assets held by American entities, banks and their overseas branches were frozen and imports of Iranian oil banned.

I gathered from the newspapers that President Bani-Sadr and Foreign Minister Sadeg Qotbzadeh were doing their best to solve the crisis. However, because the central government was divided in its strategies towards Washington, nothing seemed to work and, as the days passed, the 'students of the Emam's line' became bolder in their hold of the hostages, to the extent that they began threatening to try them as spies if Washington did not meet their demands. Bazargan's government was rendered impotent by infighting, jeopardising the rule of the moderates.

Luck was on the side of the hardliners. An American attempt to rescue the hostages had come to naught. Apparently, an aircraft and some helicopters had landed in the desert, West of Tabas. Two of the helicopters had failed to function and one helicopter and a C-130 aircraft had crashed, causing eight American airmen to be burned alive in the flames. The scene of the disaster was extensively televised and the failure of the mission was proclaimed as a miracle for the revolution. The lawn of the university campus was covered with the grizzly pictures of Ayatollah Khalkhali inspecting the burnt bodies of the U.S. would-be rescuers.

This intrusion caused a revival of fears of American, Royalist and Zionist plots against the regime and led to further purges and 'purifications', especially in the armed forces. Naturally, mass executions followed.

A few days after the American disaster, just before dawn, we were awakened by the excruciating sound of aircraft flying so low that I thought they might hit the roof. We were so frightened that I rushed everybody into the basement, expecting some sort of bombardment. Nothing happened and the next morning the radio announced that the dawn's air traffic 'raid' had been an airforce exercise.

It seemed that, these days, our state of mind was permanently one of bewilderment and numbness – that is, until shock brought us out of it. Every day witnessed a new and terrifying event that shattered the nerves of the people. For the silent majority, living during a revolution is like being a matchbox floating on the ocean waves. The box floats here and there until the force of the waves disintegrates it. Like many of my kind, I had become like the matchbox – but, somehow, there was something in my heart that was telling me not to give up, not to disintegrate.

What frequently happens in revolutions is that different extreme factions unite to bring down the hated old system; then, once that short-term success is achieved, the unity of the factions falls apart and the fight for power begins again until the strongest establishes its supremacy. This same process was now afoot in Iran. Unified hatred gave way to individual rivalries and confused goals. The extremism which had been vital for the initial revolution was now imploding. The leftist groups were pushing for radical measures, calling for sweeping nationalisation, distributive justice, the cancellation of 'imperialist' agreements and the purging of people connected with the former regime. They were feeding the revolutionary turmoil and undermining the government of the moderates.

The leftists were everywhere, especially in the Komitehs and the universities. Thousands of young radicals would turn up at Teheran University to listen to Mojahedin-e-Khalq's

282

leader, Mas'ud Rajavi, whose ideology was based on a classless Islamic society, a potent programme with popular appeal. The campuses had turned into huge platforms for political debates. The Hezbollahis viewed the leftists with animosity and thought of the universities as centres for agitation. They were pressing for the closure of these centres. The issue became so important – so hot – that it was taken up at a meeting of the Revolutionary Council, where it was decided to give the left-wing political organisations three days to vacate university buildings and grounds. Classes had already stopped and political meetings followed one after the other.

Most active lecturers were leftists and they were preparing to put up a fight. Iskandar and I, however, were as apolitical as ever, believing that some good would come out of all the change. Our immediate concern was with what would happen to our salaries should the universities close. We drifted naively, not acting, merely watching.

Khomeini was on the side of the fundamentalists and frequently attacked the 'Westernised universities which were training our youths in the interest of the West'. On many occasions he had compared the intellectuals to 'donkeys carrying books on their backs'. Encouraged by the Emam's latest anti-university speech, the Hezbollahi club-wielders attacked the Teheran Teachers' Training College and lynched one of the students. As a result, bloody confrontations broke out in campuses all over the country, the worst of which took place on April 21 at Teheran University, where many lost their lives.

The following day, the Teheran University campus hosted Bani-Sadr and his followers celebrating the cleansing of the campus of its left-wing elements, and proclaiming the start of a 'cultural revolution' to 'Islamise' the universities.

Shortly after the proclamation, the universities closed indefinitely. As far as salaries were concerned it was announced that, after a thorough 'purification' of the undesirable elements, those acceptable to the system would receive their base wages, for which they would be required to work at government-designated institutions. The next step taken by the regime was to prohibit the employment of females not in Islamic wear. This meant the end of my academic career.

University salaries are low everywhere in the world, and no academic can maintain a comfortable standard of living without some kind of salary supplementation. We were no exception and now, with the closure of the universities and colleges and Iskandar's earnings from extra lecturing having ceased, I did not know how we would live. So I began selling the rest of my carpets and some of my gold coins. The price of gold had increased tenfold but, unfortunately, within a short period of time the property market crashed and I could not liquidate my lands. Rumour had it that, soon, all uncultivated land would be confiscated and given to the Disinherited.

One afternoon, when Taghi and his wife returned from Goldonak, he came to my house bearing bad tidings. Mashallah had set fire to my garden. I was aghast. Why on earth would he burn my trees, I asked myself.

Iskandar and I drove to Goldonak at once to see for ourselves. We found the garden barren, dotted here and there with black ash where once had stood the trees. I knocked at Mashallah's door. He opened it, greeted us politely and invited us in. We refused and remained standing outside. I asked him what had happened to my trees.

He began scratching his grey head and replied, 'Khanum, I was not here when it happened. When I arrived home my sons told me that some guards from the local Komiteh had come and set fire to the trees, thinking the land belonged to NeNe, the daughter of the cursed Hussain.'

I could not believe my ears. This so-called faithful retainer was cursing the man for whom he had worked for thirty years.

'Mashallah, why did no-one from your household tell them the truth? Your wife is always at home and your sons themselves are in the Komiteh. Surely they could have protected the garden?'

'Khanum, I am not responsible for what my family could have done, or have not done. The deed is done. Why don't you go to the Komiteh and complain, rather than accusing me of negligence?'

I was getting very angry. Iskandar saved the situation: 'Laila, Mashallah Khan is right. The deed is done and we cannot do anything about it now. Perhaps Mashallah can plant new trees for you.'

'Yes, perhaps.' Having agreed thus, I turned and got into the car, slamming the door behind me.

Iskandar stayed behind a little longer.

'He is as guilty as hell. I'll bet the Komiteh guards were his own sons and that they burned the trees so that the land could be called uncultivated. Then it would be confiscated and given to them.' I was convinced.

'Laila, the land is still yours. What has happened is not really important. People have lost more than a few trees and they are still smiling. Just try to forget about it. Next spring we will plant new ones.'

He was right. So much had already been lost that a few trees did not matter at all. At least I did not have to pay this loyal employee his monthly wages anymore.

Life had changed. People had changed. The new society hated us, and for as long as this revenge-fever existed, nothing constructive could be done. The lower classes wanted revenge for having been poor, the bazaaries wanted revenge for having been disregarded by the Shah, and one's neighbour simply wanted revenge because he did not like you. What was more, everyone felt justified in their vengeance.

We - the Taghoties - were traitors, whores, thieves, spies and whatever else they wished to call us. Stealing from us and lying to us were sanctified by the revolution, which still needed tangible short-term results. Making up dossiers for 'Corruptors on Earth' had become a daily practice. Evidence could be fabricated overnight and one could be collected and sent to Evin without reason.

The situation was getting more desperate by the hour and neither Iskandar nor I could come up with any plans for the future. The truth was that we could not make up our minds whether to leave everything behind and become refugees in a foreign country or stay, accept the system and hope for better days to come in a country that we deeply loved.

A simple telephone call one Friday decided for us.

It was from Mrs Cheragi, Betsy's American teacher.

Our conversation was short and to the point. The U.S. Embassy had ordered its citizens to leave the country within four weeks. To facilitate the exodus, non-citizen spouses and next of kin were to be granted U.S. visas. Betsy was American and Mrs Cheragi imagined that, as her parents, we would qualify. The Swiss Consulate was looking after U.S. affairs, and she suggested that we go to see them as quickly as possible as the situation was very serious. At the end of the conversation she asked me not to tell anyone about her call. I promised, and thanked her for thinking of us.

We were shocked by the news and spent the whole afternoon speculating as to what might be the cause of such a drastic move. Perhaps the Americans were expecting an army coup or, even worse, a civil war. We had to leave. I could not expose the children to war – and, besides, none of us was strong enough to survive another hell.

But how could we leave Iran without any money, and without valid visas?

Mrs Cheragi's suggestion was well-intentioned, but it seemed to us that it would be highly dangerous to approach the Swiss Consulate now that they were looking after U.S. affairs. The 'students of the Emam's line' might attempt to occupy it, too, and, naturally, they would find our applications for U.S. visas on the computer. If this happened we would end up in Evin, accused of co-operation with 'the Great Satan'.

Suddenly, in the midst of our confusion, I remembered that Kaman's representative had fallen in love with my house. What if he could be persuaded to buy the house and deposit the money for me in Europe? I immediately told Iskandar of my idea and we decided to contact the man with the offer.

The prospect of getting some cash out of the country made us courageous enough to decide to apply for U.S. visas and, the next day, we took Betsy's U.S. passport and all the required documents, including our university degrees as evidence of our Western education, to the Swiss Consulate. Fortunately, the reception area was empty of visitors except for one young man, hiding behind his newspaper. A clerk asked us the reason for our visit and then told us to wait. After a few minutes we were summoned. One look by the consul at the age of the passport-holder disqualified us. Betsy could not apply for an immigrant visa for us until she was twenty-one years old; we would have to wait for another twelve years. And there was no way that we could obtain visitors' visas under the present circumstances.

In spite of my disappointment at this rejection, I had the presence of mind to ask the official what could be done about Betsy's passport in case we wished to leave the country. If such a document was found on us while going through customs, our safety might well be jeopardised. He agreed that the possession of any U.S document was dangerous these days, and advised us to bring the passport to him should we decide to leave the country. He would put it in a diplomatic pouch and have it delivered to the embassy which was nearest to our destination. We would be able to collect it from there on our arrival. At least one problem was solved.

Now we had to approach the British Embassy. Though my parents did not know it yet, we hoped to be able to stay with them in London.

At home, I called my brother, Ali, and told him of the conversation I had had with Mrs Cheragi. He immediately suggested that we leave the country as soon as possible. Mother, who must have been listening on the extension in her bedroom, came on to the line and pleaded with me to get on the next flight for London. I reminded her that we needed visas these days and that that could take a long time. I suggested that she ask Ali to try to find a doctor who would be prepared to certify that I was suffering from some sort of illness requiring urgent surgery. The doctor's certificate might facilitate the acquisition of our visas. She promised to look into it at once.

Soon after talking with my family, I received a telephone call from Tari's partner informing me that Tari had been taken to jail again. Apparently, his telephone had been bugged since his previous release, and the Komiteh was now in possession of the tapes of all his conversations, including everything that had been exchanged between him and his mistress and the one call he had made to me inquiring about Kaman Aga.

I asked him what they had charged Tari with this time. He did not know and warned me not to call NeNe, who had arrived in the country the previous night. She and the children had returned to an empty home, where a guard was waiting to hand her the tapes. Fear for myself and pity for my cousin were making me feel nauseous. Hurriedly, I thanked the caller, said goodbye, and ran to the toilet to vomit. Nothing but acid came up. I rinsed my mouth, washed my face and returned to my bedroom, where I dropped onto the bed and began to cry.

Poor NeNe. First her father, now her husband – and for the second time. Obviously, this new regime's intelligence service was much more sophisticated and alert than SAVAK had been.

Suddenly, the doorbell rang. I began to tremble. It must be them, I thought. They have come for me believing, perhaps, that I had received a commission from my dealings with Kaman.

God, what have I done? Please, please, save me.

I heard footsteps.

They were here. They were coming for me.

The bedroom door opened slightly and in crept NeNe. For a moment I could not believe my eyes, then I jumped up to embrace her.

She had lost a lot of weight. Her athletic body seemed to have shrunk, her beautiful dark eyes were red from crying, and her short, curly hair was half-grey. She was two years my junior, but looked much older. Once, she had been the envy of the town, with her handsome, successful husband and highly-regarded parents. Now she was a beaten woman – lost, dependent, and alone.

Well, I thought to myself. 'Call no man happy till he dies . . . '
The great Greek law-giver Solon understood life in relation
to political forces. And I was learning it over and over with
the experiences of the last few months.

NeNe sat on the armchair facing the garden. The climbing
roses covered the walls, the annual bulbs were flowering and
the garden looked quite beautiful. There are many harmless
little sub-political pleasures which all humanity can share. But
politics, the grab for public power, can stop the spirit from
enjoying such small comforts. We took no joy in the spring.

NeNe described how the guard had given her the tapes,
demanding that she listen to one, in particular, in his presence.
She had sent the children to their rooms and then listened
to her husband's love talk with his mistress. The guard had
taken sadistic pleasure in observing her reactions. To
disappoint him she had listened in silence. The guard's last
words to her before leaving the house had been: 'Your husband
made love to his mistress in your bed. For that alone, he
deserves to die.'

She also told me about the money which had been sent
to her via Kaman. She had given half of it to her lonely, penniless
mother, once the 'Khanum of Ehteshamieh'.

My cousin was cool and composed, a dignified lady in
spite of her great distress. I respected her courage and patience,
her prudence, her understanding and generosity of heart. From
the way she was talking, I gathered that she had already forgiven
her husband. She loved him too much not to. I tried to comfort
her by attempting to explain the nature of the times in which
we were living, and the extent of the frustrations and the
fears which we had all had to face. I reasoned that, more
than likely, his affair had taken place not out of love for the
woman, but out of desperation – to release tension, a mere
physical need. After all, he had been living alone for almost
a year. She was inclined to agree with me.

After drinking the tea which Fe had brought for us, we
decided to walk to Grandma's – a little like children seeking
comfort. The old princess was lying on her bed, looked tired

and sick. She suffered from high blood pressure, but I suspected that it was really loneliness which was taking its toll on her health. With the exception of NeNe and myself, all her offspring had left the country. She missed Aunt Firouzeh most of all, and knew she would never see her again.

In a way, Grandma was lucky. At least she still had her household staff, who looked after her with affection and loyalty. After the success of the revolution, the majority of servants had become informers against their employers, in the hope that they would be sent to jail and that they could then become the new occupiers of their masters' homes. Others, who still trusted their own masters more than the guards, had nevertheless turned to blackmail.

Grandma's pallor vanished as she saw her two favourite grandchildren entering her empty room. To make her happy, we gossiped about the family members who were living overseas and gave her all the good news we could think of – which, under the circumstances, was very little. When it began to get dark, I left for the bakery to buy bread for dinner.

There was a lot on my mind. Iskandar was going to visit the British Embassy the following day and I had not yet been able to liquidate any of my assets or contact Kaman's man. There was talk that the government was going to stop all property transactions. This meant that I had to sell something before it was too late.

Drowned in thought, I only vaguely heard a car honking behind me. Alarmed, I turned to see Javad Aga behind the wheel of a car, a young couple in the back seat. My heart missed a beat. Forcing a smile, I waved to him. He pulled over to the curb, stopped the car and got out. Obviously, he wanted something, so I crossed the road to meet him. We shook hands and he introduced the couple as Mr and Mrs Kaman. I nodded to them and waited to see what Javad Aga wanted from me. He began by telling me that Mr Kaman was looking to buy a property in Shemiran and that he had told him about my beautiful house. He wondered if I might be interested in selling. In fact, he said, he had been going to telephone me that very evening to see if the idea appealed. If so, he would like to make an appointment to inspect it.

Excitement combined with paranoia rendered me speechless for a moment, then I pulled myself together and invited them to join me for a drink at the house. They accepted my invitation and he politely opened the car door for me.

When we arrived home, I gave them the grand tour, surreptitiously watching Kaman's facial expressions, then took them into the formal sitting room where we sat relaxing and drinking Arak. I told Kaman that I would only be interested in selling the house if he was able to send the money overseas before I left Iran. He told me that he would let me know of his decision the next day. Still feeling slightly stunned, I urged him not to contact me by telephone. I told him about Tari and the tapes. We arranged that I would call him myself at four the following afternoon.

They were just about to leave when Iskandar arrived home from playing tennis at Veissi, the club we had frequented for seven years. The club owner, a Mr Veissi, was now in jail for owning this 'Nest of Corruption', in which whores were used to seduce men with their bare legs. Women were not allowed in anymore.

Iskandar's expression told me that he was very surprised to see my guests. I quickly informed him of the purpose of their visit and a broad smile lit up his face.

We saw our visitors out of the house and returned to the sitting room where, in a celebratory mood, we drank the remaining half-bottle of Arak.

In order to beat the crowd at the British Embassy's visa queue, Iskandar left home at five the next morning, but returned around noon, empty-handed. The purpose of the queue that day had simply been to obtain a number, which would be called the following day. He would have to repeat the ritual tomorrow. The letter from the English doctor had not yet arrived and I was becoming nervous. Finally, at 4 p.m., I called Kaman. He wanted the house! I was ecstatic. God willing, everything would be well again.

Just before dinner, we received a call from Bayat, the bank's chauffeur. He informed Iskandar that the prosecutor general's office was investigating all the Omran Bank's directors, deputies and managers and suggested that if Iskandar had to take any precautionary measures he should do so immediately.

Fortunately, we did not have to worry about taking any 'precautionary measures', as Bayat had politely put it. But this meant that Iskandar was now on the list of individuals who were prohibited from leaving the country.

Before we sold the house, we had to make sure that he would be able to leave Iran. We spent the whole evening contacting those friends who had been turned back at the airport because they had been on the list. From what they told us, it seemed that the traveller knew nothing until the travel agent submitted his passport to the airport authorities for the usual security check. Then, a couple of nights before his departure, the wanted passenger would receive a call informing him that he had to attend the office of the prime minister for clearance before he was permitted to leave the country.

Then, the choice was his. He could either forget about his passport or take the risk of presenting himself to the authorities. Some people who had shown themselves had been cleared, while others had ended up at Evin.

After much reflection, Iskandar decided to book a seat, submit his passport and wait for the call. If he was on the prohibited list, he would face the so-called Clearance Committee, whose decision would determine his plan of exit from Iran. Should he be cleared, he would fly out. Otherwise, he would take the mountain route.

The wisdom of this plan was that it eliminated any possibility of surprise. It also gave us time to organise ourselves and set a suitable departure date.

The next day, again at five in the morning, Iskandar left for the British Embassy and the travel agency. But at noon he again returned without the visas. The man in charge of the tickets had cancelled all the previous day's numbers because he had discovered that someone had taken ten numbers to sell on the black market.

We cursed our luck and decided not to pursue the matter until we had received the doctor's letter. However, in the meantime, Iskandar tentatively booked himself on a flight to London on June 5.

From the first of June until the evening when the call came, we were glued to the telephone, our spirits rising and falling at every call, all of which were irrelevant to our present purpose. Finally an officer did call, asked for Iskandar and, very politely, informed him that if he wished to travel he had to go to the office of the prime minister. Now it was Iskandar's turn to test the justice of the regime.

I knew he was good. I knew he was brave. And I knew that he was innocent. But did any of that matter now? The following day, I gave him my pocket Koran for safekeeping, whispered a prayer and sent him out of the house to present himself at the designated address.

I was so worried about what might happen to my dear husband that I could not keep still. Fe felt sorry for me and suggested that I go for a walk. I wandered around until I found myself in front of Niavaran Palace. A man sitting by the gate was selling beautiful tulips in colours I had never seen before. The flowers were from the palace garden. I purchased two bunches and walked back home.

The parked Fiat indicated that Iskandar was at home and not at Evin. Joyously, I opened the door and, shouting his name, ran upstairs. My darling was sitting in his usual armchair, smiling at me. I ran to him and hugged and kissed him a thousand times. The official in charge, he said, had treated him with great respect and had simply told him that he had to obtain clearance certificates from all the institutions, except the university, which had employed him within the past ten years. That was all, thank God.

It took two weeks of nerve-wracking, humiliating trials by various committees before he was cleared and given an exit visa. He had four weeks to leave the country before the visa

293

expired; to renew it he would have to undergo the same procedure. God only knew who might be sitting in judgement then!

Iskandar was very lucky. His popularity with his subordinates, as well as his personal generosity to those who had needed help but had not qualified to receive it from the bank, combined to save his skin. For example, at the beginning of his career there, one of his assistants had approached him for help. His wife desperately needed an operation for cancer and he simply did not have the funds to pay for it. Iskandar and I had combined forces with my parents and Amir to finance the operation in Israel and had, in effect, saved the woman's life. This man, once a humble clerk, was now the president of the Omran Bank's Clearance Committee! The letter from the English doctor arrived at last and, on its basis, the British Consul granted visas to Iskandar, Parissima and myself. For some unknown reason, Betsy was denied, but I did not dare to insist in case he changed his mind about ours.

I reminisced about the days of the Shah's reign when we had not needed British visas at Heathrow Airport. The customs officials had simply looked at one's passport and asked: 'Madam, how much money are you planning to spend in London on this trip?' Then, a glance at the bank cheque or the bank account document ensured a six months' permit to stay. Now, we had to beg.

Once the travelling arrangements had been made, we met with Kaman to discuss the details of our transaction. He wanted me to turn the deed of the house over to him and to trust him with the transfer of the funds. I refused. He accused me of not having faith in him. I told him I trusted no-one, and that if he wanted the house he had to accept my terms. He hesitated, then called me a 'lion of a woman' and agreed to my conditions. First, we had to go to a notary public's office where the legal transaction would take place. There, to make sure that no-one suspected our deal in foreign currency, he was to give me a cheque for the agreed sum in rials. This I would keep until the money was deposited in Ali's bank account. Then the cheque would be returned to him. This was the safest arrangement I could think of. In case anything went wrong, at least I had the sum in rials.

For a change, matters were sorting themselves out at a dizzying pace. My neighbour, a tenant of Mother's, was Dutch and well aware of Betsy's visa problem. The kindly man, of his own accord, offered to help us by personally taking her Iranian passport to the Dutch Embassy and obtaining her a visa. Once in Holland, he said, she would be able to travel to England on her U.S. passport. The idea was brilliant and I accepted it with gratitude.

This gave rise to a new plan. We decided that Iskandar and Betsy would travel to Amsterdam together and wait for me and Parissima to join them there. I had to enter England before August 7 which, according to the English doctor's letter, was to be the day of my cornea transplant operation. Kaman had promised that the money would be in Ali's account before July 7.

The plan was immediately put into action and our Dutch visas were obtained within twenty-four hours. Betsy's U.S. passport was submitted to the Swiss Consulate and Iskandar was instructed to collect it from the American embassy in Hague. For the first time in many months, stamina returned to me. All the neighbours' servants with whom I had established good relations were mobilised to help us pack. Iskandar asked his parents if we could leave our valuables at their house and, rather reluctantly, they agreed.

On a bright June day, I drove Betsy and Iskandar to the airport. The departure lounge was so crowded that it was almost impossible to move. The large hall was crowded with would-be passengers, surrounded by luggage and relatives who had come to see them off. Lines of people stretched in all directions.

At the luggage check-ins, thorough searches were being conducted by the revolutionary guards. I noticed that some were even ripping open the linings of suitcases in the hope of finding money, jewels or other goods which were not allowed out. I thanked God that I had already taken my most precious belongings to London on my previous visits.

Since movement was so difficult, I remained standing in a corner, enjoying the warmth of Betsy's hand in mine and watching Iskandar take care of the formalities. I was afraid of being left alone in Iran, but I did not dare to express my apprehension in case Iskandar changed his mind and stayed behind to protect me. He was still in danger and had to leave the country now; these days, one could not leave anything to chance. Even if the worst came to the worst, at least two members of my family were going to be safe.

Time was running out and Iskandar and a rather pensive Betsy had to leave the lounge. Our goodbye was long and emotional. I wondered what Betsy was thinking. She was just a child. She could not possibly conceive of the risks that were involved. I waited until the loudspeaker announced the departure of their flight and then, very slowly, walked to my car.

I told myself that I had to be strong and careful. Very careful. The future of my family depended on my efficiency. Iskandar had left with only 1, 000 pounds sterling. I prayed that Kaman's money would be transferred on time, so that I could leave Iran before Iskandar ran out of cash. They could not enter England without me and the doctor's certificate stipulating my need for an operation. The customs official was bound to ask them the reason for their travel and, if they had none, they would be sent back to Iran.

When I reached home, my spirits were lifted by the electrifying commotion going on in the house. Taghi and his wife, along with Fe, Akbar Aga, the husband of Grandma's personal maid, and a couple of the neighbours' servants were all busy packing for me. The only servant who was missing was Nematallah. Recently, he had been bad-mannered, impertinent and hostile. Why was he absent?

My antiques and carpets were to go to my in-laws and the rest of my belongings, including all my electrical appliances and my stock of frozen food, were to be distributed among the people who were helping me. This was saying goodbye to a lot of money, but that did not matter. I wanted these people to remember me well, as I would remember them.

Every day I called Kaman's office to see if the money had arrived, and every day the answer was: 'It will be there tomorrow.'

I was beginning to get worried. We were well into the first week of July and I had booked for the 20th. The planes were all full and the next available seats after that were not until September 1. I had to leave Iran on the 20th.

The days passed slowly, in a long, lonely haze. My headaches had become more frequent and, sometimes, I experienced dizzy spells. But most of my suffering was from loneliness and fear.

My in-laws probably wished that I had never existed. Since the day that I had taken my valuables to their house, I had neither seen them nor talked to them on the telephone. Fortunately, Tari had been released and he and his family had escaped the country on horseback.

I will never forget those unhappy days when, desolate, I would sit by the pool reflecting on the past and not daring to think of the future. What can be righteous about political action which is based on vengeance, and which intrudes into every corner of people's lives? I firmly believed that the state should be the servant of the people, not the people its whipping boy.

Somehow, I did not regret selling my house. I had owned it, perhaps, for as long as I was meant to. Now it belonged to Mr and Mrs Kaman and, when the time came, it would belong to someone else. We are all joined in our love of creature comforts. I felt consoled that someone else, then someone else again, would live in and love my beautiful house. Perhaps one day, I told myself, when the Emam declares a national amnesty and when the persecution mania subsides and stability returns to the country, I might return and buy it back and be one more dweller in the chain.

On July 11 I was informed that Kaman had been taken

to prison in Bandar Abas. I was assured that it was a case of mistaken identity and that he would be freed in no time at all. Apparently his namesake was a SAVAK butcher.

On July 14, Kaman was executed.

No money ever reached the overseas bank account. I deposited his cheque. It bounced. I could not go to the authorities – it was too dangerous. Thus I, too, joined the ranks of the Disinherited. What were we going to do in England without a nest egg? I consoled myself with the thought that at least I had my carpets and my jewellery. They would see us through for a short while.

I called Ali and told him the story. At first he found it hard to believe, then he urged me to leave Iran at once. I asked to speak to my father. The generous man assured me that he would look after us until we found employment. I called Iskandar and gave him the news. He took it calmly and, as always, tried to comfort me. But we both felt that life had been too cruel to us.

On July 18, when the last of my furniture was being removed, Nematallah and two guards armed with machine guns forced their way into the house. In loud, harsh tones they began accusing me of various sins – of helping the widow of the executed Hussain; of hiding alcohol in the house; and of attempting to flee the country. Tahgi and his wife, along with four other neighbours and Akbar Aga, a Komiteh guard himself, managed to stop them from getting too close.

I was petrified. Parissima was screaming and Fe was shaking with fear as the other servants argued with the revolutionary guards. I cannot remember what was said. I can only recall that Akbar Aga saw the men out of the house and slapped Nematallah on the face, calling him 'Namak nashnas' – ungrateful. When the armed men had left, I lost consciousness. Some hours later, I found myself in bed, Parissima and Fe sitting on the floor nearby. When she saw me stir, Fe rose and left the room, reappearing a moment later with Akbar Aga. He apologised for entering my bedroom, then went on to urge me to leave the house, the next morning if possible. Nematallah could not be trusted, he said, and might return with an order for my arrest. I thanked him for his help and his loyalty. He said goodbye and walked out of the room.

We were left by ourselves, two women and a child.

Nematallah might come back? I was too scared to stay in the house any longer. We had to leave that night. I got up, took a shower and called my mother-in-law to see if we could spend the remaining two nights at her house. Unfortunately, no-one was at home.

I could not go to Grandma's house. Her safety could not be jeopardised. I called Ellahe, the only friend I had left in Iran. She greeted me warmly and told me that they would come and pick us up within the hour. Together, Fe, myself and Parissima carried the heavy suitcases down the stairs. My little girl, in anticipation of a reunion with her father and sister, was bubbling with joy. How different is the child's world from that of the adult's.

I instructed Fe to call Taghi to come and supervise the distribution of the goods I had left for all those who had helped me. The bedroom furniture had been sold to Kaman's wife, who Fe was to call after I had left the country. She would, no doubt, make arrangements for their removal. Poor woman, she had become a widow at the age of twenty-five. It was quite likely that all her accounts had been closed and that she would not be able to pay for the furniture, but that did not matter any more. Only our safety mattered.

We double-checked that everything had been taken downstairs.Then I made a final tour of my once-happy home, remembering the wonderful times I had spent with my family and friends in those sunny rooms. It seemed as though the house had a soul of its own and was crying out for me. My home, I sighed. My beloved home. How easily did I lose you. Once the authorities find out about your new owners, they will come and confiscate you for the Foundation of the Disinherited. Am I not disinherited, too?

Slowly, I descended the curved staircase to the once grand

hall and went out into the flourishing garden. Mother's tasteful landscaping had made a lush paradise out of Grandpa's barren land. I walked the length of the path to my vegetable garden and picked a stem of mint to tuck between the pages of my pocket Koran. It would be a memento from my home. Will I ever have another one, I wondered?

Fe's voice interrupted my thoughts. My friend was waiting for us at the gate. I stood for a few minutes longer, trying to feel the essence of the garden with every nerve in my body. Then I pushed sadness from my mind and, very quickly, walked to the gate.

Fe had already locked up and had placed the suitcases in the boot of the car. She was going to stay with us at Ellahe's for our last two nights. I could not take her with me as the British Embassy had refused her a visa. She had had the choice of returning to the Phillipines, or remaining in Iran. She had chosen to stay.

In the car, I asked my friend to stop by Grandma's house so that I could see her one more time. I took Parissima in with me. I wanted her to remember her great-grandmother. My beloved Grandma was lying on her bed watching television. I could not tell her that this was a farewell. As I had done when I was a child, I sat on her bed, massaging her thin limbs. Then I kissed her, from the tips of her toes to the top of her head, wishing as I did so that I could turn the clock back. I was crying inside, knowing that this was the last time I would be able to touch this woman I loved as much as my own mother.

She took my face in both hands, kissed it and invited us to stay for dinner. I made up an excuse and refused. Parissima jumped up onto the bed and gave her a big hug. Tears were in my eyes, but I could not let them loose. I had to leave quickly, otherwise my emotions would overcome my composure. After a final, tight hug, I left the only real treasure I had in Iran. I never saw her again. Grandma died in 1984, a very lonely princess. She never saw any of her family again, four generations of them.

We drove down Avenue Ehteshamieh for the last time. Grandpa's trees had matured and the avenue looked absolutely beautiful. I wondered what the municipality would call it, now that they were renaming the streets in honour of the martyrs of the revolution. Ellahe was very kind and tried to cheer me up as we drove. I appreciated her efforts, but I was in no mood for conversation. I had an excruciatingly painful headache and I had no taste in my mouth. My body was rigid with tension, prepared for flight.

Our last day in Iran passed without event. I stayed in bed most of the time. My health seemed to be deteriorating and I was worried that I would not make it to the airport. Painkillers were proving ineffective.

Our British Airways flight was at 11 a.m. and the travel agent had advised us to be at the airport by six in the morning. My friend and her husband drove us to Mehrabad. Our farewell was sad, but I could not afford unnecessary sentimentality. I had to keep going.

The man who inspected my luggage was sympathetic. He made only a superficial inspection of my cases, then closed them neatly. I wanted to cry in gratitude at his unspoken kindness, but I could not weaken now. Once the luggage had been dealt with, it was time for the body search. A mean-looking young woman in Islamic dress showed me into a small, partitioned room and began sliding her hands over my body, sides, front and back. Disappointed at not finding anything, she took a pair of surgical gloves from a wooden chair nearby, and put them on. She told me to take off my underpants. I began to shake and begged her not to subject me to such humiliation. She gave me a sarcastic smile and ordered: 'Pull your pants down, or I'll do it for you.'

I suddenly felt sick and began to breathe deeply in an effort to control myself.

'Hurry up, woman!' she screamed.

Trembling, I obeyed.

'Spread your legs.'

I obeyed again.

She knelt down and proceeded to shove her index finger into my vagina, pushing it as high as she could and turning it around and around, deliberately and sadistically causing me pain. Then, satisfied that I had nothing hidden there, she pulled her finger out and stuck it up my rectum. When she had finished, she smirked and left the room. I felt as though I had been raped.

A spasm of nausea hit me and I bent over to let the liquid spew out of my mouth. I began breathing deeply again, then wiped my mouth with a handkerchief, pulled myself together and left the room. I had never been so sure until now of the wisdom of our decision to leave Iran.

Parissima was patiently waiting for me. My headache was getting worse and I had difficulty in keeping my eyes open, but I had to make it to the passport section. I simply had to.

We joined the queue to have our tickets checked and waited. At last, tickets checked and our seats allocated, we joined another queue. After about half-an-hour we reached the official in charge of the passports. He asked me for my name.

I managed to stammer, 'Mahdavi, Laila and Parissima.'

He turned to the pigeon holes and turned back with the documents.

Thank God, the last bridge to safety had been crossed.

I found two empty seats and walked over to them. Parissima was behaving like an angel. She must have sensed that I was ill. She sat next to me, fidgeting with the hem of the coat which I had made her wear in preparation for the cold weather in Amsterdam.

After a delay of three hours, the loudspeaker announced that our flight was now boarding. The passengers rose automatically and began to form a long line. At last, I was dragging myself and Parissima up the steps of the aircraft and inside. The plane took off, and I lost consciousness.

Just before landing in London, where we had to change airplanes for Amsterdam, I came to. The passenger sitting next to me left her seat and, shortly afterwards, returned with a hostess. They began fussing around me. When I became fully aware of my whereabouts I told the hostess I felt very ill and wished to disembark in London. Both my child and I had valid British visas, I explained. She replied that, because my ticket was for Amsterdam, I was not allowed to disembark in London. However, she said, they would take me to the sick-room at London Airport and I would be able to stay there until I felt fit enough to fly to Holland.

After we had landed at Heathrow, a wheelchair was brought for me and an orderly took me and my daughter to the airport's clinic. I asked the matron who was attending to me to call my brother and inform him of my whereabouts, and to let my husband at Amsterdam Airport know of our delay. I gave her Ali's telephone number and Iskandar's full name. She assured me that she would let them all know where I was, and then she gave me an injection.

I woke up at around ten-thirty, feeling better. The matron returned and asked me if I felt well enough to take the last flight to Amsterdam, at 12 midnight. I gazed at Parissima lying next to me on the clinic bed, fast sleep, thanked the matron and told her that I felt able to travel.

Another wheelchair was brought and we were taken to the appropriate aircraft.

When we landed in Amsterdam and the door of the airplane opened, an airport official entered, calling my name. I almost had a heart attack, believing that the arm of the revolution had stretched this far to grab me. Fearful, I decided to keep quiet. He called my name again and a hostess led him to where I was sitting. I was trembling again and everything was starting to go round and round. The man asked me how I was. I was surprised. How did he know I was sick?

'I feel better, thank you.'

'You have a husband who loves you very much,' he said.

How did he know I was married? He took hold of Parissima's hand and told me to get up and follow him. The rest of the passangers were standing up, preparing to leave the aircraft. I had to follow him quickly, otherwise we would be hemmed in. I collected my hand luggage, handed it to him, walked the distance to the door of the aircraft, then sank into the wheelchair which had been brought for me. The official pushed me through to the lounge, where Iskandar and Betsy were waiting for us. Betsy was the first to see us. Excitedly, she pointed in our direction and they both ran towards us.

Why were they weeping, and why had this man come to fetch us? Nothing made sense anymore. Reunited, we flung our arms around each, but I was too sick to feel excited.

The mystery of the strange man on the airplane was soon solved as Iskandar revealed what had happened. Many hours ago, he and Betsy had been waiting for us in the arrivals lounge at the time that our original flight was due to arrive. He had spotted our suitcases, but waited in vain for us to appear. Worried, he had contacted British Airways staff seeking information about his two missing loved ones. They had gone through the passenger list but had been unable to find our names on it; they had then called London Airport, but had not been able to discover anything about our whereabouts. No-one seemed to know what had happened to us between Iran and Holland. To assist Iskandar, British Airways had put an international telephone line at his disposal.

After waiting for three hours, and not finding us on any of three other flights from London, Iskandar had called Ali, then Ellahe. She had told him that she and her husband had left me at the airport and seen me head towards the passport section. But that was all she could tell him.

For six hours, we had been lost to all! My family had assumed that I had been taken to Evin.

Finally, the London police, who had been contacted by Ali, informed him that they had succeeded in locating us at the Heathrow clinic. This news had instantly been communicated to Iskandar and, eventually, our names had appeared on the passenger list of an incoming airplane. When it landed, the relieved British Airway official who had been helping Iskandar had boarded the aircraft to collect us. It seemed that the matron at Heathrow had called neither Ali, nor Amsterdam Airport.

Happy to be together again, we drove to the hotel where Iskandar and Betsy had been staying. I still felt dreadful and Iskandar immediately arranged for a doctor to visit me. His examination revealed that I had suffered a nervous breakdown. I was kept under sedation for two days, after which we were due to leave for London. Our last worry was whether or not the British officials would let us in. What if they refused? We would have to return to Iran. But to where in Iran? And to what?

The flight to England was smooth and the children were very excited, but Iskandar and I were grave and silent. No-one must guess at the anxiety and fear which burned inside us. That would give rise to suspicion.

Very composed, we joined the queue for immigration. When our turn came, the officer inundated us with questions, then ordered us to follow the man who was standing next to him. Our visas, it seemed, had to be approved by a higher authority. Alarmed, we followed the second man to a corner where he asked us to sit and wait. We obeyed and waited for a long time, not daring to speak. Finally, he reappeared with our passports which bore a three months' permit to stay.

Again I reflected on the days of the Shah, when the polite questions: 'How much money are you going to spend on this trip, Madam?' and, 'How long do you wish to stay in London?' guaranteed a six month permit.

But it did not matter. Nothing mattered anymore except being together and being safe. Nothing mattered but the nebulous dream of being able to live without fear; of once again being able to tuck one's children into bed at night, knowing the dawn would come without incident; of being able to walk hand in hand with one's husband through the streets; of having a garden again.

The war with Iraq broke out a few weeks later.

Bibliography

Alam, Assadollah: *The Shah And I* (I.B. Tauris & Co Ltd, London, New York, 1991);

Amirsadeghi, Hossein: *Monarch in Power* (Amirsadeghi Editions, Teheran, 1977);

Bakhtiary Esfandiary, Princess Soray in collaboration with Louis Valentin. Translated from the French by Hubert Gibbs: *Palace of Solitude* (Quartet Books Ltd, London 1991);

Bakhash, Shaul: *The Reign of the Ayatollahs: Iran and the Islamic Revolution* (Basic Books, New York, 1984);

Bani-Sadr, Abolhassan: *Islamic Government*. Translated by M.R. Ghanoonparva, MAZDA Lexington, KY., 1981);

Batmanglij, Najmieh: Food of Life (Mage Publishers Inc., Washington, 1986);

de Villiers, Gerard with Touchais, Bernard & de villiers, Annick. Translated from the French by June P. Wilson and Walter B. Michaels: *The Imperial Shah - An Informal Biography* (Weidenfeld and Nicolson, London, 1976);

Farman Farmaian, Sattareh,with Munker Dona: *Daughter of Persia* (Crown Publishers Inc., New York, 1992);

Follett, Ken: *On Wings Of Eagles* (Collins, London, 1983);

Forbis, William H.: *Fall of the Peacock Throne: The Story of Iran* (Harper & Row Publishers, New York, 1980);

Halliday, Fred: *Iran: Dictatorship and Development* (Penguin Books, London, 1979);

Huyser, General Robert E.: *Mission To Tehran* (Andre Deutsch Ltd, London, 1986);

Lambton, Ann K.S.: *Qajar Persia* (I.B. Tauris & Co. Ltd., London, 1987);

Parsons Anthony: *The Pride & the Fall - Iran 1974-1979* (Jonathan Cape, London, 1984);

Radji, Parviz C.: *In the Service Of The Peacock Throne* (Hamish Hamilton, London, 1983);

Roosevelt, Kermit: *Counter Coup: The Struggle for Control in Iran* (McGraw-Hill, New York, 1979);

Templeton, Peter Louis: *The Persian Prince* (Persian Prince Publications, Printed in Great Britain, 1979);

Shari'ati, Ali: *Marxism and Other Western Fallacies* Translated by R. Campbell. (Mizan Press, Berkeley, Calif. 1980);

Shawcross William: *The Shah's Last Ride, The Story of the Exile, Misadventures and Death of The Emperor* (Chatto & Windus, London, 1989);

Sick Gary: *All Fall Down* (Random House, New York, 1985);

Sullivan, William H.: *Mission to Iran* (W.W. Norton, New York, 1981);

Taleqani, Mahmood: *Islam and Ownership*. Translated from the Persian by Ahmad Jabbari and Farhang Rajaee (Mazda, Lexington, KY., 1983);

Wright, Robin: *In The Name of God*, The Khomeini Decade (Bloomsbury, London, 1990).